Roswell, First Shot Fired

A John Hunter Adventure

Mark Jackson

Trilobitebooks Ltd

For Jenny,

And of course, Brooke, Ciaran, Isabelle, Victoria, and Ollie.

This edition first published in 2022

TrilobiteBooks Ltd

Mark Jackson, 2022

Cover Design by TrilobiteBooks

Prologue

7th July 1947

Yussel cupped his head in his hands, supporting the extra weight his eleven-year-old neck was struggling to cope with. He winced as his fingertips caressed the parallel lines of scar tissue running the length of his skull. Although anesthetized, the buzzing sound of the medical saw cutting through bone still invaded his dreams. He shuddered. The operation remained the last, or rather what he hoped to be the last, in a series of mutilating acts transforming him from a homeless street urchin into the disfigured monster of his captor's creation.

He groaned and massaged his forehead, desperate to relieve the pressure exacted by the bulbous, black eyeballs protruding from his face. At least it was better than the sound chamber. The chamber proved the breaking point for countless of his fellow inmates; many descended into madness, most of them never seen again. It was a fate he didn't want to share for good reason. The doctors hadn't picked up on it, but the chamber trials appeared to be having a positive effect on him. He could do things - see things others couldn't. A week earlier, a guard discovered a bar bent out of shape in his cell door. He'd been blamed and, unable to protest his innocence, received a beating before being transported to his current location. He admitted to dreaming of ripping the bars from his door but swore he'd never touched them. He shifted in his seat, regretting the movement as the safety harness cut further into his shoulders. Whatever lay in store, he would meet the challenge and beat it. He did not have a choice. He couldn't allow them to break him as they had the others. He'd been through too much already. He would survive this. He must survive this.

Yussel forced his head back into an upright position and reached into the darkness. His long fingers closed about the skinny thighs of his two companions. The smell of their fear permeating the space was almost palpable. Yussel opened his mouth and uttered a low-pitched guttural sound. Without a tongue, it was as comforting a noise as he could manage. The boy to his right responded with a soft whimper, reassuring him at least two of them were still alive.

Unable to communicate further, he returned to the question of where they were. Why were the straps about his chest and waist so tight? Were they being transported somewhere? What might the white coats be testing for this time? He released the legs of his companions and caressed the rounded metallic walls and ceiling of their cell. He frowned to the extent his disfigured face would allow. A metallic bubble? He thought back and remembered a momentary surge in the pit of his stomach, a feeling associated with a take-off. Were they inside some kind of aircraft? A faint, yet constant thudding noise reverberated around the space. The sound of whirring propellers, perhaps? Such bloated airplanes existed at the base. Before the operations began, he'd spent hours staring at them through his cell window, fascinated by how the huge metal elephants ever left the ground. He sniffed the stale air, but it offered no further clues.

Yussel grimaced and wriggled his toes. The effects of the painkillers injected into him were wearing off.

He drew both legs to his bare chest and enjoyed the silence. These were the moments he lived for back on the base. They equated to solitude and, more importantly, meant they were leaving him alone. He hated what they'd made him, hated them for their experiments and constant drugs. If God truly was the entity of vengeance portrayed in scripture and saw fit to spare him from the fires of Hell, he would dedicate whatever of his life remained to seek retribution. If ever a people needed to pay for their sins, it was his captors.

Yussel blew the air from his lungs and swallowed hard, his heart skipping as he registered the enormity of what he was doing. Enjoying the silence... the thudding whine of the engine had disappeared. He winced as the bubble shook around him, his chest restraint again cutting into him as invisible winds buffeted the exterior. What was happening? Were they falling? Were they crashing? His knuckles whitened against his armrests and he locked his jaw, bracing himself for impact.

***

It was a clear, star-filled night, in the small American town of Roswell, New Mexico, and Solomon Garnett, a young sophomore, was determined to make the most of it. He may have consumed one too many illegal beers at the house party and perhaps shouldn't have been cycling at this time of night, but what did it matter now? This was a matter of the heart and screw the consequences. Tonight was the night his sweetheart, Lilly-Rose Adams, would forgive him and take him back. Even thinking her name gave him goosebumps. What did it matter if he'd kissed her sister? A year had passed. Surely enough time to forgive - maybe even forget.

He glanced at the road sign above his head and belched. Grove Way. She lived on Oak Street, the next road down. Not far now. Dulled by alcohol, Solomon's initial nerves had long since shifted toward what his friends termed misplaced confidence. But what did they know? He'd been chasing her since grade school, dutifully carrying her bag and doing her homework since he could hold a pen. This couldn't be the end, not when he'd only just got her to admit to being his girl, albeit with the caveat the relationship was still open on her part. No, here's how this would play out; he would sweep Lilly-Rose off her feet, embracing her whilst explaining away the misunderstanding with her twin; making it clear the experience meant nothing, not the first nor the second time. She would no doubt accept his version of events and forgive him. Reconciliatory snuggling would follow and the balance of the Universe would be restored. What could go wrong?

Solomon stopped to catch his breath. He carried a few more pounds than someone of his age should and didn't want his first impression to be that of a panting asthmatic. He leant his bike against a fire hydrant and tapped his ear in irritation. An odd buzzing noise reverberated through his skull. Where was it coming from? He scanned the road for traffic but saw nothing. No pedestrians. No cars. He was alone; alone with his bike and a variety of amorous feelings. He banged the side of his head. The buzzing refused to shift. If anything, the volume increased.

Then Solomon's world changed forever. A dark object filled his field of vision only for an instant, but long enough to imprint itself on his brain. It looked like a disk, a black, spinning disk, illuminated only by the light of the moon. It appeared to be out of control, whistling overhead before diving groundward and disappearing behind a row of houses. Solomon shook his head in disbelief. Did that just happen? A trick of the light, perhaps?

An explosion ripped through the night, dispelling any doubt. He took a step backward, tripping over his bike as a fireball and a plume of smoke pinpointed the crash site. Adrenaline tore through his body, clearing his alcohol-fogged mind in an instant.

The crash site looked close and Solomon knew what he had to do. There might be survivors. His mind raced. Could it have been a plane? It hadn't looked like any kind of plane he'd ever seen. Russian perhaps? Shit - perhaps the Air Force just shot down an enemy aircraft.

Solomon grabbed the handlebars of his bike and threw a leg over its hefty frame. He kicked away from the curb and pedaled towards the smoke as if his life depended on it.

Chapter 1
12th April 2014

D r. John Hunter sat alone with his thoughts in the sparsely decorated reception of the Aloma Retirement Home. Although his contact with Professor Solomon Garnett had faded since the breakdown and the Professor's subsequent reclusion, the shock and pain he'd felt upon learning of his passing were real enough. After he graduated from Cambridge in Archaeology, Hunter spent a year at the University of Florida, cutting his teeth in academia under Solomon's watchful eye. Although just over forty years his senior, they became firm friends and Hunter credited him for instilling the foundations of many of his beliefs, particularly those cemented in the Professor's specialism, Ancient Egypt. When the call arrived, the decision to drop everything and jump on board the next flight to Miami had not been difficult.

The funeral's attendees befitted a lecturer of Solomon's popularity, and both the Catholic priest and his ex-wife, Lilly-Rose, gave moving eulogies. The wake proved a little more raucous and a good excuse for Hunter to catch up with old colleagues and exchange stories and anecdotes whilst toasting the Professor's good name. Toward the end of the evening, while rescuing a Dorito from a salsa dip, one of Solomon's care workers approached him. The woman was a rotund, friendly individual who, after establishing his name, requested he visit Solomon's retirement home before returning to the UK. Apparently, the Professor had bequeathed Hunter something in his will.

So here he was, reading a dog-eared fishing magazine and awaiting the re-emergence of this self-same woman with his inheritance.

'Dr Hunter?'

Hunter ditched the magazine and rose to greet the petite Indian woman poking her head around a 'Staff Only' door. 'That'll be me.' He smiled. 'Sorry, I was expecting the other lady.'

'English eh, cool accent. Gloria asked me to give you this. She got waylaid with a toilet emergency.' She thrust a small brown envelope into his hand.

'Nice to know, and perhaps a little too much information,' said Hunter, taking the envelope and exaggerating his Surrey accent. 'But I'm much obliged, madam.' The woman giggled and disappeared back behind the door.

Hunter rotated the package in his hands and frowned. This made little sense. What could Solomon possibly have left him? He slipped his index finger under the flap of the envelope and ripped it open.

A little overzealous in his assault, the envelope split and spat its contents onto the reception's gray carpet tiles. A key attached to a piece of folded card rolled to a stop beneath a nearby chair. Hunter retrieved his prize and held the key to the light. It didn't look like anything out of the ordinary. A standard, bronze, Yale-type key embossed with the initials WFB. 'WFB?' he thought. Perhaps a company acronym? It certainly wasn't one that leapt off the page. The circle surrounding it made it look like a logo, but he was clutching at straws. He unfolded the card, hoping it might shed more light on the matter. Hunter scratched his head. The message was an incomprehensible series of meaningless letters and numbers:

"SPTXFMM – 181858."

'Conclusive proof old Sol slipped over the sanity line, I guess,' he whispered. He shrugged his shoulders and slipped the key into the inside pocket of his linen jacket. The mystery would have to wait. Whatever it opened, he could figure it out back in England. Hunter only had one more day left in Miami, and he fully intended to make the most of it.

He shouted a cheery "Dick Van Dyke" style thank you at the giggling receptionist and stepped out into the midday sun. Although hot compared with England, the Florida sun in April was not too uncomfortable. He remembered periods during the summer months where he'd outright refused to leave the sanctuary of UF's air-conditioned offices and lecture halls. He'd lived most of his adult life in and around Cambridge, and humidity was not a mistress he enjoyed. It certainly wasn't one he wanted to return to in a hurry.

Hunter stood on the pavement and drank in the relaxed atmosphere as he waited for a cab to appear around the bend. Miami was a strange city, as was the diversity of its populous, one might be forgiven for thinking they were somewhere other than the United States. The Art Deco buildings, the laid-back atmosphere and the friendly disposition of its residents put it at odds with the pace and pressures more prevalent in cities such as New York and Chicago.

'Spare change, guy?'

Hunter shook his head free of the daydream and turned to find a downtrodden man in his mid-forties lazing against the outside wall of the retirement home. Dressed in an assortment of ripped and stained rags, Hunter felt a wave of pity wash over him. The US was not an easy place to live when one was destitute. He pulled out his wallet and removed a ten-dollar bill, shoving it into the man's outstretched hand.

'Just don't let me down and go spending it on booze,' said Hunter.

The man's accent changed. 'Thank you so much. You don't know how much this means, Dr Hunter.'

Hunter stepped backwards, jerking his hand away. 'Who are you? How do you know my name?'

'A word to the wise, Dr Hunter; you are in Solomon's world now and you mustn't trust anyone. And I mean no-one.'

'Solomon's world? What do you mean?' The man backed away as a car rounded the bend. 'Where are you going? Get back here and explain yourself.'

'Is this man bothering you, sir?' asked an officious voice in a southern drawl.

'What? No, I mean...' Before he could finish his sentence, the homeless man turned tail and fled, leaving him alone with a pair of officers from the Miami Police Department.

'There's no need to protect him, sir,' said the larger of the two officers, shoving his head through the window of the squad car. 'Most of our homeless community are harmless enough, but one or two can get a bit touchy-feely with the tourists.'

'I'm fine, thank you, officers.' Hunter shook his head, a little shaken by the experience. 'Something he said just caught me unawares, that's all.'

'You need a cab, sir?' said the second officer, hailing a passing yellow taxi.

'That would be great. Thank you so much for your help. I should be okay from here.' He waved a final salute of thanks and climbed into the waiting cab.

'Not a problem, sir. You have a good day.'

Hunter fingered the outline of Solomon's key through his jacket. 'Hilton please, driver.' What was the old man involved in this time? And why the hell had he seen fit to drag him into the middle of it?

Chapter 2

Hunter tapped Solomon's key against the rim of his beer glass and continued twirling it wistfully through his fingers. Someone knocked into him as a cheer erupted around the Fontainebleau Hilton's glow bar, interrupting his daydream and snapping him back into reality. Evidently, the Miami Heat must have taken the lead in their playoff game.

He glanced down at his notebook and scratched his nose. He'd made his only breakthrough before his first drink arrived but was still struggling to make sense of its significance. The message left by Solomon was encrypted, but in an overly simplistic fashion using a code taken straight from page one of cryptology 101. The real message could be read simply by substituting each figure with the letter or number following it. Once run through this rudimentary cipher, "SPTXFMM – 181858" therefore becomes, "ROSWELL – 070747." But so what? What could it mean?

Hunter was well aware of Roswell's reputation as a Mecca for conspiracy theorists the world over. Who wasn't of the post-X-Files, Mulder and Scully generation? Believers claimed the small town in New Mexico played host to an alien crash site back in the forties; a crash publicized in the press but later retracted by the Air Force as part of an alleged government cover-up.

Hunter was indifferent to the subject; he neither believed in the existence of alien life nor dismissed the possibility they might exist. In his opinion, there were plenty of mysteries still to be solved on Earth without looking for more beyond its fragile atmosphere.

With the basketball game failing to hold his attention, he ran a quick Wikipedia search for Roswell on his phone. It was a captivating, albeit brief, story. The crash supposedly occurred on the 7th of July 1947. He raised an eyebrow; that at least explained the numbers on Solomon's note. He continued. The United States Air Force maintains to this day the debris found at Roswell came from an experimental surveillance balloon. It was an explanation that probably would never have been questioned had the Roswell Army Air Field public information officer not issued a conflicting press release earlier in the day. His press release asserted that the attending 509th Operations Group recovered a "flying disk".

'Are you finished with that, sir?'

Hunter jumped at the intrusion and looked up to find one of the bar staff hovering next to his table. 'All done thanks,' he said, nudging his empty glass towards the man. 'Could I order another please?'

'Certainly, sir. Budweiser, was it?' Hunter nodded. The server smiled. 'So what are you hiding away?'

Hunter frowned. 'I beg your pardon?'

'Sorry, I didn't mean to pry. I've got one for my baseball cards. Worth a fortune, some of them.'

'You've got one of what?' asked Hunter.

The man nodded at Solomon's key. 'A Wells Fargo Bank safe deposit box. Sorry, I just recognized the key.'

Hunter shook his head, feigning stupidity. 'Of course, my apologies. My head is somewhere else.' The man smiled politely and returned to the bar. Hunter tapped the key smartly on the table, his interest pricked anew. So it opened a safe deposit box... What could Solomon have deemed important enough to hide away in a safe deposit box? Hunter's heart rate climbed. Might it contain something to do with the Roswell crash?

He rose to his feet and waved a hand, trying to catch the eye of the barman. 'Sorry mate, something's come up. Can I cancel that beer?' The man nodded. 'By the way, which branch is your box in?'

The barman looked confused. '40th Street, why?'

'Is that the closest?' The barman nodded and gave him a thumbs-up as Hunter slid a ten-dollar bill across the counter. 'Thank you, you've been very helpful. Any chance you can do me one more favor and call me a cab?'

'No need, sir. There's always at least three or four waiting out front.'

Hunter rolled his eyes. 'Of course, and thanks again.' He turned to leave and froze as a hand gripped his bicep and eased him towards the exit.

'Fancy a little company on your trip, Hunter?' He instinctively relaxed his muscles, ready to strike if the situation escalated. The act did not go unnoticed. 'I'd heard you received Special Forces training.' The man chuckled and leaned into Hunter's ear. 'Still, if I were you, I wouldn't try anything just yet. Whatever you can do, I can do it quicker.'

'We'll see,' hissed Hunter.

'Feisty aren't we? You've nothing to worry about though. I'm not the threat.'

Hunter winced as his arm was jerked unnaturally. 'Could have fooled me.'

'Just pretend we know each other. We are being watched. Continue walking and do something natural. Laugh or something.'

Hunter forced a smile and whispered a reply through clenched teeth. 'What do you mean, we're being watched? Who would want to watch me?'

The man pushed him through the exit. 'Check your jacket pocket.'

Hunter did as he was told. 'It's empty.'

'Check again.'

Hunter re-inserted his hand and made an exaggerated show of his search. 'See, nothing...' Then he found it. It was no bigger than the head of a pin, but nonetheless, it was something. He withdrew his fingers and looked at the tiny piece of metal in his hand. 'What the...'

The stranger grabbed it, rolling it between his fingers. 'It's a tracking device. It was slipped in your pocket when the first cheer for the Heat went up.' He threw it into the air and caught it. 'Don't worry, I'll dispose of it once we're clear of the hotel. No point in letting them know we're onto them just yet.'

Hunter shook his head in confusion. 'Them? Who is this "them"? And for that matter, who the hell are you? Give me one good reason why I shouldn't just scream for the police.'

The man smiled. 'Solomon said you'd react this way. Look at my face. Are you sure you don't you recognize me, "guy"?'

He moved into the light of a nearby bulb. Hunter narrowed his eyes. The man was of medium build, with a craggy, clean-shaven face and a headful of graying, curly black hair. A knee-length trench coat concealed his clothing. The light exaggerated a slight lump protruding from the stranger's chest. Whoever he was, this man was armed. Then it hit him. 'Shit, you're that hobo from outside the care home!'

Chapter 3

Chris Cartwright threw the earpiece into his computer screen and released a controlled exhalation, just as his therapist had taught him. Idiot! Why was he always tasked with running the idiots? To be fair, Company men always behaved this way on secondment, always looking to cover their backs and slime their way out of awkward situations. He understood the premise of avoiding culpability, but why couldn't they just do their jobs? This limey bastard was meant to be a side issue for fucks sake. Just bug him and follow him. What wasn't clear about that?

'If he leaves the room, you follow him,' he shouted. 'What are you, simple? Do your job!' He shoved his chair away from the desk and plucked a lukewarm mug of coffee from the adjacent filing cabinet. Why the department was investing any time in this Brit was beyond him. He wouldn't have looked twice at the guy, particularly with his insight into the deceased, but his opinion seemed to count for very little these days. He was just there to make sure the orders were carried out, not to question them. Chris' days as a field operative were long behind him and now it was simply a case of whiling away the days until retirement. He still believed he could be of use in the field, but a bloodbath in the desert convinced his superiors otherwise.

He glanced at the photo of John Hunter in the file on his desk. The man was an interesting target for sure. A stint in the British Navy sandwiched a doctorate in archaeology and classical languages from Cambridge University and a return to academia amidst a storm of claims he'd discovered some link to the lost city of Atlantis. Chris sniggered and shook his head. 'Atlantis... No wonder they kicked him out of Cambridge. Don't suppose decent schools like that tolerate having nut jobs on their books. Shame the same can't be said of this place. What d'ya reckon, Julio?'

The thick-necked, ex-college line-backer he shared his office with glanced up from his paperwork. 'Sorry, what? I wasn't listening.'

'Doesn't matter. Are your boys doing anything fun? Mine are still following the British guy - and struggling, I might add. Useless idiots. Why are we using Company boys anyway?'

Julio snorted. 'No idea, but I know a few favors were called to get them here. Our guys must be involved in something big for none of them to be available.' He tapped a few keys on his keyboard, then hit return. 'This batch seems to be particularly crap. They're getting softer every year. Need a good war to harden them up. What do you think?'

'True dat. Vietnam certainly pounded me into shape. Literally and figuratively,' said Chris.

'Figer what? Shut it, Ivy League.'

Chris smiled and rolled his chair back under the desk, retrieving his earpiece and slotting it back into place. The bleeping dot on his screen representing Hunter was on the move. With any luck he'd be heading for the airport, so Chris could finally file this distraction as complete. Perhaps then he could get back to tracking down Solomon's real accomplice. Whatever the deceased possessed, it was a big deal, and no stone was being left unturned by his bosses. He hadn't seen activity like this since the cold war. It was just a shame he'd been given a set of green CIA agents to run. He was certain some of the other "Top Secret" files occupying the desks of his colleagues would make much more interesting reading than the one issued to him.

The task of actually following Hunter on the ground had fallen to a certain Lewis Bentley, some youngster a couple of years out of Yale. No doubt another silver-spooned graduate of the secretive CIA backed society, the Skull and Bones. Not that he was in any position to quibble about nepotism, his career via Harvard Law School was littered with chance encounters and promotions endorsed by individuals or groups all too happy to grant a favor for a favor. He didn't like it, but for the moment it was the way the system worked and who was he to rock the boat? There was the law for the people, then there was the law for the lawmakers. Democracy at its finest.

Chris squinted at the screen as the red dot turned onto Northwest 42nd Avenue. Surely the limey wasn't heading for the airport; he wasn't scheduled to leave until the morning. What the hell was going on out there? He tapped his earpiece. 'Charlie One. Come in, Charlie One.'

A hiss of static accompanied Bentley's smooth voice. 'Charlie One receiving.'

'Where's the mark? Are you in pursuit?' asked Chris. 'Where's he going?'

'I'm tailing him a couple of cars back. He hailed a cab outside the hotel, got in with a male I didn't recognize. Clean-shaven, short hair, no features discernibly out of the ordinary.'

'Photo?'

'Nothing clear. I'll send through the best I could get.'

Chris shook his head and covered his mouthpiece. 'He contacts me when the guy leaves the room but neglects to tell me he picked up a friend. Prick.'

Julio smiled. 'Like I said, they're all the same.'

Another hiss of static crackled in Chris' ear. 'Sorry, sir, say again?'

'Forget it. Keep eyes on the mark. The cab has reached the terminal. Just make sure you don't lose them. Get your phone out and pretend you're on a call. You're in a suit, you'll blend in fine.'

'Affirmative. Exiting the vehicle now.' Chris heard the faint voice of the cab driver thanking Bentley for the tip. 'Target vehicle is stationary. No attempts made to exit.'

Sixty seconds passed. 'Any movement?' asked Chris.

'Nothing, sir.'

'Shit. Take a walk, nice and slow. I want a visual on the mark.'

Chris heard a long exhalation and rolled his eyes as he awaited confirmation of the inevitable. 'It's empty.'

'Just get inside and get some answers.' Chris heard the tapping of a knuckle on glass and a window winding down.

'Excuse me, any idea what happened to my two friends?' asked Bentley. 'I think they've played a joke on me.' Chris nodded his head in approval. Not a bad cover for a green agent. Particularly as Bentley must be stressed off his balls right about now.

A snigger followed as an Eastern bloc accent boomed through the earpiece. 'They get you good and proper. Guys give me a fifty and get out other side of cab. Tell me drive to airport and wait at terminal.' The man laughed. 'Are you groom? Bachelor party, no?'

A door slammed shut. 'Sorry, sir. The bug must be on the back seat. What do we do now?'

Chris massaged his temples 'From your point of view, I couldn't care less. From my point of view, the shit and the fan are about to collide.'

Chapter 4

Hunter's face tightened as the agent, apparently detailed to monitor him, entered a waiting taxi and pulled away from the hotel. He looked young. Perhaps why he'd fallen for a trick like that. Hunter glanced at his new companion.

He grinned and pulled him to his feet. 'See, what did I tell you?'

'I suppose I should thank you.' Hunter brushed the dust from his trousers. 'So what do I call you?'

'Most people know me as Ethan.' He smiled, 'But if you fancy calling me hobo, call me hobo.'

'Most know you as Ethan? And what do the rest know you as?'

Ethan shook his head. 'Not important.'

'Okay, well, until I learn your real name, thank you, Ethan.' He shook his hand. 'Now we've moved from strangers to acquaintances, Ethan, can you tell me what the hell is going on?'

'All in good time, Doc, all in good time. First things first, we need to get to that little Bank of yours while time is still on our side. It won't take these people long to realize their mistake.' He cracked a knuckle. 'I'm just glad they deemed you low priority. If they'd allocated more than one agent, the situation may have got a little fruitier.'

Ethan gripped Hunter's arm and pulled him towards the nearest cab, opening the rear door and shoving him inside.

'Where to boys?' asked the cab driver in a high-pitched voice.

Ethan raised an eyebrow and smirked at Hunter. 'What can I say but welcome to Miami.' The cabbie winked, his dark unkempt beard in stark contrast to the red lipstick and blue eyeliner framed by the enormous blonde wig perched atop his head. 'You off out after your shift, mate,' asked Ethan. 'Or is this some new dress code I've missed out on?'

'I get off in an hour. Performing with my crew at one of the hotels in town. You guys interested? I could get you in cheap.'

'Some other time. Great outfit though,' said Hunter, screwing his nose up at the pungent smell of cheap perfume assaulting his senses. He'd thought London was liberal, but Miami took it to a whole new level. 'Any chance of a ride to Wells Fargo Bank on Biscayne Boulevard? You know it?'

'No problem guys, can get you there in ten,' replied the driver, forgetting himself and allowing his voice to deepen.

The yellow cab pulled into the slow-moving night traffic. Hunter cracked a rear window and settled back into his seat. 'Come on, Ethan, you've got to give me something. At least give me a clue as to what I am going to find at the Bank? Has Solomon thrown me to the lions? Am I in danger?'

Ethan ran a hand through his hair, appearing to contemplate his response. 'I don't really know what to tell you, man. I'm as in the dark about all this as you are. Sol left me a bunch of money with instructions to get myself cleaned up and then find you. He suspected you'd have a tail, and he wasn't wrong.' He paused for breath. 'All I know is I'm playing the role of your shadow until I'm told otherwise.'

'My shadow? But why? You must have a vague idea what's going on. It'd be a start if you told me how you know Sol.'

'Vague is right. I've known Sol for years. Ever since he hustled me playing pool back in Roswell. We were either going to be friends or enemies. Lucky for me, he selected the former.'

'You're from Roswell?'

'Hell no, Nebraska born and raised. I don't look that old, do I? No, I was a military man back then, a lowly guard at one of the bases out in the desert.'

Hunter smiled. 'That fits. Area 51, by any chance?'

Ethan rolled his eyes. 'Yes, but before you ask, I let no aliens pass through the gates. The base is a secret because the CIA and the Air Force built their spy planes there. Nothing more. I'll admit I saw some weird shit, but hand on heart, I never caught wind of a visit from ET?'

'You don't need to convince me, I'm not a believer either. Solomon was open to the idea, but it was a topic where we just agreed to disagree,' said Hunter. When were you posted there?'

'Early eighties. I was there when Major Whitley first flew the F-117 Night Hawk.'

'The stealth fighter?'

Ethan whistled. 'She certainly was. The Wobblin' Goblin, as the flyboys called her.'

'Wobblin' Goblin?'

'Because it shuddered like a bitch at low speed.' He laughed. 'Looked like a flying triangle from below. It's no wonder the public thought it was alien tech.'

'Wells Fargo Bank on the right,' interrupted the driver. 'That'll be eight-fifty.'

'Keep the change,' said Hunter, handing him a twenty-dollar bill, 'and I hope the show goes well for you tonight.' The two men eased from their seats and alighted on the deserted pavement. 'Are you sure we can get in at this time of night?'

'I hope so. I believe the key you have should get us inside,' said Ethan. 'Shouldn't matter what the time is. A perk for those prepared to pay a little extra, I guess.'

Hunter shrugged and pulled out the key, inserting it into a Yale style lock marked "Depository." 'Here goes nothing.' He twisted the key, and the door swung open to reveal a small but plush reception area. A black leather sofa faced an unmanned desk. It must have been recently refurbished, as the space had that "new car" kind of smell hanging in the air. They entered, their respective footfalls setting off an electronic beep, and no doubt alerting whoever should have been behind the desk to their presence.

Hunter scratched the back of his neck and moved towards the sofa. 'I guess we just wait here then.'

Before he could sit, a short, balding man clad in a tight-fitting security uniform bundled through the door to the left of the desk. 'So sorry, so sorry.' He paused for breath and fiddled with a clasp on his trousers. 'My apologies, you caught me a little short there. I do hope I haven't kept you long? I don't get many visitors at this time of night.' He straightened his tie and sat at the desk. 'Now, what can I do for you?'

'Not a problem, we only just arrived.' Hunter stepped forward and placed the key in front of the guard. 'With a bit of luck I'm hoping you can clear up a little mystery for me,' said Hunter. 'I'm flying back to England tomorrow and I've been left the contents of one of your deposit boxes in a friend's will.' The guard typed something into a computer. 'It should be me apologizing for the lateness of my visit, but my late friend didn't make it clear as to what the key was for, and now this is the only window I have to open the box before my flight.'

'No problem, sir,' said the security officer. 'What name is the box under and I'll need ID?'

'Solomon Garnett I expect. What do you mean ID? Not for Solomon, surely?' said Hunter.

'Or evidence the box has been passed to you. Something legal.' He grinned. 'I can't let just anyone inside, can I? I'm sure it isn't, but the key you have may have been stolen for all I know.' He frowned and peered at his screen. 'Saying that it may not matter; I don't seem to have a record of a Solomon Garnett on our system.'

Hunter mirrored the man's frown. 'Really? Can you try checking again please? His name has to be there. Could it be at another branch?'

Hunter felt Ethan lean towards his ear. 'John, before you get us thrown out, might I suggest you search under your name? Solomon was a canny old boy. He'd have known this situation would arise.'

Hunter nodded and returned his focus to the guard. 'Sorry er... Mr Symes, is it?' he said, noticing the man's name badge. 'Can you go back a step, please? Solomon may have put it under my name, John Hunter.' He patted his jacket and felt the outline of his passport. 'Luckily, I have my passport.'

Symes paused, huffing under his breath as he typed in the fresh details. This time he looked up from the screen with a smile on his face. 'Excellent, you're here. And a Doctor to boot; impressive stuff.' He took Hunter's passport and scanned it into his system, returning it with a conspiratorial wink. 'This will be a first for the both of us. I've never taken anyone into the high-security section before. Your friend must have something pretty special tucked away.'

'We'll soon find out,' replied Hunter, trying to maintain his cool as Symes punched a security code into a keypad next to the depository's entrance. The door made a loud buzzing sound and clicked open. Ethan shoved Hunter through the door, hard. He lost his balance, and in turn, knocked Symes to the floor, the guard's arms flailing and any semblance of his previous authority lost.

Hunter twisted to face Ethan, his mouth and eyes twitching in anger. 'What did you do that for? Bloody idiot.'

'Just keep going,' Ethan hissed. 'The fucking computer just lit up like a Christmas tree. It won't be long before we've got company.' He looked at Symes and held up a hand in apology. 'Sorry dude - my bad. Tripped over my feet.'

Chapter 5

Hunter rubbed at the pain in his right arm where he knocked it against the door and lifted his hand in an apology to the security guard. Symes scowled and unlocked a pair of large wrought-iron gates separating the trio from the scores of depository boxes beyond.

'These are the first level boxes, the cheaper choice. We get anything from jewelry to porn.' He registered the surprise on Hunter's face. 'Weird, I know, but you'd be surprised at the lengths people go to when it comes to covering up their dark side.' He waved a hand at the boxes. 'There are five hundred in total, all arranged in size order; small, medium and large.'

'Does that mean Solomon's box is somewhere else?' asked Hunter. 'You mentioned it was in a high security section.'

'Affirmative. We keep the high value stuff in the safe.'

'The safe?' said Ethan.

'Well, it's technically a small vault. It's not exactly Fort Knox, but there's still not many skilled enough to crack it.' He grinned. 'Fun fact, the vault at Fort Knox requires a team of ten to unlock it.'

'So your door requires how many?' said Ethan. 'Fun fact - I'm hoping for...'

'Just one,' said Symes, not picking up on Ethan's sarcasm. 'Well, just me and your code. You enter the code into the computer outside. The box is then located and delivered by some kind of robot thing. The vault door opens and your box will be waiting for you inside.'

Hunter raised an eyebrow. 'Nice. I'm guessing no-one could sneak a look at other boxes whilst inside then?'

Symes looked at Hunter, crossing his arms defensively. 'If you're worried someone may have pulled out your friend's box, you shouldn't be. They'd have to fight their way through a least two feet of steel to do that. And if that was a reference to the incident last week, the assailants lost their lives in the reception area. Any more questions?' before Hunter could answer, the guard turned on his heel and headed for the high security section of the depository.

'Wow,' Ethan mouthed at Hunter. 'Hence the new furniture and fresh paint. Touchy fellow, isn't he? Fun fact.'

Hunter grinned and followed Symes down a short corridor hidden amongst the less secure boxes. It was capped by yet another steel framed door. The guard swiped his card, and the locking mechanism buzzed. Hunter peered inside, expecting to find yet more steel and concrete. It was a pleasant surprise to find the room tastefully decorated with a combination of expressionist art, chrome fittings, and black leather. Evidently, you really did get what you paid for with Wells Fargo.

'Our clients use this area to view or add to contents of their boxes.' Symes pointed at a panel on the wall. 'Enter your passcode on the screen and the computers will do the rest. Do you want me to hang about or would you prefer a bit of privacy?'

Hunter nodded. 'Yeah, I think we'll be al...'

'No,' interrupted Ethan, shooting Hunter an angry glance. 'Could you hang about just for a few minutes? God alone knows what the old man put in this box. If it's dangerous, we might need you.'

The guard shrugged his shoulders. 'No problem. Although if it's all the same to you, I'd prefer not to know what's inside. Bank policy, I'm afraid.'

Ethan smiled, rolling his eyes. 'I think your bosses have been watching too many gangster movies.'

Hunter stood in front of the computer and felt Ethan's warm breath on the back of his neck. 'How are we going to get around this?' he whispered. 'I don't know the passcode.' He tapped the screen. The Bank's red square corporate logo disappeared to be replaced by a series of blank boxes. Hunter shook his head in frustration. 'Thirteen bloody digits and they can be letters or numbers.'

Ethan leant over and touched the screen. 'Thirteen digits... Hey didn't I see you mulling over a set of numbers back at the hotel?'

Hunter balled his fists, shaking his head at his apparent stupidity. Of course, the crash date! Why hadn't he thought of that sooner? The late light must be affecting him more than he realized. He rummaged in his pocket and pulled out his notebook. 'It's the crash date. It has to be the crash date.'

'Really,' said Ethan. 'Isn't that a little obvious?'

'A little,' said Hunter. 'Although the message was encrypted - albeit using a fairly basic cypher.' He opened the notebook. 'ROSWELL 070747. It's thirteen digits.' He tapped the code into the computer and waited. Nothing happened. He turned to Symes and raised an eyebrow.

'Give it a minute,' said the guard. 'The robotic things in the back have to retrieve the box before you can get inside the vault.'

'So the code was correct?' asked Ethan.

'Looks that way,' said Symes. 'This place would have lit up like a Christmas tree if it wasn't.' He smiled. 'Although I understand the system gives you a couple of attempts before it goes nuclear.'

The massive circular door to the vault made a loud clunking sound, and the smell of well-oiled hinges permeated the space. 'Better stand back, guys,' Symes directed. 'It opens on its own steam and believe me, you don't want to be clipped by five tons of steel. I can only imagine what it would do to a man caught in its arc.' Ethan nodded and stepped clear as the massive door eased open.

Hunter let out a drawn-out breath. The small, brushed steel cavern was dominated by a conveyor belt knifing its center. Atop a steel counter at the belt's end lay a small, innocuous, black metal box.

'There she lies.' Hunter shot a sideways glance at Ethan and entered the vault. 'I don't know about you, but I'm hoping for the Holy Grail.'

Symes called after him. 'You've only got ninety seconds before that door closes again.'

'Jesus,' hissed Ethan. 'You'd think he'd have told us something like that first.'

Hunter plucked the box from its resting place. Whatever it contained, it certainly wasn't heavy. 'I guess we'd better move. To be honest, my claustrophobia isn't doing me any favors at the moment.' They stepped clear as the vault door rumbled and edged shut behind them. He made a beeline for an armchair and sat down, carefully placing Solomon's box on the glass-top table in front of him. His heart thumped hard in his chest. It was the same feeling he experienced in the field on day one of a dig. The rush of the unknown, the endless possibilities of what might be found and the chance, however slim, of unearthing artefacts with world and life-altering potential.

'Come on,' Ethan said. 'What are you waiting for, fireworks or ticker tape?'

Hunter cracked a knuckle and slipped Solomon's key into the lock, twisting it until it clicked. He held his breath, teased the lid open and reached inside. 'Let's see what you've been up to, Professor Garnett.'

'What is it? A book?' asked Ethan, craning his neck for a glimpse of the contents.

'Not just any book,' said Hunter, pulling it free of its prison with a flourish. 'This is Solomon's notebook.' Bound in dark leather, the small notebook bulged with an assortment of browning loose-leaf papers, the accumulation threatening to rip it apart at its spine. A frayed shoelace held it together, but that too had seen much better days. Hunter rubbed the day-old stubble on his chin. 'He was always very protective of this thing. Wouldn't let anyone near it and as far as I remember, it never left his person. He used to joke it would change the world, but only when the world was ready.'

Ethan raised an eyebrow. 'He might not have been joking.' Hunter nodded and let the possibility hang in the silence. 'So,' said Ethan, breaking the moment. 'Is there anything else?'

Hunter slipped the notebook into his pocket and tipped the box forward. 'Doesn't look like...' He paused, raising an eyebrow as he heard a clinking sound. 'I spoke too soon.' Hunter reached inside and carefully removed a shard of shiny metal. 'Feels like Aluminum,' he said, weighing it in his hands.

Ethan took it from him and examined the find, turning it over and over in his hands. 'There's something stamped on it.' He tapped it. 'Look here, down at the bottom.'

Hunter looked closer. It wasn't surprising he'd missed it; it was tiny. A crest of some sort. He squinted, trying to get the engraving to catch the light. 'A crown hovering above a Middle Eastern style sword... What do you think? Looks Arabian to me?'

'Perhaps Turkish,' said Ethan. 'Any idea what it means?'

Hunter smiled. 'If this is part of the Roswell ship, at least we can rule out alien involvement. This mark is very much of this planet.' He pursed his lips. 'A question for Google perhaps?'

Hunter glanced at Symes as something beeped somewhere on his person. The guard flicked a switch on his belt and the sound stopped. 'Sorry guys, there's someone in reception. Busy night, eh?'

Ethan tapped Hunter's arm. 'We need to leave, and we need to leave now.' Hunter jumped as a loud bang decimated the silence of the depository, and a puff of dust rose from the crack under the door. 'Shit, they must've taken the outside door off its hinges.'

'What the hell was that?' Symes looked at Hunter in disbelief before tentatively opening the door and scurrying off in the direction of the reception.

'We're trapped like rats,' said Hunter. His gaze raked the room and landed on the door to the vault. 'Maybe we could hide inside?' He ran to the computer console and entered Solomon's password. He started as the door behind him crashed against the wall, the lock no doubt blown by the owner of the heavy footfalls that followed. Hunter's finger hovered above the enter key.

'John Hunter, I presume. Be a good chap and turn yourself around. Nice and slow please, and hands where I can see them. I suggest your friend do the same. Any funny business and I will end you both.' Hunter raised his arms and turned to meet the source of the command, his confidence draining to nothing as his eyes processed the size of the man-mountain blocking the doorway. He held Symes in front of him, the guard's collar pulled taught in one of the man's meaty hands. Hunter searched for a weakness but came up blank. The man was built like an NFL all-star; at least six-five with the chest of a fully-grown stag. Symes dropped to the floor, a powerful shove sending him scurrying for cover as the all-star pointed a silver .44 Magnum at Hunter's chest. At this range, the customized hand cannon could down an elephant. Hunter's wiry frame certainly wouldn't pose too many problems. 'Is that the box? Have you opened it?'

'What's your deal, man?' Ethan interrupted. 'We're here opening a box an old man left to a friend on his deathbed. Nothing more.' Hunter winced, expecting the worst.

'Have you opened the box?' the gunman repeated.

'Yes,' said Hunter, 'but we only found...'

'This,' interrupted Ethan. He glanced at Hunter, nodding at the computer screen. Hunter understood immediately. 'There was only a piece of metal inside, a piece of metal with a funny stamp on it. I assume the fact you are trying to steal it means you know what it is?'

'Throw it to me and easy does it.'

Ethan glanced at Hunter again and very deliberately threw Solomon's prize to their captor. The arc was perfect, just short of the man's outstretched arm. He took a step forward, momentarily lowering his gun as his focus switched to making the catch. Hunter nudged the computer screen and the "password accepted" message flashed onto the screen. In unison, Ethan rolled from the sofa, his hand inside his jacket. Three loud bangs filled the air, the sound bouncing around the walls in a crescendo of apocalyptic proportions. Ethan's jacket shredded at the breast. With no time to remove it, he'd been forced to fire through his holster. The first shot missed the target, the bullet pinging off the vault door, but the second and third found their mark, hammering into his torso like punches from a heavyweight. He crashed against the wall but refused to buckle. Ethan lifted the open depository box from the table and hurled it with all his might at their aggressor. With unerring accuracy, one of its corners caught the gunman on the head, drawing blood. He yelled in pain, the gun dropping from his grasp and bouncing noiselessly against the thick carpet. His arm hung at an awkward angle as he slid to the floor, the fight temporarily knocked out of him.

Ethan sprang into action, simultaneously reclaiming the Roswell shard and pulling Hunter towards the exit. There was a loud clunk and the vault door swung open, the bleeding man in its arc.

'You can't leave him,' Symes shouted, finding his tongue again. 'The door will crush him.' Hunter pulled on Ethan's arm, forcing him to stop.

'Don't be a fool, Hunter, leave him. He'd have killed us all once he got what he wanted.'

'You help me pull him clear or I destroy Solomon's book.' Hunter shouted.

Ethan faltered and gave in. 'On one condition.'

'Which is?'

Ethan threw his gun in the air and caught it by the barrel, bringing down the hilt and smashing it hard against the back of the fallen man's skull. 'That I'm certain he's unconscious.' He shoved the gun back inside his jacket and half-heartedly joined Hunter and Symes in pulling him clear of the opening door. 'I just hope he's grateful.'

Hunter turned to leave. 'Wait up,' said Symes. 'Where are you two going? The police are going to want to speak to you. It may have been in defense, but you shot this guy. I can't just let you go.'

Ethan smoothly pulled his gun back out and stroked a few beads of sweat from the guard's forehead. 'I shouldn't worry, Mr. Symes, the police won't get involved. Our man here will see to that.' He kicked the unconscious gunman in the gut. There was a muffled groan. 'Awake already. You're a tough one, aren't you? Since you can hear me, I'll make this simple. You move - you die. Got it?' The man managed a weak nod as Ethan's hand snaked about his person. Snorting in triumph, Ethan pulled a card wallet from an inside pocket and flicked it open.

Hunter gasped at the sight of their captive's face emblazoned upon an instantly recognizable ID card. Above the headshot, a black strip highlighted three heart-stopping words in white, bold print, "CENTRAL INTELLIGENCE AGENCY."

Chapter 6

'We have an agent down!' Chris screamed into his headset. 'Can you not understand English? Agent down. Twenty minutes to mobilize is a disgrace? Just forget it. My target will be long gone by then. I'm based in Miami, I'll go myself. You lot can tidy up the mess later.' He paused, listening to the woman from head office. 'No, he's not dead. Apparently the target saved his life. He thinks we're dealing with a man who can be reasoned with.' Chris paused as the faceless woman spoke again, the blood boiling in his veins. 'What do you mean, "why did I let him go in alone?" I suggest you tone down the attitude, lady. Listen back to the tapes; it was your office who deemed this low priority, not me. Screw this, just do what you want. I'm going to pull my spook out of this shit storm and do your job for you.'

Chris ripped out his earpiece and threw it into a drawer. 'Bureaucratic ass.' He rotated his chair to face his roommate. 'Julio?' Julio looked up from his screen. 'Can you spare me twenty minutes to cover my back? A member of my team has managed to get himself shot. This one's a rarity, a CIA boy with a spine. I told him to wait for backup, but he claimed there was no time.'

Julio grinned. 'Thought he could handle your scrawny archaeologist, did he? Hasn't he seen Indiana Jones?'

'Indiana picked up a friend, unfortunately. A friend with a gun.' Chris spun a set of car keys around his index finger. 'So, you coming or what?'

Julio patted his pocket and grabbed his keys. 'How did you...? I take it you want me to take the Porsche then?'

'If you're offering,' said Chris. 'Just promise me you won't do your, "Driving Miss Daisy," impression.'

A couple of minutes later and both men were safely installed inside Julio's 2005 model 911 turbo, the engine revving aggressively as he gave it some gas.

'So what do I need to know?' asked Julio, releasing the clutch and accelerating harder than he needed in the freeway's direction.

'I don't know much myself. This Hunter guy used his passport as ID in a bank. Looks like a depository box was hired in his name.' He shook his head. 'That wily old bastard must have done it to throw us off the scent.'

Julio nodded. 'It worked. Didn't you run checks on friends and acquaintances?'

'Obviously, I followed the checklist. Hunter was overlooked. They've not been in touch for over a decade, so he wasn't flagged.' He snorted. 'Given how he's acting, I'd say this whole messed up situation is as much a mystery to him as it's been to us. Our agent in the bank thinks Hunter has the notebook everyone's been searching for. We have to act fast or the shit storm swirling building about me could get epic.'

'The Solomon Garnett notebook? Jesus.' Julio slapped Chris on the leg, and the car sped up. 'Now I get it. Next time lead with that and I'll put my foot down sooner. So who's the guy babysitting Hunter? Rival agency or loner?'

'I ran a quick check on the back of a few CCTV images. You aware of a former Russian spy going by the code name, Ahab?'

Julio shot a glance at Chis, his eyes twitching in recognition. 'Ahab. You're shitting me. He's been on my radar for years. Nearly got him a few months back, but he was tipped off.' Julio shook his head. 'We need to be careful, Chris. This boy is a dangerous sonofabitch; he dropped three of my agents before his disappearing act.'

'Why were you after him?'

'He infiltrated one of our bases in the desert. Found something he shouldn't have.'

Chris winced, his shoulder bashing against the car door as Julio rounded a corner. 'Careful, I'd prefer we arrived in one piece. Did you have clearance to kill on sight?'

Julio shook his head. 'No, he's got something physical. Exactly what is beyond my paygrade but I know he's trying to sell it to the highest bidder. I was tasked to find him, retrieve the item and then bury him.'

'What went wrong?'

'As I said, he must have been tipped off. Bastard laid a trap and carved up all three of my men. No remorse.'

'I wonder why he let my boy live then?'

Julio twisted the steering wheel, the tires screeching as they rounded another corner at high speed. 'Christ knows. Maybe he doesn't want Hunter to know what a cold-blooded asshole he really is.'

Chris gripped the door handle as his stomach lurched. 'Come on, Julio. At least give this guy the chance to kill us.'

Julio smiled. 'Don't worry, this guy is a pro. He'll be long gone.'

Chris pointed at the illuminated BankAmerica sign up ahead. 'There it is. Just park up outside. And leave the light flashing. I'd prefer if the local cops stayed out of this.'

Chris extricated himself from his bucket seat and shook his head in disgust at the state of the Bank's front doors. He touched the ragged edge of one of the hinges. 'When an agent tells me he's going to break into a building, I'd normally expect something a little more refined than, "Hulk smash".'

Julio laughed at the poor impression and both men unsheathed their Glock 22 sidearms in unison. 'You ready?'

***

'What do we do now?' asked Hunter, rubbing his nose. 'This alleyway stinks.' He'd developed a touch of sinusitis from the long-haul flight and it was playing up, probably aggravated by stress.

Ethan continued watching the two armed men enter the bank. He frowned. 'Must be bring your dad to workday. Those two can't be field agents.' He shrugged. 'Better for us, I guess.' He pulled up his sleeve and glanced at his watch. 'We need to get to a safe house to examine Solomon's book. Kind of those old boys to provide us with transport.'

'You're not seriously...' Hunter watched, open-mouthed as Ethan strode across the street and pulled open the driver's door as if he didn't have a care in the world. Seconds later, the car's engine rumbled into life. Trying not to dwell on the implications of colluding in the theft of a CIA automobile, Hunter sprinted for the passenger door and jumped inside. He glanced at Ethan. This man certainly had game and whatever his background, he was certainly not a run-of-the-mill tramp. He jumped as a face appeared at the car window. It was Symes.

'They're in your car!' the guard screamed. Ethan pulled out his gun.

Hunter pulled at Ethan's arm. 'What are you doing? Just drive.'

Ethan pulled his arm free and fired three shots through his open window. Symes ducked for cover and scrambled back inside the bank. 'I wasn't going to shoot him. I'm buying time.'

The Porsche fishtailed into the center of the street. The rear window disintegrated and Hunter cursed as a bullet whistled past his ear and lodged in the ceiling. Ethan cornered hard and the two ageing agents disappeared from view.

He grinned. 'That shot will piss off whichever of those two owns this mid-life crisis.'

Hunter shook his head and pushed a finger into the bullet hole. 'That was a little close for comfort.'

'Sorry,' said Ethan. 'But you cost us those extra seconds.' He turned another corner. 'Now sit back and try to relax. By my reckoning, we have at least ten minutes before we need to ditch this thing and the fireworks will start again. I just hope they are still intent on keeping the police out of this.'

'Out of what? And who are they? The CIA? And for that matter, can you give me a little insight into who the hell you are?'

Chapter 7

The notebook flipped in the air and landed with a satisfying thud atop the rectangular coffee table. Hunter's gaze flitted between Ethan and the book. The time had come for answers.

'We're safe now,' said Ethan. 'There's no way they'll find us here. I've called this shipyard home for about six months now and not encountered even a sniff of interest.'

Hunter looked at the dank walls of the abandoned block of flats, the stale odor of damp permeating the air, doing little to convince him of Ethan's promise of security. 'Who owns it?' he asked.

'One of the shipping conglomerates. This place used to be somewhere for the company's executives to rest up before inspecting the troops.'

'Used?' said Hunter.

'Yes, used to be. It was given to me as payment for a little job I carried out a few years back.'

Hunter's ears pricked. 'A little job!? What are you, a hitman or something?'

'A hitman?' Ethan laughed. 'God no; just a few internal corruption issues I helped smooth out. I caught a few crew members enjoying a secondary paycheck smuggling drugs. This flat was my bonus for getting to them before US Customs.'

'A few shallow graves in the Nevada desert was it?'

'This isn't the Godfather. There were a few bruises involved, but they were all delivered to their paymasters in one piece.' He tapped Solomon's book. 'Now, rather than question my credibility, may I suggest you crack open this journal? Solomon left it to you for a reason. Let's find out why.'

Hunter tentatively lowered himself into a moth-eaten armchair and rubbed his tired eyes. He needed sleep, not homework. How could he concentrate after everything he'd been through this evening? He slapped his cheeks and picked up the journal. Ethan's coffee had better be strong. This was going to be a long night.

***

7th July 1947

Solomon turned the handlebars left, panting heavily as he rounded the last bend. The crash site loomed ahead, and he pulled hard on the brakes, his rear wheel locking and bringing him to a skidding stop in front of a series of hefty lumps of rock. He swung his leg clear of the bike and let it fall, leaving it and sprinting towards the thick smoke billowing beyond the scrub-covered dune. A loose pebble skated from under his shoe and he lost his balance. Solomon tumbled forward, his hands slapping against the sandy topsoil as he desperately fought to regain control of his body. He fell hard on his shoulder, and rolled down the dune, a rock slicing through his white shirt and cutting into his skin. With barely time to yelp in pain, he collided with a man-sized boulder jutting from the desert floor. It drove the air from his lungs and instantly ended his tumbling descent. He pressed a hand against the cut and winced, the blood already seeping through his clothing. Using the other hand to right himself, Solomon twisted his body and caught his breath, his brain finally able to process the full horror of the flaming wreck dominating his field of vision.

'What the hell?' he whispered. The crash site was littered with a strange assortment of debris, scattered like confetti about the downed aircraft - if indeed this was an aircraft at all. It looked more like a disfigured silver disk, a Frisbee domed top and bottom. Solomon rose to his feet and hesitantly took a few steps closer. His heart rate quickened. All his instincts urged him to flee, to run for the hills and back to the warm embrace of Lilly-Rose. But he knew running wasn't an option. What if someone was still inside? And worse, still inside and alive. He couldn't just let them die. He coughed and pulled a handkerchief from his pocket, covering his mouth and blocking the worst of the smoke from entering his lungs. Solomon pressed forward and circled the structure. There didn't appear to be an entrance. He crouched beside the single wing and tapped it. A brief echo answered his blow. It was solid but hollow.

A purple light flickered under the craft, bathing Solomon's feet in a strange ethereal glow. He started as he heard a muffled clang of metal on metal. Solomon pushed away from the frame and shuffled backwards in shock. There was a survivor. So where was the entrance? Panic overwhelmed him. It had to be underneath. He fell to his knees, pressing his cheek to the dirt, and desperately clawing at the smooth metal, looking for a way in. Then he saw it, a silver lever depressed into the skin of the machine. He slid forward, buoyed by the discovery and the frantic frequency of the clangs. Whoever was inside was panicking.

Solomon grabbed the lever and yanked as hard as his perilous position would allow. He closed his eyes, praying the enormous machine was stable enough not to roll and crush him. The lever jerked free of its alcove and he pulled again. The mechanism moved through ninety degrees and clicked, locking in place.

Solomon rolled from under the hull and glanced back at the lever. 'Please do something. Don't just pop the fuel cap.' He scrambled backwards, startled as a jet of stale air hissed from a widening set of cracks on the underside of the dome. It looked like a ramp - or was it steps? Solomon dropped on all fours, straining to see through the smoke. Could the pilot be alive? And for the first time it crossed his mind, if he was, was he human? He shuddered, shaking off the thought. That damned Orson Welles radio show had a lot to answer for.

Solomon remembered it well. Nine years ago, Welles terrorized America with his infamous radio play, 'The War of the Worlds'. Broadcast on All-Hallows-Eve 1938, Welles' dead-pan voice interrupted a music show with a breaking-news bulletin claiming a Martian army was invading New Jersey. The show caused panic from coast to coast, with people fleeing cities and causing gridlock all over the United States. It was a vivid memory, and he still remembered his father's panicked voice telling him everything would be fine, as they scampered towards the city limits.

'Herrr...'

Solomon shrank away. What the hell?

'Herrr... me.'

Herr me? Was the creature speaking English? Or was it just a fluke of coincidence? Solomon heard a clunk and the sound of whirring gears. He trained his eyes on the partially open ramp. There! Something moved inside the craft. It looked like the dome of a bald head. It caught the light, and Solomon's eyes widened in disbelief. It was a head, but he couldn't identify its shape as human. A pale, hairless sphere the size and shape of an oversized football. He steeled himself. But so what? The creature needed his help, and alien or otherwise, he was damn sure going to give it.

He dove onto his stomach, reaching his arms and extending his fingers towards the collapsed figure. They closed around skinny, malnourished shoulders. It felt like the body of a child. Solomon pulled, his eyes momentarily blinded by a bright explosion and then further by a stream of thick, dark smoke seeping from the aircraft's core. The structure must be on fire. He pulled harder, praying the creature was the only thing on board. It had to be. There was no way he could physically squeeze his frame through the hatch if it wasn't.

The creature let forth a strange guttural sound and its body slid free. The sound filled Solomon with a sense of relief. It certainly sounded human, but then again, how different could a Martian in pain be? Solomon stumbled backwards, rising to his feet and dragging the alien clear of the wreckage. He pulled it to the relative safety of a dune and lowered its head gently to the ground before collapsing beside it. He coughed, his lungs expelling the dirty smoke. A thunderous explosion filled the Roswell night and Solomon shielded the creature from the searing heat and debris raining down about them.

Something landed with a thump close to his head. He opened his eyes, his heart quickening as they focused upon a lethal shard of metal quivering in the ground. Grabbing it, he shoved it inside his jacket without thinking. He caught the eye of the creature groaning underneath him and again fought the urge to run. But there was something in the creature's eyes stopping him. The huge, black, hypnotic orbs stared up at him, unblinking and intense.

The lips moved, once more emanating the same eerie, guttural sound Solomon first heard from inside the wreckage. 'An g,'

'An g,' said Solomon. He spoke slowly and loudly. 'I don't understand? Do you speak English?' The creature moved, looking for all the world like it was nodding. Its misshapen head bobbing back and forth atop a pencil-thin neck. 'Are you trying to nod?'

The creature's head bobbed back and forth a little more vigorously. One of its skinny arms moved. The skin looked almost translucent in the moon's light. The mouth opened and a finger pointed inside.

Solomon bent forward, shrinking away as his brain processed the horror of what it was showing him. There was no tongue, just a ragged fleshy stump where it should have been. Who could have done such a thing, and more to the point, why?

The whine of a distant siren focused his mind back to the present. 'For your sake, I hope that's an ambulance. I'm not sure I can help you anymore.'

Having seemingly spent any remaining reserves of strength, the creature's arm flopped onto its stomach. It looked exhausted. Solomon stood, and for the first time examined his new companion without fearing for his life. If you ignored the head, he mused, the body could easily pass for that of a young boy. He gazed into the unblinking eyes. But how could one ignore the head?

Solomon glanced right, turned as a large vehicle skidded and screeched to a halt, illuminating him in the beam of a pair of bright headlights. Four sets of heavy boots crunched into the sandy gravel.

'Military Police. On your knees and hands above your head. We have you surrounded.'

Chapter 8

Solomon felt a meaty pair of hands grip his shoulders, leading him and shoving him, against his will, into the back of the forest-green ambulance. He yelped as his thighs thumped against the tailgate, his cuffed hands unable to prevent the painful collision as he toppled inside.

'What are you doing?' he shouted. 'I've done nothing wrong. I've got rights.' His voice cracked, fear getting the better of him. 'I have got rights haven't I? What are you going to do with me?'

The spade-like hands returned, grasped him under his armpits, hauling the remainder of his body inside the vehicle and up onto a stretcher. 'I need you to calm down, sir. You're safe now. We just need answers to a few questions. That's all, just a few questions.'

Solomon focused on the man addressing him. He was in uniform. Maybe this was legitimate. Solomon grimaced as his left cuff was removed and reattached to a bar on the stretcher. The soldier then pulled Solomon's right arm straight and wound a Velcro secured pad about his bicep. A heart monitor beeped somewhere above his head. A light illuminated his captor. He was short, but broad, with dark, greying hair and kind eyes. Solomon's heart rate slowed.

'Good lad,' said the soldier, noting the drop in the speed of the beeping on a notepad. 'You thirsty? Can I get you a drink?' Solomon nodded and accepted a slug of warm water from a flask on the soldier's belt. 'I'm Kevin. Can you tell me your name?'

'Solomon Garnett, sir.'

'You from Roswell?'

'Yes, sir.'

'And can I ask what you are doing in such a remote locale at this time of night, Solomon?'

'A g-girl, sir. I was on my way to see my girl. Then this disk thing flew over my head and crashed into the desert. I knew no-one was about. I wanted to help.'

Kevin's eyes narrowed, his gaze boring into Solomon for a good ten seconds before once again relaxing; his inbuilt lie detector evidently satisfied the explanation was the truth. Solomon continued, making sure to leave nothing out. There was no way he wanted to be interrogated in whichever base these men were from. What would his mother say? He could almost feel his father's belt on his behind, even thinking about it.

'So... can I go now?' Solomon asked. 'That's everything, I promise.'

Kevin snapped his notebook shut and scrunched his face apologetically. 'Not yet, I'm afraid. I've just got to report my findings. Once complete, I expect they'll give you a lift back to Roswell.'

'No problem. Whatever you need.' Solomon rattled his cuffs. 'Any chance of removing these?'

Kevin smiled and shook his head. 'Sorry, I need authorization first. If I let you go and it turns out you're a Russkie spy, my career would be over.'

He turned and jumped from the ambulance, leaving Solomon alone with his thoughts. He took a deep breath and lifted his head from the stretcher. The rear door was open and he could just about make out the creature. It was more or less in the same prostrate position where he'd left it, but now surrounded by a buzz of activity. A barrel-chested man with a thick neck and officer's cap stood motionless at the creature's feet. He saw Kevin salute the man. He must be the officer in charge. Without warning, a breathless soldier appeared on top of the dune. He shouted at the group and made a frantic hand gesture, indicating something on the road behind him.

'Sir, it's the press. They're on their way. The boy must have tipped them off.' Solomon shuddered. Although his conscience was clear, this development would not aid his cause in getting home anytime soon. The man continued. 'We need to hide the body. What do you want me to do?'

The officer's chest heaved, and he shook his head. 'Shit, I don't know. Tell the bastards what they want to hear. We're bang to rights on this one and if they discover the truth, we're all screwed.' He turned to Kevin. 'You there, stick this thing in the ambulance with the boy. We don't want any photographs.'

'So the boy is coming with us?' said Kevin.

'Yes, he's coming with us. What are you, an idiot? Perhaps you would prefer the press got their wormy little paws on him? Now get rid of this thing, those headlights are close.'

Kevin covered the creature's body with a blanket and lifted it onto the stretcher next to Solomon. He looked genuinely apologetic. 'I'm sorry, lad, looks like you're coming along for the ride.' Solomon shrugged and said nothing, watching Kevin fiddle with the locking mechanism on the rear doors. He slammed them shut, the vibration enough to shake the blanket free of the creature's head. Solomon stared transfixed as the massive globe-like eyes bore into him, their intensity causing him to shudder. He tried to break contact but found he couldn't move, his head locked in place by some invisible force.

'*Herr me...*'

Kevin jumped. 'What the hell was... Is it still alive?'

'I saved him from the craft,' said Solomon.

'Yeah, but... I just assumed. What's it saying? How do you know the gender?'

'What are you going to do with him?' asked Solomon, ignoring the questions.

'Christ only knows. I guess we need to find out what it is, where it came from, determine if it's a threat and if so if there are any more.'

'So you're going to kill him?'

'Err, no,' said Kevin, a little unconvincingly. A radio crackled into life amidst a hiss of static. He held up his hand; gesturing for silence. 'Listen to this. I asked a friend to record the arrival of the reporters.' He turned up the volume on a device wired into the wall of the ambulance, twisting the dial until the sound of an authoritative voice filled the cabin.

'We will publish a press release in the morning, gentlemen, and I would appreciate it if you would all now leave.'

'That's Walter Haut,' said Kevin. 'He's one of the good guys in intelligence.'

'What have you found, Walter?' asked a reporter. 'A rancher rang our office claiming our boys shot down an alien aircraft?'

'That's you in the clear,' whispered Kevin, nodding at Solomon. He turned his attention back to the speaker.

'I can neither confirm nor deny such an allegation,' said Walter.

'So admit you have found something at this site?'

'A flying disk has been recovered, but that is all I can tell you. As I said, we will give a press release tomorrow at noon.'

'A flying disk,' whispered Kevin. 'Well, it's more than I thought he'd say. I suppose Major Marcel did tell him to feed them something.'

'Do you think he's part of an invasion then? Or maybe pre-invasion reconnaissance?' said Solomon, nodding at the creature.

Kevin snorted. 'I certainly hope not. Not sure how effective our armor will be against ray guns.'

***

Hunter looked up from Solomon's diary. 'Ethan?' Ethan's face appeared around the door. 'You wouldn't happen to have a copy of the Roswell press release would you?'

'I thought you'd never ask?' He disappeared into the back room. 'Which version do you want?'

'Which version?'

'Yup, they released two.'

'Are you serious, two?' said Hunter. 'And no-one questioned it?'

Ethan grinned and dropped three sheets of paper on the table in front of him. 'Not at the time. Why would anyone question the infallible word of our most honorable and incorruptible military leaders?'

Hunter picked up the first. "The intelligence office of the 509th Bombardment group at Roswell Army Air Field announced at noon today, that the field has come into possession of a flying saucer."

Hunter devoured every word. The article followed the gist of what the intelligence officer, Walter Haut, promised the reporters in Solomon's diarized account. Notably, there was no mention of his mentor's involvement. The release detailed the discovery of a "flying disk" by an unidentified rancher in the vicinity of the town of Roswell, New Mexico.

The rancher notified the local sheriff, Sheriff Geo. Wilcox, who in turn informed the military.

'So the rancher must have arrived and disappeared before Solomon pitched up,' whispered Hunter, piecing a timeline together in his mind.

"Believing the find to be outside of his capability, Sheriff Wilcox passed authority of the recovery to a certain Maj. J. A. Marcel, an intelligence officer of the 509th Operations Group. On completion of his assessment, Marcel ordered the disk be flown to higher headquarters for further analysis."

Hunter glanced at Ethan. 'Higher headquarters? Where was it taken?'

Ethan shrugged. 'No-one really knows. I know they eventually flew the remains to the infamous Area 51 facility via Edwards Air Force Base, but where it was taken first, I've honestly no idea.'

'Area 51? Isn't that a myth? Actually, don't worry, we can come back to that later.' Hunter returned to the press release, reading aloud. 'Haut made it clear no details of the saucer's construction or appearance were to be revealed to the press. The matter was to remain a classified military matter.' Hunter paused. 'They didn't give much away, did they?'

Ethan smiled. 'Try to think in terms of the implications of what they aren't saying? On the day they were simply trying not to stir up any panic amongst the public. We were a pretty simple race back then. The prospect of an alien invasion would have goddam near caused the country to collapse into anarchy.' He pushed the second paper within Hunter's reach. 'And then later that same day, this came out.'

Hunter snorted as he read the first few lines. 'Jesus, it's not even subtle.'

The article documented a second press conference, this time held by the Commanding General of the Eighth Air Force, Roger Ramey. He stated his men had recovered the remains of a weather balloon from the Roswell crash site. The General even supplied a little of the salvaged debris to corroborate his story. A meagre offering of singed foil, rubber and little bits of wood, apparently enough to convince the newspapers he was telling the truth.

Hunter tutted and pursed his lips. 'Was that the end of it? Well, until the crackpot alien conspiracy fanatics got involved?'

'Not quite,' said Ethan, pushing a third piece of paper into his hand. 'This hit the press a couple of weeks later.'

Hunter raised an eyebrow. The last newspaper extract documented an eyewitness account from what the journalist termed, "a respectable and well thought of couple from Roswell".

A week or so after the event, Mr. and Mrs. Dan Wilmot reported seeing what they thought was a flying disk. Around ten o'clock in the evening of the 7th of July, the pair had been enjoying a nightcap on the porch of their residence, 105 South Penn. They were shocked when a large glowing object whooshed above them. It appeared to be travelling in a north-westerly direction at a high rate of speed.

The pair ran into their yard to follow its path. Wilmot estimated the craft to have been in sight for just under a minute, flying between 400 and 500 miles per hour and at an altitude of around 1,500 feet.

He described it as oval in shape, a little like two inverted saucers faced mouth to mouth. Guessing the craft to be between fifteen and twenty feet in diameter, Wilmot detailed how the skin of the craft glowed in a manner he could neither understand nor explain. All he could do was keep repeating, "It did not look of this world."

Ethan smiled. 'One hell of a speedy weather balloon.'

Chapter 9

The ambulance bumped and jolted over what Solomon could only assume was a makeshift desert road. Having lost his bearings long ago, he couldn't even make a rough guess as to its destination. He could hear the rumbling diesel engines of at least a couple more trucks and guessed he was part of a convoy. He glanced at the alien creature lying next to him. Was it dead? It certainly looked dead.

He thumped his head repeatedly into the thin pillow atop his improvised bed. This was ridiculous. Why was he here? He should not still be here. He'd only been trying to help. What more could he do other than promise to keep the events of the night a secret? Who would believe him even if he did break their trust? He was nineteen, known to have been very drunk just a few short hours ago and on his way to make a fool of himself in front of a girl. He huffed and rattled his cuff, still firmly attached to the rod welded to the right side of the stretcher.

The ambulance slowed to a stop. Solomon slapped his free hand against the cabin window, desperate and close to tears. 'Kevin. Kevin let me out. Please. I won't tell, I promise.'

The curtain blocking his view slid to one side. 'We're nearly there, friend. We've arrived at the entrance to the base. Just hang in there for me. I doubt they'll keep you for long.'

'What base? Where are we? We've been travelling for ages.'

'Sorry, that's classified. I shouldn't worry about it though. The less you know, the better.' The curtain slid back into place and Solomon slumped down onto his stretcher. He could hear Kevin speaking to someone, but it was nothing more than an ID check. The ambulance gathered speed, and they were off, bumping down yet another dirt track.

The ambulance skidded to a halt, and Solomon started as the rear doors crashed open. He shielded his eyes as bright spotlights illuminated the interior of his temporary prison. The creature twisted onto its side and let out a low moan. It was a pitiful sound. Solomon squinted, looking beyond the lights, and made out a series of shadowy figures bustling about in front of a large warehouse, or perhaps a super-sized aircraft hangar. He blinked, the heart-rate monitor beeping furiously as the fear of the unknown overwhelmed him. Kevin stepped into view. The familiarity calmed him, but not enough to stop a tear roll down his cheek.

'I want to go home.' Solomon sniffed. 'Am I going to die?'

Kevin slipped an arm around his shoulder and unlocked the handcuff. 'Don't be silly, lad. We're just being cautious. You've just witnessed a highly sensitive military event. You should feel privileged. There aren't many who know we're not alone.'

'So he really is... Alien?'

'We don't know where from, but yes.' Kevin nodded, raising an eyebrow. 'He really is.'

The revelation hung in the air. Neither party said anything more as Kevin led Solomon from the ambulance. The soldier pointed at something inside the huge hangar. The doors were open and Solomon watched the trucks from the crash site file inside. He stopped in his tracks and pulled Kevin back. He considered himself an aviation buff and prided himself on the breadth of his knowledge.

'What are they? I don't recognize any of them, not one.' He paused to take in the spectacle. 'Are they experimental or from...' Unable to bring himself to say the Alien word, again he opted for something safer. 'Elsewhere?'

'I suggest you forget anything you see tonight. They are just relics of the war. We utilized this place as a center catering for target practice for our bomber crews. I believe they were something to do with that.' Solomon huffed and shook his head in disbelief. Given what he had learnt tonight, why was this man continuing to trot out the party line bull-crap. He opened his mouth to press him further, but the impromptu interrogation faltered as a petite, brown-haired woman joined them. 'Ah, Senior Airman Jenkins,' said Kevin. 'She'll take you through the confidentiality paperwork.'

'Will I see you again?'

Jenkins steered him in the direction of the hangar and a brightly lit office just inside the entrance. Kevin winked and waved. 'Who knows? maybe one day you'll end up working for us.'

Solomon walked a few paces and turned, breaking free of Jenkins' grasp. He ran back to Kevin, ready to thank him for his kindness. He was speaking with the man he'd called Major Marcel. Solomon stopped, frozen in his tracks by ten life-changing words.

'Do you think he bought it?' asked Marcel.

'Yeah, he bought it...' Marcel coughed over Kevin's words and nodded at Solomon. He turned, his face reddening. 'Hello again.' He grinned a toothy, charismatic smile. 'What have you done with the lovely Miss Jenkins?'

'I just wanted to say thank you,' Solomon stammered. 'I didn't thank you.'

'No problem, all part of the service.'

Solomon nodded at the ambulance. A group of men transferred the Alien from the stretcher and into a steel casket. 'What are you going to do with him?' Jenkins grasped his arm and pulled him towards the office.

Kevin grimaced. 'I'm sorry to say, but he'll be examined and buried. I'm afraid the Alien died in transit.'

Solomon wrenched his arm free but continued to follow Jenkins. 'He didn't die in transit,' he whispered. 'What the hell is going on?'

***

'Is that it?' asked Hunter, turning the page to find it blank.

'Afraid so,' said Ethan.

'You might have to work with me a bit here. Just to clarify, you worked at Area 51 and knew of no Alien activity.'

'Correct.'

'So what was Roswell?'

Ethan grinned. 'Would the answer, "an intensely messed up situation," suffice?'

'Wait, the shard of metal Sol retrieved from the flying disk. Was that what was in the box? Did they not think to search him?'

Ethan nodded. 'I believe it could be. And no, they didn't. I'm guessing they overlooked it in all the excitement of a potential invasion.'

'Invasion?' Hunter pulled out the shard of metal and sat it next to the notebook. 'So to be clear, Solomon witnessed the UFO in the air, saw it crash, saved one occupant and we still don't believe in the alien cover-up theory?'

'Correct.'

'May I ask why?'

'May I refer you to the ten words fueling a lifetime of obsession, "Do you think he bought it? Yeah, he bought it."' Ethan sat back in his chair. 'What would you take from those words, Dr Hunter?'

Hunter cocked his head to one side. 'Solomon was fed a story.'

'Correct. But what story did the Air Force feed him?'

'That the creature he found was alien to this planet...' Hunter placed his hands behind his head, deep in thought. 'Okay, so the creature was human. I still don't understand. Why then were the US Air Force afraid?'

A gravelly baritone echoed about the room. 'The truth, dear boy. These men were afraid of the truth.'

Hunter sprang to his feet and spun on his heels. His face drained of its color. Standing before him was a ghost; the living, breathing ghost of Solomon Garnett.

Chapter 10

Chris lowered his glass, the single malt serving its purpose and reigniting his senses. Aged twelve years, the bottle of Old Pulteney was not his favorite whisky in their range, but pretty darn close. Now if the bottle's label had read aged twenty-one years, it really would have hit the spot. Voted World Whisky of the Year 2012, Chris' palate had never and probably would never again experience such a majestic drink. The unfortunate by-product being that everything else now felt like a poor imitation.

'You want another?' asked his boss. 'This is the bottle you told me about, right?'

Chris smiled. 'Close enough. How are you finding it?'

The man swilled the bronze liquid in his glass and inhaled. 'Full-bodied, with traces of fruit; apples and pears. Slightly fragrant with spicy overtones.'

Chris shook his head and glanced at Julio. What an idiot. Not only were these the tasting notes recited word for word from the distillery's website, but they were for a different bottle. How these people made it into positions of power was beyond him. This particular incarnation was three months into the job. Geoffrey Johnston, a direct recruit from Langley and the Company were supposed to be lucky to have him. This stunt with the whisky was evidently his attempt to climb down from his perch in the clouds and bond with his troops.

Chris emptied the remains of his glass. 'Very good, sir. You obviously know your stuff.'

Geoffrey looked pleased and refilled their glasses. 'So where are we with the Hunter problem? It appears we miscalculated his importance when allocating the agents.'

'Bastard stole my car,' grumbled Julio. He jabbed Chris with his finger. 'And then this bastard put a couple of holes in it.'

'I apologized,' said Chris. 'Anyway, we got it back didn't we? And I'm sure the Company will stump up for the repairs.'

Geoffrey nodded. 'You catch this guy and hell, we'll go all out and buy you a brand new one.'

'Thank you, sir. Good to know you have our backs.' Chris shifted in his seat. 'To summarize, our report will confirm the bank's security guard witnessed Hunter remove two items from a safe deposit box. A book and a shard of metal.'

'What's this about, sir?' Julio interrupted.

'Please, sir, any information will help,' added Chris. 'If we're going to track these guys, we need to know what we're up against. What are we missing? And why are the bigwigs, if you'll pardon the expression, shitting bricks?'

Geoffrey cracked the knuckles on his right hand and rose from his desk. He turned to stare through his window at the alleyway two floors below. 'You'd think my pay grade would demand a better view.'

'Come on, sir,' said Chris. 'Give me something my men can use. I'm flying blind at the moment. I need intel and need it quick if you want results.'

Geoffrey turned, his friendly demeanor replaced by cool annoyance. 'Lose the attitude, Cartwright. You know as well as I do this operation is black. No one outside the Chief is party to the full picture.' He sniffed, then drained a second glass of whisky. 'However, I have been authorized to tell you what I know. Not that it's much, or even worth knowing.'

Chris frowned. 'What do you mean by that?'

Julio slapped the table. 'He means he ain't sure if those sons of bitches upstairs have fed him some bull, just to make us go away.'

Geoffrey looked uncomfortable and nodded. 'Something like that.'

'So, what did they tell you?' said Julio.

'To put it succinctly, this Solomon guy we've been tracking was found at the scene of the Roswell weather balloon crash site in 1947.'

Julio shook his head and closed his eyes. 'Don't tell me.'

Geoffrey nodded. 'Yup, turns out it wasn't a weather balloon at all, but some kind of a UFO. A UFO with a survivor.'

Chris whistled and slapped his thighs. 'Wow, sweet, and that's why the URS Corp is involved... Am I right in assuming the items retrieved from Wells Fargo were proof?'

Geoffrey turned back to his window. 'I told you it was fantastical. Upstairs believes the shard of metal to be part of the Roswell craft.'

'Are we really buying this? There must be more. Something doesn't add up,' said Julio. 'Even if the shard was part of a flying saucer, surely by chucking money in the right direction, we could easily discredit the find. Hell, I could pull the wing off my car and claim it was from a Ferrari. Doesn't mean it is. Come on guys, we're talking sixty years ago here.'

'I know,' said Geoffrey. 'There's definitely more to this than I'm cleared for.'

'So what do we do?' said Julio, looking at Chris.

Chris frowned and drummed his fingers on the arms of his chair. 'I guess nothing for the moment. We need Hunter to re-surface.'

'Fine, at least this time we'll be ready,' said Julio. 'And more specifically, ready to neutralize his accomplice.'

Geoffrey reached into the top drawer of his desk and pulled out a file. 'I assume you mean the Russian.' He threw the file to Chris. 'Julio, I know you've been tracking him, but a little more intel won't hurt. You both have full clearance. He's a slippery one; a double agent... or rather, he's meant to be. No one is really sure whose side he's on now. There has been a "shoot to kill," authorization hanging over him for months now. And not just from our agency, the Russians have issued a similar directive.' He pointed to the cover of the file. 'Probably why someone's stamped "presumed dead" on his file.' The phone rang on the desk. Geoffrey snatched it up. 'I thought I said no disturb...' He nodded and replaced the receiver. 'Back to your posts, gentlemen. Your targets have surfaced. Agents are already en route and this time we have eyes in the sky. They won't escape.'

***

Hunter grasped Solomon's hand and pulled him into an impromptu hug. 'You old dog! How are you still alive? I just saw you buried. What the hell have you got yourself into?'

He patted his stomach and grinned. 'Just a dressed-up manikin with a few rocks to simulate this I'm afraid.'

'But why?'

'Let's just say, like Icarus, I flew a little too close to the Sun. My choices were pretty limited by the end; fake my death or let others take the choice out of my hands.'

Hunter pushed away from his former mentor. 'Come on, Solomon, enough of the theatrics; just tell me what's going on? I've been to hell and back for you this evening.'

'I know and I'm sorry.' Solomon glanced at the floor, avoiding eye contact. 'Unfortunately, I may need one more favor.'

'A favor? Don't you think you've had enough of those already?'

Solomon pursed his lips. 'You're right, and again I'm so sorry for pulling you into all this. Your safe deposit box was one of a hundred I've rented all around the country; each of them taken out in the name of one of my previous students. I needed the artefact, and you were the only one who could open the box. I knew my death would bring you back.'

'But why me?' asked Hunter.

Solomon stepped forward and took Hunter's arm. He shrank away, uncomfortable at the mania emanating from the old man's piercing green eyes. 'You've read my journal, but still barely scratched the surface of what's been going on. Hell, even after forty years chasing shadows, I probably haven't either.'

'So you're an ufologist.'

'No, John, I'm not. That's just my cover. I know what I found wasn't Alien and I've spent my life trying to find answers and justice.'

'And now you have.'

Solomon frowned. 'Not quite, but I am close and those bastards out there know it.'

Hunter exhaled and shook his head, trying to take in all he was hearing. 'Can we just take a couple of steps backwards? I'll say it again. Where exactly do I fit into all this?'

'Serena Harmony. Do you remember the name?'

Hunter stared blankly at Solomon. The name was familiar, but why? 'Serena Harmony...' He paused; surely it must be someone from UF. 'Wait, was she a lab assistant at the University?'

'Bingo,' said Solomon. 'And I might add, a lab assistant that once held a torch for a certain, John Hunter.' He chuckled, smoothing down his cream linen shirt. 'I say torch, but as I remember, it was more of a raging bonfire.'

'Seriously? Well I'll be... I never knew.'

'Lost in one of your books I expect. You were a wonderful student, John, but your social skills were... shall I say, lacking?'

'Thanks very much. Although I don't remember you being much of a hit amongst the socialites either.' Hunter ran a hand through his hair and rubbed his tired eyes. 'So where does Miss Harmony fit in? What do you want with her?'

'It's not what I want with her exactly. What I'm after is a date with her employer, and more specifically with their computer servers. I need information...' A beeping sound emanated from Solomon's belt and stopped him mid-flow. He glanced at Ethan. 'You said you weren't followed.'

'There's no way... we took their car.'

'And you scanned both John and the car for bugs?'

'Yup, only one and I left it in the cab.'

'What about his phone?' Ethan's eyes twitched. Solomon turned to Hunter, panic in his voice. 'Your phone, John?'

Hunter pulled it from his pocket. 'I just turned it on. Why?'

'Shit.' Solomon grabbed it and threw it against the wall. 'They know your number, you idiot. Hell, even a fucking five-year-old could track you armed with that information.' He drew a Colt semi-automatic from a holster under his shirt and flicked the safety off. 'We've been compromised. We have to leave and leave now.' He ran to the door of one of the bedrooms and yanked it open. The sight of his gun raked the walls beyond and, satisfied it was safe, he disappeared inside.

Hunter could feel the knot in his stomach returning. He'd thought he was safe. How can he have been so stupid to overlook the phone? For that matter, how had Ethan been so stupid as to overlook the phone? He looked at Ethan, but he refused to meet his gaze. Hunter watched as the man shifted his weight between each leg. A bead of sweat left a trail of moisture from his hairline and disappeared into one of his thick, dark eyebrows.

'I warned you not to trust anyone,' hissed Ethan. He lunged at Hunter, a balled fist aimed at the archaeologist's jaw. Hunter saw the telegraphed attack coming and sidestepped the blow. Now the element of surprise was on his side. Ethan did not know the extent of Hunter's pugilistic training. He'd banked on landing a knockout punch and, in doing so, overextended himself. Hunter twisted his body along the line of attack and brought his knee sharply into Ethan's midriff. He took the blow without reacting, but still bent forward far enough for Hunter to slam his right elbow hard between his attacker's exposed shoulder blades. Ethan collapsed to his knees, his eyes wild with fury. He punched out in desperation. Hunter sidestepped, deflected the blow, and gripped the flailing wrist. This time Ethan could not help but scream as Hunter twisted his arm through a hundred and eighty degrees, shoving a shoe into the man's armpit as he anchored the lock.

Solomon reappeared in the doorway, his handgun raised. 'John? What the hell is going on? Ethan, what are you doing?'

'I'm afraid to say it, but it appears you've got a snake in the grass,' said Hunter.

'Ethan?' whispered Solomon, his eyes expressing disappointment at the apparent betrayal.

'Fuck the both of you.'

'But you know what they've done?' The old man looked almost physically wounded by this turn of events.

'What can I say?' hissed Ethan. 'They pay better than you do.' Hunter twisted Ethan's wrist further and heard a crack. Ethan screamed in pain and passed out.

Hunter winced. 'Even I felt that one.' He glanced at Solomon. 'What shall I do with him?'

Solomon threw him a length of twine. 'Tie him up. We don't have much time.' He turned but paused in the doorway. He glanced at Hunter. 'Actually, perhaps I should err on the side of… screw it!' He raised his weapon and fired a single shot. It struck Ethan with a wet thump in the back of his head. The body convulsed and twitched as blood seeped into the carpet, a halo of claret expanding about the dead man's head.

Hunter let Ethan's leg drop to the floor. 'What the…' He looked between Solomon and the body, shock enveloping him. 'Jesus, what have you just done?'

'He knew everything, John. Everything, that is, apart from Serena.' He tapped the gun against the side of his head. 'If I hadn't pulled the trigger, Serena would have lost her life within twenty-four hours. I've come too far to abandon my plans for the sake of a traitorous rat.'

'He's not the first man you've killed, is he? I can see it in your eyes.'

Solomon shook his head. 'There have been others. But all were justified.'

'As long as they were justified,' said Hunter, his words laced with sarcasm. 'It's nice to know you aren't a complete psycho.'

'Stick with me and you'll understand eventually,' said Solomon with a grin. 'For now, it's safer if you only know the basics.' He turned, and this time re-entered the bedroom.

Hunter shook his head and attempted to compose himself. What the hell was happening? Before its destruction, his phone confirmed his picture currently occupied the thirteenth position on America's most-wanted list. There must be more to this than the sixty-year-old conspiracy much of the world already believed to be true. He stepped over Ethan and followed Solomon. What else could he do?

Hunter hesitated and stared in disbelief at the sight greeting him. The walls were lined with high definition monitors; the hardware attached to them whirring as they deleted gigabyte upon gigabyte of surveillance data, photographs, and documents. Solomon raised his eyebrows in mock frustration. 'This used to be the center of my operation. I'll be with you in a second; I just need to detonate the hard disks before we can go.'

'Detonate?'

'It's the only way to ensure the data can't be retrieved.' Hunter saw a puff of smoke and the screens went dark in unison. 'Okay, we're done. Right, let's go; Ethan's friends are already in the building.' He passed a handgun to Hunter. 'Here, you'll probably need this. Just stay close to me and whatever you do, don't look back.'

Hunter wiped away the beads of sweat gathering on his face and checked the gun was loaded. 'Where are we going?'

Solomon pulled a broom from a cupboard and prodded a hatch in the roof. 'Up.'

'Up? To the attic? But won't that trap us?'

Solomon hammered the handle of the broom through a window and cleared the glass. 'And that's our decoy escape route,' he said. 'Have a bit of faith, John. I knew this day would come eventually. This plan has been in place for months.'

'Aren't you worried Ethan may have told...'

'He didn't know about it.' Solomon interrupted, ducking to avoid a ladder as it slid from its resting place in the attic. 'Lucky for us, on top of everything else, I'm a paranoid old bastard.'

Hunter tailed Solomon up the steps and retrieved the ladder, carefully clicking the hatch shut with as little noise as possible. It proved the right move as an explosion rocked the building, and seconds later the apartment's front door was kicked from its hinges. Solomon raised a finger to his lips as something flashed and hissed beneath their feet in the room below.

'Keep your breathing to a minimum and cover your mouth and nose. That's a tear gas canister,' whispered Solomon. 'We need to move and move fast. It won't be long before it seeps through the cracks and inhaling tear gas is really not that high on my bucket list.'

He turned and pulled Hunter toward a framed poster of a UFO. The words, "I WANT TO BELIEVE," were printed in bold under the otherworldly craft. Solomon smiled at the confusion on Hunter' face and shrugged. 'It should really say, "I want the rest of you to believe," but the store was all out of them.' He pulled it from the wall and revealed the bricked-up divide separating him from the apartment next door. The elderly academic pushed at the center of the brickwork. Hunter's forehead creased into a frown, the expression replaced by surprise as the bricks gave way and fell noiselessly into the adjoining attic. Solomon winked. 'I laid out some pillows to break their fall. I told you I was prepared.' They climbed through the hole and not a moment too soon as the effects of the tear gas took hold. Solomon stuffed pillows in the gap to delay the advancing gas.

'Now what?' asked Hunter. His gaze landed on the large window set into the slope of the roof. 'Are we jumping? There's no way you're making that at your age!'

Solomon grinned and pulled something from his pocket. 'I may be approaching the end, John, but I'm not there yet.' It was a detonator.

Hunter's eyes widened as the extent of his friend's mania became apparent. He made a grab for the brick of plastic but tripped and fell to the floor. 'Is that a detonator? What are you doing? We're nowhere near clear of a blast radius.'

'You need to trust me, John. The only casualties will be next door. I reinforced that apartment better than Fort Knox. That includes the entrance to the attic.' Hunter heard a click and scrambled for the window. The explosion was as intense as it was spectacular. Concentrated in the tiny space and with nowhere to go, the energy from the blast escaped via the windows. A tsunami of flame struck the adjacent building, cladding two floors in white-hot flames. The air stank of chemicals and a combination of glass and molten metal showered the street below with gut-wrenching consequences. Screams of pain and terror scaled the building.

Solomon winced and joined Hunter at the window. 'Bugger. I didn't see that coming.'

Hunter shoved it open, craning his neck in a futile attempt to discover the extent of the devastation Solomon's bomb had inflicted. 'You idiot, Sol. It was a bomb, and a bloody big one at that. What did you expect? At least there don't seem to be any bodies down there. Although I doubt the men in your apartment fared so well.'

Solomon looked on the verge of tears. He was in shock. Seemingly, this was one slice of carnage even Solomon's poor excuse for a conscience couldn't justify. Hunter grabbed him by the shoulders and shook him. 'Sol, as horrible as this situation is, I need you to block it out. Pay for a little time with a shrink later, but right now I need you with me. There could be more of Ethan's hired guns kicking around this building, and I don't fancy our chances if they find us.' He shook him again. 'Now focus. What's the next part of your escape plan?'

Solomon twisted free of Hunter's grip and took several deep breaths. He wiped his eyes and shuffled over to the attic exit. He pulled it up and, using a ladder, descended to the floor below. Hunter looked back at the open window. 'Okay,' he whispered. 'So I guess we aren't jumping then. That's definitely a good thing.'

Hunter landed nimbly on the floor of the second apartment and found Solomon rummaging through a large oak cupboard in the room's corner. The Professor acknowledged him with a friendly nod. 'Ah, John, nice of you to join me. Welcome to part two of the plan.'

'You're sounding chipper again; you worked through your emotional turmoil pretty quick?'

'No-one died, lad.'

Hunter rolled his eyes and brushed down his clothes. 'That you know of... So what is it?'

'What is what?'

'Part two of the plan. Jesus, this is like getting blood from a stone.'

'We just walk out.' Solomon grinned. 'Join the crowd outside, admire the devastation and just walk away.' He threw an overcoat and grey wig at Hunter's feet. He picked them up and screwed up his nose. 'Don't look so disgusted. It's mostly the homeless and the elderly living around here. They don't tend to wear Hugo Boss.'

Hunter held a hand under his nose. 'You could have at least washed it first. Did its last owner actually die in it?'

'I'm going to plead the fifth on that.'

Hunter felt his nose twitch in repulsion as he pulled the festering garment on. 'I really hope that's just a bad joke.'

The buzz of an electric shaver filled the apartment, whining in protest as Solomon hacked at his thick beard. A bit of a sound risk, but it made sense. Solomon's beard was his trademark and pictures of him past the age of twenty without it were non-existent. Hunter studied his former mentor as the bristly hair collected about his feet. He wasn't the man he remembered. Lank, unwashed, grey hair sat atop a wiry body and supported a gaunt face with a weak chin, the real reason behind the thick beard. The Professor looked older than his years, but although prioritizing his work above health during his life, he still carried a decent amount of definition in his muscles. For a man in his eighties, Hunter certainly got the impression he could still handle himself.

Dispelling the myth somewhat, Solomon let forth a hacking cough and doubled over. Hunter slapped his back, fearful he may be choking.

'Thanks, John, but it's just the smoke. I need to get out of here.'

Hunter pulled on the wig, repressing his gag reflex as its festering smell entered his nostrils. He placed a hand on the small of Solomon's back and ushered Solomon towards the exit. 'At least the state of your lungs will make this a little more realistic. He pulled open the door, instantly slamming it shut as a barrage of flame and heat stonewalled their exit. 'Bugger; I take it you didn't reinforce the doors either.'

Solomon frowned. 'I'm afraid not. It was all about protecting this flat from the initial blast.'

'The upside being it will also delay Ethan's mates.' Hunter shook his head, unsure of his next move. 'We're still going to have to make a run for it. How about dousing our clothes in water? And perhaps a little shampoo for this horrific hairpiece.'

Solomon pointed to a door to his left. 'Bathroom's over there.'

Hunter raced to the door. 'Now pray the water is still on.' He tried the shower, closing his eyes in relief as a jet of water sprayed from the head. He turned it toward Solomon and drenched him through before returning his attention to their escape. 'Am I right in thinking the stairs are to the left of the door as we go out?'

'Yes,' said Solomon, pulling a sodden hood over his head. He threw a flannel at Hunter and returned to the front door. 'Cover your nose and mouth. Are you ready?' Hunter nodded back. 'On three then. Three!' Solomon pulled open the front door and shuffled into the inferno beyond.

Hunter winced at the ferocity of the inferno blazing beyond. Maybe he was wrong and jumping through the window might be the safer option. Solomon's flat might be reinforced, but he doubted the integrity of the rest of the building. Taking a deep breath, he buried his face in the damp flannel and took a leap of faith, jumping through the flaming doorframe. He landed heavily, a little too heavily.

An almighty crack filled the air, and Hunter found himself in freefall. He crashed onto the floor below and yelped in agony as the impact jarred his spine. He rolled to his right and scrambled to his feet, rubbing his lower back. Glancing up at the hole he'd fallen through, he jerked backwards as the hall carpet severed and whipped past his face in a haze of flame. He needed to be quick; the remains of the upper floor could give way at any point. Hunter squinted, fighting to keep his eyes open and ignore the burning sensation in his sockets. The stairwell door appeared like a mirage in the smoke.

Hunter grabbed the handle, launching himself inside like a burning avalanche of wood, carpet and plaster cascaded into the hallway behind him. He dared not look back, ignoring all pain as he descended two to three steps at a time. Stumbling as a stair gave way under his weight, he pulled his foot free and cried out in agony as something cut through his boot and into his foot. The situation was desperate; the smoke, claustrophobic in its intensity, clawing at his lungs and daring him to breathe. He needed fresh air, and he needed it now.

The fire escape door crashed open and Hunter stumbled into the alleyway beyond, coughing and hacking as his lungs adjusted to the fresh sea air. He fell to his knees and lifted his head. He raised a hand, waving it in a silent cry for help. Noticing a large black woman, his waving became more frantic. She did nothing but stare in open-mouthed shock. Why wasn't she moving? He must look worse than he thought. Her gaze flitted to his rear, and she screamed, turning tail and running. Hunter rolled his eyes, expecting the worst, and turned, following her line of sight. He ducked as his singed wig flew past his head, kicked from the stairwell by a canoe sized military boot. The owner of the boot levelled a silenced Heckler & Koch MP5 at the center of his forehead.

The soldier emerged from the darkness and into the light of the alleyway, his imposing dimensions matching up to the size of the boot. 'You must be the archaeologist.' He nodded at the flaming building, each word tinged with a Russian accent. 'This your doing?'

Hunter grimaced, trying but failing to get to his feet. He pointed in the direction of the fire escape. 'You best watch yourself, my friend is dangerous.'

'You think I was born yesterday, Comrade? Place your hands on your head.'

Hunter shrugged and raised his hands as a blur of metal shimmered through the air, connecting hard with the side of the soldier's unprotected head. The man's knees buckled, and he fell forward, unconscious before his face hit the pavement.

'You look like shit,' said Solomon, metal pipe in hand and standing victorious above his victim. 'Can you walk?' Hunter nodded and let Solomon pull him upright. He was certainly stronger than he looked.

Chapter 11

Chris stared at the flaming building in disbelief, shielding his face as another fireball erupted from the three-story building. 'Jesus, URS don't pay me enough to deal with this kind of shit.'

'I hear ya,' said Julio. 'How many did you send up?'

'Only four, thank Christ. The other three are covering the exits; two at the front and one at the rear.'

Julio wrinkled his nose and shook his head. 'On the plus side, at least it's an easy one to cover up. Leaking gas pipe should do it.'

'Recovering four bodies might prove more problematic,' said Chris, looking up and down the road. 'This is a pretty busy street. Even at this time of night.'

'I'm sure the URS and the Agency will cope. They breathe lies at Langley. This'll be a walk in the park for them.'

Chris tapped his earpiece. 'Looks like we're back in business; the chopper has spotted them.' He rolled his eyes. 'Shit, there's another man down at the rear. Helicopter in pursuit. They're travelling towards the MacArthur Causeway on 836 in a beaten-up blue Dodge.'

Julio pointed the remote at the Ford Taurus they'd arrived in. The sidelights flashed as it unlocked. 'Shall we?'

Chris pulled open the passenger door and slid inside. 'It's no Porsche is it?'

'Piss off.'

***

'Where is he?' said Solomon, twisting his neck back and forth as he attempted to locate the source of the whipping blades somewhere above their heads. 'I can hear him, but I can't see him.'

'He's right above us,' said Hunter, pointing through the closed sunroof. 'The Pilot is holding his position. Seems content just to track us.'

'Probably waiting for a car to catch our scent,' said Solomon.

A road sign whizzed past the window and a pair of cones tumbled in their wake. 'Did that say what I think it did?' Hunter's voice picked up pace as panic set in. 'Sol, where are you going? You idiot, that sign said they haven't built this road yet. We're heading for the sea.'

'Trust me, John.' Solomon twisted the wheel, forcing it to lurch to the right. Hunter held on for dear life, shutting his eyes as the car smashed through a locked wire gate, its padlock no match for the ton of steel slamming into it. Daring to open his eyes, he braced himself as the Dodge skipped over a high sidewalk and dropped several feet into a semi-deserted construction site below.

'Solomon, talk to me,' shouted Hunter, his knuckles white as he gripped the edge of his seat. Then all became clear. 'Shit, Solomon, is that what I think it is?'

The tires span, spitting smoke as Solomon slammed the gearshift into first, the bonnet aimed directly for a huge black hole, its entrance lit only by a few yellow flashlights. 'Certainly is, Hunter, me old lad. Welcome to the Port of Miami tunnel project. Let's see that bloody chopper follow us now.'

The car hit another ramp and jumped a good foot into the air, landing with another bone-jarring crack as the overworked suspension failed to soften the blow. Unable to handle the constant pummeling against the fender, a wheel exploded. Hunter started, turning to see the rubber roll out from under the car and disappear into the darkness. The unprotected rim hit the temporary tarmac, sending up a cascading arch of sparks into the night sky.

'Solomon,' said Hunter. 'We need to get off the road. This heap of crap will not last much longer.'

The car broke through the barrier blocking the tunnel entrance, scattering a couple of late-night workers and leaving them shaking fists at the fleeing car. The helicopter veered up into the night sky and disappeared.

'We've only got to get another four hundred and fifty feet,' said Solomon, shouting over the screech of metal on tarmac. 'They've installed emergency exits every four hundred and fifty feet. A couple of months ago, I stashed away some equipment in the first of them.' Solomon slammed on the brakes and the car came to a stuttering stop, the engine still running.

'Don't you think they might notice the car?'

Solomon pulled hard on the handbrake and reached into the car's rear, fumbling for something. 'They might if we left it here, but... Oh, where is it? Ah...' He retracted his hand and raised a brick into Hunter's line of vision. 'Time to get out.'

Hunter smiled knowingly as Solomon wedged the brick against the accelerator pedal. The engine whined in protest, the rev counter flying into the red. He jammed it into first gear and released the handbrake, leaping from the car in a Bond-Esque stunt belying his age. The car gathered speed, fading into the darkness until only the erratic sparking of the front wheel was visible.

Hunter looked at Solomon in triumph. His face fell; the elderly academic hadn't recovered from his fall, his body still lying limp on the damp ground. He darted to his side and gently maneuvered him onto his back. He tapped Solomon's cheeks. 'Solomon, you bloody fool, snap out of it.'

The old man opened his eyes, blinked a few times, and grinned. 'I bet Bruce Willis never put up with this kind of crap. He makes it look so easy up on the big screen.'

'He's nowhere near your age... plus he has the option of using a professional stuntman.'

Solomon closed his eyes, but grinned. 'Damn, I knew I forgot something.'

'Can you walk?'

'I'll do my best,' said Solomon, raising his head and wincing in pain.

Hunter slipped an arm under his armpits and gently pulled him to his feet. 'Let's just get out of here and worry about fixing you up later.' They took a couple of paces toward the exit. 'At least you haven't broken your legs.' Hunter kicked the door open and eased Solomon into the corridor beyond. 'Where now?'

'Head for the stairs,' said Solomon. 'The gear is inside a locker on the second level. I disguised it as an electrical cupboard.'

Hunter took Solomon's weight, and they negotiated the stairwell together. Holding up his fist, Hunter stopped in his tracks. He could hear an engine roaring, the sound-amplifying as it closed in on their position. He urged Solomon forward, concerned their pursuer might smash through the wall concealing their escape at any moment. The noise faded. Hunter glanced at Solomon in triumph and pumped his fist. The driver must have bought Solomon's diversion.

He hauled his injured mentor up the last flight of stairs and the Professor grinned as his disguised locker emerged from the gloom. 'If you need a place to hide, where better than in the pocket of your enemy.' He shoved a hand into his trouser pocket and it re-emerged with a key.

Hunter relieved him of it and unclasped the padlock. Inside, he found three wetsuits and a sports bag containing flippers. He returned one wetsuit to the cupboard. 'Ethan won't be needing that. So, I take it we're going for a jovial midnight paddle?'

Solomon kicked off his shoes and pulled the suit over his legs. 'Just help me get this on, will you?'

'Have you thought this through? The plan is just to swim away, take a dip in the harbor at night?' He bit his lip. 'You do know what else calls those waters home?'

'Sure, couple of sociable bull sharks. We will be fine. You're not telling me you're scared of a few little fish?'

'When said fish can remove my limbs, yes, yes I bloody am.'

'Would you prefer we try our luck against a hail of bullets?'

Hunter's tight suit made an off-putting ripping sound as he pulled it over his thighs. 'Fine, but if we meet any, I'm leaving you to be sociable on your own.' He grabbed the bag of flippers and helped Solomon through a door labelled as the exit. He could hear the sound of lapping water and see a small jetty up ahead. Were they going to get away with this? The water lapped against his bare feet. It was still warm from a day of hot sunshine; certainly nothing like the freezing cold, sewage-laden offerings he was used to back in England. Even in the harbor, the water was clear and free of any obvious pollutants.

Solomon slid into the water first and beckoned him to follow. Hunter pulled on his flippers, held his nose, and jumped alongside his friend. The splash coincided with the stutter and hum of a rotary engine igniting. It was the helicopter.

'I would say that probably means they've discovered the car,' said Solomon.

'We're not really just going to swim are we?' said Hunter. 'We're sitting ducks.'

A flashlight whizzed above their heads and both men ducked their heads underwater in unison. Solomon prodded Hunter in the ribs and pointed to the space under the jetty. Hunter followed the finger and a grouping of bubbles escaped his nose. Nestled out of view and concealed by a black paint job, lay a pair of diver propulsion vehicles, twin scuba cylinders and isolation manifolds. If he hadn't been close to drowning, Hunter would have kissed the old man to his left.

Chapter 12

Chris slammed the underside of his fist against the locker door and dropped the wetsuit into Julio's waiting arms. 'And you're certain the site supervisor knows nothing of this locker?'

'Nothing,' said Julio.

Chris bashed the door harder, feeling a degree of satisfaction as it buckled under the force of the blow. 'Hunter can't have known or planted these suits. I'd be surprised if he even knew this place existed this time yesterday.'

Julio shrugged. 'Probably not.'

'So how in the shit has he got a support network to sort stuff like this out? And in less than twelve hours of getting off the plane.'

'Short answer. He hasn't.' Julio discarded the wetsuit and handed Chris the printout in his hand. 'This was pulled from CCTV at the entrance.'

Chris peered at the dark, grainy image and shook his head. 'What does this tell us?' He tapped a silhouette of a man in its center. 'Who's this? Is it the Russian?'

Julio winced and pursed his lips. 'You're goner be pissed.'

Chris rolled his eyes. 'Go on.'

'The Russian is dead.'

Chris' brow furrowed involuntarily. 'Don't tell me.'

'Yup, burnt to a crisp in one of those apartments.'

He tapped the image again. 'Are you saying this is him or it isn't?'

'It isn't. I just received some follow-on intel from Johnston. Turns out the Russian was working for us. Planting seeds to uncover whatever it is this damn operation is about? I guess Hunter must have figured it out and ended him. Poor guy took a bullet to the head before going up in smoke.'

Chris shook his head. 'This job is an absolute joke sometimes. So, who is the guy in the picture?'

'Look closer.' Julio tapped the face. 'It's another dead man. Solomon Garnett.'

Chris let out a controlled exhalation through his nose and closed his eyes, attempting to collect his thoughts. 'You're sure? This is the dead academic from Florida U?'

Julio nodded. 'Turns out upstairs knew he was still alive but deemed it classified. They were trying to flush him out. He's got something they want and it's something they want bad.'

'This internal covert crap is getting on my nerves. Do they think we are bloody amateurs? Tell me to execute a target and I'll plan it. Tell me the target is wearing a bomb and I'll do it differently. If there are bodyguards, the plan changes again. It's all about intelligence. The more I know, the better I can do my job.'

'You're preaching to the converted here. This sucks ass. Men have died because of the intel they've chosen to hold back. If we'd known about the undercover Russian spook, there's no way we'd have stormed the building.'

'So what now?' asked Chris. 'It's clear Hunter, and now this Professor, has been one step ahead of us all the way. For all we know, they probably organized a submarine to collect them from this pier. They could be anywhere by now.'

'If we are to believe anything Johnston fed us,' said Julio. 'This shit storm has something to do with Roswell. If these guys are heading anywhere or indeed even if captured, I'd bet my house on them ending up at the Groom Lake base.'

'Good point.' Chris cocked his head to one side. 'With that in mind, why don't we take a trip and do some digging of our own? I still have some decent contacts in that neck of the woods. There's one in particular who might swing it for me to take control of any interrogations conducted.'

Julio licked his lips and nodded. 'So we're back in the field?'

'What d'ya reckon, old-timer? You up for a last hurrah?'

***

The Sun nudged above the horizon, its warm rays inadvertently gnawing at the dawn mist shrouding the bare countryside far below. Hunter glanced at his passenger in the rear-view mirror. Solomon stirred and shifted in his seat. 'You feeling better, Sol?'

Solomon stretched his right arm and grimaced, retracting it to rub the muscles in his neck. 'I'll live. Just a bit stiff. A few cuts and bruises, but nothing serious. My leg feels much better. The swim probably helped keep the swelling down.'

'Are you ready to tell me what we're doing in the middle of this wasteland yet? I mean, I know you said, "head for Gaithersburg," but what exactly is in Gaithersburg?'

'Gaithersburg, Maryland, my dear John, is where Miss Serena Harmony currently resides.'

'I suppose I should have guessed,' said Hunter, tapping the steering wheel. 'But unless you've turned into Oprah and are trying your hand at matchmaking, I'm none the wiser. Who does she work for? And for that matter, why should I give a shit? I couldn't care less if your precious aliens exist or not. Governments lie all the time; yours, mine, who cares? Yes, I'm sure exposing an Alien crash would sell a few newspapers, but so what? Is it something I really want to risk my life for?'

'I need you to trust me, John. The less you know at this stage, the more likely you'll be able to walk away if my plan goes belly up.'

'This better not be about aliens or I'll kill you myself.'

'It's not about fucking aliens,' hissed Solomon through clenched teeth. 'That much I can tell you.'

Hunter knew Solomon's ignition point, and he knew he'd just reached it. A change of tack was required. He took a slug of water from the bottle lying on the passenger seat and offered it to Solomon. He took it gratefully. 'So who does she work for?'

'The URS Corporation.'

'URS?' John clicked his tongue as he mulled over the acronym in his head. 'No, never heard of them. What do they do?' asked Hunter.

'No reason you would have done. They're an engineering, design and construction firm.'

'A big one?'

'Eleven billion a year, just inside the top 250 companies in the US.'

Hunter whistled. 'I'm guessing they have happy shareholders. So where does Serena fit in?'

'She works in a section you may have heard of. URS' EG&G division.'

Hunter pulled a face. 'EG&G... No, still doesn't ring any bells?'

'It would to any competent ufologist?'

Hunter held up his middle finger. 'Guess that proves I'm not one then.' Solomon grinned and winced in pain, coughing as he straightened his spine. 'You don't sound great, Sol. You sure you don't need to see a Doctor?'

'I'm already registered dead. What are they going to do?'

'Good point.'

Solomon cleared his throat and bent forward, wrapping his arms around the headrest of the front passenger seat. 'Right, UFO conspiracy 101. Three MIT alumni set EG&G up in 1934. Two students; Kenneth Germeshausen and Herbert Grier, and their Professor, Harold Edgerton. Edgerton was a pioneer in the world of high-speed photography and the key to the company's success.'

Hunter nodded. 'Okay, but I don't see the link. What has high-speed photography got to do with Roswell?'

'Nothing,' said Solomon. 'EG&G were dragged into the secret underworld of the United States government to record one of the most important scientific events in human history, the atomic bomb.'

Hunter nodded as the pieces clicked together in his head. 'The Manhattan Project.'

'Bingo,' said Solomon. 'They used EG&G equipment to image the implosion tests in the Nevada desert. In fact, they later used the same tech to develop a more reliable trigger for detonating the nukes. As such, the company's relationship with the Nevada test site continued throughout the fifties and sixties, hired as the primary subcontractor of the Atomic Energy Commission.'

Hunter changed gear and pulled off the interstate, following the sign for Gaithersburg. 'And in so doing they morphed from a small tech start-up and into some kind of clandestine, government endorsed arms company?'

Solomon nodded. 'Over the years they've been linked to several covert, so-called "black" projects. But not just secretive stuff mind, bizarrely, over the years, they've provided the US with a range of services from facility management to security and even pilot training.'

Hunter scratched the lengthening stubble on his right cheek. 'I assume you're about to tell me EG&G managed Area 51.'

'Designed it; built it; managed it. If anything is, or was, hidden in the desert, these are the guys in the know.'

'Ethan told me all they did there was test spy planes.'

'He's right. The CIA developed the U2 and the A-12 Oxcart at the site.'

'Surely that would account for the secrecy? Why do you think there is any more to this "conspiracy"? If I were developing spy planes in the desert, I'd probably deny the existence of the base and then make damn sure it was as far away from humanity as possible.'

'There's more to it than that.' Solomon tapped Hunter's pocket and pulled out the silvery shard of metal Hunter retrieved from Wells Fargo Bank. 'You remember this?'

'How could I forget?'

'Do you remember the symbol stamped on it?'

'The Eastern sword and crown? Yes, I meant to ask you what that was about.'

'You mean you don't recognize it?' asked Solomon, feigning surprise. 'Dr Hunter, I'm astonished!'

Hunter rolled his eyes. 'No, which makes you so much wiser. Just tell me. You're meant to be the teacher, after all.'

'It's the symbol of a small town in Russia, a place called Astrakhan.'

'Astrakhan?' He closed his eyes, massaging his temples. 'I recognize the name, but for the life of me can't remember why. Was it Lenin's birthplace or something?'

'No, he was born in Simbirsk. The symbol is a manufacturer's stamp?'

Hunter shot Solomon a sideways glance. 'Are you saying the ship you saw crash at Roswell was Russian? Are you drunk?' He laughed. 'So all these years of preaching at me and you've actually been holding onto the proof there was no extra-terrestrial involvement.'

Solomon cocked his head to one side and wagged his finger. 'Tut tut, John, jumping to conclusions without all the evidence is not how a true academic should operate.'

Chapter 13

18th March 1992

Solomon unzipped the tent flap and tentatively tested the temperature with the end of his nose. It was certainly fresh - a stiff early morning breeze blowing in from the North. It would soon warm up though. During his stay, the temperature fluctuations levelled out around a comfortable 80 degrees Fahrenheit which meant he was still thoroughly enjoying his break in the wilderness.

It wasn't every day a United States academic was invited into mother Russia. In fact, prior to the dissolution of the Soviet Union the previous year, it would have been virtually impossible. He knew how fortunate he'd been with the timing and was determined to make the most of it. With the new government still in a state of flux after Gorbachev's death and the disbandment of the KGB six months earlier, this might be his only opportunity to operate under the radar of Kapustin Yar's security. He'd been told a mere bottle or two of vodka could work wonders on the integrity of the base's poorly paid guards. Times were hard, and he was determined to exploit the fact.

He glanced at his companion, Oleg Anosov, and grinned. The soldier's meaty outline remained zipped tightly inside his sleeping bag, his puffy red face protruding through the hood, giving him the appearance of a giant Russian doll. On their first day together, Oleg joked Solomon wouldn't make it through one night in the hinterlands, but here they were, three days in and who was the first up?

He tapped the book in his hand against his thigh and re-read the title of the opening chapter; "Kapustin Yar – Russia's Roswell." Oleg wrote the tome under a pseudonym and published it outside of the Soviet Union to protect himself. He'd opened with a chapter detailing a third encounter of the first kind, an encounter alleged to have occurred back in 1989. Oleg claimed he'd been part of a military unit who'd borne witness to a flying disk hovering for hours over the arsenal of their base. He'd submitted a report to the KGB with a full description, eyewitness accounts and even a hand-drawn picture of the craft. The account read like a replica of Solomon's encounter with the craft back in Roswell.

It was an encounter of which Solomon was already aware. The KGB attempt at suppression failed, and a synopsis hit his desk in his capacity as chair of the American Institute of Ufology. Solomon knew instantly that this was the breakthrough he'd been waiting for. He needed to see the base for himself and perhaps even get inside. He vocalized the wish amongst his members and came up trumps; a retired defector passing him the details for Oleg Anosov, the soldier who had filed the original report. On receipt of a reasonable fee, Oleg had proven a most amenable ally and even agreed to escort Solomon to the scene of his encounter.

Solomon pulled on the Russian uniform purchased during their overnighter in Moscow. The black market yielded a genuine military uniform and accompanying ID of a Russian Polkovnik, the equivalent of a US Colonel. He patted down the creases picked up in transit and made sure the three gold stars on the green and red striped shoulder boards were visible. The plan was to let Oleg do all the talking, fussing about him in the guise of an aide, while Solomon hid behind a façade of stoic silence. He just hoped a Polkovnik was a high rank to warrant such a display of arrogance.

Nudging the Russian in the ribs, Solomon opened up the tent flap and allowed the early morning sunshine to flood inside. It was almost six and time they were on their way. The plan relied on arriving at the entrance just before the change of guards; the idea being to take advantage of any fatigue and their proximity to food and rest. Oleg pulled himself upright and released his arms, rubbing at his eyes.

'What time is it?'

'Just gone six. We've less than an hour to get to the gate.'

The Russian stretched and pulled a cigarette from a battered Sobranie branded packet. He threw the packet to Solomon. He caught it and, with a strong tap, popped a cigarette into his hand. He smiled as the Russian struggled to free himself from the tent's tight interior, tripping and stumbling through the open flap. Brushing himself down and glossing over the mild embarrassment, he sparked a zippo and lit his cigarette.

'Today is a good day for answers, do you not think, Professor?'

Solomon followed suit and inhaled slowly, letting the rough tobacco penetrate his lungs and momentarily numb the fear in his stomach. 'If they really possess what I think is inside that base, then this, my friend, is only the beginning.'

'You are certain you saw the same object in Roswell?'

Solomon nodded. 'I did. A silver disk flying under its own steam. I was only young, but I still remember it as if it were yesterday.'

Oleg patted his arm. 'Not something you forget in a hurry, eh comrade. The KGB swore us all to secrecy, but now they are no more...' He paused as if searching for the right words. 'How do you say in America, fuck'um?'

Solomon grinned and dipped his head. 'Close enough.' He took a long drag on the cigarette and glanced toward Kapustin Yar. 'You say in your book it hovered over the arsenal of the base?' Oleg nodded. 'Then shone or fired some kind of bright ray vertically down from its underbelly?'

'Yes, I remember the men speculating it was assessing our capabilities or perhaps making a record of our technological capabilities.'

'That's a leap and a...' Solomon caught himself. Whether he believed was immaterial, but it was essential Oleg continued to assume he was a fellow devotee. 'I mean... that must have been... out of this world.'

The Russian beamed back at him as he finished dressing. 'That's what it says in my book.'

Solomon returned to the tent and grabbed a briefcase containing a set of fraudulent orders; orders printed on headed paper from none other than the Office of the President himself. He set his jaw and steadied his gaze on the domed roof of the arsenal in the distance. 'Shall we?'

The two men broke cover a couple of hundred meters from the gate. Oleg charged ahead, waving papers at the guardhouse and trying to attract their attention. He greeted the guard with a rigid salute and followed it with a slap on the back and a laugh, demonstrating familiarity. What a stroke of luck, thought Solomon. The guard must remember Oleg. The plan was off to a flyer. He clenched his buttocks, puffed his chest and marched rigidly towards the checkpoint. His Russian was basic, but he followed Oleg's description of the breakdown of their official car and caught a warning not to aggravate the angry Polkovnik. Oleg passed the guard a couple of bottles of vodka, "for his trouble," and placed the fake orders in front of him.

The guard glanced at the request detailing a Kremlin ordered inspection and turned to face Solomon. He stood straight to attention and saluted. 'Хотите быть в сопровождении или будет Олег делать?'

Solomon looked down stonily at the man and returned the salute, trying to buy time. Oleg's name was clear, but given the speed of delivery and the local accent, he was at a loss as to what the rest of the sentence might mean.

Oleg jumped to his rescue, answering before the uncomfortable silence forced a reply. 'Я его руководство.'

I am his guide! The guard must have been asking if they needed a guide. He nodded at the guard and shot him as disdainful a look as he could manage in the circumstances. It was enough. The guard handed him the papers and saluted again, this time standing aside to let Solomon pass. He strode past with as much confidence and arrogance as he could muster, a tough ask given the tornado of fear whipping about the pit of his stomach. It was imperative he at least looked as though he belonged. Although their methods are sometimes deplorable, at this moment Solomon was grateful for the Soviet's insistence on instilling an innate respect for authority amongst its people. A man of his standing would show little more than contempt for the lower ranks, and he knew he must maintain the illusion to ensure acceptance.

Oleg joined him and pointed the way. 'Well done. You could not have performed better. The guard even insulted you.' He grinned. 'A sure sign your disguise was accepted.'

Solomon felt sick. 'Just tell me where we're going?' he grunted. It was hitting home just how dangerous a situation this was; shifting from Hollywood to reality in the blink of an eye, or rather with the proximity of numerous Russian machine guns. Discovery meant life imprisonment at best. However, given their location in the back end of nowhere, a bullet and shallow grave seemed much more likely.

'I suggest we pull the file from the records and then head for the underground bunker.'

'Forget the file,' said Solomon. 'I say we go to the bunker first. If I get caught, I want it to be for a respectable reason, not just for raiding a damn filing cabinet.'

'But the evidence? Surely we need the file.'

'If my instincts are right, and they are rarely wrong, I doubt the papers we're after will have been kept amongst missile test reports anyway.'

Oleg pulled a face. 'Are you pulling rank on me, comrade?'

'Just lead the way and hope to God our ID is good enough to open the remaining doors.'

Oleg nodded at a small, non-descript building a hundred meters or so from their position. 'They hide the entrance within the shed over there.'

'Where are the guards?'

'Below ground. We did not want it showing up in any photographs taken by your spy planes.' He tapped Solomon's arm with a smile. 'You are a lucky man. The first American to enter this base without bullet holes.'

Solomon raised an eyebrow as they reached the hut. 'I'll keep that in mind.'

Oleg wrenched open a stiff wooden door and ushered him inside the shed. Solomon noticed the wood merely coated a heavy iron superstructure, several inches in thickness. He was impressed; an atom bomb would struggle to level this structure. His gaze swept about his new surroundings. A bare room with a few token tools hanging beside a blacked-out window on one wall. The only unusual feature lay on the floor; a circular, steel disk covered in dirt and set into the center of the space.

'Step onto the disk and keep your arms by your side,' said Oleg.

Solomon followed the order and stood as instructed. 'What is this? Some kind of elevator?'

Oleg clicked on a torch and shone its beam into each corner of the room. He grunted as he found what he was looking for and pushed against something hidden in the door's shadow. He joined Solomon on the disk. 'Try to keep your balance, the mechanism isn't so good.'

'You've been down before?' said Solomon. 'I thought you said...' The ground beneath his feet jolted, juddered, and then gave way completely. He didn't even have time to scream.

Oleg put a hand to Solomon's mouth, suppressing any sound, and hauled him upright as the elevator's speed regulated. 'I've been to the guard's room, but no further. As I said, you have to be of a certain rank to proceed further.'

Solomon nodded as a chink of light appeared around the disk's edges and the concrete tube gave way to reveal some kind of holding room, complete with magazines and a water cooler. He stepped from the platform, battling to ignore the childlike butterflies fizzing about his abdomen. He needed to maintain an air of arrogant professionalism. He was a colonel in the Russian Army after all.

He shivered and noticed a stern painting of Yeltsin, the President watching over the room and making it clear to visitors of the recent change of management. An imposing steel counter overlooked the space and Solomon banged his fist on its surface. The sleepy-looking guard behind the glass started, jolted from his daydream with a look of panic as he recognized the rank of the officer in front of him. He scrambled to his feet, stood to attention, and saluted.

Oleg stepped from the elevator and approached the guard, speaking in Russian. 'Voloshin, my old friend, how are you? Another exciting day behind this godforsaken desk?'

Voloshin glanced nervously at Solomon. 'It is my duty to carry out the orders of Mother Russia. I do not question them; I execute them.'

Oleg slipped Solomon's orders into the tray beneath the bulletproof window separating them from Voloshin. 'Then you will like these. Yeltsin himself wants the facility checked out. Something to do with the UFO sighting back in 89. The release of the KGB file has stirred up a bit of a shit storm in the Kremlin.'

Voloshin glanced down at the papers and picked up a telephone receiver. 'I'll need to confirm this with Professor Zigel. We are not aware of any scheduled visits.'

'I believe that was the idea,' said Oleg. 'Our newly elected president wanted to ensure no artefacts... how can I put this diplomatically... went missing prior to the arrival of the Polkovnik.'

'Open the door or answer to Yeltsin himself!' Solomon barked in Russian. It was a line he'd been practicing and given the instant look of fear it engendered, his effort appeared to have paid off.

The steel door buzzed and creaked open a couple of inches. 'Sir, yes, sir. But I'm afraid I can only let you through this door,' Voloshin stammered. 'The second can only be accessed by the scientists.'

'You have the emergency card,' said Oleg.

'Yes, but...'

'Use it,' hissed Solomon, starting to enjoy his role.

'But this isn't...' whispered Voloshin.

'Use it or face the wrath of your government,' said Oleg. 'The element of surprise is what our leaders are after.'

'But if I use it, the scientists will be alerted anyway,' he said, sounding almost apologetic. 'It's one of the security measures.'

Oleg grimaced. 'Okay, call this Zigel fellow... but only tell him he has a visitor, not the nature of the visit.'

Voloshin stabbed something into the numerical pad in front of him and held a telephone receiver to his ear. Solomon looked away and took the opportunity to examine the vast slab of steel doubling as the main entrance to the bunker. It must be at least a foot thick. He pulled on the handle, his muscles tensing as they struggled with both its weight and the aggressive return mechanism. Oleg slid through the gap and he followed, the enormous door slamming shut and locking behind them. Going back was now no longer an option.

Chapter 14

The second room was a little more comfortable. Solomon lowered himself into one of the three brown leather armchairs clustered around a small television. A Russian news program reported on a recent shooting in Moscow. He rubbed his temples and looked at Oleg with concern. This was not part of the plan. He was going to have to meet with one of the base scientists. There was no way his Russian would be up to such scrutiny.

The inner door buzzed, and his heart sank. He had nothing, nothing that is but his rank. Solomon stood and turned to salute the rotund, squat little man standing before him. The scientist's moustache quivered. He was either scared or angry, perhaps both. The salute wasn't returned. Solomon didn't know the scientist's standing in the military, but surely that couldn't be a good sign.

'Who are you and why are you here?' said the man, talking in Russian. 'Yeltsin sent someone over a year ago. He is satisfied with what we are doing now. We were not advised of your visit.'

Solomon understood snatches of what was said but knew his cover wouldn't hold up under the pressure of direct conversation. 'I presume you are Professor Zigel. And yes, there is a reason you were not warned,' he calmly replied in English.

Zigel took a step backwards, his face turning a sickly pale color. 'You're an American? Voloshin... Voloshin, sound the alarm. Intruder!'

Solomon raised his arm. 'Stay where you are, Voloshin. Нет, оставаться там, где вы находитесь.' He turned back to face Zigel. 'I'm ex-KGB, you fool. I've spent the last ten years in Washington perfecting my accent. My apologies if you believe I've carried out my job too well. I want to converse in English solely because I know my escort will not understand. Are we clear?'

Professor Zigel's gaze flicked between Oleg and Voloshin, his eyes twitching as he processed the request. 'What do you want?'

Zigel's reply was in English. Solomon's heart fluttered. Had it worked? Could the scientist have bought his explanation? He felt a bead of sweat trickle through his hairline and swept a hand through his fringe, mopping his brow under the guise of a scratch. It was sink or swim time. 'Moscow is thinking of reallocating funding. They have asked me to assess the spy craft.'

Zigel's eyes widened. 'Are you serious? But they only pulled the funding last year. Are you saying there is a chance I can finish the project?'

'Just convince me of its worth and it's yours,' replied Solomon, trying to remain deadpan while his innards turned cartwheels. He'd been intending to threaten the removal of funding, but Zigel's interpretation was so much better. The scientist would surely bend over backwards now he believed there was a pot of gold in the offing. Solomon nodded at the mysterious door. 'After you, Professor.'

Zigel swiped his identification card, and a panel slid open to the right-hand side of the door. The scientist planted his face inside and a line of blue light swept across his face, probably scanning both the shape and his retinas. The door clicked and Solomon pulled it open, stepping aside to allow the Professor to lead the way. He cracked his knuckles, reminding himself not to come across as too eager. Indifference would be the key to pulling this off, no matter what lay beyond the door.

He need not have worried, bar the drab concrete décor, the laboratory he found could have been lifted from the science faculty of any major University around the world. Three white coats occupied the space. They glanced up, but appeared unfazed by the intrusion and returned to their work.

'What is this place?' asked Solomon. 'What are you working on in here?'

'Since our funding was pulled, these labs are where we carry out the core of our research,' said Zigel. He waved his hand in the direction of his peers. 'These men and women are the finest minds Russia has to offer. Over the years they have been responsible for many breakthroughs in the field of weapons research.'

'What are they working on?'

'I'm not entirely sure. We tend to focus solely on our own specialisms.' The Professor turned to address a female member of his team. 'What are you working on?' He glanced back at Oleg. 'And reply in English.'

'Английском языке?'

'Yes, in English.' He nodded in Oleg's direction. 'For security reasons.'

The scientist frowned but complied. 'I'm working with the blood agent, cyanogen chloride.'

Solomon raised an eyebrow and glanced at Zigel, seeking more clarity. 'A form of chemical warfare, Polkovnik,' he replied, understanding the signal.

'Yes,' the scientist continued. 'In a warhead, this agent is as toxic as it gets. At present, I am trying to perfect its ability to penetrate the filters installed in modern gas masks.'

'What does it do?' asked Solomon.

'Victims may expose many symptoms: coughing; nausea; vomiting; loss of consciousness; convulsions; paralysis and/or death. We are concerned with exacting the latter of those.'

'Beautiful,' whispered Solomon. 'And we have a plentiful supply of this kind of weaponry?'

The scientist nodded. 'Over twenty thousand tons. Although rumor has it that the Chemical Weapons Convention to be held next year may change all that. They are talking about a blanket ban on production, stockpiling, and use of this type of weaponry.' She grinned at Zigel. 'It's lucky Dr Mengele is no longer here. He'd have been bouncing off the walls.'

'Mengele...' Solomon felt his forehead crease into a frown as he processed the name. 'Not Josef Mengele the Nazi? Was he posted here?'

Zigel nodded. 'Yes, sir. After the war ended, the Americans rejected the chance to work with him. Of course, Stalin snapped him up.'

'What did he do for you?'

'You don't want to know,' said Zigel, hanging his head. 'His experiments were brutal. I was a mere junior technician back then and certainly didn't have the stomach for such barbarism.'

'I take it he was allowed to continue with his program of human experimentation?'

Zigel laughed. 'Certainly. Why else would he have been here? Stalin backed him, truly believing that sick bastard would eventually create a super-soldier.' He shook his head, evidently reliving the past. 'But his methods... his methods were something else. In the end, Stalin himself even deemed them too extreme, sending him to Brazil to live out his days in hiding.'

'Stalin found them inappropriate. Jesus, they must have been bad?'

'When I was involved,' said Anna. 'He was testing chemical agents on live human subjects. The idea being to determine what a body could withstand.'

'There was a medical wing-back then,' interrupted Zigel. 'Now those boys could tell you some stories. He did all sorts; expanded the skulls and eye sockets of children and inserted adult brains and eyeballs, just to see what would happen. I heard he once connected the urinary tract of a young girl to her colon. For what reason, God only knows. The man was pure evil. A proper sadistic bastard.'

'Sounds like a must invite for any dinner party.'

'Absolutely. We were all glad when he left. He was meant to work with me for a while, but I refused.'

'Why? What was your project?'

'He claimed he could create the perfect pilot for my craft.'

'No doubt one of his big-headed freaks?'

'Probably, but I never let him near my work.'

Solomon couldn't resist and shot a knowing glance in Oleg's direction. Given his encounter in Roswell, Mengele must have got his way in the end. He needed to find out more. They were so close to finding answers. He returned his focus to the Professor. 'Can I see your work? Perhaps the funding from our chemical weapons program should be redirected... since they are soon to be outlawed.'

Zigel smiled. 'That would be good, although I can't see our chemical program ending. The Kremlin won't risk the Motherland being at a disadvantage, no matter what papers our politicians sign.' Zigel pointed toward a set of double doors and nodded his thanks to Anna. 'I won't show you, but our nuclear testing lab is on our left and the missile engineers work in the space to the right. My working environment lies beyond these doors.' He scanned his ID card and a steel door slid open, revealing a huge, dark void beyond.

Solomon squinted in the darkness and tried to pick out shapes. 'It looks like an enormous space. What exactly is your expertise?'

The Professor's eyes narrowed. 'Ariel reconnaissance. Surely you...'

'Yes, yes; sorry, I'm on autopilot. Please lead the way,' said Solomon, inwardly berating himself for the slip. Zigel shrugged and entered the hangar, his footfalls triggering a series of motion sensors. One by one, row upon row of artificial lights flickered on, illuminating the space in a Mexican wave of bright, white luminescence. Solomon took a step backwards. His body numbed and reached for Oleg's arm to steady himself.

Zigel grinned. 'I'm guessing this is not what you were expecting?'

'I certainly wasn't expecting a museum.' Recovering his composure, Solomon stepped further into the hangar and his mouth dropped open. It was the Shangri-La of Soviet spy plane technology. His gaze drifted from a Tupolev Tu-16R Badger to a Tupolev Tu-22 Blinder-C, its engines proudly sitting beside the vertical tail. Behind them sat a rare Mikoyan-Gurevich MiG-25, an aircraft with a top speed of about Mach 3; hell, Zigel even had a Myasishchev M-17 in his collection, the Soviet version of the American U-2. Certain members of the CIA would kill to be standing in his shoes right now.

Solomon inhaled and drank in the scene, a feeling of childlike excitement fizzing in his gut. He ambled further into the hangar and stopped dead, excitement morphing into triumphant ecstasy. A series of strange triangular, circular and even hexagonal shaped aircraft strafed the hangar floor, each a failed experiment of some long-forgotten engineer. His eyes narrowed - but where was the original he'd come so far to see?

'You certainly have an impressive collection, Professor, but I cannot see the craft mentioned in the KGB report. Where is it?'

'Behind the Tupolev drone.' He sighed. 'Ironic, given the drone is the reason I lost the funding for the project. "Why invest in piloted aircraft?" Short-sighted bastards, the lot of them.'

'Short-sighted?' questioned Solomon. 'So what can it do that the drone cannot?'

The Professor smashed a balled fist into his open hand. 'I tried to tell them, but they wouldn't listen.'

'Calm yourself. You must remember your place. What did you tell them?'

'Forgive me, Polkovnik.' He calmed himself with two deep breaths. 'This craft is the ultimate spy plane. Speed, stability, and stealth. The disk has it all. We've come a long way from the Nazi prototype, but there is still work to be done. With further funding, I am certain I can build a smaller unmanned version.'

'Nazi prototype?' questioned Solomon.

'Yes, did you not know? The design was dreamt up by a pair of brothers under Hitler's command.'

'Are you referring to the Horten brothers?' said Solomon. 'Didn't they build the first jet-powered flying wing?'

'You know your history, Polkovnik. In fact we have a captured Horten Ho 229 on the far side of this room. The first aircraft to break 500mph.'

'And they designed the flying disk?'

'They did. It was an extension of the fixed-wing idea. Hitler challenged them to come up with something capable of VTOL.'

'Vertical take-off and landing.'

The Professor nodded. 'And they came up with the disk. It was a primitive design, but the science was decent.'

The pieces were slotting together in Solomon's mind. 'I assume we acquired their services after the war and they engineered a similar craft for the Motherland.'

Zigel pointed at a small craft in the center of the hangar. 'As I said, it's behind the drone.'

Solomon stared at the familiar shape. A ghost from his past. 'And this is what Stalin sent to the States.'

'Yes. Stupid idea if ever there was one. I was against it from the start. A petty stunt to get one over on an American President no one would care about ten years later. The bloody bomb strapped to it never even went off.' Zigel sighed. 'Not that it mattered since it crashed in the desert anyway.'

Solomon froze, suddenly very aware of his own mortality. He was lucky to be alive. He glanced up at the massive steel struts supporting the domed roof of the hangar, not quite believing this scientist, or engineer, or whatever the hell he was, had just revealed the truth behind the Roswell crash in such a blasé fashion. It was just a side issue for him. A mere footnote in his country's history. 'Stalin wasn't worried the Americans would reverse engineer the craft themselves,' he asked, trying to keep his cool.

'No,' replied Zigel with a chuckle. 'The US Air Force already possessed the same designs as us. If they wanted to make a VTOL disk, they could have done so at any time. The Roswell stunt was just an ill-advised attempt to strike fear into our enemy. The Kremlin wanted to analyze the fallout, testing the resolve of our enemies under pressure and hopefully reveal weaknesses we could exploit in the event of an invasion.'

'I have not heard this before. Why then did Stalin hide his intentions under the guise of an Alien invasion?'

'You were obviously in the wrong department, Polkovnik. It is common knowledge. Stalin believed the effect to be twofold. The first was to spread panic amongst the American public and second, he wished to breathe fear into the military with the bomb. They knew where the craft originated and that it was a show of force; irrefutable proof Soviet bombs could be detonated in the heartland of America.'

Solomon smiled. 'And then it crashed in the desert without the bomb exploding.'

'Indeed. Now that was a debriefing I did enjoy. The target city was meant to be Las Vegas.' He shrugged his shoulders. 'It still kind of worked, just not as planned. Perhaps not the public, but we certainly ruffled a few military feathers. Some believe the Roswell crash underpinned the start of the cold war.' He laughed. 'One of their Colonels is even quoted as stating the incident was the first shot fired in the campaign.'

Solomon snorted and placed his hands on a waist-high barrier separating them from the aircraft. 'What do you think President Truman did to enrage Stalin?'

'Don't quote me, but I believe it was something to do with the program, Operation Crossroads, the atomic bomb testing in the Pacific. Stalin believed the Motherland was Truman's target. Hence his quest to prove our capability of retaliating and breaching American airspace.'

Solomon drummed his fingers against the steel tube and turned back to face the Professor. 'It certainly worked, and a forty-three-year stand-off resulted just because two men couldn't trust one another.'

The Professor raised his eyebrows and pulled a look of indifference. 'Who am I to question the decisions of our esteemed leaders?' He smiled. 'Particularly since the situation worked for me and my personal aims.' He nodded at the array of aircraft. 'Do you want to see the last iteration of my disk in action?'

Solomon choked and coughed to cover it. 'It's still working? I thought the funding was pulled.'

The Professor winked. 'Yes, but that didn't stop me from working on it. The project was virtually complete anyway. Hence the test in 89.'

'Do it, show me,' said Solomon eagerly, urging Oleg to fall in step behind him. God only knew how his Russian companion was coping with the information overload he'd just received. Solomon always suspected the truth, but Oleg's world and entire belief system had just been blown apart by Professor Zigel's revelations.

Chapter 15

Solomon brushed his fingers lightly over the shimmering aluminum skin of the disk-shaped, fixed-wing aircraft. It wasn't quite as he remembered. It felt sleeker and less bloated than its 1940s counterpart. He stepped back to admire it in its full glory. It was certainly aesthetically pleasing, a sexy, aerodynamic design for the nineties. A far cry from the usual chunky, yet functional designs Russian engineers typically opted for. Perched atop a shimmering black metallic tripod, the craft could have come straight out of the pages of the National Enquirer. The domed, blacked-out cockpit bulged proudly from the dinner plate design, its reinforced glass canopy designed to allow the pilot a clear, unobstructed view of the skies about him.

Solomon frowned as a red light flickered and traced its way around the edge of the dinner plate. 'What's that?'

'Three sixty thermal imagery,' said the Professor, sounding more like a proud father than an engineer. 'Plus it looks cool and don't you think it just screams Alien tech? I got the idea from the Hasselhoff show, Knight Rider.'

'Don't know it,' lied Solomon.

'Try and catch it. Aside from being American, it's a good show.'

Solomon glanced back at the Professor, still unsure if the reference was a test. The Professor ignored him and held up a small, metallic box. He looked closer and recognized it as an advanced version of the 12-channel radio control that he himself used to fly. A scale F-16 Falcon model now sitting in his garage. He glanced between the Horten disk and the control unit. 'You haven't?'

Zigel grinned. 'I have.'

'So this is what you wanted me to see? You've converted the disk into a drone.' Solomon cocked his head to one side. 'But didn't you say this was what you needed further funding to achieve?'

'Additional funding will allow for a complete rebuild. The craft will be smaller, faster and with an extended range. You rightly deduce that this is merely the converted original. Still far superior to anything currently used in the field, but I can make it so much better.'

'Any weaponry?'

'It was originally unarmed, but my team has added a single GSh-30-1 30 mm cannon under the pilot and two R-73 air-to-air missiles. It cannot carry much more or it would compromise the weight. The machine is very delicate.'

'What is it powered by?'

'You may need an engineering degree to understand.'

'Try me,' said Solomon.

The Professor flicked a switch on his remote. 'Why don't I just show you?'

Solomon scuttled backwards, colliding with Oleg as a pressurized seal on the underside of the craft hissed, instantly transporting him back forty years. It was the same flickering purple; the same ghostly smoke; the same snug entrance. He gulped and closed his eyes, half expecting to see the head of the dying creature lolling listlessly on the lowering ramp.

'Are you alright, Polkovnik?' asked the Professor. 'You look as though you have seen a ghost.'

Oleg gripped his arm. Solomon nodded to his companion, his eyes confirming he was fine.

'Zigel? Zigel, what the hell are you doing?' Solomon turned to see an irate, balding scientist striding in their direction and snapping his fingers, pointing at Oleg. 'That man is not cleared to be in this hangar.'

'He is with the Polkovnik,' snapped the Professor. 'Don't interfere. If Yeltsin is thinking of reinstating my funding, it is his business, not yours. Go back to your cameras, Dimitri.'

Dimitri stopped in front of Oleg. 'What's going on, Oleg? You have no right...'

'The papers,' whispered Oleg, stammering in Russian. He pushed the fake orders into Dimitri's outstretched hand. 'These papers include my orders to escort the Polkovnik wherever he wants to go on base.' Solomon winced. His friend was sweating.

'It is fine,' interrupted Zigel. 'We are speaking in English. This soldier does not speak English.'

'But he does sp...' Dimitri paused mid-sentence; staring hard at Oleg's reddening face. He turned, his gaze shifting toward Solomon. He took a step backwards and shifted his weight, turning tail and running in the direction of the guard's office. 'Traitors! Guards! Shoot on sight.'

Solomon looked into the shocked eyes of Professor Zigel, shrugging as the scientist's eyes glazed and the man crumpled to the floor. He plucked the remote from the unconscious Professor's spindly fingers, and rose to find Oleg stood like a statue, the butt of his handgun still clasped in his right hand, like a club.

'We have to get inside the craft,' hissed Solomon. Oleg hesitated. 'Move man, we've got no choice. Stay and we'll both be executed. KGB or not, I don't suppose your government is quite past making its enemies disappear.' He shoved the Russian toward the ramp. 'It'll be cramped, but there must be room enough for two.' Oleg ducked inside. The bewildered face of a guard popped out from behind one of the aircraft. He was carrying an AK-74. Solomon panicked and his leather-soled dress shoe slipped on the smooth edge of the ramp. His arms flailed and his shoulder hit the hangar's tarmac, the remote squirting from his grasp and under the disk. He felt Oleg's hands grip his right arm, pulling him to safety as a smattering of bullets pinged and sparked off the ramp.

'Close it up,' screamed Oleg.

Solomon stared at Oleg. Before his brain could assess the level of danger, he dove for the remote. He knocked it further and sent it teetering further from reach. He grimaced and made a last-ditch attempt to grab it. His hand closed about it and the relief was intoxicating, albeit short-lived; a second volley of bullets forcing him to pull it clear and retreat.

He examined it and shook his head. 'Shit, Oleg, the tags are all in Russian. I can't read Russian,' Solomon hissed. A bullet ricocheted inside the cockpit.

Oleg screamed in agony and grabbed his bare forearm, blood oozing through his fingers. 'Fuck! Just do something. You saw him lower the walkway thing. Just press some buttons.'

Solomon did as he was told, pushing the first button in his eye line as he hauled himself into the pilot seat. He jumped as something exploded under him. 'What the hell was that?'

'You've found the cannon!' Oleg shouted. 'Look.' Solomon followed his finger and gasped as he saw the round smoking hole in the adjacent aircraft. Oleg punched a button on the control. 'This one controls the ramp control.' A whirr of gears confirmed Oleg's guess, and the ramp eased shut under them. 'And this is the engine,' said Oleg, flicking open a protective casing and prodding at the large black button lying underneath.

The craft lurched forward, wobbling around its central axis. Solomon gripped the arms of his chair as his stomach attempted to escape his body. 'Jesus Christ! Are we airborne?'

The machine stabilized. Oleg peered through the tinted glass of the canopy. 'We're airborne. Only a few feet, but we're rising.'

'Why is there no engine noise?' Solomon peered at his surroundings for the first time. It was so dark. He was the proud holder of a private pilot's license, but recognized barely anything in this cockpit. Where was the primary flight display? The airspeed and altitude indicators? The navigation display? There didn't even appear to be a fuel gauge.

'What are you doing?' shouted Oleg. 'Use the remote and fly this thing. Remember, it's a drone. They have ripped the guts out and put them inside that thing on your lap.' Solomon shook his head, snapping out of his trance. 'We need to get out now. Certainly before that arsehole scientist raises an army above ground.'

Solomon squinted and gazed through the tinted glass at the hangar beyond. 'How the hell do we get out? We're underground.'

'The far wall opens. Just blast the crap out of it.' Solomon stared back at the exasperated soldier blankly. 'This thing fires missiles, doesn't it?' Oleg hissed. 'Fire one.'

Solomon could feel the stress and pressure of the situation taking hold. The symptoms were familiar and a panic attack was on the way. 'But...' Oleg shoved one of the joysticks to the right and, putting the disk into a sharp turn, simultaneously depressed the trigger for the cannon. A series of thunderclaps accompanied a spray of 30 mm rounds punching indiscriminately into the hangar wall and fuselages of the surrounding aircraft. A group of soldiers burst into the hangar, instantly hitting the ground as the huge wing of a TU-95 crashed alongside them. Now facing what he hoped was the correct wall, Solomon braced himself as Oleg tapped the button next to the trigger for the gun. Solomon held his breath and prayed, expecting a sidewinder missile to launch from somewhere under his feet. Nothing happened.

Oleg tapped it again and looked down at Solomon, his face draining of blood. 'There's no target! Bloody thing won't fire without a target.'

'Shit,' said Solomon. 'What do we do now? Those bastards will not stay down for long and I bet they're carrying something that will fire.'

Oleg returned his hand to his injured arm and grimaced. 'I know the code to the doors.'

'How? I thought you hadn't been inside this hangar.'

'I haven't. But I have been asked to open it from the other side. I just hope the code is the same.' He stood on his toes and looked through the canopy.

'Why would it be the same? And what the hell are you doing now?'

'It was so long, no one ever felt the need to change it. Opening the doors was deemed low risk. Come on, where is that damn terminal... Got it, aim this thing to my left.'

Solomon could feel his blood rising. 'Are you joking? You won't get ten feet without a hundred bullets in your back.'

'If you have a better idea, comrade, I'd like to hear it. We are a sitting target up here. I either try or this disk thing will be our tomb.' Solomon ducked as a smattering of 7.62 mm rounds ricocheted off the dome, emphasizing Oleg's point. 'Unless you want to find out if we are RPG proof, I suggest you try maneuvering towards the exit. Keep those soldiers suppressed for as long as you can and I'll jump down and input the code.'

'You're a crazy sonofabitch,' said Solomon, wiping a layer of sweat from his neck. 'But I swear I'll do my best for you.' His hands were shaking, but he knew this was their only option, their only hope of survival. He gently pulled back on the right-hand joystick and pulled the other to the left. The disk responded instantly, both rising and spinning to face the approaching soldiers. They scattered as another volley from the cannon forced them to find cover.

'Oleg, we aren't moving. Where the hell is the throttle on this bloody thing?'

'Push the third button or twist the dial top right. Whatever you do, do it quick. There are two RPGs being levelled at us.

Solomon saw them and fired the cannon in their general direction. Two rounds erupted beneath him, followed by silence. He pushed the button again. 'Shit.'

'What?' said Oleg.

Solomon swung the craft around again to face the alleged false wall. 'We're out of ammo.' He depressed the third button and braced himself for a burst of speed. What happened instead was something neither of them could have guessed. The red light whizzing around the edge of the craft turned blue. He squinted through the gloom of the dark cockpit. It looked like it was speeding up. Within seconds it no longer looked to be travelling, the light spinning so fast his eyes could only register it as a single block of color. Without warning, the light disappeared and reappeared as a single ball directly in line with Solomon's chair.

'What the h...' Before he could finish his sentence, a shaft of pure energy burst from the disk's edge. The hangar wall didn't stand a chance. Whatever reinforced construct from which they were made evaporated on impact. The beam powered down as quickly as it had appeared, leaving only a perfectly round hole and, more importantly, an exit.

Oleg was the first to react. 'Twist the dial, twist the damn dial.'

Solomon's hands shook uncontrollably, but he knew he had to put aside the borderline miracle he'd just witnessed and focus himself. Oleg was injured and he needed to step up to the plate. He twisted the dial to the right. The craft jerked forward; the movement accompanied by a strange purring sound. 'What was that?'

'Oleg nodded at their reflection in the skin of another aircraft. 'The legs have just retracted inside the disk. We're good to go.' They were almost at the exit, the craft rising and falling as it responded to Solomon's deft touch. Oleg gripped his shoulder. 'RPG away!' he shouted.

'They ain't taking us that easily,' said Solomon. He spun the dial full to the right. His neck snapped back into his headrest, his cheeks ballooning as an extreme number of Gs ripped into his face. The remote slammed into his chest, the two joysticks pinned on full lock. They were rising and spinning at a speed he could only imagine. Kapustin Yar now only a speck on the ground far below. He needed to slow down, but his fingers were pinned. A black haze danced across his eyes. He was blacking out. It was now or never and never was beyond contemplation. Using every ounce of strength in his arm, he pushed against the pressure, his fingers almost there, but not quite. He screamed a guttural roar and, powered by sheer will alone, forced them to travel the last inch. He could feel the groove of the dial against his fingernail and he scratched it. The craft powered down instantly, the remote dropping to his lap. His head lolled, and he closed his eyes, his muscles no longer feeling like his own.

'Oleg?' mumbled Solomon. 'Are you... okay, comrade?' He heard something crumple to the floor behind him. His friend must be in a bad way. The initial impact with the wall could even have been fatal. He massaged his neck and tried to stand. It was so dark. In theory the craft should now be bathing in the rays of a mid-morning sun, so why was it so dark? He stood gingerly, placing the remote on the chair, and moved towards the prostrate Russian. He knelt and felt for a pulse. Solomon closed his eyes and let out the breath he'd not realized he was holding. It was there; faint, but it was there. A dull white light pierced the cockpit canopy, edging its way across the floor. Solomon raised his head and dropped to his knees, refusing to believe what he was seeing. They were passing over the sea of tranquility, skirting so close to the surface he could almost smell the cheese the moon was made from.

Chapter 16

Solomon started as an extended moan disturbed the peace. He gently slapped Oleg's face and the hardy Russian stirred at his touch.

'I wouldn't try moving just yet, comrade. Wait for your wits to return.'

Oleg coughed and clutched at his back, rubbing it in obvious pain. 'What happened? Where are we?'

'Certainly not Kansas, Dorothy.' Solomon grinned and waved a hand at the transparent dome above their heads. 'See for yourself. You won't believe me otherwise. You, sir, have just become an astronaut, or in your case, cosmonaut.'

Oleg blinked, grimacing as he shifted his weight onto his elbows. 'That's the moon?'

'Yup, and with it, the proof you were right all along. There is no way you Russkies could have come up with this. If you have, your scientists are light years ahead of those in the States.'

'You think this could be Alien?'

'Maybe, or perhaps technology lost to us and rediscovered?' Solomon grinned. 'If Professor Zigel really had the brains to dream up this aircraft, do you think the Russian's would have sat on it for this long? No exaggeration, but a dozen of these things would probably be enough to take out the entire US air force.'

'So you think this could be the only one?' whispered Oleg.

'Must be. Makes sense why it was never used in anger. They couldn't risk losing it. This disk is a game-changer to the highest degree. It can out-fly, outrun and probably out-gun anything currently available - and by some distance, I'd say.'

'So why cut Zigel's funding?'

'I'd guess it must have been political. He's obviously been working on it for forty-plus years. Funding on that kind of scale can't come cheap. If the Kremlin were looking for cuts when the Union dissolved, his pot of money must have stood out like a flashing beacon. Aside from converting this thing into a drone, it doesn't look like he's made much progress in reverse-engineering the tech.'

Oleg tentatively touched the back of his head and lifted his hand into the light of the moon. Blood coated the tips of his fingers. 'I may need a Doctor.'

Solomon returned to the pilot's seat and strapped himself in. 'I'll take things a little easier this time. Make sure your back is against the wall and pray re-entry isn't as tricky as the shuttle pilots make out.' Taking a firm grip of the controller, Solomon gently twisted the throttle and eased the joystick left, rotating his view from the undulating craters of the moon until he faced Earth.

The scene was breath-taking, its beauty increasing with every passing second, the evocative outline of the awe-inspiring Scandinavian coastline filled his field of vision. The region was suffering in the grip of a particularly harsh winter, and he could make out row upon row of white-tipped mountains, multiple frozen lakes and deep fjords etched into the landscape. Swept up in the drama and majesty of the return flight, Solomon neglected to address a vital decision. Where the hell were they going to land? He pulled back on the stick and reversed the throttle. They were in orbit but with no place to go.

'What are you doing?' asked Oleg.

Solomon stared down at his home planet, fascinated as it passed from daylight and into the dark of the night. The sparkling lights of North America twinkled up at him; major cities such as New York and Chicago, chunks of white light against the black of the countryside and the swathes of water surrounding them. He craned his neck and identified Miami, Tampa and Orlando. Home. He would give anything to be there now, sat in his comfortable office and simply dealing with the mundane day-to-day existence of his academic life. Hell, at present he'd even take a stay with his parents in Roswell. Roswell... Roswell... Of course, Roswell! Why hadn't it crossed his mind before? The Nevada desert; Area 51; Groom Lake. It was certainly worth a shot. Where else in the world could he get away with landing what was potentially an Alien spaceship? It was perfect. He reversed the throttle, slowing the craft and throwing it out of orbit.

Oleg bashed his head at the sudden drop in speed and yelped in pain. 'Take it easy, comrade. You'll be the death of me.' He rubbed his head. 'Do you have a plan? Where are we going?'

'You ever heard of Groom Lake?' Oleg coughed, bulking at the reference. 'That's right, my Russian chum, we're heading for the eye of the storm. If ever outsiders like us are going to get access to the elusive Area 51, it'll be as the result of arriving in one of these babies.'

The craft jolted as it punched into the Earth's atmosphere, the blunt underbelly burning red-hot somewhere beneath his feet. Solomon smiled; it was a perfect example of design engineering for re-entry. The United States made the same discovery in 1951; coincidentally, or perhaps not so coincidentally, around the same time the Roswell ship was first taken to the Groom Lake complex. A pair of American scientists, Allen and Eggers, calculated a blunt shape made a very effective heat shield. The greater the drag equating to a more limited heat load. In layperson's terms, the spacecraft re-enters at such a high speed the layer of air it is pushing through cannot escape the blunt surface. Instead, it remains trapped, pinned against the base and cushioning the craft from the shock wave and associated heat layer created.

Beads of sweat built up around Solomon's body as the temperature rose inside the small machine. He could see the corona discharge, the infamous St Elmo's Fire, licking and creeping up and over the edges of the disk. The craft shuddered, and he strengthened his grip on the remote-control unit, shutting his eyes and praying for the ordeal to end. Surely they must be closing in on the Kármán Line, the hundred-kilometer boundary between the Earth and space. Suddenly they were through, the red-hot belly of the saucer steaming as it plummeted through the night sky, the silence of space replaced by the high-pitched whistle of the wind.

'Should we be making that noise?' shouted Oleg.

'I don't think so. The hull must have been breached,' said Solomon, pulling and pushing the levers and buttons in front of him. 'It's not responding to my commands.' They were spinning out of control, every second taking them a few hundred meters closer to their deaths. Solomon's movements grew more and more frantic. There must be a starter motor somewhere. He threw the remote aside and bashed the bare dashboard in front of him in frustration. It lit and flickered back into darkness. His heart leapt. Did this mean the Russians hadn't removed the original controls? They were still there and appeared to be touch control. He drummed his hands against the console. These were the actions of a desperate man and he knew it. The starter could be anywhere.

Without warning, the console sputtered into life, silver light shimmering in a series of waves across its surface. They had power. Solomon glanced in Oleg's direction. His triumph was replaced by horror as he realized the reason behind their change of fortune. The Russian lay prone on the ground, his body convulsing with a pair of thick cables grasped in his hands. He returned to the console, his mind fogged by shock at the sacrifice of his friend. Two circular lights dominated its surface. They must be the primary controls. He centered himself and slowly traced a finger over the surface of the left pad. The saucer jerked sideways, instantly responding to his command, but the craft was still in freefall.

Solomon cleared his mind, focusing on the stall training he'd received at Roswell's model aircraft club. Not ideal, but possibly his only option in the circumstances and surely the principles must be transposable. What was it his instructor drummed into him? His eidetic memory kicked into gear.

'The key to recovery is regaining positive control of the aircraft. You must first reduce the angle of attack. Decrease the wing angle to regain lift.' At that point, Solomon's model Republic P-47 Thunderbolt smashed into the ground. The instructor hadn't even flinched. 'Too much forward pressure will hinder recovery by imposing a negative load on the wing. You must learn to smoothly apply maximum allowable power to increase the airspeed and minimize altitude loss. Once recovery is complete, adjust your power and return the aircraft to the desired flight path and establish level flight with full coordinated use of the controls.'

Solomon slid his index finger backwards on the left pad whilst simultaneously trying to level the saucer using the right pad. 'And now for a burst of maximum allowable power,' he whispered. 'God, I hope this works.' He shoved both fingers forward, powering down almost immediately as the sudden G force forced both hands backwards on the pads. He coughed and punched the air in delight. It worked. The craft was stable and flying level. The mountainous peaks of the Sierra Nevada mountain range ominously whipped by on either side of the domed cockpit. A few more seconds more and his body would probably have decorated one of those peaks. At least he more or less knew where he was. Solomon slowed and set a course for the old nuclear testing facility at Groom Lake. If the rumors were true, he doubted he'd be flying solo for very long.

Chapter 17

Solomon's instincts proved correct as the roar of two single-engine F-16 Falcon fighters invaded the silence of his cabin. They appeared on either side of the saucer, their familiar bubble-shaped cockpits easing into his line of sight until he could see the pilots inside. He held up a hand, hailing the pilot to his right. The man responded, clenching a fist and then pointing to the ground.

Solomon smiled and mumbled through clenched teeth, 'I assume that means I should follow you.' He exaggerated a nod and mirrored the gesture, dipping the nose of the saucer with a flick of a finger. 'Now show me where you're from, boys.' As if on cue, America's most secretive airbase exposed itself, a row of landing lights appearing from nowhere on the desert floor. 'Oleg, my friend, I really wish you were seeing this.'

The lights brought back a memory of a description he'd heard at a recent conspiracy seminar in Utah. "We stood on Tikaboo Peak night after night with our cameras at the ready. On the third night at precisely three in the morning, a row of lights illuminated the surface of the valley. A wave of excitement spilt through our party and we heard an aircraft roll down the runway. We could see its shadow as it accelerated, but it disappeared on take-off. The lights cut out as soon as its wheels left the ground and the valley was plunged back into darkness." This was the closest members of the public ever came to exposing the elusive base and each was arrested as a result.

The lead F-16 lowered its landing gear and touched down on the desert runway, decelerating hard as a trio of parachutes ejected from its rear. Solomon followed the aircraft as it taxied through the empty desert. There were no signs of life; no evidence this was the base where the world's first extreme altitude spy plane, the U-2, was born.

The fighter came to a halt, its engine powering down until only the red-hot glow of the exhaust nozzle remained. Solomon eased the saucer toward the ground, aware he didn't have a clue how to operate the landing gear. He set his jaw and braced for impact. Instead, he heard only the whirr of gears and felt a gentle bump as the saucer's undercarriage met the desert floor. His heart rate normalized. The undercarriage must be automated, perhaps linked to some kind of proximity sensor. The second F-16 pulled alongside him, powering down and blocking any chance of an exit.

Solomon jumped from his seat and focused on Oleg. He was in a bad way. He must have received one hell of a shock when he connected the cables. Rolling the Russian onto his side, he raised the man's knees into his chest.

'The medics will take care of you, Oleg. You're not in Russia anymore. We have proper doctors over here.'

The comment solicited the briefest of smiles and an accompanying whimper of pain. 'Don't... Don't let them hide this, Sol,' he stuttered. 'If I don't make it, saving your ugly American ass has to mean something.' He forced another smile. 'My father will be turning in his grave. His only son sacrificing himself for a Пиндос.'

'Don't you die on me, Oleg. Come on you commie bastard, we've won goddamnit. We're safe. You're out of Russia and we've stolen the saucer. I need you to help spread the word and tell the world.'

Solomon tapped a pad on the wall beside the raised ramp. It activated with a hiss of pressurized air and he slid, feet first, through the widening gap. He landed awkwardly, twisting and rolling onto his back. The cold barrel of a 9mm semi-automatic pistol pressed against his forehead.

'He's a fucking red,' exclaimed his captor. 'Look at the uniform. What is he, a major or something?'

Solomon blinked up at the silhouette of the pilot standing above him. 'I paid for the rank of colonel.' He shoved the gun aside and tried to stand. 'Is this the way you treat American heroes round here? You should be rolling out the red carpet after what I've been through.' He glanced around. The runway lights extinguished and the sense of desolation was complete. 'So this is Area 51? Not exactly catching you on spring break, am I?' said Solomon, trying to emphasize his southern accent. 'Where is your commanding officer? I've delivered a goddamn bona fide flying saucer. The least I should expect is someone of rank to meet me.'

'Sorry, sir,' said the pilot, lowering his weapon a little. 'We didn't know...'

'Just find me a medic. My associate is still on board and the poor bastard is half dead. He took a bullet in the arm, banged his head and possibly suffered a heavy electric shock.' The pilot moved to holster his firearm but indicated that his companion should remain vigilant. 'I'm not armed, you prick. There's no way they would have let me inside Kapustin Yar if I had been.'

'You've come from Kapustin Yar?'

'Where do you think our red friends were hiding this little beauty?'

'Jim, make the call,' said the second man.

Jim shrugged and clicked the radio attached to his shoulder. 'Target secure. Approach with caution.' Solomon scanned the vista. A series of torchlights flicked on, torchlights attached to assault rifles and carried by a large division of heavily camouflaged soldiers. So that was how they'd decided to play it. He'd been wondering why his initial welcoming party was so small.

He raised his arms and turned through three hundred and sixty degrees. 'I am unarmed, boys, so go easy on those triggers. I'm on your side.'

'On the floor. Hands on your head,' barked a soldier. Solomon complied and hit the deck, the pain in his ankle disappearing as his adrenalin heightened. A pair of hands patted him down, searching for hidden weapons.

'He's clean.'

Jim stepped forward and hauled Solomon to his feet. 'I'm sorry, sir, but I'm sure you can understand our concern given your uniform.' He pointed into the darkness. 'I've been asked to accompany you to our debriefing room. It's not far.'

Solomon noticed the rank sewn into Jim's flight suit. 'Lead on, Captain.'

***

Forty minutes later, Solomon stretched out his legs, exhausted and cradled a cup of strong coffee inside a small interrogation room in the depths of the base. The US Air Force was now in full possession of the facts and the interrogating officers had only just left him alone, probably to seek further guidance from someone higher up the command chain. Given the magnitude of his revelation, maybe even the President was being briefed.

Solomon swung his head in the door's direction and nodded at the middle-aged officer entering the room, his golden oak leaf insignia showing he held the rank of Major.

'You the delivery guy everyone's talking about?'

Solomon frowned and nodded. 'And you are?'

'Rumor is that you were in Russia looking for answers.'

'I found a few.' Solomon cocked his head to one side. 'I'm sorry, and you are?'

'If you want a few more, you come and see me.' The officer slid a card into Solomon's breast pocket. 'I've seen shit I just can't live with anymore. That ship of yours is just the tip of a very blood-soaked iceberg.'

The handle of the door creaked, and the officer fell silent. Solomon's original interrogator strode inside, visibly taken aback when he realized Solomon was no longer alone. He saluted. 'Evening, Major. Is everything okay?'

The Major coughed. 'Captain Wellman, isn't it? Your man was shouting for attention. Apparently needs to relieve himself. I suggested he hold it and await your return.'

'Thank you, sir. I can deal with it from here.'

The Major saluted the junior officer and made for the door. 'As you were, Captain, and make sure you take decent notes, your name may well go down in the history books if you're lucky.' He paused. 'Then again, it's more likely they will bury this whole thing like everything else happening in this god-forsaken hole.'

Chapter 18

Hunter raised an eyebrow and peered at Solomon through the rear-view mirror. 'You are either the biggest and best bull-shitter in history or...'

'Or you may have to revisit a few of your preconceived prejudices?' whispered Solomon.

'Something like that,' Hunter mumbled. 'What happened after the interview? They can't have just let you walk out the front door.'

'In a manner of speaking, they kind of did. They bought my silence with a trip to the White House. It was the tail end of the Bush administration and he presented me with a medal and a pat on the back. Fed me some crap about being a hero and proud I was American.'

'So you stayed silent?'

'I did.' Solomon laughed. 'You wouldn't believe it now, but presidential approval actually meant something to me back then?'

'What changed?' said Hunter.

'I met with the Major.'

'So you did meet him,' said Hunter. 'When?'

'Only recently.' He rubbed his chin. 'About a week before they forced me to fake my death.'

Hunter nodded and blew the air from his lungs. 'That explains a few things. I don't suppose you're going to tell me what he said?'

'You aren't ready for it,' said Solomon.

'Not ready for it? Are you kidding? You're asking me to believe in the Roswell alien crash? What could be bigger than proof we're not alone?'

'Grow up, Hunter. Roswell was and still is a Soviet inspired fraud. The real saucer crashed in Italy during WW2 and was picked up by the Nazis. It was just rotten luck the Russians recovered it during the fall of Berlin and I can't emphasize enough how damn lucky the rest of us are that they never figured out how to replicate the technology.'

'How do you…' He rolled his eyes as he realized. 'Of course, the Major. But they sort of did with the Roswell saucer.'

'Yes, and look how that turned out. It crashed, and the bomb didn't even detonate.'

'Fair point.' Hunter drummed his fingers on the steering wheel. 'So am I right in thinking you believe that Serena Harmony's employer conspired with the US government to cover up the incident?'

Solomon nodded. 'Yes, and so much more. EG&G have been inextricably linked to numerous black operations for decades. They still are.'

'And now you want to expose the truth? Ok, then what's the plan, Sol? Persuade Serena to give us her ID, break into a highly secure facility and ask for directions to their secret files?'

'In a manner of speaking, yes, that's exactly what I intend to do.'

Hunter glanced at his watch. It was just after six in the evening. He knocked on the dark blue door again, louder this time. A sliver of paint flaked from the surface and spiraled to the ground. He shrugged at Solomon. Serena was either at the office or refusing to answer. They would just have to wait. He turned to leave and heard something rattle. He paused and looked back. The door inched open, locking against a chain. A familiar grey-blue eye bore into him, looking him up and down with suspicion.

'Serena? Is that you?' asked Hunter. 'Serena Harmony?'

The door closed, and the chain tinkled while being drawn free of its bonds. Hunter started as the door crashed open and a stocky pit bull of a woman lumbered through. She collided with his waist and clamped a chubby pair of powerful arms around his chest.

'John Hunter.' She panted, a little out of breath. 'You're the one person I never thought I'd see on my doorstep. Pinch me.'

'Wow...' said Hunter, struggling to extricate his body from her vice-like grip. 'It's nice to see you as well.'

Serena retracted her arms and blushed. 'Sorry, I didn't mean to... I mean... Sorry, I just can't believe John Hunter is standing on my front porch.'

Hunter felt a little like a piece of meat as her ravenous eyes roamed his body. 'I had no idea you felt this way.'

'Why would you? After all, why would someone like you ever be interested in a girl like me?'

'Don't be silly, Serena, that's unfair,' said Hunter. Serena's eyes lit up, and he instantly regretted the comment. This was a dangerous game he was playing. He didn't want to lead her on, but given the role she was to play in Solomon's plan, a woman scorned would be next to useless. 'I'm sorry, Serena. Perhaps I should get to the point before I make a fool of myself. Could we please come inside?'

She stood aside, and her brow creased. 'Wait, we?'

Hunter glanced back at the car as Solomon slammed his door. 'I assume you remember, Professor Garnett?'

Serena started, her gaze flitting between the two men. Hunter noticed her left eye twitch. She almost looked scared. 'You haven't...' she stuttered.

Solomon shook his head. 'Same issue as last time.'

'Good. I mean...' She glanced at Hunter. The fear was palpable now. 'You agreed never to bother me again.' She wagged a finger at Solomon as he approached. 'If you think you can barge in demanding things of me just because of...' She nodded at Hunter. 'Why is he here?'

Hunter placed a hand on Serena's shaking shoulder and shot an angry glance in Solomon's direction. 'My apologies, but it appears Professor Garnett has been a little tight-lipped with the information he's chosen to share with me.' He moved into her eye-line. 'I don't know what he's done, but can we do this inside? We really do need your help, Serena.'

'That man wanted me to break into the office of my boss and steal a file. I mean, as if I would. Who does he think I am?'

Hunter gently steered her backwards. 'Please, can we do this inside? Perhaps with a stiff drink? I certainly need one, and I think we have some explaining to do.' He glared at Solomon. 'And that means you as well, Sol.'

Solomon shrugged and followed, a wry grin etched on his lips.

The two men took a seat on a threadbare forest-green sofa. Hunter winced, shuffling uncomfortably as a rogue spring threatened to pierce his behind.

'You take milk and sugar?' called Serena from the kitchen.

'Black please,' said Hunter.

'Same for me,' added Solomon.

'Why didn't you tell me you'd already made contact?' whispered Hunter.

'I didn't want to muddy the waters,' Solomon hissed back. 'For all I knew, you might have refused to meet her out of some misplaced sense of justice.'

'Justice? What the hell did you do to this woman?'

'I can field that one,' interrupted Serena, placing three cups on the coffee table. 'Professor Garnett here threatened to kill me if I didn't give him access to a confidential file from the archives of my employer. I threw him out on his ass. Mad bastard, you're lucky I didn't call the cops.'

'I am truly sorry for how I acted, Miss Harmony. All I can tell you is that I was desperate. I didn't know where to turn. When I discovered you were his PA, I just couldn't believe my luck.'

'Was that before or after you remembered I always thought you to be a misogynistic prick?'

Hunter held up a hand. 'Enough,' he barked. 'This is getting us nowhere. Serena, I suggest you take a seat.' Serena frowned but followed the instruction. 'I'm sorry to tell you Solomon's threat was half right, but it's not him you need to fear. Your name may already be compromised. There are people looking for us and at least one of them knew we were heading here. That particular man is dead, but we have no idea whom he may have told.'

'Dead? Who's dead? What's going on, John?'

'Can I just ask how much you know?' asked Hunter, shooting a glance at Solomon. 'What exactly did our esteemed Professor tell you?'

Serena's eyes narrowed to slits. 'That madman fed me some bull crap about Roswell. You know, the site of the Alien crash?' Hunter nodded. 'Claimed it really happened, and he was a witness. He said he was chair of some nut job UFO group and they wanted to expose the government cover story for what it really was. He thinks my boss is sitting on the evidence.' She sipped her coffee and stared Solomon in the eyes. 'If it weren't for his ridiculous threat, I'd have laughed in his face.'

Hunter maintained his deadpan expression. 'But it's all true, Serena. I swear to you on my life. Everything you've recalled is the truth.' He pulled the shard of metal he'd taken from the deposit box from his jacket and handed it to her. 'That was part of the ship.'

Serena turned it over in her hands. 'You have got to be joking. No way.' She raised an eyebrow. 'You've just pulled this off a car or something.'

Hunter shook his head. 'Nope. Bonafede Roswell crash artefact.'

Serena's eyes narrowed. 'If this was anyone else telling me…'

'I know,' said Hunter. 'You have to trust me. I can't tell you why, hell I'm not even sure why, but this EG&G file is so much more than confirmation the US government has lied to its people. The contents could be life or death.'

'So this is X-files? But for real?' said Serena.

Hunter nodded. 'For real. So… do you think you can help?'

'Life or death, you say?' Hunter nodded again. 'Whose life? Yours?'

'Yours, Mine, Solomon's and Christ knows how many others.'

'Mine? Are you…' Hunter held up a finger and silenced his former colleague. It was the part of Solomon's plan he'd objected to, but he could see no other way of convincing her. Maybe if there were a few more hours to play with, but the clock was ticking and they needed to move and move fast. The group chasing them could be hours, minutes, or even seconds in their wake. Exposing the conspiracy might be their only path to freedom. Once public, surely their deaths would only exacerbate the fragile position of those incriminated by the truth.

Hunter pointed at a tall chrome lampshade in the room's corner, using the distraction to fish something from his pocket.

'What is it?' whispered Serena.

'I thought I heard something, a high frequency whine.' He paused, pretending to listen intently. 'There it is again. Can you hear it?'

She grimaced, listening to the silence and hearing only a ticking clock. 'No, nothing. What is it? I can't hear anything.'

Solomon raised a hand to his ear, cottoning onto the ruse. 'Quiet! John, I hear it too.'

Hunter rose from his seat and made his way to the lamp, making a show of feeling around its rim. 'Got it,' he whispered, pretending to pull a small bead-like object from the shade. He tossed it to Serena.

She lifted it to the light and examined it, rolling it between her fingers. 'What the hell is it? A metal pea?'

'You've been bugged, Serena. God knows how many more of those are scattered around your apartment.' She looked up, genuinely alarmed by the revelation. This was his moment. He needed to capitalize on her vulnerability while he could. 'We need to get you out of here, Serena. I'm sorry, but you're part of this now. I don't know what to tell you. The only way out is to expose EG&G. The alternative is too horrific to contemplate.'

'You mean?'

Solomon sliced his index finger across his throat.

'I'm afraid so,' said Hunter, hoping the Professor's melodramatics had revived none of Serena's previous suspicions.

'We can go now,' she said. 'The Colonel...'

'The Colonel?' interrupted Hunter.

'Yes, my boss is a retired colonel, Colonel Patterson. He likes us to use the title.' Hunter exchanged a puzzled glance with Solomon. 'Anyway, the point being, he left early for a dental appointment, so I know he isn't around. That's why I'm home so early myself. Normally he has me working to around eight. You're lucky, means people won't be surprised to see me in the office at this time of night.'

'Perfect.' Hunter turned to Solomon. 'So what's our cover story? Assuming, "asking to see it," was just one of your little jokes.'

Chapter 19

The silence in the car bordered uncomfortable. Hunter changed gear and glanced at Serena, desperately trying to think of a conversational topic to ease the tension.

'So how did you end up working for the bad guys anyway?' She shot him a glance, instantly making him regret his ill-advised attempt at humor. 'Sorry, poor joke, but it might actually help if you can fill us in a little about the company.'

'Fine, but remember these people are my friends. If you make me choose between them or you two, my choice might disappoint you.'

'Noted,' said Solomon.

'Okay, so I joined the defense and services team after leaving Florida University,' said Serena. 'And luckily survived the URS buy out in 02. That was a chaotic time; people were hired and fired virtually every day. It only settled down once URS relocated us to Maryland and renamed the team URS' EG&G. We're still called that, although officially the EG&G badging was dropped in 09.'

'Why was that?' said Hunter.

Serena shrugged. 'No idea. Above my paygrade I'm afraid.'

'Perhaps to sever links to their murky past,' said Solomon.

Hunter shuddered as their red sedan drove past the huge corporate lettering adorning the entrance to the URS site. The complex was enormous and a homage to the achievements of the modern industrialists; a gargantuan structure of glass and steel housing a workforce of eleven thousand. They sped past workshop after workshop, listening to Serena's commentary as to the various engineering projects they accommodated; ranging from temporary field bridges to tanks and ammunition.

Hunter slowed as the gates to the central building loomed up ahead. A pair of armed guards staffed a barrier to what looked like a fenced off car park. He rubbed his temples and felt butterflies in his stomach. They were already trespassing and capture could mean prison, or worse. He glanced at Serena. She looked fairly calm or at least wanted to project that she was on the surface. He could only guess at what might be going on behind her oversized sunglasses.

The car pulled up to the security barrier and she wound down the window to show her pass.

'The Colonel got you back has he, Miss Harmony?' asked the guard.

'You know how he is, Phil.' She jabbed a thumb at Solomon and Hunter. 'I've got two externals to come and look at his computer. He's wiped a drive and requested the help of some forensic computing experts to reverse his mistake.'

'Haven't we got anyone internally who can do that?' said Phil.

Serena shrugged. 'I assume the old boy checked. I just do as I'm told. What do I need to do to get them checked in?' She smiled and looked at her two passengers. 'They look like dodgy bastards to me, so I suggest you do a thorough background check.'

Phil grinned. 'Fuck that. You know the game's about to start, don't you?' He tossed in a pair of visitor badges. 'Just make them wear them at all times or it's my arse on the line.'

Solomon leant forward. 'You a Ravens man?'

'Hell, yes, sir. We got the Steelers tonight and those fuckers are goner pay for beating us at the M&T.'

'Give them a shout from me, will you soldier? I've given up my spot at my bar for this job.' He snorted. 'Unfortunately, the wife's love of my credit card means I can't afford to say no, even at my age.'

'I hear you, sir.' Phil lifted the barrier. 'I hope it's a quick job so you make it back for half time.'

'Drive,' hissed Solomon, simultaneously grinning at the soldier and giving him a thumb's up.

Hunter accelerated and eased the car under the barrier. He turned to Solomon. 'Kudos to the quick thinking. He shouldn't give us a second thought now.'

Solomon nodded. 'Yup, dear old Phil will only remember us as a couple of fellow Ravens fans pissed at being unable to see the big game.'

Hunter patted the Professor's leg. 'Genius, Sol, genius. You and all, Serena, very cool.'

Serena shrugged. 'Nothing to it. Phil is a friend of mine anyway. He wouldn't suspect anything dodgy from me.' She let out a sigh and pulled into the parking lot. 'I just hope I haven't landed him in it. He really is one of the good guys.'

'Don't worry, H,' said Solomon. 'We'll be in and out. I don't want anyone risking their job over this.'

'Apart from me, you mean,' said Serena. 'And don't call me H. Makes me sound like one of those wannabes from American Idol.'

Hunter stepped from the car and drank in the huge, imposing horseshoe-shaped building dominating his field of vision. A string of fountains ran the length of the central courtyard, their jets rising and falling, each performing its part in an intricate pre-programmed dance of water and light.

Serena shoved a visitor's badge into Hunter's hand. 'Please put this on. We don't want to draw any unnecessary attention.'

Hunter surreptitiously jabbed a finger at the heavily guarded and well-lit atrium at the building's center. 'Do you know another way inside? I'm not sure we can rely on another accommodating sports fan.'

Serena nodded toward the right-wing. 'I tend to use the side entrance. A couple of years ago, I kicked up a stink about how much time I was wasting by using the main entrance. HR didn't care, but the Colonel took pity and eventually sorted me out with a passkey.'

'Perfect,' said Solomon.

'I should warn you there is a camera over the door.'

'Not to worry,' said Solomon. 'I've got this part covered.' He pulled out his phone and keyed a number into the touch screen. 'Do either of you remember Biggles?'

'Of course,' said Hunter. 'I loved those books as a child.'

'I don't think he's ringing a fictional character you twit,' said Serena. 'Biggles was a UF oddball who spent all his free time in the IT suite on flight simulators.'

'Ah, of course,' said Hunter. 'He once helped me debug an underwater surveying program. He was a bit of a whiz kid if I remember rightly.'

'He was and still is. His technical genius was the only reason the faculty put up with him playing games during work hours.' Solomon put the phone to his ear. 'Biggles? Yes, I'm good, you? Excellent. Yes, I'm inside and in a bit of a bother. Need some help blinding a camera. Any chance you can have a quick fiddle?' He paused and covered the handset. 'Do you know the door number?'

'Eighty-three, I think,' said Serena, pulling out her passkey. 'Yes, eighty-three. It's written here on the back.'

'You get that Biggles? Yup. Yes. Okay. Cheers mate, I owe you one. Keep close to the phone, remember I'll need you for the data transfer.' Solomon looked at the building. 'Wherever door eighty-three is, its camera is now on a one second loop. Biggles has a trace on my phone. If there are any more cameras dotted along our route, he'll shut them down as we go.'

'Nice,' said Hunter 'Simple, yet effective. I hope you're paying him in more than beer tokens.'

Solomon grinned. 'He'll get a few peanuts as well.' He waved a hand at Serena. 'Come on, let's get this over with. I don't want to spend any more time inside this place than needs be. This is a snatch and grab mission. We clear?'

***

Chris Cartwright stared ashen-faced at his partner in crime, Julio Mendes. He knew he didn't have a choice, but this was the type of organization he'd been banned from having any contact with during his time at Area 51. It was even more ironic that its chair was a current employee of the base. The Roswell branch of the American Institute of Ufology was located inside an eclectically decorated building in South Maine. He could tell by the décor that its members were struggling to tread the fine line between credibility and making the institute appealing to the wallets of the town's innumerable tourists. Given the number of blow-up green aliens with their black almond eyes and cliché "I want to Believe" posters, he guessed credibility had been the loser in that particular battle. He circled the room, awaiting the arrival of the contact he'd been given, and paused in front of a print taken from the Roswell Daily Record. "RAAF Captures Flying Saucer On Ranch in Roswell Region."

'July the 8th 1947,' whispered Chris.

'What d'ya say?' said Julio.

'Nothing, they've just got a copy of the paper from the day they found the alien ship.'

'Do you believe any of this shit? Little green men and autopsies,' said Julio. 'I certainly saw nothing.'

'This shit,' a female voice snapped, 'is why you are here, I assume?'

Chris jumped and turned to face the dark doorway to his rear. The aggressive voice did not match the slight frame of the elderly lady emerging from the gloom. Her demeanor was more akin to a friendly grandmother than a spikey purveyor of misinformation.

'Mrs. Collins?' he asked. He received a nod in acknowledgement. 'I must apologies for my associate. He is unused to seeing such... how can I put this... extreme beliefs?'

'Call it what you like. This meeting will not last long. I am far too long in the tooth to waste my time trying to convince those with closed minds. Good day gentleman.' She turned and made to exit the room.

'Wait,' called Chris. 'Are you aware of a man called Solomon Garnett?'

She stopped in her tracks and turned to meet his gaze. 'Professor.'

'I'm sorry?'

'His name is Professor Garnett. Do not do him the disservice of forgetting his title,' said Mrs. Collins. 'What do you want with him?'

'We're looking for him,' said Julio.

'Then you can start by looking six feet under. Solomon recently passed away. He was one of our most high-profile members and our organization's chairman throughout the Nineties.'

Chris eased Julio behind him, forcing him to back down. Antagonizing this woman would not get them anywhere. 'I'm sorry, Mrs. Collins. Can we start again?' She frowned but seemed happy enough for him to continue. 'Professor Garnett is very much alive and well.' Chris noted a lack of surprise at this revelation. 'He's discovered something big, and not wishing to be alarmist, but there are people on his trail trying to silence him. We managed to throw them off his scent, but now have no idea of his whereabouts.'

Mrs. Collins let her thin lips form a spiteful smile. 'Sounds like Solomon alright. He was always on the edge of some adventure or other.'

'He's done this before?'

'I'm afraid I can't help you any further, gentlemen. If the Professor has slipped off the radar of two men supposedly "helping" him, why do you think he'd be on mine? The last time I saw him, he was in a casket being lowered into the ground.'

Chris changed tact and pointed to a photo on the wall. 'That's him, isn't it? And, if I'm not much mistaken, your good self. Where were you? It looks like a vacation spot. You must have been close at one time.'

'We were close in our younger years, but it wasn't a vacation. More of a field trip.'

'Really, whereabouts? Somewhere up north, by the look of the greenery,' said Julio.

'Rendlesham Forest, England.'

'What, New England?' asked Julio.

'No, you fool, as in the United Kingdom,' Mrs. Collins snapped.

'The UK? They have UFO sightings in the UK?' said Julio.

'Young man, you have already angered me enough with your disrespectful arrogance. Do not make it worse by displaying such a comprehensive level of ignorance.'

Chris pointed to the door and shoved Julio toward the sunlight. 'And I apologize once again. Julio is one of those who believe such encounters occur only in the presence of drunken American rednecks.' Julio stood his ground and glared at Chris, refusing to budge.

Mrs. Collins stared into his eyes, and the hint of a smile cracked on her lips. 'Is this your way of saying you are a believer?'

Chris allowed the hint of a smile to form on his lips. 'Let's just say I've seen one or two things which have left me open to the possibility.' He paused, choosing his next words carefully. He didn't want her closing up again, particularly since Julio seemed determined to derail his attempt at a light touch interrogation at every turn. 'And I'm also open to the possibility of finding out anything which may lead me to Solomon.'

She jabbed a finger toward a pair of seats. 'Fine, I'll see what I can find out.'

Chris took his seat. 'Why were you in the UK?'

'Sol was obsessed with saucers,' said Mrs. Collins. 'He spent all his free time reading, researching, building models and writing papers.'

'What happened in the forest?' asked Julio.

'We arrived in the January of 81, a month after receiving several reports from different and unrelated sources. They each detailed unexplained lights and alleged landings of unidentified craft inside the forest. The reports alone warranted a visit, but the clincher came when we looked up the site on a map.'

'The geography? Why? Was it unusual?' asked Chris.

'It was located on the edge of a military base, RAF Woodbridge.'

Chris nodded. 'Okay, so why was that significant?'

'Solomon believed, and as far as I know, he still believes the United States is the prime culprit in covering up the existence of flying saucers.'

'But doesn't this disprove the theory if the British Air Force were involved?' said Julio.

She laughed. 'It might, but at that time RAF Woodbridge just happened to be under the control of the United States Air Force.'

'I'm still not sure I understand. Why did you go? Were you hoping for a saucer to make an appearance?' asked Chris.

'God no,' said Mrs. Collins. 'We broke into the airbase.'

'You did what?' said Julio.

'I wasn't always this old, boys.' Mrs. Collins smiled, her stony façade replaced by a look of sweet innocence. 'I've been involved in my fair share of espionage.'

'Nice. So what did you find?' asked Chris.

'I now know how the Brits decorate their prison cells.' She sighed and rose to her feet. 'The rest I'd rather not discuss. If you boys truly want to help Solomon, you're better off just leaving him to get on with whatever he's plotting. He's a tough cookie, that one, but he's hurting. Truth be told, he's been hurting for years. Solomon is looking for answers and justice, nothing more. You've told me he faked his own death, and I'm not surprised. He died the day he found out. Now he just wants to make someone pay. The government, the US Air Force or those sons of bitches at EG&G.' Chris and Julio exchanged glances at the reference. It was a fleeting acknowledgement, but enough to raise suspicion. Her eyes narrowed. 'Who did you boys say you work for again?'

Chris coughed and stood, stumbling over his words. 'We didn't, but I can reassure you we have Solomon's best interests at heart.'

'Get out!' she screamed. 'I saw the way you looked at your buddy. You're EG&G aren't you? I should have known; I've been interrogated by you bastards before.' She pulled Chris from his seat and ushered him to the door. 'This is a change of tack, though; pensionable wolves in sheep's clothing. You should be ashamed of yourselves.' She shoved Chris into the street and wagged a finger at him. 'My instincts may have dimmed, but my memory is still intact and I don't forgive easy. If I see either of you again, I swear it'll be from behind the barrel of a shotgun.'

Julio followed Chris onto the sidewalk. 'Chill lady, I swear we're here to help.'

'Like hell you are. Go slither back to your paymasters. Make sure they know if Solomon's disappeared, then it's because he's onto them.' She paused and looked Chris in the eye. 'And if he is... you and them, you're all fucked.'

She tried to slam the door, but Chris was quicker and wedged his boot in the gap. 'Mr. Collins,' he said. 'David Collins, does he still live here?'

The door opened fractionally. 'How do you know my David?'

'Chris pulled an envelope from his jacket. 'We used to work together. Can you please give him this? My name is Chris Cartwright. It is imperative he receives this letter. I promise we're not the enemy. The life of Solomon is hanging in the balance.'

'Professor Garnett.' Mrs. Collins snatched the letter from his hand and kicked his boot from the door, this time slamming the door shut.

Julio looked at Chris in bewilderment. 'What just happened? Who's David?'

'A friend, and with any luck, our passport inside the base.'

Chapter 20

Hunter clipped the visitor badge to his overalls and admired Serena's place of work. Every new corridor revealed yet another set of workshops and laboratories containing high-end electron microscopy suites, bookended supercomputers, robotics studios and an array of testing units.

'These are what they call the "phase one" labs,' said Serena, reading his mind. 'They're where the true brainiac scientists ply their trade.'

'Do you have access?' asked Solomon.

'Why? Am I not breaking enough rules for you? But for the record, no. Aside from security issues, giving access to mere mortals is a massive health and safety risk.' She pointed to the door they had just passed. 'That lab is predominantly concerned with weapons development and chemical warfare. Who knows what I might inhale if I went in without the right gear.'

Hunter bulked at the comment and raised an eyebrow. 'Chemical warfare? Are you serious? I thought the States accepted the ban on the use and possession of chemical weapons back in ninety-seven.'

Serena smiled. 'They did, and I expect the politicians on the Hill still believe we comply.'

'But surprise, surprise...' said Solomon.

Serena ignored the comment and continued. 'Don't get me wrong, the Colonel doesn't believe they'll ever be used, but should we face a threat on home soil... Well, the technology is there if required.

'A dangerous game,' said Hunter. 'Imagine the devastation should weapons of this type fall into the hands of a terrorist group.'

Solomon tapped the glass panel insert on the laboratory door. 'We're an arrogant race, John. You should know that by now. If a foreign power or terrorist group did ever raid this place, I'm more or less certain we'd already be at war...' He glanced at Serena. 'I don't know, but I'd be willing to bet these rooms all have self-destruct mechanisms in the event of a breach?'

Serena nodded. 'I'm told they can cleanse the labs in less than ten minutes.'

'Cleansed.' Solomon grinned. 'I like it. It sounds so detached and innocent.'

Hunter rubbed his head. All these conspiracies were weighing down on him. 'Can we push on? Where's your office, Serena? Are we close?'

She turned a corner and stopped in front of an opaque glass door. A black stenciled name dominated its center: Colonel Patterson. She swiped her passkey and its lock clicked. Solomon gave it a gentle push, opening it fully as a motion sensor activated the lights. 'I think we're in luck. The office is empty.'

'Excellent, so he hasn't returned,' said Serena.

'Hasn't returned?' said Hunter. 'What do you mean "hasn't returned"? You told us he'd gone for the day?'

Serena shrugged. 'Yeah, but you never know.'

Solomon entered and held the door as Hunter entered. It was a super-sized office, several times larger than Hunter's own space back in England. Whatever it was this Colonel did at EG&G, it must be significant to warrant this level of square footage. Leather-clad books lined the walls, interspersed with an impressive collection of landscapes and animal busts. Hunter scanned the nearest bookcase and caught a few keywords; psychoanalysis; surgical procedures; hypnosis; Reich archaeology; geomancy; Egyptian architecture and extrasensory perception. It was certainly an eclectic mix of reading material. He hadn't known what to expect, but it certainly wasn't this. It was like stepping back in time, a sea of dark leather, oak-paneling and animal heads invoking an image of an eighteenth-century European townhouse. Bulky armchairs dominated the center of the room, separated by a Lion skin rug complete with roaring head. They faced an oversized oak desk adorned with trinkets and trophies, each carefully placed in an effort to further intimidate any visitors daring to enter the occupant's mini kingdom. He certainly wouldn't have felt comfortable having a meeting in such a daunting environment.

Serena beckoned for Hunter to enter a secondary room in the far corner. This must be her office. He passed through a frosted glass door and paused at the threshold, shocked by the number of filing cabinets greeting him. There must have been at least thirty, together forming a wall around a small desk covered in paperwork. 'So this is where the real work takes place.' He nodded at the Colonel's office. 'Is all that just for show?'

'Gaudy, isn't it?' said Serena. 'I keep telling him to remodel, but he insists the décor helps him dominate negotiations.'

'I can see why,' said Solomon. 'A man willing to buy and flaunt an illegal lion skin rug is not someone I'd like to cross.'

'He didn't buy it,' said Serena

'I beg your pardon?'

'He shot it and skinned it himself. The Colonel is a big game hunter.' She shook her head. 'He killed all these poor creatures up on the walls.'

Hunter raised an eyebrow. He was certainly getting a measure of this man.

'To the matter at hand,' interrupted Solomon. 'How far do these files go back?'

'About ten years,' said Serena.

'Not far enough,' said Solomon. He drummed his fingers on the glass door. 'Plan B. Can you get us access to his computer?'

Serena pointed to the Colonel's computer and pushed past Hunter. 'You're in luck. Every morning I have to delete any irrelevant emails he's received overnight. Obviously, I can't do that without his passwords.'

Hunter put his arm around her shoulders. 'This will definitely implicate you now. You don't have to do this...'

'What are you talking about? Yes, she does,' said Solomon.

Ignoring Solomon, she turned and met Hunter's gaze. 'Time was I'd have run through a brick wall for you, John, and back again if you asked. If you say this is important, I believe you. If my instinct is wrong, I'll just have to face the consequences.'

He kissed her lightly on the cheek. 'You were always one of the good ones.'

'Excuse me while I throw up, but can we please get started? Time is of the essence and all that. Bad guys chasing us, etcetera etcetera.'

Serena shot Solomon a hate-filled glance. 'You, on the other hand, I would happily push through said brick wall and over the cliff on the other side.' She placed a notebook and pen on a green leather inlay beside the computer's wireless keyboard and pushed the power button. It sparked into life, and the familiar Macintosh start-up chime echoed about the room. A couple of seconds later the URS Corporation logo appeared alongside a username and password box. Serena punched in the required information and stood aside. 'We're in. Now it's down to you two. I imagine whatever you're after will have further protection though, especially if it's as sensitive as you are making out.'

Solomon plugged a USB stick into the back of the machine and sent a message on his phone. 'This is where Biggles comes into his own. He knows what we're looking for. He just needed a way past the firewalls.' The pointer on the screen burst into life, manically whizzing about the screen as pathways opened, accessing files and saving their contents.

'Cool, remote access,' said Serena.

A stream of code replaced the home screen, a series of familiar words intermingled amongst the gobbledygook. Roswell, Saucer, Alien and Yussel.

'What's Yussel?' asked Hunter.

'The alien's name,' said Solomon.

Hunter turned slowly to meet Solomon's gaze. 'The what? You know its name?'

'It was part of the information given to me by the Major.'

'It sounds Jewish?'

'Ten points to Dr Hunter. Yup, our alien was a young Jewish lad called Yussel, or Joseph, if you prefer the western version.'

'So your alien... isn't an alien?' asked Serena, looking confused.

'Was he Russian?' asked Hunter. 'If the Russians built the saucer, I guess it follows the poor kid might have been a victim of one of those horrible Nazi experiments Professor Zigel mentioned.'

Solomon's phone buzzed. He slammed it on the table. 'Shit, he's drawn a blank.'

'What do you mean, he's drawn a blank?' said Hunter.

'What the hell do you think I mean? We've got diddly squat. It's a dead end. All my search fields have returned nothing. Even Area 51, and I know for sure these EG&G bastards were definitely in bed with the military on that one.'

The phone buzzed again. Hunter picked it up. 'He's asking if the info we need is untethered.'

Serena frowned. 'What's that mean?'

'Has your boss got another machine that isn't linked to the web or the company database? Could be a hard disk in a safe. Anything along those lines.'

'He's got a safe, but if you're looking for files, you're out of luck. As I said, my files only go back ten years. The EG&G files from the fifties and sixties are stored offsite. And when I say stored offsite, I understand they are in Nevada somewhere. I don't know where.'

'Nevada?' said Hunter.

'Area 51,' said Solomon. He sighed. 'Maybe I was being naïve. Thinking about it, why would the military allow the URS Corporation access to such information? It was probably never even transferred during the sale. Our file is probably sitting in some underground warehouse gathering dust in the desert.'

'So why the hell are we here?' asked Hunter. 'What exactly did this Major tell you?'

Solomon slumped into the Colonel's chair and spun to face the screen. 'He told me the smoking gun could be found in Patterson's office.'

'Right, so what are we missing? Where is the safe?' asked Hunter.

'It's behind the elephant head,' said Serena. 'But there's nothing in there of consequence. Only money and a few invoices on a memory stick.'

'Invoices?' Hunter pulled the animal's head aside. 'Why would he keep invoices in a safe? Can you open it up?'

'No problem.' She keyed in the code and the door sprang open.

Hunter's heart pounded as he scooped out the contents, a roll of $20 notes and a memory stick. He placed everything in front of Solomon. 'I'd guess there's about ten thousand here and the invoices must be on the stick.'

Solomon plugged the memory stick into the computer and opened up a file. He frowned. 'They're gibberish. Damn, they must be encrypted.' He smacked the arms of his chair. 'If this is the Major's smoking gun, the smoke isn't particularly thick.'

'Let me look,' said Hunter. 'I took a module or two in modern and ancient cryptology as part of my degree. It's a fascinating subject.' Hunter turned the screen to face him and stared at the series of letters and numbers covering the open window. He grabbed a pen and started noting down possible patterns.

'Do you have any dealings with these invoices?' asked Solomon.

Serena nodded matter-of-factly. 'Of course; I'm the one who pays them.'

Hunter turned to look at her. 'Then why am I doing this if you already know what they say? Who are the payees, and why in God's name didn't you say anything?'

She shrugged and made a face. 'There's nothing to say. I could give you a few figures, but not much more. They channel all the monies from our account to a bank in Indian Springs.'

'Indian Springs?' said Solomon.

'Some redneck town in Nevada.'

Hunter tutted as Solomon shoved him aside and tapped the name into Google. He grunted in triumph. 'What a coincidence. It just happens to be the closest town to the Nevada test site.'

'Area 51?' said Serena.

'Area 51,' said Solomon.

'Got it,' said Hunter, punching his fist into his closed hand.

'You know what they say?' said Serena.

'Not exactly, but I recognize the encryption.' Hunter raised his notebook and tapped the page with his pen. 'The Colonel is still using DES.'

'DES?' asked Solomon.

'Data Encryption Standard. It used to be the principal symmetric-key algorithm for the encryption of electronic data. The NSA developed it in the seventies.'

'What do you mean by used to be?' asked Serena.

'It was deemed unfit for purpose during the nineties and replaced. Don't get me wrong, it is still a very secure encryption device.'

'Get to the point. Is it breakable or not?' said Solomon.

'Definitely,' said Hunter, 'but it won't be quick. I remember my lecturer telling us about a public attempt to decipher a DES key back in the late nineties. It succeeded, but took about twenty-four hours.'

'Biggles,' said Solomon. He tapped a number into his mobile and lifted the handset to his ear. 'Hi, yes it's me again. I've inserted a memory stick into the machine. Can you upload it? Yes... Yes... It's full of encrypted files.' He glanced at Hunter. 'My colleague tells me it's been encrypted using DES... Good, you know it. Tell me when you're done.'

The screen sprang back into life; the pointer darting about the screen as Biggles prepared to upload the files.

'Biggles really is a genius,' said Serena. 'I never really gave him the time of day at UF. I think the only time I spoke to him was at the party we hooked u...' She exchanged a look with Solomon. Hunter noticed him duck away from her gaze and squirm in his seat.

Hunter looked at them both. 'Hooked up? We never hooked up, did we? Did we?'

Serena looked at the floor.

'You sure did,' said Solomon. 'It was your leaving do. You were so drunk. I'm not surprised you don't remember.'

'Did we really?' Hunter touched Serena's arm. 'Please don't be embarrassed. I should apologize.'

'It's not that... we er...' The click and buzz of the lock on the office door left the end of the sentence hanging in her mouth. Hunter reacted first and crumpled to the floor, crawling into the alcove beneath the Colonel's desk. Neither Serena nor Solomon's reactions were as quick.

'Serena, is that you?' croaked an elderly baritone. Hunter picked nervously at the skin on his lip as a pair of brown brogues strode through the door. They stopped as their owner spotted more than just his secretary in the space. 'Solomon? Solomon Garnett? Is that really you? My god man, what the hell are you doing here, my friend?'

'It's been a while, Oleg.'

Hunter's heart skipped several beats as the penny dropped. The man laughed. 'Oleg, now that's a name I've not heard in some time.'

'You'll always be Oleg to me,' said Solomon.

'Come now, Professor, you know Oleg died a long time ago. I'm the all-American war hero, Colonel James Patterson, now.'

'I'm surprised you sold out for so little, Colonel James?' said Solomon. Something hit the carpet near Hunter's head. It was Serena's swipe card. She was offering him a way out.

'Sold out, Solomon?' said Oleg. 'Whatever do you mean? I've been nothing but an asset to your cause. I'm a believer, remember? I even gave Serena a job in the wake of your... how shall I put this? Crisis of conscience over the babies.'

'What's he talking about?' hissed Serena.

'Enough, Oleg,' interrupted Solomon.

'You didn't?' said Serena.

'Oh Solomon,' said Oleg. 'You really never told her? I'm sorry, did I just let the cat out of the bag? You should thank him, Serena. Solomon's endorsement is the only reason I agreed to take you on.'

'I said enough, Oleg. We've found your invoices and we know what EG&G are funding?' Hunter noticed Solomon stiffen, his words wooden and almost sounding scripted. Perhaps this was a speech he'd practiced giving for years. 'You're finished and this operation will crash and burn in your wake.'

'Thank you for the heads up.' Oleg's brogues took a step backwards. 'Which I guess means you have both signed your death warrants.'

'James, no! You can't shoot us,' said Serena.

The Russian snorted. 'I won't shoot, Miss Harmony. Not unless you give me a reason. No, I'm afraid the pair of you will be taking a little trip.' Hunter heard a door crash against its hinges and two pairs of black, military-issue boots joined the brogues.

'Phil?' said Serena. Hunter winced, gripping her swipe card and knowing his opportunity to use it had just died.

'Serena... I'm so sorry to do this, but you have to come with me,' said the guard from the gate. 'Hey... where's the third one?'

Chapter 21

Chris pocketed his mobile and pulled open the door of the diner. Julio was ensconced in a booth at the far end, waving to get his attention. He slid into the seat opposite and downed the espresso waiting for him, banging the empty cup on the table in frustration. 'The old lady was right.'

Julio's eyes narrowed. 'About what?'

'Solomon Garnett has just been picked up.'

Julio cocked his head to one side. 'That's good news, isn't it?'

'They were picked up in Maryland.'

'So? Why does that make a difference?'

'They were picked up inside a URS office.' He continued tapping the base of the cup against the table. 'More precisely, they were picked up from an EG&G office.'

Julio itched his cheek, probably mulling over this latest turn of events. 'Does it really matter? What could they have found out? We store nothing contentious in Maryland, do we?' He stroked the stubble on his chin. 'Unless they broke into one of the research labs…'

'No, nothing quite so obvious. They pulled something from a safe though. A memory stick full of financial files. Classified of course, and seemingly above my paygrade.'

Julio shook his head. 'I really don't understand these bastards. We're at ground zero and after god knows how many years of service, we still can't be trusted?'

Chris nodded and expelled the air from his lungs. 'You know the rules.'

'The rules suck ass, and you know it as well as I do.' Julio took a slug of black coffee. 'Have they have recalled us?'

'Yup,' said Chris. 'Although we're not returning to Miami.'

'Oh, so where?'

'It appears David Collins came through for me. We have ten minutes before a chopper picks us up.'

Julio rose to look through the diner's front window. 'Are you serious? They're really sending a chopper for us?'

Chris nodded. 'Julio, my old friend, after twenty years on the sidelines, we've been asked to make one last trip to Groom Lake.'

'They want us to report to Area 51?'

'On the basis Solomon knows me... or rather I know him.'

'You know him? Why didn't you say?'

'I didn't realize it was the same guy, but we both know him. Do you remember the two men who landed that Russian saucer at the base in the eighties?'

Chris sat forward in his seat. 'Solomon is the American one! You are shitting me. He stole that thing from Kapustin Yar, didn't he?' He slapped the table's surface. 'Damn, so he's the one we've been chasing?'

'It suddenly makes sense why the top brass is running scared.'

'I'm guessing his head contains a few things they don't want leaked. But why now? He's had twenty years to blab. I wonder what changed?'

'I've just been told, apparently we are now in the need to know bracket, which is nice,' said Chris. 'Company intel turned up evidence of third-party manipulation.'

'So he's being played,' said Julio. 'Who is it? Russia? China? Europe?'

'Still unconfirmed. Exposing the threat is one of our objectives.' Chris rubbed his eyes. Perhaps he was getting too old for this. There were several skeletons hidden in the Nevada desert with his name etched into them. He'd have to be very careful not to breathe any life into a period of his life where shame and guilt took precedence. 'Come on, Julio, we've got to get moving. This chopper won't hang around forever.'

***

Hunter scowled as a firm hand shoved him forward. He stumbled, collapsing forward onto the lowest of a trio of steps leading into a URS branded Lear Jet. The same hand-pulled him upright and hauled him inside the cabin. He slumped into a chair opposite Solomon and Serena. The soldier guarding him unlocked his left handcuff and reattached it to the arm of a chair before forcing him to sit. He noticed Solomon and Serena seated across from him and nodded an acknowledgment. He forced a grin. It was the first time he'd seen his companions since their capture in the Russian's office.

'You both okay?'

'Not bad, but I admit I've had better days,' said Solomon, patting his cheek with his free hand. 'Took a bit of a whack to the head, but I'll live.'

Hunter exchanged a look with Serena. 'I'm fine,' she said. 'Phil drove the van I was in, and as usual, he was the perfect gentleman. Didn't make me feel any better about deceiving him though.'

'Good.' Hunter glanced through the small window to his right. 'Any idea where they're taking us? No one would say a word to me.'

'I'm guessing the Nevada Test Site,' said Solomon. 'If EG&G are planning to interrogate us outside the law, where else better than America's favorite blind spot?'

'I think you're right,' said Serena. 'Phil advised me to co-operate. Said if we don't, this could be a one-way trip to the bottom of Groom Lake.'

Solomon frowned, 'But Groom Lake is desert.'

'I guess that's the point, Sol,' said Hunter.

'Oh.'

'Jumping on the bandwagon of minor revelations...' Hunter looked at Serena, unsure of how to phrase his question. She squirmed in her seat. 'Oleg mentioned babies, and it's been playing on my mind. What was he talking about? What cat did he let out of the bag?' The question hung in the air as the pilot requested the aircrew to prepare for take-off and the small jet taxied towards the runway. 'What was he talking about? Have I missed something?'

Serena brushed a couple of tears from her cheeks as the jet engines revved to a crescendo. The pilot released the brakes and the plane accelerated hard down the tarmac. Hunter gripped his armrests as the jet left the ground and eased into the clear blue sky, its nose pointed toward Nevada. Solomon shifted in his seat and gazed stoically at the cabin floor.

'Why is Serena so upset, Solomon? Come on, you're obviously involved. What's going on?'

The Professor took in a slow, deep breath and looked at the panel above Hunter's head, still avoiding eye contact. 'Miss Harmony lost twin babies when she was younger. Oleg was using the knowledge to get a rise out of her.'

Serena slapped the arm of her chair. 'Are you still going to lie about this? You know I didn't lose them. Just tell him the truth.'

Solomon cracked his neck using his free hand, and at last, met Hunter's gaze. 'Your one-night stand with Serena bore fruit. Are you happy now?' Hunter felt numb, his senses overwhelmed by an all-encompassing shock. 'Serena didn't want to keep them. You were back in England with your whole life ahead of you. I convinced her to continue to term and put the children up for adoption.'

This couldn't be happening. Things like this just didn't happen to people like him. 'You did what?'

'He sent our babies to a children's home,' said Serena.

Solomon shot her an angry glance. 'More specifically, I asked Oleg to fast track the procedure and get the kids into a good home.'

'What? Where?' Hunter shook his head, rubbing his forehead with his free hand. Was this really happening? 'Wait, sorry, this is a lot to take in.' He banged his fist against his chair and gritted his teeth. 'Why didn't you tell me? You're meant to be a friend.'

'I am, John. I had your best interests at heart; both of your best interests. You didn't deserve to be tied down to babies born of a one-night fling. Your career was just taking off. John, you were... no, you still are like a son to me. I couldn't see your life ruined before it even began.'

'Jesus, Solomon. Did it not occur to you I might want to be involved? You are talking about my children here. How they were conceived is irrelevant; they were, and I assume still are, a part of me.'

Solomon wiped moisture from his eyes. 'I'm so sorry, John. I swear I didn't know.'

'How do we fix this? Serena.' He reached out and grabbed for her hand. 'I'm so sorry you went through this on your own. If I'd only known...'

A guard broke their grip. 'As amusing as this is, please keep to your seats. No touching.'

Serena raised her head and scowled at the guard, clearly fighting back tears.

'Ignore him. Were they boys, girls or both?' asked Hunter.

'Identical...' Serena's head dropped again. 'They were twin boys, John, identical twin boys.'

Hunter shook his head in disbelief. 'My god - so where are they now, Sol? Where did Oleg place them? And for that matter, why the hell did you trust a Russian turncoat with the welfare of my children?'

Solomon sniffed and brushed a tear from his cheek. 'I swear, John, I didn't know. If I'd known I'd never...'

'What didn't you know, Sol?' Hunter pulled against his restraints. 'Solomon, pull yourself together and spit it out. What didn't you know?'

'He got Serena her job. He said he'd take care of everything. John, he's a monster.'

'He said you got me my job?' interrupted Serena, her voice spiked with emotion. 'What exactly did you do to get me my job?'

'He said he'd look after you during the pregnancy; get you the best doctors, the best care available.'

'And did he?' asked Hunter, turning to Serena.

She nodded. 'Yes, I was forever going in for check-ups and various vitamin shots.'

'Okay, Solomon, I'll ask you once more and I want the truth,' said Hunter. 'What exactly do you know?'

'I knew it was too good to be true.' The Professor sniffed and wiped his nose on his sleeve. 'I'm afraid I made a deal with the devil himself.'

'Where are my children, Solomon?' said Hunter, his heart thumping.

Solomon clawed for Hunter's arm, unable to contain his emotions. 'I don't know, John. There're assumed dead. I think they killed them. I think EG&G killed them.'

Hunter pulled his hand away, a cool feeling of numb detachment washing over his body. He didn't know how to react. It didn't feel real. He'd been a father for two minutes; now he was a grieving father. Shouldn't he be screaming, shouting and tearing at his hair? Maybe, but he didn't have the energy. He just felt drained, traumatized and empty. He grabbed Solomon's hair, pulling the Professor's head from his chest and forcing him to stare directly into his eyes. 'Why am I here? Did you concoct this plan to appease your guilt? Is this some kind of attempt to avenge them?'

Solomon nodded. 'I didn't know how to tell you. I couldn't... there are rumors...'

A blood-curdling scream exploded to Hunter's right, and he watched in stunned horror as the Professor was attacked by a flurry of kicks and punches. 'You killed my sons, you sonofabitch.'

The EG&G guards rushed to Solomon's aid, unlocking his cuffs and pulling him clear of Serena's clawing hands. She lunged at one of the guards, grabbing the gun strapped to his belt, and pulled it free. The other guard dropped Solomon and unsheathed his own weapon, squeezing the trigger without hesitation. Serena turned to look at John, her eyes wide and full of fear. Her head lolled, and she flopped lifelessly back into her seat.

'What have you done?' shouted Hunter.

'Not to worry, Doc, she'll be out for a couple of hours. It's only a tranquilizer.' The guard grinned and plucked the gun from Serena's twitching hand. 'She's lucky we're in the sky. On the ground, that would have been a nine-millimeter bullet. Shame really, I was enjoying the show. All it needed was Jerry Springer.' The guard dragged Solomon to his feet and guided him back to his seat. 'You'll be alright now sir, although I'd suggest avoiding your colleague for a while when she wakes.'

'Thanks,' said Solomon. 'But I probably deserved it.'

'Probably,' said Hunter. 'You're lucky she didn't dig your eyes out.'

'You want a band-aid for the scratches?' asked the guard.

'Thanks, but I'll be fine. A drink would be good though?'

'Make that two,' said Hunter. The guard moved away. 'I hope you realize the only reason you're still conscious is because what we're doing is right. Even if your reason is a little fucked up.' Solomon nodded and sniffed. 'If there's even a slight chance we can shut down this operation and expose EG&G for the child abusers they are, we have to take it.'

Solomon raised his head, looking toward the guards in defiance. 'If we don't, I promise you, I will die trying.'

'Now we're on the same page, can you tell me what the Major told you? Or was it simply news of the death of the twins?'

Solomon wiped blood from his scratched cheek and smeared it across his fingertips. 'No, he told me Oleg held the key.'

'The key to what?' Hunter took an exasperated breath. 'Stop talking in riddles. You must be able to give me a little more than that.'

'Have you not questioned why, or rather how a Russian defector managed to occupy a post of such sensitivity?'

'What position, Solomon? I don't even know what Oleg does?'

'He is the architect of death.' Solomon clasped his hands together and placed them behind his head. 'He is the man who holds the purse strings of Armageddon. He is the architect and administrator of multiple black research projects which no government in the world would ever admit to commissioning.' Solomon gazed into Hunter's eyes. 'The facility where your children were held is not on US soil.'

Hunter could feel himself welling up again. 'It's not even on US soil! So how can we prove a link? Surely it will just be denied?'

'The memory stick is our smoking gun, John. You have to trust me. If anyone can decode it, Biggles can. And when he does, I would stake my life on him finding a list of payees, including several American children's homes and orphanages.' Hunter rubbed his eyes. He couldn't bring himself to ask the obvious question and confirm what he'd already guessed. 'I'm sorry, John. He was buying lab rats. American-born lab rats to experiment upon.' The Professor grabbed Hunter's hand. 'There are so many layers to this and they still believe I'm part of their plan. We must use that to our advantage.'

Chapter 22

Chris towered over the desk and glared down at the man in front of him.

Area 51's Base Commander, Colonel Hooley, stood and squared up to him. Although his greying buzz cut betrayed his age, the broad, lantern-jawed career soldier was certainly still a force to be reckoned with. 'Do we have a problem here?' he barked. 'You have been ordered to stand down, soldier.'

Chris relented and pushed away from the desk. 'These people know nothing. The old man was bluffing.'

'They know enough,' the Colonel retorted.

'They know a hell of a lot more thanks to your ridiculous decision to bring them here. The files they uploaded were intercepted. It was nothing more than a list of invoices.'

'The files on that memory stick were classified black. We were authorized to bring them in and I expect their IT expert to join them.'

'They are historic invoices.' He shook his head. 'Why you are jeopardizing the base, and worse still, signing off on three home soil executions, is bordering on ridiculous.'

Colonel Hooley returned to his seat. 'You have no idea how much they know?'

'They certainly didn't know what was on that damn memory stick! They wouldn't have uploaded it otherwise. All we needed to do was block it, scare them and hand them over to local law enforcement.'

'Sit back down and calm yourself before I have you escorted off my base, soldier.'

'I am not a soldier anymore,' said Chris, spitting out his words. 'Your predecessor took that title away from me years ago.'

'You're old, Cartwright, it comes to us all.'

'Is that what it says on my file?' Chris shook his head and shrugged. 'They moved me on because of my age? So you only know the highlights then. I wondered why you agreed to have me back.'

'I've been advised you are the most successful interrogator in the base's history. You are here because of your previous experience with one of the prisoners. I need to know if there is more to this group. Aside from their IT support, are there any more of them who might cause us a problem? You're a legend, Major, but don't forget who has the power here. I don't want to regret my decision. Convince me why I shouldn't give them up to the desert.' The Commander paused and stroked his greying beard. 'What's it going to be? You think you can you live up to your reputation?'

Chris sighed. 'I believe you're barking up the wrong tree, but yes, if they are hiding anything, I will probe it out of them.'

'You've got twenty-four hours.'

'Thank you, Colonel. You'll be rewarded in heaven.' Chris turned to leave the room.

'Cartwright?'

'Colonel?'

'If they give you any problems. Just say the word, they won't be missed.' Chris nodded and strode into the wide hallway fronting the Base Commander's office. It was moments like this when he didn't miss his time in the field. He'd long lost the ability to act without remorse, to kill without conscience and torture without flinching. The Colonel was making a few too many assumptions as to how many of his previous traits were still alive and kicking in his veins.

The door clicked shut, and he turned to find Julio patiently waiting on a nearby bench, a Guns & Ammo magazine in his hand. 'Good news?' asked Julio, setting down the publication.

'We've got twenty-four hours,' said Chris. 'But I need a few minutes with you first before we see them. You need to know a few truths. You got time?'

Julio pointed to an empty interrogation booth to their left. 'This is your show, my man. Lead on.'

***

Hunter paced about the small cell. The echo of Solomon's words raced through his mind. He smashed the bottom of his fist against the ironclad door and screamed in frustration.

'You cannot keep me in here. As a foreign national, I have rights. I am British, goddamn you. I demand you phone my embassy. This is unacceptable.'

A strip of metal set into the door clanged as someone yanked it aside. A pair of dark eyes appeared in the opening, twitching in anger as they locked onto him. 'Would you shut the hell up, you limey prick? You'll be processed when we are ready.'

'I have rights.'

'You have no rights down here, my friend. Whatever you've done, I'd settle in for the long term. I don't fancy your chances of leaving.' The strip of metal slammed shut.

Hunter slid to the floor, his head drooping between his knees. 'I don't fancy your chances of leaving,' he mimicked. What the hell was going on? Surely, the guard must be bluffing. The base was still a government facility. He smacked the side of his head. 'Don't be so bloody naïve, Hunter. Of course, this place was beyond the law. Think about what you've been told.'

Something rattled above his head and he felt a sudden pressure on the small of his back. 'Get clear of the door, limey,' barked his guard. 'Seems you have your wish. Time to move.' Hunter yelped as the door slammed into his shoulder, shoving him aside. He felt the soldier's hand under his armpit and a sharp pain as he wrenched him to his feet. 'Come on, you really don't want to keep these boys waiting.'

The soles of Hunter's shoes fought for traction on the polished floor as he received shove after relentless shove. He tried to shrug off the soldier's grip, but the hand clamped tighter around his bicep. 'You trying to get away from me, limey?' Hunter turned to retort but chose silent compliance at the sight of the 9mm Berretta levelled at his chest. 'Good boy. Now you're getting it. Take the next right and stop by the first door you see.'

Hunter complied, his mind alert and eyes searching for an escape route. He'd served for seven years in Her Majesty's Royal Navy and accumulated a decent number of hours operating behind enemy lines, albeit as an archaeologist. The role hadn't proved the easy option though. Several months in a Brazilian prison and an array of torture scars were a testament to that. Hunter felt confident of overpowering his guard, but what good would it do? His knowledge of the Area 51 facility was minimal at best. Hell, a couple of days ago he'd have questioned the existence of the place, let alone believed his life might soon come to an end amongst its secret corridors. He scanned the walls. They were grey and barren, bearing nothing of use, bar the occasional fire extinguisher. A silvery steel tube hung above their heads, humming gently as it pumped fresh, cool air into the underground complex.

'Right here,' said the guard. Hunter rounded the corner and shuffled sideways to avoid colliding with a plain wooden bench. The guard tutted, pushing past him and heading for the metallic door opposite the bench. He held it open and beckoned Hunter to enter. 'Dr John Hunter as requested, sir.' Hunter glanced at the weapon on the guard's belt and instinct took over. He pretended to trip and fell against the guard, propelling him backwards and trapping his legs. The two men clattered to the floor. The guard reacted first, jumping to his feet and waving the barrel of the assault rifle strapped around his neck.

Hunter stayed down and raised his hands above his head. 'Sorry, sorry.' He pointed to his right foot. 'Shoelace. Look. Sorry.'

The guard looked at Hunter's shoe and nodded. He lowered his weapon and glanced at the other man in the room. 'Sorry, sir.' He glanced back at Hunter. 'Just do it up and get to your feet.'

'If you are quite finished cuddling the prisoner, Sergeant,' snapped the interrogator.

Hunter made a show of getting to his feet, using the distraction to shove the guard's Beretta into his trousers, concealing it with his shirt.

'Well?' said the interrogator, eyeballing Hunter's flustered guard. 'Why are you still here? Get out.' There was something familiar about the voice. He recognized it, but where from?

The embarrassed soldier backed through the door, his gaze locked on Hunter. 'I'll be outside if you need me, sir. Be careful with this one.'

The door closed, and the interrogator grinned at him. 'Nice move.' Hunter frowned. 'Put the gun on the table please, Dr. Hunter. My imbecilic associate may have been taken in by your little performance, but I'm a little harder to fool.'

He opened his mouth to speak, but the opportunity was lost as the interrogator whipped a similar Beretta from his belt and pointed it at Hunter's forehead. 'Tic toc, Hunter. The gun tucked into your trousers. Place it on the table.'

'Okay, okay, just keep calm,' said Hunter, raising his hands in supplication.

The door to the chamber burst open and the hapless guard bundled inside, his rifle primed and ready to fire. He froze in his tracks at the scene greeting him. 'He's got my...'

'Gun?' said the interrogator. 'You bloody idiot. You'll be lucky if you're only scrubbing floors after this, Sergeant.' He returned his gaze to Hunter. 'I said put it on the table.'

Hunter obliged; his movements slow and steady. The interrogator didn't worry him, but the guard to his rear was liable to shoot at a sneeze. He eased the weapon free of his belt and handed it over, releasing the magazine as he did so. The interrogator nodded at the vacant chair and Hunter sat.

'My gun?' said the guard.

'Just get out, Sergeant. Don't make it worse for yourself.'

The guard left the room for a second time, head bowed and aware of the impact this incident might have on his fledgling military career.

'What now?' asked Hunter. 'I take it a lawyer is out of the question.'

'Afraid so, Dr John.' The man grinned and passed him a piece of paper, his voice laced with sarcasm. 'I've heard tell you've been a very naughty boy. Breaking into government facilities, stealing state secrets, blowing up buildings...' He paused. 'Have I missed anything?'

Hunter stared at the man in disbelief and looked at the paper again, doing his best to digest the new information and unexpected turn of events.

"Your friends are safe. We're being recorded. Say nothing and play along. Make something up. I'll buy you time to think."

'For the purpose of the tape, the suspect is shaking his head and refusing to comment,' the interrogator continued.

'Suspect?' said Hunter. 'What exactly am I being accused of here?'

'You are a spy, Hunter, and unsurprisingly, we would like to know who you are working for? We want details of your objectives and what you know of the affairs of EG&G. Comply and your one-way ticket to Guantanamo might be ripped up.'

'A spy? You are joking. This is preposterous. Google me, I'm an archaeology lecturer from England, not a spy. I'm only in this bloody country for a funeral.'

'Ah yes, the funeral of the man you were caught assisting. Should I call him Professor Garnett, or perhaps Lazarus is more appropriate?'

'Well, ye...' Hunter stumbled over his words. 'But I didn't know...' The interrogator mouthed the words "keep going, this is good". He shook his head in confusion. What the hell was going on? Where was this guy trying to lead him, and why?

'And you have not always been a college boy, have you?' the man continued.

'I...'

'You received training from the Special Boat Service and served in the British Royal Navy, did you not?'

'Yes, bu...'

'You're a British agent, aren't you, Hunter? You're an undercover agent spying on the United States, aren't you, Hunter.'

'I certainly am not.'

'If you intend to leave this facility in anything more fashionable than a body bag, I need answers, Dr Hunter. I need details of what you are after and the aims of your group. Who is in charge? Where do you report?' He slammed a fist into the table and jabbed a finger at the last sentence on the piece of paper: "Make something up."

Hunter glanced at the sentence and let out a breath, circumstances reminding him of a brief stint as an understudy for Ernest in Oscar Wilde's classic comedy. Cambridge footlights certainly had a lot to answer for. He centered himself and blocked the situation, focusing on performing a role. Heck, he'd seen enough James Bond films. He could pull this off. He returned the interrogator's gaze and grinned.

'You got me. My real name is Ernie and I'm working for the Cookie Monster.'

The corners of the interrogator's mouth lifted. Not much, but enough for Hunter to know he was on the right track. 'So you think you're a funny man, Hunter? I'm so glad.'

'Glad?'

'Yes, Dr Hunter, it means I can do this.' The man bent forward and Hunter heard something click. The interrogator closed his eyes and exhaled noisily. 'Thank Christ for that. Well done.'

Hunter rubbed his temples. 'So who are you and what was that noise? What the hell is going on?'

'You may know me as the Major. It's the name the Professor knows me by.' The Major withdrew a hammer from under the desk and smashed it against the table. Hunter jumped and pushed away from the table, knocking his chair to the floor.

'What the hell?'

'The click you heard,' said the Major. 'It was the power switch for the recording equipment. We use it when we need to exert a little extra pressure on men in your position...' He paused and grimaced. 'And said pressure needs to be... off the record?'

Hunter righted the chair. 'Okay, so you were looking for an excuse to turn off the device?'

'Exactly.'

'Perfect, now tell me what's going on? Solomon told me you were his contact on the inside.'

'You're lucky boys. I no longer work in this facility. My partner and I were drafted in as we were close by and know more than most about the subject matter.'

'Okay, but why take the risk of helping us? You could have walked away and recruited more cannon fodder for your cause.'

The Major averted his gaze and itched the back of his head. 'I guess I'm making my peace with God. I've been forced to stare evil in the face many times during my life and let's just say I didn't like what I saw.'

'Does the death of my twin sons come under that banner?'

The Major rose to his feet and nodded. 'The testing unit is the tip of a very large iceberg.'

'So Solomon was telling the truth? The American government is supporting the abduction of its own citizens for human experimentation?'

'If, by government, you are referring to the set of pompous assholes currently sitting in Washington, then the answer is no.' He cocked his head to one side. 'The real power base in this country comes from a much more sinister place.' He grabbed the hammer and smashed it once more into the surface of the table. 'And I should know, I used to be one of them.'

'You were one of them,' hissed Hunter, getting to his feet. 'You are one of those responsible for what happened to my children.'

'I'm not proud of my past, Dr Hunter, and for what it's worth, I'm sorry.' Hunter balled his fist as the red mist descended and swung at the old soldier. The Major saw it coming and swatted it aside with ease. 'I probably deserve a beating, but I suggest for now you control yourself, Hunter. I may be closer to the grave than many of the soldiers around here, but I'm still agile enough to beat an upstart like you into the ground.'

'We'll see.' Hunter swung again, emotion getting the better of him as he telegraphed another blow. The Major ducked and struck Hunter's forearm hard with the knife-edge of his hand, finishing the move with a lightning-quick strike to the windpipe. Hunter backed away and collided with a wall, holding his neck and spluttering as he struggled to draw breath. He sank to his knees and felt tears roll from his eyes. He was with the murderer of his children and there was nothing he could do. 'Why?' he coughed. 'Why? How could you authorize such a thing?'

'I was young and believed in the cause.' The Major shook his head. 'I don't know what more I can say. The US was on the brink of nuclear war and they gave us carte blanche to do whatever we could to prevent it. Nothing was out of bounds. If we sensed a chance to get one over on the Soviets, we would take it. Ethics were not a luxury we could afford. If we'd set boundaries on how far we could go, you could be goddamn sure our enemies would go beyond them.'

'So you killed kids?' Hunter screamed through his tears.

'We did not kill kids. Our scientists were detailed with trying to maximize their potential as human beings.'

'You were killing babies.'

'We were tasked with creating an army of super-soldiers, an army with greater stamina, strength, intelligence and accuracy. They would be unstoppable. Our spies reported the Soviets were ahead of the curve. I'm sorry, Hunter, but it was a race the Russians forced us to run.'

Hunter wiped the tears from his cheeks. 'I don't know how you can defend this?'

'What if we hadn't, and the Russians succeeded?' He paused and closed his eyes. 'Although there is no excuse why the program is still running now.'

Hunter stared at the Major in a state of stunned shock. He could barely bring himself to ask. 'Are you actually confirming this is still going on?'

The Major hung his head. 'Defending such atrocities without knowing the full facts whilst on the brink of war was easy. Now I'm not so sure.' He held out a hand. 'Help me, Dr Hunter. Help me expose this and we can end this vile program.'

'But you are on the inside,' said Hunter, taking his hand and rising to his feet. 'Why don't you do it? Surely people will believe what you have to say.'

'If only,' said the Major. 'If I tried, I'd be dead within twenty-four hours. I know because I've seen it happen.' He shook his head. 'No, this needs a public figure. Someone the world already knows, someone with a direct link to the atrocities, someone with the credibility of both a military and academic background - someone like...'

'Someone like me,' said Hunter, finishing the sentence. He bit his lip. 'Just how long have you been planning this?'

'Years. I dressed the stage, but I've waited far too long for the right players to surface. Everything just came together when I happened upon Solomon's dirty little secret.' Hunter shook his head, leaning back in his chair and smiling in mock frustration. 'Now, now. Before you apportion blame, I honestly believe he acted with the best intentions. It was just unfortunate he chose Colonel Oleg as his confidant. It was that damn

Russian who really went to town. To be honest, I can't believe both babies survived their birth.'

Hunter looked at the Major in confusion. 'Survived the birth? Why, what did he do?'

'It wasn't the birth as such, but more about experimental drugs pumped into the poor mother. They were designed to enhance the attributes of the babies in the womb, but Christ only knows what they really did to her innards.'

'Enhance the attributes? Are you serious?'

'Keep up, Hunter. They were part of the program. This was a chance to experiment on babies in the womb; equipping them with the tools required to maximize their potential from day one.'

'But it failed.'

It was the Major's turn to look baffled. 'Failed?'

'They both died, didn't they?'

The Major grinned. 'Both died? Why do you keep saying that? I know for a fact at least one survived.'

Chapter 23

Hunter rattled the door to the cell containing his friends and slowly eased it open, hiding his identity for the moment.

'Bloody hell,' said Solomon. 'Are you trying to give an old man a heart attack? What is it you people want now? And where is our friend? We were told he was being brought here.'

Hunter poked his head about the door and smiled, placing a finger to his lips. He entered and grasped Solomon's hand, pulling Serena into his chest with his other arm. 'Whisper. Are you both okay?'

'I've been better,' said Serena. 'Not sure my comments on trip advisor will be all that positive, though.'

'Do any of you need anything?' asked Hunter, glancing at the airman who'd followed him inside.

'Is a machine gun out of the question?' said Solomon. 'Or a helicop...' The color drained from the Professor's face as another man entered the cell.

'I'll take it from here.' The airman nodded at his superior and left the room.

'What are...' said Solomon, the rest of the sentence muffled by Hunter's hand.

The Major placed a small speaker on the desk. He flicked a switch and a recording of his voice penetrated the silence. 'Major Chris Cartwright, retired, location classified, date and time classified. Interrogation of Dr John Hunter, the suspected leader of an as yet undetermined British spy ring.' Solomon's gaze flitted between Hunter and Major Cartwright, his confusion exacerbated upon hearing a recording of a door opening and someone announcing Hunter's arrival on the speaker.

Chris motioned to zip his lips and pointed to the exit. They all dutifully filed into the corridor and waited as the door was locked behind them.

'What's going on, Major?' hissed Solomon. 'This was not part of the plan? How did you get inside?'

'Plan? What plan? Your plan to double-cross me by faking your death? It would appear we're both skiing off-piste now.'

Solomon broke eye contact. 'Sorry, I just didn't know who to trust. Paranoia is a tough mistress to placate.'

'More so when your confidant turns out to be a mercenary spy. You should never have broken contact.' Chris glanced furtively up and down the length of the corridor. 'I have to get you out of here. We still have a slim chance of pulling this off and I've invested too much to fall at the last hurdle.'

'Can I ask why are you doing this? Don't get me wrong, I'm very grateful,' said Serena, backtracking a little. 'I just don't get what's in it for you.'

Chris smiled. 'Just a simple matter of conscience, Miss Harmony. I'm not getting any younger and I need to make amends for a few questionable life decisions... you know, before I meet the big man upstairs.'

'He's on the level,' said Solomon. 'The Major has been working with me for years on this project. I wouldn't have got anywhere near this close without his intelligence reports.'

'So why ditch him?' said Serena.

Solomon slapped Chris on the back. 'Believe me, this is a man with a ton of making up to do before meeting his maker, but I admit my recent opinion may have been ill-advised.'

'I understand the lack of trust. Hell, in your position I'd probably feel the same, but do you mind if we do the inquisition thing later?' said Chris, shrugging the Professor's arm from his shoulders. 'My partner is busy buying us a little time and I'm not sure how long he'll be able to keep the wolves from our door.' He nodded at the ceiling. 'This place is riddled with cameras. My advice is to act natural. We can make it to the interrogation booths without raising suspicion. However, once we pass them and someone notices... we may need this.' He pulled his gun from its holster and waved it at Solomon. 'Lead on, Professor, we're heading for the base archives. This is probably the last time I'll be in this building, and there's a file I'd rather like to get my hands on.'

Hunter nudged Serena as they walked and whispered, 'One of our boys survived.' She exchanged an exasperated glance with Solomon.

'What?' interrupted Solomon. 'One survived? And still lives?' Chris nodded. 'Have you any idea of the purgatory I've been living? That decision has haunted me from the day I made it, and now you tell me one survived. Why didn't you say anything?' Solomon moved to shove Chris in the chest. The former soldier moved deftly to his left, catching Solomon by the wrist and twisting the joint, forcing him to his knees. The Professor yelped and yielded.

'I didn't know myself until recently, you sanctimonious asshole. Why would I tell you anyway? Your guilt is the fuel that brought you here. You know it and I know it. And why would I trust you with such information? You've already double crossed me with your ridiculous fake funeral charade?' Solomon's silence spoke volumes. Chris let him go and stepped out of reach. 'Nothing to say, Professor?'

'Enough, the pair of you,' said Hunter. 'The camera above your heads is buzzing like crazy, so I know someone's enjoying the show. Now make them believe everything is fine. This corridor will be crawling if you don't.'

Chris pulled Solomon to his feet and gave a thumb up to the camera. 'Good call, Hunter.' He pulled a gun and pointed it down the corridor. 'For the record, I am sorry, Sol. I did what I did for the good of the mission; it certainly wasn't out of spite.'

Solomon rubbed his wrist. 'It's fine. I'm still responsible for ruining the lives of both boys. I deserve everything coming my way.'

'Too right you do,' said Serena, kicking out at the Professor. Hunter blocked her path. 'Everyone, calm down. Put this on hold until we're free.' He looked at Chris. 'Can you change the subject and tell us why we are risking our necks for a file? Where is it?'

'Walk and talk,' said Chris, shoving Solomon forwards. 'And to answer your question, Dr Hunter, we need to get inside Hangar Eighteen.'

'Hangar Eighteen?' Solomon whistled. 'It actually exists?'

Chris nodded. 'They still kept the Roswell debris you found in there. Well, alongside a few other choice discoveries the USAF has made over the years.'

'Like what?' asked Solomon.

'Your Russian disk for one.'

'Jesus! Is it still in one piece?' asked Solomon. 'I assumed it would have been ripped apart by now. Haven't you guys tried to reverse engineer it?'

Chris snorted. 'They tried and nothing but an expensive heap of shit came out of that particular science project.'

'But they tried? Did they get any parts of it working?' asked Hunter.

'Sort of.' Chris frowned. 'You ever hear of the Avrocar?'

Hunter thought back for a second. The name was familiar. Then it came to him. 'Ah, of course, that was a disk. I remember seeing it on the History channel.'

'That's right, designated, "Project Silver Bug", you'll have seen one of the few working incarnations. Our engineers helped the Canadians build a flyable saucer inspired by the Russian design.'

Serena looked at Hunter. 'What's he talking about? Flying saucers aren't real, are they?'

Hunter nodded. 'Are you really surprised?'

'But doesn't that blow all the conspiracy theories into touch? Any sightings can surely be explained away as experimental aircraft.'

'You'd think so, wouldn't you?' Chris grinned and flipped his phone to show a picture to Serena. 'This is the picture attached to its Wikipedia entry.'

'It has a Wikipedia page,' said Serena

Solomon nodded and tapped the image. 'It's a pretty basic concept; a silver dinner plate with a massive air intake at its center.'

'Thank you, Solomon,' interrupted Chris. 'There are sound scientific principles behind it though.' He zoomed in on the saucer's center. 'The lift and thrust came from the turbo rotor.' Serena frowned. 'The spinning blades in the middle. The engine generated enough power to blow exhaust out to the rim of the disk, which in turn allowed the machine to rise vertically.'

'The dates don't match up though,' interrupted Hunter. 'I thought the Avocar was canned in sixty-two.'

'Close,' said Chris. 'I believe they originally pulled funding in sixty-one.'

'But Sol didn't drop off the Russian disk until the early nineties.'

'True, and a few months later funding resumed. Surprise, surprise, the move coincided with a tenfold increase in UFO sightings.'

'So it is all bullshit,' said Serena. 'This alien crap is all just a case of our military testing new kit.'

Chris shrugged. 'Ninety-nine percent of it probably is bull.'

Serena tilted her head to one side. 'And the one percent.'

'The one percent...' Chris paused as they rounded a bend in the corridor. 'Cannot be explained in public.'

Solomon and Hunter exchanged surprised glances. Had this guy just admitted to extra-terrestrial contact? Did the one percent include the Professor's Russian disk? Surely that was a terrestrial invention. Admittedly blessed with crazy speed and the ability to leave the Earth's atmosphere, but that didn't mean it originated off planet. The advance of science and technology had been so rapid over the last century, the envelope of what was possible never ceased to amaze him. A century earlier, man couldn't fly, and yet a mere sixty years later, the residents of Earth bore witness to the first moon landing. Anything was possible when the right minds and the right funding came together.

'We're coming up to the interrogation chambers,' said Chris. 'Just act natural and keep your heads. I need to get us buzzed through the barred door at the end of this corridor. Hangar Eighteen is a few hundred feet further on. Whatever I tell the guards, I suggest you just nod and agree. Say as little as possible.'

Hunter exhaled and massaged his eyebrows. His sinusitis was playing up and he could feel a headache building. He grimaced. That was all he needed.

Major Cartwright paused in front of the glass partition separating him from the guard reading local sports news on a tablet. He tapped the bulletproof Perspex with his ID card. The man jumped at the movement and pushed a button to his right.

'Sorry, sir. I didn't see you there.'

'Not a problem, Staff Sergeant. Any chance of popping the lock? I'm in the middle of an investigation and I need these folks to see a file we've got squirrelled away in one of the hangars.'

A small drawer shot out under the window. 'No problem. Place your ID in the slot please, sir. I'll just bring up your security clearance and then you're good to go.' Chris dropped his card where instructed and stood back as it snapped shut. The guard scanned the card. 'Major Chris Cartwright; retired.' Chris nodded. 'You haven't been on base for a while, have you, sir?' He winked. 'I assume the fat cats upstairs called you back for something special?'

Chris grinned. 'A bit of corporate memory. A case I worked on a few years back has reared his head again.'

'Which hangar did you want access to, sir?'

'Eighteen.'

The Master Sergeant screwed up his nose. 'Damn, sorry sir, it looks like they rescinded your clearance.' He raised his eyebrows. 'Wow. You used to have full clearance.' He looked impressed. 'Jesus, we don't have many with that kind of access. You must have met all the Aliens we keep down here.' He was joking, but Hunter could see a glint of hope in his eyes as he looked down at Chris. Not all those working at Area 51 were aware of what their paymasters dabbled in. 'It's the one thing all us guys get asked about back home. Never anything about the cool aircraft, or the weapons testing actually going on.' He snorted. 'No, it's always about how many little green men we've seen.'

Chris leant in towards the speaker. 'Can you keep a secret?' The man nodded. 'The Roswell crash was a Russian-made saucer containing three young boys who were originally part of our human experimentation program. The Russkies kidnapped them and strapped them to a Nuke in an extravagant attempt to expose the program and scare our great nation into declaring war.'

The Master Sergeant gazed into Chris' deadpan face for a moment and erupted into laughter. He tapped the divide. 'You nearly had me there, sir. Super soldiers and Russians. You should be writing the next Bond movie.'

Chris smiled. 'You're too sharp for me, soldier. Can you try to get me a couple of hours' access to eighteen? I'm here at the request of the Base Commander and I'm sure he'll rubber-stamp my request if you ring him.'

'Will do, sir. I'll need his consent anyway. Just give me a minute.' The line went dead, and he turned away to pick up a phone.

Chris turned to Solomon. 'Just got to hope the speech I gave the BC earlier was enough to convince him I know what I'm doing.'

Solomon was still in shock. 'You just gave away official secrets to a low-level drone.'

Chris gave him a sly wink. 'Relax, he didn't believe me. Even if he did, who'd believe him? I should have told him I still meet some of the little green men for Friday night drinks. Although he'd probably have believed that.'

The enormous gate blocking their way buzzed aggressively and swung open. 'You've got an hour, sir,' crackled the Master Sergeant's voice over the intercom. 'The BC was surprised, but just said to monitor your movements. Mind how you go. And watch out for those Russian spies.'

Chris grabbed his ID card from the drawer. 'Thanks, soldier. We'll be quick.' He ushered Solomon and the others through the gate. 'Just as I expected,' he whispered.

'Are you serious?' asked Solomon. 'You expected to be granted access?'

'The current Base Commander has no idea what's in Hangar Eighteen. He's just an over-promoted bureaucrat who the real power brokers haven't put in the loop.'

'Why do you say that?' said Solomon.

'Because if he did know, we'd all be riddled with bullets by now.'

Chapter 24

Hunter gazed through the small window and into the blackness beyond. What secrets lay on the other side of the strengthened glass, entombed within the all-encompassing darkness of Hangar Eighteen? The Roswell saucer? The corpse of Solomon's bogus alien friend? He sighed, turning his back on the unanswerable questions and instead watched Major Cartwright pull yet another file from the array of grey-metal cabinets lining the walls of the hangar's office. Once again, he leafed through the contents and grimaced, dropping the file and moving onto the next.

'Why don't you let us help?' asked Serena. 'This is taking forever.'

'Because I still have an ounce of sanity,' Chris retorted. 'These files are all classified way beyond top secret.'

'What more can there be? We're stood inside Hangar Eighteen for Christ's sake,' said Hunter.

'Dr Hunter, what you think you know is just the tip of a very large iceberg. There are files here even the Commander-in-Chief doesn't have clearance to view.' He slammed another drawer shut and shuffled to the next cabinet. 'And some of them signed off by yours truly.'

'These document the skeletons in the USA's cupboard?' asked Solomon.

'Not all of them, but yup,' said Chris. 'History is written by the winners. Just look at Nazi Germany. If they'd won the war, imagine how many of their atrocities would have been covered up.'

'Surely you can't compare anything the US did to crimes like the Holocaust?' said Serena.

Chris met her gaze for a moment before refocusing on the filing cabinets, his silence spoke volumes.

Hunter's ears pricked as a door slammed. 'Can you just get on with it? We're running short on time.'

Chris grinned and flapped a brown file in Hunter's face. 'This is the little beauty we're after.' He pulled the sheets from their protective plastic casing and placed them side by side on the floor. Every sheet was marked, "Top Secret - unauthorized disclosure will cause exceptionally grave damage to national security."

'Jesus,' said Hunter. 'Tell me again how we've been allowed inside this room?'

Chris pulled out his phone, pointing its camera at each sheet in turn. 'The Base Commander has no clue what is hidden away in here. He was barely out of diapers when most of these documents were signed off.'

'Are you taking pictures?' said Solomon.

'Better. I'm scanning them and sending copies to five separate email accounts instantaneously.' He glanced at Solomon and winked. 'Our cold war spies could only have dreamed of tech like this. Now it's just standard bloatware on a phone.'

'Okay Granddad,' said Hunter. 'Just hurry it up. Whoever slammed that door can't be far away.'

'Oh shit.'

Hunter tensed. 'What? Did you hear something?'

'There is a page missing.'

'Is that all? It's probably still in the fi...' The door handle rattled as someone pushed against the locked door and a key was inserted.

Chris reacted first and swept up the papers at his feet, thrusting them back into the cabinet. He plucked a random file and threw it at Hunter.

'What?' said Hunter.

'Just improvise,' Chris whispered.

Hunter stared at the title emblazoned across the front sheet in disbelief. 'But these are...'

The door crashed open. Three armed soldiers burst inside, the barrels of their M16 A2 rifles flitting between targets as they screamed for everyone to hit the floor. Hunter dropped the file and complied. They were trapped and with no chance of escape.

Chris remained on his feet and, with his hands held high, walked with confidence toward the lead soldier.

'Stand down!' the soldier screamed. 'Face in the dirt. Now.'

'What's the meaning of this?' asked Chris, his voice calm. 'We have the explicit permission of Base Commander Hooley to be in here.' He swiped the barrel of the soldier's weapon away from his face. 'I suggest you lower your weapon, Sergeant, or I'll have you cleaning restroom floors till you retire.' The man faltered and complied. 'Correct choice. Now tell me where your orders came from?'

'Sir, please comply. I have a shoot to kill on your group.'

Chris motioned for Hunter to rise. 'Get to your feet, John. This man needs to hear what you have to say.' The soldier's gun twitched, sweat building in the man's hairline. 'We have every right to be here and if our permission has been rescinded, I insist the BC tell me to my face.' He stared into the Sergeant's eyes. 'Who gave the order?'

All three soldiers looked nervous, probably wrestling with their order to kill one of their own. They stood down in unison and lowered their weapons. 'Sorry, sir, we were informed you were stealing files. Our orders came from the Base Commander.'

Chris rolled his eyes and jabbed a finger toward Solomon and Hunter. 'These two are university professors with Top Secret clearance. They are here helping me in a professional capacity.'

'But they were brought in as prisoners?'

Chris shook his head and sighed theatrically. 'Sergeant, can I rely on you to keep what I say confidential?' The soldier nodded. 'What I am about to tell you must go no further.' Chris turned and plucked the file from Hunter's grasp, grimacing as he read the title. He maintained his composure and handed it to the guard. Hunter was impressed. This was a man clearly used to thinking on his feet.

The Sergeant looked confused. 'These are...'

Chris nodded. 'Invasion plans for Canada, I know. I drew them up myself at the height of the cold war.' He pointed to a signature on the front sheet. 'That's me.'

'Canada? Really.' The Sergeant showed the cover of the file to the other soldiers. 'What the hell did we want with all that snow and ice?'

'It's not the snow and ice; it was about what the snow and ice were bordering.'

'The USA?'

'Yes, but more specifically, Alaska.'

The soldiers looked confused. 'Alaska?'

'And Alaska borders?'

'Russia,' said Hunter.

'So what?' said the Sergeant. 'What's that got to do with invading Canada?'

'Don't depress me, Sergeant.' Chris narrowed his eyes, a shake of the head showing his disdain. 'Have you any idea how many times Soviet special forces have been repelled in Alaska?' The soldier shrugged. 'They were ten a cent during the fifties and sixties. And if successful, Alaska would have fallen and marked a precursor to a full-scale invasion of the United States.'

'And so you proposed conquering Canada? I still don't get it.'

'We couldn't allow the Russians to get a foothold in North America. Canada was there for the taking and our government knew it. The Canadian military would have been no match for the Soviets.'

Solomon snorted. 'Yeah, that and you guys had a stash of nuclear weapons hidden under the ice in Greenland.'

Chris turned his head in surprise. 'How did you...'

The Professor grinned. 'We declassified the base last year.'

'If true,' interrupted the Sergeant, 'then why was the plan canned?'

'The world changed,' said Chris. 'I wasn't aware they'd declassified the Greenland project, but the plans were shelved when the nukes moved south in sixty-six. Our scientists deemed the ice too unstable an environment to store weapons.'

'And Canada lost its tactical advantage,' said Solomon.

Chris nodded. 'There was still the Thule airbase, but you're right, it turned government thinking on its head. I amended the paperwork to prepare for a counterstrike in the event of Canada's occupation. In fact, the folder in your hands details the planned assault of Toronto should the city fall under foreign control.'

The soldier pursed his lips and flicked through the pages. He suddenly looked up. 'Wait, are you telling me this threat has re-emerged?'

Chris shrugged, stoic in his mannerisms. 'I can neither confirm nor deny the possibility. However, in the wake of the recent Ukraine crisis...' He nodded at Hunter and Solomon. 'These men have received intelligence confirming a Russian-backed plan to take Alaska. As the closest Canadian city to New York and DC, Toronto is the next target on their list.'

Hunter dipped his head, desperately trying not to laugh. If they managed to break out of this base, Chris really should be up for an Oscar after this performance. The only worrying aspect was the plausibility of his rhetoric. How much of this was the truth?

'And the Base Commander is unaware of this plan?' asked the Sergeant.

'Colonel Hooley is unaware of his own ass,' Chris spat back. 'And you must repeat this to no one.'

The men saluted in unison. 'Sir, yes, sir.'

'Excellent. Now could you do me another favor, please? My companions and I were about to enter the hangar just as the three of you turned up. Is there any chance you can give me a hand flipping the lights?'

Hunter felt his stomach tumble towards his feet. Were they about to see the inside of Area 51's fabled Hangar Eighteen?

'Now you know more of our mission, can we please proceed, Sergeant? And I'd advise you to delay your report to the BC. I'm a little concerned your orders may have come via the Russian President himself.' Hunter couldn't resist a sly smirk. This man was a genius. What better way to manipulate an American than to accuse them of aiding a communist?

Chapter 25

Colonel Hooley replaced the handset and glanced at his pale reflection in the glass of his office door. He rose unsteadily and opened his drinks cabinet, pouring himself a shot of Kentucky Bourbon. He drained the glass and poured another. He'd personally banned drinking on the base before 1700 hours, but these were exceptional circumstances. A direct order from a four-star General, to kill three civilians and two ex-servicemen, was not something one came across on a daily basis; even on a secure base such as this.

He dropped back into his chair and puffed out his cheeks, expelling all air from his lungs. The three airmen should have reached the Major by now. He cracked his neck, attempting to free the tension and let out a deep sigh. Should he have ordered more men to assist? No, these were civilians and retired soldiers. As much as he respected Major Cartwright, three was enough. He stared at his phone receiver; daring it to ring whilst wishing it never would.

He stretched and drained his drink, banging the glass angrily atop the green faux leather panel stretched across his desk. Could the General really have been serious in his threat of demotion? He'd only been in post for a few months and his record was spotless. Perhaps he shouldn't have allowed Cartwright access to that blasted hangar; but how was he to know someone had kicked the man out of the Air Force for attempting to steal sensitive documents? Why wasn't it on his official record? Hell, if his superiors actually bothered keeping him in the loop and he'd known what the hangar housed in the first place, then this apparent crisis would have been derailed before it even started.

The phone buzzed. He fumbled for the receiver, dropping it and knocking his empty shot glass to the floor. He placed it to his ear and closed his eyes as the message was relayed, any remaining color in his cheeks disappearing into a paler shade of grey.

'I've lost contact with the team, sir.'

'Lost contact? What the hell does that mean? Are they dead? Did you hear any shots?' The soldier on the other end paused. 'No, but...'

'But what? Send in the secondary team. Use your initiative, you bloody imbecile.'

'I did, sir. They reported back before I alerted you. They locked the hangar down and the lights are on.'

'Jesus Christ, the incompetence on this base is unfathomable.' Hooley leant back and took a breath, using the moment to assess the situation. 'Okay, I'm on my way. Sit tight and make sure all exits are covered. I'll mobilize the Special Tactics unit.'

***

Hunter endeavored to maintain his cool but failed dismally. His brain could barely comprehend what his eyes were showing him. The sheer size of the hangar itself was something to behold, let alone the contents.

Chris beamed with pride. 'Impressive isn't she? I'm told we could house four replicas of the White House in here if we wanted. And there'd still be room for the Lincoln Memorial.'

Hunter stumbled forward, his gaze darting in all directions. There was almost too much for him to process. Row upon row of military vehicles, from tanks to aircraft, motorbikes to boats; it was a veritable museum of engine powered warfare. He stroked the massive wing of a very recognizable aircraft and glanced back at Solomon. 'Sol, look, it's the...'

Solomon joined him at his side. 'Wow, the original Dragon Lady. The Lockheed U-2, the grandfather of the modern spy plane.' He grinned. 'I remember being shown this the first time I was allowed in here. This is the actual U-2 flown by Gary Powers, the pilot shot down by the Soviets. We lost a hell of a lot of lives retrieving this old bird.'

'Gary Powers? Are you serious?'

'Yup. The official record labelled it a politically sensitive incident for the US. In reality, the crash brought Uncle Sam closer to nuclear war than the Cuban Missile Crisis ever did.'

'And all because of a few photographs,' interrupted Chris. 'Just a shame we took them from a machine our government claimed was a stray weather plane. Not that they could have known it crashed almost fully intact.'

'So how did they get away with it?' asked Hunter.

Chris guffawed. 'The official line, or the truth?'

'I know the official line,' said Hunter. 'You guys gave up a KGB Colonel in a swap deal, didn't you?'

'Yup, but behind the scenes, President Kennedy gave the Soviets access to a stack of non-military research. This was on the proviso Gorbachev would enter into peace negotiations. The deal went through in the February of sixty-two. Eight months later Gorbachev broke his word and the Cuban Missile Crisis began.'

'Fascinating,' said Hunter. He tapped the tip of one of the U-2's elongated wings. 'So with different leadership, this very plane could have caused the world to end as we know it.'

Chris sniffed and smiled. 'Yup. The photos Powers took that day are still in the office somewhere. Ironically, they were all pretty much crap.' He turned and pointed to the other side of the hangar. 'Look behind the Panzer tanks. Can you see the edge of a corrugated iron shed?' Hunter nodded. 'That's where they house, or rather, used to house the flying disk Solomon pinched from the reds. I suggest you make your way over there. I'll join you in a couple of minutes.'

Serena glanced at Chris and raised an eyebrow. 'You got somewhere more important to be?'

'Something like that. Just humor me, I've got to keep a promise I made a hell of a long time ago.'

***

Major Cartwright watched Serena and the two academics disappear into the maze of equipment. He turned to find the three soldiers sent to kill them, still standing on the platform fronting the office. 'Sergeant, I need access to the lab. Is that something you can help me with?'

'In normal circumstances, no, but we've been given "access all areas" passes for this mission. Our orders were to kill on sight, sir.' He paused and glanced at Hunter. 'Aside from him. They wanted him alive.'

Chris shook his head. "Kill on sight!" What was going on? The situation was more serious than he'd feared? Hooley must be receiving serious pressure from above, and why keep Hunter alive? He grinned at the Sergeant. 'I guess I should count myself lucky you didn't fall for this Russian plot then.'

'Yes, sir,'

'I like you, Sergeant.'

'Thank you, sir.'

'It pains me to do this. But long term, it's for your own good.'

The man looked confused. 'Sir?' A pair of almost inaudible pops preceded a fizzing sound. The Sergeant's two companions crumpled to the floor. He turned to the noise and pulled a handgun from its holster on his belt, but too late. Chris fired a tranquilizer dart directly into the man's throat, injecting a non-lethal dose of Azaperone into his bloodstream. He grasped the Sergeant's gun hand and twisted it into a straight-arm lock, forcing submission. The gun slipped from the soldier's grasp and clattered against the steel platform.

'No hard feelings,' Chris whispered. The Sergeant's eyes widened, shock and anger etched on his face as his body fell limply to the ground.

'You're taking your time,' shouted a familiar voice. 'Or have I misjudged the situation and you're wanting a little snuggle time?'

Chris looked up and grinned as the distinctive silhouette of Julio appeared atop the roof of the records office. 'As politically correct as ever, my friend. Another anecdote for your HR tribunal.'

'There're mounting up.' Julio dropped beside him with a grunt. 'Christ, I'm glad my field days are behind me. My knees are properly screwed.'

'Use it to your advantage,' said Chris. 'We're harmless old men to these youngsters.'

'Speak for yourself. I'm still in my prime.' Julio stepped forward and winced, grabbing at his right knee. 'Well, most of me.' He nodded at the three bodies lying at his feet. 'What are we doing with them?'

'I'll wrap them. Now I suggest you get out of here and raise the alarm.'

'You want me to leave?'

'I don't want to drag you into this, Julio. You're a good man, but these are my demons, not yours.' He pulled his friend toward him. 'Find the BC and exaggerate. Tell them I'm mad, bad and dangerous; armed to the teeth; I don't know; Rambo on speed, but with better hair. Whatever you say, they'll believe it.'

'What did you do, Chris? I know you have a past and probably shouldn't ask, but...'

The question hung in the air, unanswered. Chris massaged his cheeks and gazed out into the vast hangar. 'Suffice to say, I was a nasty piece of work, Julio. I've rubber-stamped a whole heap of shit in the name of national security.' He shook his head. 'Some of which I can't ignore any longer.'

Julio shrugged. 'You were doing the job they paid you for.'

'A lot of war criminals were paid.' He gently pushed at Julio's shoulder. 'Now go and do what you have to do. My window of opportunity is getting smaller by the minute.'

'Fine... but this doesn't mean I like it.'

Chris grinned. 'Do you think Jesus and Judas had a similar conversation before the Last Supper?'

'Maybe, Major Cartwright, maybe they did.' The big man playfully shoved him back and turned to leave. 'But I ain't goner be kissing you in no romantic garden setting.'

'Thanks, man. Hey,' Julio turned his head. 'Try and buy me twenty minutes and make sure they don't come for us through the main hangar doors. Tell them they're rigged to blow.' Julio raised a hand in acknowledgment and scaled the office wall, disappearing inside the air vent he'd appeared from.

Chris bent and cuffed the unconscious soldiers, retrieving the Sergeant's ID card and his rifle as he did so. He flipped the card between his fingers and gazed up at the darkened laboratory to the rear of the records office. 'I guess it's time to run the home leg.'

He strode purposefully to the entrance, his arrogant gait doing little to repress the series of flashbacks his brain appeared intent on revisiting.

He closed his eyes, making it worse as visions of the monthly meetings they had forced him to endure invaded his conscious. The endless stream of faceless scientists terrifying him now as much as they ever had, each justifying their funding with graphic presentations of experimental procedures even Genghis Khan would have baulked at authorizing. He shook his head. The creature, if it was still alive, had endured enough. He bit his lip, recognizing his blunder. Creature? Even now, after so many years, his subconscious was still dehumanizing the subject; as if that somehow made what the Air Force was doing less of a crime. No, this was a human male and Yussel Bauman had endured enough.

Chris raised the swipe card and ran it through the reader. There was a whirr of machinery and something within the door clicked. 'Bingo,' he whispered, releasing a breath as the door gave way under his touch. He could feel butterflies in his stomach, a feeling he'd not experienced for literally decades. His heart pounded in his chest, perhaps a little too hard for a man of his age and particularly one with a weakness for the odd doughnut.

Chris slipped through the gap in the door and into the darkened laboratory beyond. He pulled out his dart gun and scanned the bank of desks clustered around the infamous central pedestal. He could make out the straps, still stained with the blood of the writhing subjects they once secured. The equipment may have been upgraded, but the laboratory was just as he remembered. He closed his eyes and let the memory of Yussel's guttural cries and perpetual moans wash over him. Anger swept through him and he felt his nostrils flare as raw emotion replaced rational thought. He holstered the dart gun and flipped the safety on the M16 A2 rifle slung about his neck.

With a roar, decades of repression spewed forth alongside a hail of 5.56mm bullets. They thumped into the pedestal, sparking in an arc of destructive rage as they ricocheted off metal and tore into the wood of the surrounding desks.

Chris ejected the magazine and smashed in a fresh clip, adrenalin urging him on as the therapeutic effect of the carnage overwhelmed his being. He aimed at the LCD screens lining the walls, each explosion of glass doing its best to erase the horrific images of operations and dissections they'd once displayed and burnt into his brain.

The rifle fell silent as the final bullet casing hit the floor. He couldn't bring himself to release the trigger, continuing to fire in vain as he attempted to blast away the pain and guilt of his past. Finally, he pulled the rifle from his neck and hurled it spinning towards the final and largest of the screens. It caught a glancing blow, cracking the frame but doing little damage. He retrieved the rifle and thrashed at the screen in a frenzy. It fell from its perch and landed heavily on the examination table, shedding its innards in a tsunami of plastic and glass. Chris slid to the floor, his breathing heavy. If this was to be the end, he certainly wasn't going down without a fight. 'That was for me,' he whispered. 'Now to keep my promise to Yussel.'

Chapter 26

C hris Cartwright first met Yussel Bauman approximately fifteen years after Solomon retrieved him from the Roswell wreckage. His role overseeing his care came about purely by chance, the position offered during a drinking session where he'd inadvertently bonded with a two-star General. The General was looking for a young officer to head up a special operation and, from his point of view, Cartwright fitted the bill. Without knowing the detail, the soon to be Major Cartwright grabbed the opportunity with both hands.

Chris took a deep breath and pushed open the entrance to Yussel's quarters. Remembering the first time he'd been ushered through this same door, he choked up, emotion getting the better of him.

3rd February 1962

'Who are you? Where is your badge? This facility is classified.' Chris turned to find a pasty-faced lab-coat marching in his direction. 'How did you get in here? Woodward, fetch security.' A second lab coat glanced in his direction and scuttled toward a fire door doubling as the exit. Chris felt a few more pairs of eyes locking onto him, the remaining scientists glancing up from their wooden workstations, intrigued as to the source of the commotion interrupting their work.

'Relax,' said Chris, holding up his hands in mock supplication. 'You got me; first day on the job.' He glanced around the plain room, its only decoration being the various whiteboards coated in equations and complicated chemical formulas. Yellowing ceiling tiles added a touch of color and indicated some of them must smoke while they worked. 'I'm looking for a... Jennings.'

'Asking may have helped,' the scientist snapped. 'It's Dr Jennings though, and I assume therefore you must be Major Cartwright?'

He nodded and flashed his identification. 'That's right, your new boss.'

Jennings snorted and fiddled with his tie. 'I wouldn't get ideas above your station; you're just a cog...'

Chris held a finger to his lips. 'Let me stop you there. I don't want to start our working relationship by shoving my foot so far up your rear you'll polish my boot when brushing your teeth. So I suggest a do-over.' He held out his hand. 'I've been told rank is irrelevant in here, so just call me Chris.'

Jennings grasped his hand and gave it a limp shake. 'Pleased to make your acquaintance, Chris. You still need a badge.'

'Fine. I assume they have briefed you as to my remit. I'm here to oversee the treatment and handling of patient X5 and the X-Man program in general.'

Jennings sniffed and rolled his eyes. 'X-Man isn't a name I approve of, and certainly not one I use.' Chris frowned. It was clear this guy was going to be hard work. 'Your predecessor re-badged the program on the back of a comic book he read.'

Chris smiled. 'I thought I recognized the name. Last year I bunked with a guy obsessed with comic books. He loaned me a few to pass time. This was one of them. "Mutants with Superpowers" if I remember rightly?'

'Spot on, and I'm sorry to say there is a framed first edition to your left.'

Chris glanced at the oddly attired superheroes scattered over the cover and shrugged. 'What does the comic have to do with your work?'

Jennings looked surprised. 'You haven't been briefed?'

'Only the basics. Why, what have I missed?'

Jennings scratched his head and pointed at the room behind him. 'Do you know what's inside that room?'

Chris shrugged. 'Patient X5.'

'You are unaware of patient X5's... capabilities?'

'You're trying my patience, Doctor. If you have something to say, spit it out.'

Jennings waved Chris forward and tentatively opened the door labelled, "Testing Suite – X5." 'Perhaps it would be easier if you just experienced the subject for yourself.'

Chris peered into the darkness. 'Is it safe?'

'Perfectly safe.' He felt a hand on the small of his back, easing him forward.

Dim, purple strip lighting lit the room, the effect adding to the ethereal feel of the space. Various bits of machinery circled the huge Perspex tube dominating the room's center, a strange humming noise emanating from numerous metal cases adorned with flashing lights. This must be the Atlas supercomputer he'd heard so much about. The higher ranks had been singing its praises, but he still had little idea what it was a computer actually did. Chris adjusted his glasses and strained to focus in the semidarkness. Did something just move inside the tube? Yes, there it was again. He stepped closer and jumped as a small, non-descript humanoid bashed into the tubular wall. Without warning, it lurched sideways, turning to look at him whilst thumping and clawing at its Perspex prison.

Chris retreated and stumbled in his haste. He balled his fists, embarrassed as he caught the Doctor smiling in the doorway.

'Not to worry, sir,' said Jennings. 'At least you didn't urinate.' Chris shot him an angry glance. 'What? The last guy I took in here did.'

In different circumstances, Chris may well have taken a swing at the insubordinate scientist, but the relevance of the incident abruptly fizzled to nothing. He stared into the tube, his gaze locked on a deformed head and the two bulbous black eyes glaring at him. He lowered onto his haunches and placed a hand against patient X5's smooth plastic prison. The scrawny creature continued to meet his gaze, unblinking and motionless.

'Fascinating,' whispered Chris. 'How are you keeping him alive? What does it eat?' The question hung in the air, unanswered. He turned, looking for Jennings and realized he was alone with the subject. 'Where has that fu...'

'*No cursing, please.*' The words came out of nowhere. They certainly weren't audible. The request simply planted in his brain.

Chris tilted his head and stared in disbelief at the deformed mute in front of him. He shook his head. 'Christ, I've had a longer day than I thought. I'm hearing things now.'

'I'm not big on blasphemy either.'

Chris lowered himself to X5's eye level, his heart rate rising. 'Do that again? Can you talk, or am I actually going mad?'

'You are communicating with a man without sound or any visual cues. As you're asking, I'd say you were crazy.'

'Son of a bit... sorry, gun. Is this the trick Jennings wanted me to see?'

X5 continued to stare blankly back at him. *'I guess so. I'm pleased they've got me some fresh meat to play with. The rest of them rarely come near me these days.'*

Chris looked at the door to the lab. 'Why? What do you do to them?'

'There are two reasons.'

This was incredible. Not a muscle twitched anywhere on X5's body. Somehow they were engaged in a telepathic conversation — well, from one side at least. Chris shook his head in disbelief, equal measures of excitement and fear bubbling in his veins. 'Which are?'

'Do you have a pen or a coin on you?' Chris reached into his wallet and pulled out a dime. *'Place it in the center of your open palm.'*

He obliged, turning his hand so X5 could see the coin. 'Now what?' He felt a tingling sensation building in his wrist. Without warning, it became too much to take and he retracted his arm, scrambling backwards and colliding with one of the computer terminals. He raised his head and his eyes narrowed in confusion. The dime hovered in mid-air, following the movements of his head, mere centimeters from his nose. It turned on its axis, gaining speed, spinning faster and faster until it was no more than a blur of movement.

'Stop. What are you doing? I order you to...' The coin levelled and shot past his ear, embedding deep into the metal cabinet housing part of the computer. Chris blinked, his gaze flitting between the coin and patient X5.

'Sorry, but I needed to do it,' said the voice in his head.

'What, why? You could have killed me.'

'Exactly. I need you to know I am not a threat. I have spared you from injury twice.'

'Twice?'

'Look up.'

Chris glanced upward and started. Part of the heavy casing hung in the air, hovering inches above his head. He scrambled to his left and the thick piece of metal dropped to the floor with an enormous crash. 'What are you and why wasn't I briefed on this?'

'They do not know the extent of what I can do.' A workbench scraped on the floor and rose into the air as if a bat in a batting cage.

Chris shifted clear of its radius, afraid it might knock his head for a homer. 'Okay, point proven, you can stop now.' The workbench eased to a stop and thumped down onto the concrete. 'Thanks.' He exhaled in relief. 'Wait, you said there were two reasons you didn't get visitors. What's the second?' Without warning, Chris collapsed, falling onto his back and holding his head as an invisible force squeezed his skull to the point of cracking. It lasted a mere second, but the demonstration was enough.

'I learnt to do that a few years ago.' Although in his head, he could sense X5's pride in his ability. *'A bonus for me, but not so much for those men who used to taunt me. The experiments became far less frequent, at least until they installed this tube thing around me.'*

Chris rubbed his temples. 'I can see why. Did you kill anyone?'

'No, they would have shot me. I just gave them a scare.'

He tapped the tube. 'So, what is this for, then? It obviously doesn't block your powers.'

'They use it to gas me; knock me out before strapping me onto that table out there.'

Chris looked past the tube to the small operating table beyond. How he'd missed its presence initially, he wasn't sure, and now he'd seen it, he wished he hadn't; the leather straps and dry smudges of blood didn't fill him with optimism that it was there to provide positive experiences for poor patient X5. The comment hung in the air. Humanizing the patient made the experimentation much harder to justify. He tried to dodge the issue. 'What's the deal here? Where did you come from, and who on Earth did this to you?'

'You don't believe I'm alien?'

Chris shook his head. 'I believe in rational explanations and evidence.'

'How then does your logical mind rationalize my recent demonstration?'

He pursed his lips and gazed into the unblinking black eyes of the trapped man before him. Chris smiled, deciding to ignore the jibe. 'What's your name and where are you from?' There was a long pause, long enough for Chris to think he'd pushed the subject too far. 'Shall we try this again tomorrow? Have I upset you?'

'Yussel.' The name arrived clear and loud in his head. *'My name is Yussel Bauman, just an ordinary American citizen from Brooklyn.'*

Chris' jaw dropped. 'Are you serious? You're American.' He turned as the laboratory door slammed somewhere behind him.

'Need any help, new man?' Jennings grinned. 'I see you've made contact with the patient?'

Chris stood and scowled at the Doctor. 'Not the best way to endear yourself to the new boss, asshole.' He started for the door and paused on the threshold. 'I'll be back once I'm fully in the loop.'

'Help me,' whispered a pitiful version of the voice in his head. *'I just want to go home.'*

Chapter 27

C hris released the door handle, and the return mechanism slammed the door in his wake. Many years had passed since he'd been unceremoniously escorted from the base. Officially charged with aggravated battery of a fellow officer, Chris accepted the Air Force's offer to sweep it under the carpet. They wanted only a guarantee he'd stay silent about his time at the base in return. It was a narrow escape. If they'd uncovered his real aims, he wouldn't have survived the night.

He pushed on, smiling at the familiar purple glow of the strip lighting. Still the same after all these years. It appeared Patient X5 was the forgotten man on campus, reduced to a myth bandied about by new recruits arriving at the base. Strangely, X5 was a myth the Air Force actively encouraged, albeit unofficially. Just as it had in the fifties and sixties, the alien myth still proved an effective means of detracting from the development of the spy plane technology critical to the existence of the base.

He shivered. Yussel always did like a cool room, and the air-conditioning unit certainly seemed to be doing a good job. As his eyes adjusted to the dim light, Chris' gaze fell upon the thin and familiar outline of a childlike body crouched at the base of the huge central tube. The poor bugger must be nearing ninety. What a life.

'*I'm seventy-seven.*'

'Yussel,' said Chris. 'You're still alive then, you wily old bastard?'

'*I don't intend to give them the satisfaction of dying without a fuss.*' The body moved. The ethereal voice in Chris' head increased in volume. '*Plus, Major Cartwright, you made me a promise.*'

'That I did, my friend. That I did.' He walked to the nearest computer and removed a USB memory stick from his pocket. He touched the keyboard and the screen flickered into life, a password request replacing the screensaver. 'So, Yussel, you managed to read any heads recently?'

'You'll like this one,' said Yussel. *'Try jpatterson89.'*

Chris typed in the username. 'And the password?'

'Meatmaster.' He snorted, tapped it in and hit enter. *'A nickname given by his wife.'*

'Nice, whatever floats their boat — and we're in.' Chris slotted the USB stick into the computer and clicked the icon as it synced. 'I'm told this will take no more than sixty seconds.' He grinned. 'I have a feeling the Meat Master will face a few uncomfortable questions next time he logs in.'

'He's an asshole. Takes delight in making me suffer. Cuts my rations if I play up.'

'Hey, I thought you were opposed to cussing?'

'Cussing is too good for this guy.'

Chris shrugged, continuing to tap away at the keyboard. 'In that case, I'll give him an electronic slap on your behalf. A few links to the dark web should do it. Give his mates a few more questions to ask.'

'What are you doing?' He twisted in fright. It was the Sergeant. The dart must have malfunctioned and not discharged a full dose. 'Who are you talking to? Are you communicating with...' A loud buzz interrupted the standoff. Chris glanced at Yussel and saw the tube twist and rise into the ceiling. 'What are you doing?' shouted the Sergeant. 'Major, stand down. We cannot free the alien. You don't know what it's capable of.' The soldier raised a handgun and aimed at Yussel.

'No,' Chris screamed. He launched his body to the left, screening the little man and blocking the path of the shot. Three shots burst from the end of the barrel and everything in his world seemed to slow. He landed with a bump, crashing into a chair and sending it spinning into the middle of the room. He patted himself for bullet holes, but felt nothing — no pain, no blood, no impact. Shit, did the bullets get through? He couldn't have failed Yussel already. He pushed himself upright and froze as his gaze locked on the trio of stationary bullets paused mid-flight. Two of them dropped and clattered against the hard-tiled floor. The third remained suspended in mid-air, its tip slowly rotating until it faced the weapon that had discharged it.

'Don't do it, Yussel,' said Chris. 'Please, you're better than this.' The Sergeant ran for cover, sliding behind a row of desks and emptying the remainder of his clip in Yussel's vague direction. The suspended bullet whistled forward in retaliation and Chris winced as it banked ninety degrees, disappearing from view. He heard a muted cry followed by the thump of a body hitting the ground.

Chris stood and brushed himself down. 'Not part of the plan, Yussel. They'll come after us with everything they've got now.'

'Oh, come on. I just saved your life. A bit of gratitude would be nice.'

'We agreed not to kill. These men are not to blame. They are only following orders. Just like I used to follow orders, remember?'

'The moral compass of a soldier can always be disguised by his orders, Major. Keep in mind I have spent much of my time inside the heads of these men. Suffice to say, some are very happy in their work.'

Chris banged his fist against the rising tube. 'Fine, but from now on, promise me you'll only use your gifts as a last resort. As I said, the more of a threat you pose, the more firepower they'll send our way.'

'Okay, okay, defense only. For now, would you please fetch my chair? The muscles in my legs won't support me for long.'

Chris pulled Yussel's wheelchair from the storage cupboard behind the tube and lifted him into it. He was so frail, much worse than he remembered. 'Just sit tight; we've got friendlies on standby by the ship. Now I just need to get you there in one piece.' He eased the chair through the doorway and scanned the area. The coast was clear. He knew they'd be exposed for at least two minutes, but it was now or never. He huffed, considering the irony. All those years spent planning, and it had come down to a two-minute dash with too many variables to contemplate. He was in the hands of fate, and its grip on him was questionable. Chris pushed the wheelchair, his knuckles white against the black plastic handle grips. 'This is it, Yussel, a one-way ticket to freedom... either that or certain death.'

'Don't be so dramatic. Just point the wheels in the right direction and sprint.'

Chris set his jaw and focused on the destination. 'Done and done.' He shoved the chair forward and focused on maintaining a steady jog, negotiating the ramp leading to the hangar floor with the merest screech of rubber. The chair hit the concrete floor with a thump, its tires buzzing as they rolled over the grooved surface. Chris started, veering sideways as a loud bang resonated about the vast hangar. The Base Commander's cavalry chose to announce its arrival by ramming the door. He dared a backwards glance as a second bang punctured the silence. The reinforced steel was holding, but he knew it wouldn't stand up against stage two - explosives. He stepped up the pace, the buzz of the tires increasing in volume. He swerved to avoid the edge of an old medic's jeep. The wheelchair clipped the bumper and rocked erratically. Chris jammed a boot into the frame, eased it back under his control.

'*Careful,*' said Yussel.

'Sorry, but we've got company.'

'*I know; I'm dumb, not deaf. Still, no reason to throw me out of this glorified shopping trolley.*'

'I've got to get you out of here. Damn...' A plume of flame exploded into the hangar, the main door spinning through the air and slamming into the wall of the records office. Chris dove to the ground, pulling Yussel from the chair and rolling under the chassis of a nearby truck. He rubbed his face in frustration — they were still a good four hundred yards from the saucer.

The southern drawl of a familiar voice rose above the crackle of the dying flames and Chris' stomach dropped into his bowel. 'Cartwright? Major Cartwright, I know you're out there. Look man, please don't be a hero. Give it up before you get yourself and everyone else killed.' The man paused. 'Chris, please, you gotta show yourself. This is your last chance. These boys have been issued with a shoot to kill order.'

Chris snorted and roared back. 'Then why the hell would I show myself, Major Carmichael?' He hit the underside of the truck in frustration. 'We roomed together, Jacob. You know what kind of shit this poor man has been through!'

'It's Colonel now, and he's nothing more than an aggressive alien life-form. That thing is dangerous, and it manipulated you from the start. You know it and I know it.'

'Fuck you, Jacob. We did this to him. Yussel was an ordinary Jewish boy. He was born in New York for Christ's sake, just like you.' Chris could see Jacob pointing in his direction. He was ordering his men to flank their position. They didn't have long.

'Chris, give him up now and I promise it'll be quick.'

Chris nudged Yussel and whispered. 'There's an old motorbike with a sidecar to our right. Can you buy me some time and occupy these bastards for a bit?'

Yussel nodded. '*I'm on it.*'

Chris flexed his fingers and cracked his joints, anticipating action. Including Jacob, he'd counted seven gunmen, but more men were surely on their way. For now, Jacob would command two men to take each flank; the other two would remain, protecting their commanding officer.

'We've identified your position, Major. This is your last chance to come...' Jacob's head twitched violently.

'Are you alright, sir?' asked one of the men flanking Jacob.

'Stand down, soldier.'

'Sir?'

'I said stand down, goddamnit,' screamed Jacob.

'*He knows we're under this truck,*' said Yussel. '*He's got a strong mind. I'm not sure how long I can hold him.*'

'He always carries a small paper-knife in his breast pocket,' said Chris. 'Jab him if you lose control, but don't kill him.' He rolled out from under the truck and, keeping low, made his way to the bike. The vehicles in the hangar always used to carry a minimum amount of fuel so the powers that be could move them about. With any luck, the policy was still in place. He closed in on the bike and gave a discrete fist pump as he recognized the markings. The bike was a Harley-Davidson XA, a model made for the US Army in response to the success of a similar BMW model made for the Germans. It was a nice bike and certainly more than capable of aiding their escape. He reached the sprung, brown leather seat, swung his leg over the olive-green machine and froze. Reflected in the window of a nearby Jeep, he caught sight of a reflection. The barrel of a rifle pressed hard against the soft skin of his neck.

'Call off the creature,' the soldier hissed through clenched teeth. Chris raised his hands. 'Do it now or I swear...'

The pressure against his neck eased and then disappeared altogether as the soldier crashed to the floor. Chris gunned the engine and the rear wheel span before biting into the concrete, snaking as the bike eased forward. He glanced in the mirror and noticed the hilt of a small ornate paper-knife protruding from the dead soldier's temple. He couldn't see the inscription, but knew it by heart, "the truth will set you free". It was presented to Jacob by his parents before he'd left for college, and the words had never felt so appropriate.

Chris twisted the handlebars, obliging the heavy machine to turn in a tight arc until it faced Yussel's hiding place. Two rifle rounds resonated about the hangar, one whistled past his ear and the other shattered the bike's brake light. Chris pressed his body against the metal frame to minimize his profile and smiled. Someone had holstered the bike's shotgun against the front wheel. He pulled it free and twisted in the shooter's direction. The sniper ducked for cover. The shotgun clicked. Chris pumped the action and fired again. Nothing... Of course, the bloody thing wasn't loaded. Why the hell would it be? But even so, it had still bought him a few vital seconds.

'Yussel, can you see him?' Chris shouted, struggling to compete with the roar of the engine.

'*I can hear him. Drop the weapon.*'

'You what?'

'*Don't question me, just drop it.*'

Chris let go, and the shotgun slid from his grasp, hovering in mid-air. It turned and rose until the barrel was level with his forehead. The sniper popped his head above cover, probably wondering why Chris hadn't returned fire. It was to be the last action of a decorated career — the butt of the shotgun smashing into his face and ending his life on impact.

Chris looked away, wincing at the sound of shattering bone. 'Just immobilize them, Yussel. These are American soldiers.'

'*That particular soldier has, sorry "had," a passion for young boys. So, to be honest, screw him, he got off lightly.*'

Chris slid from the saddle and reached for Yussel's hand. 'They're retreating. We need to use this window. Once the reinforcements turn up, they'll start spitting so many bullets even you might not be able to stop them.'

'*I didn't stop them all this time,*' said Yussel.

Chris furrowed his brow. 'What?'

'*My right leg.*' He followed Yussel's extended finger to the seeping wound on the underside of his calf. '*I was focused on your friend. Another sniper must have spotted me through his scope.*'

Chris slipped off his jacket and ripped the sleeve from his shirt, binding it about the wound. 'Don't worry, we'll sort it later. It's only a flesh wound. You'll live.'

'*Maybe, but I have a feeling the hole in my stomach might affect my odds.*' Yussel lifted the hand clamped just above his pubic bone. Blood oozed from a tight, dark hole.

Chris rolled him gently onto his side and examined the injury. 'It's not great, but I can see an exit hole, so it could be worse. Keep your hand pressed hard against the wound. We can worry about it once we're free. Until then, a few things are vying to end you before bleeding out will be an issue.' He lifted Yussel and lay him down inside the sidecar.

'Cartwright,' shouted Jacob. 'One more chance. I've given my men the order to stand down. I know we can't rival the talents of your creature, but we have mobilized two more units. Even if you make it to the ship, you know we'll shoot you down as soon as we have a missile lock. There's no way I'm letting you leave this base. Come on, Chris, you are out of options. Be reasonable and make the right choice.'

Chris revved the bike hard. 'Some things are just worth dying for, Jacob.' The wheels bit and the bike lurched forward. He could see the Russian saucer dead ahead, Solomon urging him on from the base of the ramp. Only a hundred feet. He could hear voices and the thudding of heavy footfalls behind him. Jacob's reinforcements must have arrived, but he dared not look back. He pulled the brake, forcing the bike to slide through ninety degrees and stop inches from Hunter.

'Take him inside.'

Hunter lifted Yussel from the sidecar. 'Jesus, is this...'

'Yes, this is your Roswell alien. Now get him inside. It won't be long before we're targeted again. They don't yet know he's been hit.'

'He's been hit?'

'Twice, but he's stable... ish,' said Chris. 'Keep him warm and put pressure on the bullet holes, back and front.'

'You aren't coming with us?'

'I need to activate the hangar door.' The bike's rear wheel fishtailed as he lined it up with the activation console, three hundred feet beyond the saucer. He glanced at the gathering force behind him. At least he was beyond the range of the average grunt. He ducked as a machinegun rattled, spraying a swathe of fire in his general vicinity, bullets sparking off machinery on either side of him. He flinched as the left-hand wing mirror exploded. The sniper was back. With meters to go, Chris pulled the brake and hopped off the bike, letting it slide out from under him. Dashing to the console, he entered Yussel's stolen passcode. The screen went blank for a couple of horrifying seconds. Chris thought his plan may have failed. The screen turned white, and he smiled, relieved as a shortlist populated the screen.

"Environmental Control;

Lockdown;

Alarm;

Hangar Door Control."

He tapped the touchscreen and selected, "Lockdown". As expected, someone in the main control room had locked the base down. However, this particular hangar was the only one with a local override, an override accessed only via the console in front of him. He reactivated the hangar control and returned to the menu, this time selecting the option giving him full control over the hangar doors.

In the corner of his eye, Chris noticed a solitary muzzle flash and the pop of a high-velocity bullet. His shoulder lurched forward, smashing against the console and spinning him about. He collapsed to the ground, his left arm hanging lifelessly at his side. He could see the saucer in his eye line. At that moment he knew he would not make it back. He closed his eyes and tried to focus, shutting out the pain. 'Time to get going, Yussel. Looks like we have a decent sniper unit in our midst. I'm done. Raise the ramp and get ready to pull some Gs.'

There was a momentary pause before the reply seared into his brain. 'Not an option. I can hold them. Get yourself back to the ship.'

Chris shuddered as a second, third, and fourth bullet ploughed into the wall above his head. 'Negative. Shut up shop and get the hell out of here. They have multiple crosshairs on my position. You might be able to stop a couple, but I'm estimating over ten. Leave now or the entire team will die. The mission comes first. I've done my bit, now do yours.'

Chris could almost feel Yussel running through his options. *'Major Cartwright, it's been an honor... and thank you.'*

He lifted his right arm, making a fist as the saucer's power source flared into life and the ramp rose into the ship's body. 'Good luck my friend.' He tensed and pulled himself in front of the console.

Several shots popped from around the hangar, each finding its mark. Chris collapsed to one knee and fell sideways, spluttering and convulsing as his lungs filled with blood. He fought death for a few moments more; he needed confirmation. His mouth creased into an imperceptible smile as the rumbling sound of the hangar doors opening reverberated in his ears. He closed his eyes and gave in to the darkness. Major Chris Cartwright finally found the peace he craved.

Chapter 28

'What the hell is going on?' shouted Hunter, clinging to the wall of the cramped craft as it rose and wobbled in the air. 'Major Cartwright is still down there. We can't just leave him. They'll lock him up and throw away the key.' He patted his ear. 'Am I going mad? Can anyone else hear that?'

'Hear what?' said Serena.

'This is weird, but I'm hearing a voice in my head. It keeps repeating the same words, "he's dead, he's dead".'

'It's me, you fool; your friendly neighborhood alien.' Hunter jumped and stared down at the tiny figure lying hunched up at his feet. *'You need to put me in the pilot's seat, and be quick about it.'*

'How are you... you're a telepath?'

'Bingo,' said Yussel. *'You tend to hone differing skillsets when your eyes and tongue have been removed. Now put me in the damn seat.'*

'But it could kill you,' said Hunter.

'Is it communicating with you?' asked Solomon.

'I am not an "it", Professor Garnett. My name is Yussel.'

Hunter smiled. 'Did you hear that?'

Solomon took a step backwards and grabbed for something to hold on to as the saucer lurched to one side. 'Shit, so it is a telepath. The rumors were true...' Solomon suddenly doubled over, holding his head and crying out in agony.

'I am not an "it". Or a "thing". I am a... I am a...'

'Okay, that's enough, Yussel,' said Hunter. 'Let him go and I'll put you in the chair.'

'*Shit, you're the guy.*' The words were spaced, the little man shocked by something he'd discovered in Solomon's head.

'What do you mean, I'm the guy?' Solomon dropped to the floor, rubbing his temples as Yussel released him. 'What are you doing in my head?'

'*Reading you. You're the boy from Roswell. You saved my life.*'

Solomon nodded, his face still screwed up in pain. 'I am, and you're making me regret it.'

'*You made all this possible?*' Yussel squirmed as Hunter placed him in the solitary pilot seat in the center of the deck. '*Not that I didn't curse you for years, wishing you'd just let me die.*'

'I thought the same when I found out how you were treated.'

'*I don't want pity,*' said Yussel. '*The Major changed my outlook. He gave me a purpose, a mechanism to avenge my treatment and a reason to stay alive. He promised this day would come. This plan has been in place for decades; all variables are accounted for. All we awaited was the catalyst.*'

'You accounted for the Major's death?' said Hunter.

'*Of course; although regrettable, my own death would have been harder to overcome. However, we should not focus on the sacrifices littering the route; this is about the journey's end; freeing the innocent and flaying the guilty. The truth will out, Dr Hunter, the truth will out.*'

The saucer nudged the hangar wall, interrupting the speech and knocking Hunter from his feet into Serena. It tilted forward and back before finally stabilizing to face the exit.

'Jesus, watch it,' said Serena. 'Whatever this guy is saying, can you do me a favor and ask if he knows how to fly this thing?'

'That's a good point,' said Solomon. 'I delivered this thing to the Americans, but there was a remote-control unit back then.'

Hunter's heart sank as the rumble of the hangar doors ceased. The sound restarted. More soldiers filed into the hangar, the muzzles of their weapons flashing as they took potshots at the disk. At least, if nothing else, the craft was proving bulletproof. Hunter grimaced as something sparked off the hull near his head. They needed to escape and now, it wouldn't be long before something designed to pack more of a punch entered the fray, and he didn't fancy their chances of repelling much more than small arms fire.

'Just make it go,' shouted Serena, 'those bloody doors are closing back up again.'

'You forget I've had access to all their research for the past sixty years.' A silvery strap appeared around Yussel's waist and shoulders. *'That includes the flight manuals.'* Yussel's body jerked. He was evidently still in a lot of pain, a fact his emotionless face could not convey. *'I suggest you three sit against the wall... and brace yourselves.'*

'Shit, they've fired an RPG!' screamed Hunter, pulling Solomon and Serena into his chest and bracing for the inevitable impact.

***

'What do you mean, the lockdown has been overridden? On whose goddam orders?' Jacob screamed into the radio. 'My orders? Soldier, are you fucking insane? Why would I...' He turned, letting out a pained breath, and looked toward the still figure of his former roommate, slumped over a computer console. 'Mother fu... Okay, whatever, just get those damn doors closed again.' Jacob clicked off his radio and turned to address the two men behind him. 'We're out of options. This is now damage limitation. Takedown the saucer.'

'But, sir, the saucer is to be preserved at all costs.'

'Are you disobeying a direct order, soldier? Take it down or we risk losing it forever.'

The two men exchanged a brief look of resignation, and both lowered to one knee, simultaneously hauling a rocket-propelled grenade onto their shoulders. Jacob moved to their rear and searched for cover. Lockheed Martin's Predator SRAW RPGs needed three seconds to track a target before firing, the time required to predict the point of interception by measuring the target's speed and direction. With a slow-moving tank, this delay would prove no problem. However, given the machine currently in their crosshairs was no tank; three seconds could mean the difference between American and Russian airspace.

Jacob shielded his ears as the rockets ignited and watched in satisfaction as they arrowed toward their target. The impact was deafening. Moulton metal rained down on the hangar floor, igniting ageing ordnance and setting off a secondary scene of devastation as bullets ricocheted amongst the spoils of wars long gone.

Jacob rubbed his eyes, trying desperately to rid himself of the explosion of light burnt into his retinas. 'Did we hit it? Can I have a kill confirmation from someone please?' The scene slowly eased back into focus. 'I want a kill confirmation, god-damn-it!'

With a creak, the decimated right-hand door of the hangar fell forward, crushing a row of Huey helicopters and throwing a tsunami of dust in Jacob's direction. The wreckage of the saucer was conspicuous by its absence.

Chapter 29

Hunter coughed, retching as the bone-crushing grip of the multiple G forces imparted on his body finally released him. He collapsed forward and crawled to the pilot seat, using it to pull himself upright. He stared out at the blanket of white, fluffy clouds stretching as far as the eye could see. 'Where the hell are we?' he croaked. 'Or am I dead?'

He felt Solomon's large, sausage fingered hand clamp against his shoulder. 'You're alright, lad. The saucer is designed to reduce the impact of high G maneuvers. Plus, we've only been flying for a few seconds.'

'If we're not dead, then where the hell are we?' asked Serena. She wiped vomit from her mouth. 'Ask the little man. He doesn't seem to want to talk to me.'

'Tell her we're over the Kenyan Savannah and apologize to the lady. I can't do women,' said Yussel. *'I do not know why. Different genetics I guess. Lucky for me, the scientists at the base never worked that out.'*

'Where are we?' Hunter glanced at the frail body seated in front of him. 'And how did you hear what she said?'

'I'm not deaf and apologies. I overshot a touch.' Yussel paused as the disk banked to the left. *'Give me a break though, I may know the theory inside out, but this is my first time flying this thing.'* Hunter watched the small man's chest heave back and forth. *'And no, this blood loss is not helping.'* Yussel's head twitched and drooped. The craft plunged downward.

'Shit, this can't be good. Has he passed out?' Hunter gripped hold of the chair as his feet left the floor. Solomon and Serena both lost their footing and tumbled to the rear, the increasing G force pinning them against the wall. They were in free fall. 'Solomon, Yussel's unconscious. What do I do?'

'Yup, thanks for the update, John. What am I, blind?'

'Not much we can do back here,' said Serena. 'We're stuck.'

Hunter fought against the pressure threatening to overwhelm him and pressed a hand against Yussel's bare chest. 'His heart's not beating.' He glanced back at the Professor. 'Do you still carry an EpiPen?'

'You could kill him.'

'He's dead now, and what's the alternative? Mid-air CPR?'

Hunter watched Solomon's hand creep towards the inside pocket of his jacket. As long as he'd known the ageing academic, Solomon had made sure all those around him knew of his potentially deadly allergy to bee stings. In the event of a sting, the EpiPen would deliver a dose of epinephrine to counteract the poisons. He stressed it must be delivered in the thigh. Elsewhere and it could cause the heart to beat uncontrollably and result in fatality.

The sunlight disappeared as the ship tumbled through the clouds. 'Jesus, Solomon, at this rate of decent, I'd say we've got ten to fifteen seconds, tops. But please, you just take your time.'

Solomon pulled the cylinder free. 'How do I get it to you?'

The belly of the saucer hit a vertical draft in the clouds, pitching the craft into a roll and momentarily slowing them down. Solomon's head cracked against the floor and the EpiPen slipped from his grasp. Hunter grunted as he took a similar knock. He kicked out, trapping the medicine with the toe of his boot as it rolled toward him. The craft completed its roll, and Hunter instinctively pulled his foot towards his open fingers. His fingertips touched the EpiPen's label, but he was an inch shy of a good grip. The saucer was gathering speed again. It was now or never. He let the EpiPen slide back into the arch of his foot and kicked it. It was do or die. He reached for the pen, his heart pounding as his outstretched fingers met nothing but thin air. He'd failed.

Then suddenly a vision of Serena filled his field of vision, elation replacing despair. The saucer's second rotation allowed her to dive at Yussel, EpiPen in hand, needle unsheathed. She plunged it deep into Yussel's chest, discharging a full dose of the liquid inside. The effect was instantaneous. Yussel's head bashed into the chair, his body convulsing as he gasped for air. The ship levelled and skimmed the savannah, dispersing a group of grazing gazelles and the lioness stalking them.

Hunter groaned and lay on his back, feeling for broken bones. 'Serena, I love you. You okay, Yussel?'

'*Sorry guys,*' said Yussel. '*Bit of a close call, was it?*'

'Too close,' said Solomon, shaking off the bang to his head. 'We need to get you to a hospital, and I could do with a little attention for that matter.'

'Agreed,' said Hunter. 'Yussel, any chance you can fly this crate to Cambridge?'

'And try to keep out of sight,' said Solomon. 'Attention is not something we need right now.'

'Do you think we are being tracked?' asked Serena.

'*Definitely*,' said Yussel. '*And someone thank her for saving my life.*'

'He says thank you,' said Hunter, looking about the small cabin. 'Where's the tracking device?'

'*The plans placed it under my seat.*'

'Okay, so what do we do? How do we get it out?'

'*We don't.*'

'We don't?' Hunter grimaced, surprised by the answer.

'*These guys were so paranoid the Russians were going to steal back this crate, they rigged it with a small nuclear device. It's designed to blow if tampered with.*'

'What the actual?' Hunter whispered, his body numbing at the implications of this terrifying new reality. 'So we're flying a nuclear bomb the Americans could blow at any moment.' Serena coughed and dry retched.

'*Tell her we're quite safe for the moment. I changed the detonation code before we left.*'

'But I assume they can still track us?' asked Solomon.

The nose of the saucer dipped. '*Only in the air.*'

'So, what are you saying? We're going...' Hunter gripped hold of Yussel's seat. 'Holy crap.'

The ship slowed and gracefully slipped under the churning surf of the Atlantic Ocean. Hunter could hardly believe what he was seeing. A hundred feet above, the sun twinkled on the ocean's surface, its warm rays piercing the seawater and providing enough light to illuminate the mysterious blue world they now inhabited.

Something collided with the saucer's hull. Hunter grasped for a handhold, but failed and lost his footing. 'What the hell was that?'

'Looked like a silver king to me,' said Solomon, pulling Hunter to his feet. 'And a beauty at that — must have been at least eight feet.'

'An eight-foot fish?' said Serena. 'Are you kidding me?'

Solomon grinned and ruffled her hair. 'No. And they get bigger.'

'Well, shouldn't we be slowing down a touch if there are freaky, giant fish outside?'

Hunter stretched, cracked his neck, and massaged a few of the aches and pains covering his person. 'She's right. Can you slow down a touch? This craft is pretty old now. It might not take many more hits like that, and I don't fancy our chances if we sustain damage underwater.'

'*Come on guys,*' said Yussel. '*This saucer is designed to take the pressures of space. Do you really think a collision with a fat fish is going to make a dent?*' He paused. '*Just sit back and enjoy the ride. If you think this is bumpy, just wait until we get back in the open.*'

Hunter glanced at Solomon. Yussel was right, of course; they had no idea of the severity of the metaphorical shit storm they were flying towards. He sat himself down, bringing his knees to his chest and closing his eyes as the saucer's hull shuddered at yet another heavy impact.

'Can I at least suggest a heading?' asked the Professor.

olonel Jacob Carmichael stood over the body of his former friend and confidant. How long had it been? Ten? Perhaps even as long as fifteen years. He shook his head. The incident secured his promotion, but emotionally, the investigation took its toll to the tune of five years of therapy. However reprehensible the morality of his order might seem to an outsider, he knew killing Cartwright had been his only option. Only God came before the country in the mantra and God had chosen not to intervene.

He knelt and brushed Chris' eyes shut. 'I hope you find peace, my friend. I'm sorry it came to this. If I'd known that fool of a Base Commander pulled your file with the intention of bringing you back, I'd have personally slapped him with it.' He bent his head and rested it on the shoulder of his dead friend. 'He was right though, on paper you were the best choice for this kind of work.'

'Sir?' Jacob turned to see his aide carrying a tablet computer. 'We have a track on the saucer.'

Jacob stood and clapped a large hand on the young man's back. 'Excellent news. Where is she?'

'Africa, sir.'

'Africa?'

The man winced, 'Well...'

'What do you mean, "well?" She's either over Africa or she isn't!'

He shook the tablet. 'It's gone. Let me reset the link,' the man garbled. 'It was travelling east over Nigeria and then... nothing, it must be a glitch.'

Jacob cracked a knuckle and looked back at the tight smile imprinted on the dead man's face. 'I assume this is your doing. A parting shot from the grave. Did you tell your friends to duck out of sight under the Atlantic?'

'Sir?'

Jacob put his hands behind his head and blew the air from his lungs, thinking hard as he attempted to second-guess his old sparring partner. 'It's not a glitch. Just keep a close eye on the coast of Brazil... actually make that the eastern seaboard in general. Something tells me our little alien will pop up sooner rather than later.' He strode to the exit and stopped in the doorway. He shook a finger at the dead body. 'Have Major Cartwright buried in an unmarked grave in the base. Give him a service. He may have lost his mind, but he served his country with distinction for many years. He deserves more than a hole in the desert.'

Chapter 30

Yussel slowed the craft, but the journey from the Nigerian coastline and into the Solent, the strait separating the Isle of Wight from mainland England, still only took an hour. Hunter stared at the waves lapping against the glass dome atop the saucer, mesmerized by the hypnotic pitter-patter of rain. In the distance, he could see Portsmouth's Spinnaker tower, lit up by the occasional flash of lightning and standing guard over the harbor entrance, the home of the Royal Navy.

'Tell me again why we're parked up in full view of some of the most sophisticated surveillance equipment in the world?' asked Hunter.

'Say what?' said Serena.

Hunter pointed beyond the expanse of water. 'Look beyond the island. Can you see those chalk cliffs in the distance?' Serena squinted and nodded. 'That's Portsdown hill. Now look up a touch. You might just be able to make out a few grey funnels, antennae and a selection of satellite dishes. Sort of looks like the top of a buried ship.'

'Oh yeah, I see it. Christ, you've got good eyesight. So, what is it?'

'It's a Naval Research facility.'

'They won't be concerned with us,' Solomon interrupted.

'Sol, I know for a fact they have got surveillance technology in that facility leaps and bounds beyond anything you've got in the US,' said Hunter. He glanced back up at the hill, noticing a couple of spinning dishes receiving signals from god knows what. 'A naval mate of mine is currently involved in selling part of their systems to your CIA.'

Sol shook his head and tightened his jaw. 'Impressive, but still ludicrous to suggest they would pick us up.'

'If what John is saying is true,' said Serena, 'I kinda have to ask what makes you so confident? You do realize they have battleships in that harbor.'

'And don't forget the fully stocked armament facility at the center of the harbor. There's enough weaponry stockpiled to take on China, let alone us.'

'*Don't be so stupid,*' said Yussel, weighing in. '*First, the Professor has chosen this spot because it's one of the busiest waterways in the world. Everything from cruise liners to the smallest of fishing boats passes through these waters. Unless someone is looking, we're anonymous. Second, this ship can outrun any shell the Brits have in their arsenal. So stop this nonsense and remember we're here to find me a Doctor.*'

'Alright, Yussel, I'm sorry,' said Hunter, 'but you need to calm down. You should conserve your energy.' He turned to Solomon. 'Okay, so what's the plan, hero? I understand how we can hide in the water, but how do you intend to conceal this puppy from my countrymen once we're airborne?'

Solomon scratched the thickening stubble on his cheek. 'I don't think we can. We may have to dump her.'

Hunter snorted. 'I hope you're joking. You do realize what this thing represents?'

'I'm very aware of what we've all invested in securing this craft, but at the moment it is simply a target,' said Solomon. 'Which makes us all targets as long as we're inside her.'

'But Yussel just told us we can outrun anything fired at her,' said Hunter.

'We can run and run,' said Solomon, 'but at some point, we need to stop. We have no provisions for a start. This is as good a place as any to stock up, plus I have a contact in the city.'

'What about Russia?' asked Serena. 'The Americans won't follow us there.'

Solomon laughed. 'Yeah, but I can't see mother Russia welcoming me back with open arms? I was the one who stole this thing in the first place.'

'China then?' said Serena, her tone sharper. 'I just don't see why we're trying to get help from the fifty-first state.'

'We wouldn't last ten minutes in China,' interrupted Hunter. 'Sol's right, it makes sense to use England. I live here for a start and also know several people who will help us, no questions asked.' He tapped the dome above their heads. 'Any way we can eject the hood? Please tell me the ramp isn't our only way out of here?' Yussel dipped his head, his body on the verge of giving up its fight. 'Shit. Is that a no?'

'I'm... I'm afraid so.'

Hunter drummed his fingers on the wall of the craft. 'Okay, so we need to set this thing down on solid ground to let you out.' He slapped the back of the chair and sighed in defeat. 'Maybe it's a good thing. I'm not sure I fancy your chances swimming in the Solent. The currents around here can sweep even experienced swimmers to their deaths.'

'So, what do you want me to do?' asked Yussel. *'Keep in mind Area 51 can track our position as soon as we surface.'*

'Do you see the lights to your left?' Hunter shook his head. 'Sorry, stupid question.'

'Yes, and no. I can see through your eyes. Sort of how I've been navigating so far.'

Hunter raised an eyebrow. 'I'd not really thought about how you were guiding this thing. Just assumed there was advanced satellite navigation or something.' He jabbed his finger in the direction of something outside. It was a concrete pillar, standing stubborn and unflinching amidst the storm battering every exposed inch. 'That's No Man's Land fort, part of the harbor defenses installed during the late eighteen hundreds to ward off the French. It's a spa hotel now.'

'A spa hotel, nice,' said Serena. 'Not sure about the location, but I'll take what I can get.'

Hunter ignored the comment. 'They have a boat which can take us to the mainland. We just need to secure a passage.'

'Okay, the plan is sound, so far,' said Solomon.

Hunter frowned. 'Sound... ish. The fort has a small platform attached to the roof. We'll need to land the saucer as close to the seaboard edge as possible. Once we're out, I suggest we tip the saucer back into the sea. If we're quick enough, maybe they won't pick us up on their scanners.'

'Optimistic perhaps, but I don't think we have much of a choice,' said Yussel. *'At least tipping it shouldn't prove problematic. This craft is lighter than you might think. Part of the reason it can travel at such obscene speeds. The power to weight ratio is off the chart.'*

'Excellent, at least something is going in our favor,' said Solomon. 'I suggest we all take a seat against the wall and brace for impact.' A fork of lightning lit the sky. 'Let's hope one of those takes out some of their tracking equipment.'

'Fingers crossed,' said Hunter. 'Yussel, should I risk standing next to you? Do you need my eyes?'

***

Colonel Carmichael was not a man who showed fear often, but he certainly feared these men. The concept of human life having value simply did not exist within the confines of these offices. Men were but mere pawns in their game of political chess; pawns to be toyed with, sacrificed, and sometimes even executed at the will and whim of the players.

'I can confirm the target Chris Cartwright has been neutralized,' he continued, grimacing a little as a graphic image of his dead friend appeared on the vast screen behind him. There was not even a flicker of emotion on the faces surrounding the elongated oak table in front of him. Not that he expected a reaction. After all, this was old news. They already knew what went on in hangar eighteen, and probably in more detail than he did himself. The meeting was just a farcical exercise designed to highlight his failures and give them more leverage over him going forward.

'And then you lost the saucer?' said the Chairman.

'My men fired as soon as their weapons locked onto the target.' The Colonel barked his responses as if reporting to the commander-in-chief himself. In many ways, the man he addressed was much more powerful, and certainly more dangerous.

'Can I ask why you didn't fire sooner?'

'My orders were to protect the ship at all costs. The RPGs were a last resort, sir.'

'So instead we have nothing.' The Chairman shook his head and pounded a fist against the boardroom table. 'No alien and no saucer?'

'He's under the Atlantic, sir.'

'Nice. Should be easy to find him then. Not as if it's a vast ocean, is it? Oh wait…'

'Sir, I am sorry, sir. I did what I thought was best in the circumstances.'

The Chairman raised a hand, demanding silence. 'No matter…' He paused in thought. 'Assuming the Russians don't get hold of the creature, the situation is containable.' Jacob nodded and for the first time their eyes met. The Chairman was a grizzled, wiry gentleman of indeterminate age who'd once headed up one of the world's biggest banks. In fact, as he glanced about the space, the room was a veritable who's who of twentieth-century powerhouses. There were politicians, industrialists, technological leaders and a smattering of high-ranking members of the military that headed up various armies from all around the globe. The room was a terrorist's wet dream.

He locked his gaze back on the Chairman, refusing to buckle to intimidation. If he showed weakness, he'd lose his chance and maybe his life. 'Sir, my orders?'

'You believe the subject will head for our friends in Brazil?'

'I do, sir.'

'Good. Then I suggest you meet it off the plane, and this time put a bullet in it. Then wipe out the institute. Too many people know of its existence, and it's become a liability and a risk. Operation Paperclip is long dead — as is the Cold War. We have no need of these people and their fantastical theories anymore.' He threw a pen on the tabletop and turned his chair away from Jacob. The meeting was at an end.

Jacob's eyes widened as the implications of the order set in. 'But, sir, the children?'

'Are you deaf, Colonel? You have your orders; now leave us and execute them. Thanks to your little… misadventure, we have work to do.'

Jacob saluted and left the room, whispering under his breath. 'Asshole.'

'I beg your pardon, Colonel?'

Jacob whirled, a wave of relief hitting him as he recognized his aide. He smiled. 'You heard me. I think you're an asshole.'

The aide grinned. 'Not for much longer, I hope.'

'You have news?'

The man nodded and handed him a map. 'They've surfaced.'

Jacob slapped a hand across his friend's back. 'Excellent. Where are they? Argentina, Brazil, Mexico, where?'

'Portsmouth.'

Jacob cocked his head to one side and shrugged. 'Portsmouth? New Hampshire? Why the hell would they go there?'

'No, sir, Portsmouth, Hampshire. They're in England.'

He snorted and nodded, mulling over this development. He rubbed his face and set his jaw. 'Get me a plane.'

'There's one already waiting for you, sir. You have ten minutes until take-off.'

Chapter 31

Hunter lifted Yussel and lowered him onto the tarmac, wrapping him up in his jacket to stave off the worst of the wind and rain.

'The weather must be affecting their tracker,' said Solomon, attempting to protect his face with a hand. 'This rain could cut glass.'

Hunter nodded. 'If not, let's hope the Americans think we're still inside when the signal disappears.' He looked up at the saucer and gave it a gentle shove. It moved easily. Yussel was right. It was lighter than it looked. 'Come and help. We need to knock this thing back into the sea.'

Serena joined him first. 'We only need an hour. Surely they can't mobilize in this weather before then.'

Solomon pressed his shoulder against the craft. 'Well, I suggest we all find a god to pray to then. We're cutting it fine as it is. Now heave.' The saucer slid forward a couple of feet toward the platform edge. 'Once more... heave.' The saucer teetered on the edge and dropped with a satisfying smack into the churning surf, far below.

'I guess that's that then,' said Serena.

Hunter nodded, guessing the gist from her expression as he struggled to hear over the raging wind. He turned to Yussel and his knees buckled under him. He clawed at his ears as an unintelligible, piercing shriek overwhelmed his every sense. Someone dressed in a black rain suit crouched over Yussel, prodding at his chest.

The man stood and shouted in Serena's direction, the only person unaffected by Yussel's cries. 'What's wrong with this thing? And who are you people, and how did you get up here? You weren't on the last boat over.'

The pain in his head dissipated. Hunter rose and extended his hand. 'Dr John Hunter, University of Cambridge,' he yelled. 'I head up an archaeological unit on the mainland. Our helicopter was struck by lightning and we were forced to bail out.' The wind was strengthening. 'Any chance we can go inside? I can barely hear myself think. Do you have a phone?' The man nodded at Yussel, still seemingly after an explanation. 'My companion needs medical attention. He was injured in the crash.'

This seemed to appease the man, and he pointed to a set of wrought iron stairs on the opposite side of the platform. 'Down there. Let's get him out of this weather.'

Hunter plucked Yussel from the deck and followed their new acquaintance into the calm of the hotel; the antithesis of the storm raging outside.

'Wow,' said Serena, shaking the rain from her coat. 'I can't hear anything. This place must be built like a tank.'

The man laughed. 'That's effectively what it is. These forts were built to defend the harbor against the Napoleonic invasions. I personally wouldn't have wanted to face one in its heyday. Nine, twelve and a half inch guns set in virtually impenetrable armor against wooden ship and early ironclads doesn't seem very fair to me.'

Hunter nodded. 'About that telephone?'

'Yes, of course?' He ushered Hunter into a short corridor and held out his hand. 'The name is Walsh by the way.'

Hunter took it. 'Hunter, John Hunter.'

'So, John Hunter, what brings you out in this kind of weather, anyway? You didn't show up on my radar.'

Hunter attempted to look sheepish. 'I must confess, we didn't actually have clearance to be out here. My fault entirely. We were surveying the resting place of the Mary Rose with new equipment. We needed the data for an urgent funding application due tomorrow.'

The man rolled his eyes. 'So, you ignored coastguard advice. I should really report this.'

'Don't worry, my team has already reported the incident,' said Hunter, surprised, and a little saddened by how natural his lies were becoming. 'I just need to contact them so they know we're safe.'

The man opened a door adorned with a slab of black slate with his name printed in white ink. He nodded at an untidy desk where numerous piles of loose paper appeared to be awaiting a more permanent home. 'You can use my phone. It's hidden somewhere amongst that lot. Not sure if it'll help though. You'd have to be a madman to be out in this weather... no offense.'

Hunter ignored the jibe. 'Thank you, Kurt. This is much appreciated.'

Walsh looked momentarily confused at the use of his first name. He glanced at his nameplate and smiled, moving to one side as Solomon and Serena both entered the office. 'No problem, John, just holler when you're done.'

Hunter dialed and felt his body relax as a familiar voice picked up. 'George Goodheart. Whom has the pleasure of addressing me?'

Same old George. Hunter and George had remained firm friends since their undergraduate days in Cambridge. To say they'd been through a lot together since was an understatement. Although a geologist by training, George was a key member of Hunter's Alternative Archaeology Unit. The AAU was a Cambridge funded initiative formed in the wake of some of Hunter's previous high-profile discoveries. Although the University had long since pulled the funding, the Unit had become somewhat of a thriving business.

'Still answering the phone in a professional manner, I see.'

'John? John, is that really you? Where the hell have you been? I've been worried sick. We all have.' George paused. 'We've been receiving call after call.'

'Seriously?' said John. 'Any idea who from?'

'Are you shitting me, Hunter? You've made it onto America's most wanted list. I was hoping you might be the one filling me in. They want you dead or alive, John, dead or bloody alive. What the hell have you got yourself...'

Hunter slammed down the phone and bent over the desk in defeat. 'Shit.'

'What did you do that for?' said Serena.

'They know we're here. They've already been in touch with the Unit. How could I be so stupid? That call would have been traced in seconds.'

'Maybe you weren't on the line long enough,' said Solomon.

'Yeah, and maybe I was.' He bashed his fists against the table. 'Somehow we need to convince this Walsh fellow to take us to shore.'

'I don't know, John,' said Solomon. 'He didn't exactly seem happy standing in the rain. Can't imagine him wanting to take his boat out for a spin.'

'Then we'll offer to pay him whatever it takes,' said Hunter.

Solomon rolled his eyes. 'Who are you, Al Capone? You gonna make him an offer he can't refuse, doll-face?'

For Christ's sake, Solomon, this is not a joke. We're on America's most-wanted list. If we don't leave now, this man-made rock will turn from hotel to prison quicker than you can say...' Hunter felt his blood run cold. 'Oh shit!'

'Not the most poetic piece of rhetoric, but fine...' said Solomon. Hunter nodded at the doorway and the professor turned, confusion morphing into shock as he shuffled backwards, shielding Serena from the twin barrels of the shotgun propped against Walsh's meaty forearm.

'I believe the expletive was more for my benefit... Mr. Garnett, is it?'

'Professor,' Solomon snapped.

Hunter grimaced. 'Jesus, pick your battles, Sol.'

'Sound advice, but maybe they'll care more in prison,' said Walsh, his voice laced with sarcasm. 'It would appear the three of you are celebrities; if being on America's terrorist hit list counts as being a celebrity.' Hunter stared at him in defiance. 'Whatever, the harbor police can deal with you. I just want the reward.' He nudged the barrel in the door's direction. 'On your feet and no heroics, please. I may be carrying a few extra pounds, but I know how to use this thing.' He jerked the gun in an upward motion. 'That means now.'

'You're making a mistake, Mr. Walsh,' said Serena. 'The men after us are trying to silence us. We've done nothing wrong.'

'Tell it to the police, love. Now move.'

Hunter rolled his eyes and shook his head, making an exaggerated show of how unhappy he was about this turn of events. He slapped both hands against the desk and knocked a cup of water. He lunged, grasping it before it fell and righted the glass. Using the distraction as cover, he slipped a pen into the sleeve of his shirt with his free hand. He glanced at the spilt drink and mouthed an apology.

'Don't worry about it,' said the hotelier. 'Now on your feet, my patience is almost spent'

'Where are you taking us?' asked Solomon.

'This place still has a functional holding cell. It's under the waterline, so might be a little damp.' Walsh grinned. 'If I were you, I'd try negotiating a little discount on your final bill.'

Hunter walked past the gun. 'You've only got two rounds, funny man. What are you going to do if we run? You got the balls to take the shot?'

Walsh replied with a wink. 'I'm a Falklands veteran, Mr. Hunter. If you want to test my balls, you go right ahead. You might only lose a leg... if you're lucky.'

As Solomon and Serena disappeared through the door and into the corridor beyond, Hunter felt the cold steel of the shogun's dual barrels nudging him in the back. This was his chance. In a single motion, he turned on his heel and knocked the gun sights clear of his body. He screamed in pain as a searing heat burnt into the soft flesh of his forearm and a deafening explosion overwhelmed his senses. Hunter stumbled, tinnitus ringing in his ears, but somehow retained his focus. Unsheathing the biro, he pounced, arcing the pen's tip into the left shoulder of his attacker whilst simultaneously sweeping away his standing leg. The portly man landed on his back with a thud, his gun clattering across the floor and spinning under the desk.

Hunter swung a leg over Walsh's chest and dropped hard onto the man's rib cage. 'That's "Dr" Hunter to you, asshole. Now if you would be so kind, please hand over the keys to your lovely boat, "Mr." Walsh.'

Behind him, Solomon made a dash for the shotgun, and snapped it open, discharging the spent cartridges. 'We could do with a few more shells for this an' all.'

Hunter looked at Walsh and twisted the biro further into the open wound in the man's shoulder. Walsh winced, but to his credit refused to give in to the pain and scream. 'You heard the man, keys and ammo. Where are they?'

'Sod off, I'll die before I tell you anything.'

'Sod off?' said Serena. 'How very British. What is that, your way of telling us to go screw ourselves?'

'Fuck you,' replied Walsh.

'Better,' said Serena. 'Now that's something we Americans can understand.' She crouched behind Hunter and he stifled a smile as she grabbed the hotelier's genitalia. 'Now tell the nice men what they want to know before I take myself a unique souvenir of my trip to merry old England.'

Unable to suppress this fresh pain, Walsh screamed. Hunter exerted a little extra pressure to prevent the portly hotel manager from wriggling free. 'Top drawer,' he spat. 'They're in the top drawer of my desk. It won't do you any good though, the police will be here in a matter of minutes. Then we'll see who's laughing.'

Serena closed her fist, eliciting a final anguished cry as the prostrate man passed out. 'For the moment, it's still me.'

Hunter nodded at the desk. 'Sol, check the drawer.' He popped it open and looked up, a wide grin spreading across his face. 'What? What is it? More guns, ammo?'

'No,' said Solomon. 'It's much, much better than that...'

Chapter 32

Police Constable Peter Simpson shifted in his seat and gazed across the bow of his boat, the Loyalty. The wind and rain lashed against the windows of the bridge, rocking the boat from side to side as it negotiated wave after relentless wave. He squinted, just about making out the outline of No Man's Land Fort, a beacon of unwavering calm amidst the chaos of the storm. In this context, it was hard to believe how it hadn't succumbed to the ferocity of the ocean. The fort was a triumph of Victorian engineering in every sense of the word.

Simpson activated his radio for the second time. 'Come in, No Man's Land, come in? This is the Loyalty responding to your call. Please respond.' Why wasn't Walsh receiving? He'd have put it down to the weather, but the hotel manager only just radioed HQ regarding the American fugitives. Perhaps he needed to hail the fort directly. He looked at his three companions.

'Crane, Flintoff. It looks like we're going to have to do this the old-fashioned way. I suggest you unlock the gun case and arm yourselves, I'm getting no response from the radio. Jones, take us as close to the dock as you can. Since it's already occupied, I suggest you draw alongside the No Man's Land boat. I can't see any option other than boarding it to reach the fort.' He flicked a ceiling switch and turned the volume of the outside hailers to maximum. Even then, he was unsure if anyone would hear him above the storm.

'No Man's Land Fort, this is Ministry of Defense, Police Marine Unit, Loyalty. Your radio is non-responsive. Please be aware we intend to board your facility and retrieve the fugitives. We are armed and lethal force has been authorized. I repeat, lethal force has been authorized.' He paused. The hotel remained dark and silent — no lights, no response, no acknowledgement — nothing but the monotonous blinking of blue light on its walls, light reflected from the Loyalty herself. Simpson's heart fluttered with a surge of adrenaline. He'd been involved in drug busts and multiple instances of illegal immigration, but this was another league entirely. Three of America's most wanted and all trapped like rats on his little patch of territory. If he played this right, multiple promotions and opportunities lay ahead — maybe even a book deal.

'Take us in, Jones. Nice and slow.'

'Shouldn't we wait for backup, sir?' said Jones.

Simpson frowned and turned up his nose. 'Nah, Walsh has them under lock and key. We're dealing with unarmed captives, if we can't handle...' He looked up at the fort, his brow furrowing as a low rumble ebbed and flowed within the noise of the storm. 'Do you hear that?'

Jones looked at him in confusion. 'I can only hear the wind, sir.'

Simpson cocked his head to one side. 'It sounds like stone scraping against stone...' He looked at the dark, circular shape in front of him, searching for anomalies. Then he saw it. A dark opening in the fort's outer wall. Yes, a definite hole, about three meters by two.

'Was that hole there before? Do you see it? Just above sea level.' Jones gunned the engine. The rumble stopped, only to be replaced by an unidentifiable, high-pitched whine. 'Now what?'

'It's getting louder, sir,' said Jones. 'Like an aircraft about to take off.' Jones slammed the engine into reverse. Simpson pitched forward, losing his balance and falling into the comms console.

'What are you doing man? Are you trying to kill me?'

'That ain't no airplane, sir.'

A dark shape catapulted from the hole in the wall, narrowly missing the Loyalty's bow and skidded out into the darkness beyond. Simpson caught sight of a bright orange canopy and a huge, hissing turbine. 'Shit, they're escaping in a bloody hovercraft.'

***

Kurt Walsh's racing hovercraft scythed through the raging surf, bouncing from wave to wave with the grace and determination of an Olympic gymnast. Hunter held onto Yussel for dear life, his straps biting into his waist and shoulders with each painful thud against the seawater.

'Jesus wept. Did you see that? We nearly hit a police boat,' said Solomon. 'Is everyone okay?'

'All good bar the whiplash,' said Serena. 'Is Yussel okay?'

'Seems to be,' said Hunter. 'Just aim for the lights of the mainland, Sol. We definitely don't want to get lost in this.'

'You know this place,' said Solomon. 'Where should I point the nose?'

'The lights ahead belong to a fairground.' A Ferris wheel and roller-coaster skirting the seaboard flickered into focus. The dark mouth of the harbor opened to their left, the ominous singular blue flashing light at its center surely a police boat sent to investigate. 'Aim to the right of them,' urged Hunter. 'If we can make it to Southsea Common, we should be home and dry.'

'What the hell is a south sea common?' asked Serena.

Another wave cut Hunter's amusement short, and he cried out in pain as his shoulder smashed into the reinforced glass to his left. 'Jesus Christ. It's a park, Serena, it's a park.'

'Alright, I only asked.' She craned her neck to look through the tiny, rain-stained window behind his head. 'Are we being followed?'

'Of course we are,' said Solomon. 'Not that I can see them in this damn weather. I can barely see what's in front of us, let alone behind.'

'Just aim for the lights and try riding the waves as opposed to plowing straight through them,' said Hunter. 'We should outpace the police but, in this sea, who knows?'

'The shore is approaching. I suggest you all brace yourself,' said Solomon. 'And make sure Yussel's head doesn't smash into anything too solid.'

Unbeknown to the hovercraft's occupants, the unyielding onslaught of waves had created a natural ramp of shingle across the beachhead, piling the rounded stones to the edge of the concrete promenade fronting the Solent. The small hovercraft hit one such pile with the spirit of Evel Knievel and soared into the sky, its path lit by a fierce streak of bright lightning. Hunter felt the sensation of weightlessness before his stomach lurched and the inevitable descent began. The hovercraft's bow smashed into the concrete, collapsing the skirt amidst a flurry of sparks and the sickening screech of metal.

'Inflate, God damn you,' shouted Solomon, frantically twisting every dial on the control panel to maximum and hitting the ignition.

Hunter jumped as something nicked off the frame of his window. 'Get it going, Sol. They are shooting at us. We haven't much time.'

The giant fan spluttered and then caught, inflating the skirt and sending the small machine juddering towards the greenery of the enormous park beyond the promenade. 'We might just get away with this,' said Solomon. 'She's sagging a little at the front, but we've enough ground clearance to get us out of here.'

'Clear the park and then we'll dump it and run,' said Hunter.

'Don't think, just aim for the brightest light,' screamed Serena, her panic exaggerated as another bullet sparked off the hovercraft's hull. 'Get us out of here.'

The craft bounced and careered over the road fronting the seafront, clipping a parked car and knocking it onto two wheels. Hunter ducked as the hovercraft's rear window shattered, sustaining yet more damage from another volley of machine-gun from the Solent.

'Shit,' shouted Solomon. 'We have smoke. They've hit something important.'

'Forget it and accelerate,' said Serena. 'We can bail out when we're out of range.'

'Oh crap,' said Solomon.

'What do you mean, "oh crap?" I do not want to be hearing, "Oh crap",' said Hunter.

'They've knocked out the throttle,' said Solomon. 'I can't slow down.'

'Turn, Sol, turn. You're going to smash into that building,' shouted Serena.

Hunter braced for impact as Solomon pulled the joystick hard left. The hovercraft turned and slowed, but it was too late. The craft continued forward, its momentum propelling it in a straight line but sideways. It smashed into a pair of ornate wooden pillars supporting the porte-cochère of the Royal Southsea hotel. They buckled, snapping on impact and sending the roof crashing down into the hovercraft's skirt. Something exploded, and Hunter could hear the crackle of flames somewhere underneath his seat.

Hunter punched open his safety belt. 'Smooth, Sol, very smooth. Is everyone alive?'

'Damn,' said Solomon. 'I didn't see that coming.'

'Pop the door,' said Serena. 'We need to get out before the fire takes hold. I can smell leaking fuel.'

'I'm trying,' said Solomon, manically punching the door release. 'It's blocked.'

Hunter passed Yussel to Solomon and lay on his back, feet against the door. 'No, it bloody well isn't.' He kicked out with both feet. The blow dislodged the debris and sent the door pinging upward on its hinges. There was a rumble, and yet more plaster tumbled from above. 'Everyone out and make it quick. If the fire doesn't get us, the remains of the ceiling might.'

Hunter slid through the opening and helped Serena out after him. Solomon followed with Yussel and he placed the little man in Hunter's waiting arms. He turned and noticed a terrified looking bellhop staring at them from the doorway of the hotel's lobby. Hunter grinned in what he hoped was both a reassuring and apologetic manner.

Solomon tossed the hovercraft's keys in the boy's direction. 'Park her up for me? I'll settle up later.'

Chapter 33

Jacob Carmichael alighted upon the smooth tarmac apron of RAF Northolt and grasped the hand of the Wing Commander tasked with greeting him.

'Welcome to Northolt, sir.'

He gave the hand a firm shake and gazed about the airfield. 'It's a pleasure to visit a base with such a distinguished history. I'm led to believe this was the first RAF base built,' said Jacob.

The officer smiled. '...and the proud defender of London during the Battle of Britain.'

Jacob nodded at the office buildings lining the apron's edge. 'Shall we? I was informed I'd be briefed on arrival. This is a sensitive issue for the US Air Force and the cooperation between our teams is essential.' They began to walk. 'Who will deliver the briefing? I need to know how many of you have clearance.'

'That would be me, Colonel. The name's Kent. I head up the RAF's UOE division.'

'UOE?'

'Unexplained Occurrences and Events.'

Jacob snorted. 'You're a UFO bod. I'm sorry, but I think something has been lost in translation. I'm not in the UK chasing little green men.'

Kent stopped in his tracks and turned. 'Colonel Carmichael, it appears one of us has been left out of a very real loop. I can assure you, it is not me.'

Jacob narrowed his eyes, not entirely sure what was happening. 'Look, Kent, I appreciate a joke as much as the next man, but this manhunt is for an American citizen, not Extraterrestrial or Martian, or whatever term you guys use these days. He may look a little different, but rest assured he is very much of this world.'

'An American citizen, eh? So, you're telling me your country has a habit of removing the eyes and ears of its citizens?' Jacob berated himself internally. Had he said too much already? 'Human experimentation is a big deal, Colonel. Do you know how many laws and treaties your government has breached? Ironically, many are drafted and implemented by your own hypocritical lawmakers.'

'Thank you, Wing Commander, I am aware of the political delicacy of this situation.'

Kent tapped a code into a keypad guarding a solid steel door and shoved it open. 'With respect, Colonel, you clearly aren't.'

He ushered Jacob inside a small room with the projected image of the UOE logo filling a large screen built into the far wall. He sat as Kent leafed through a set of notes.

'Will this take long? I have a mission to complete.'

'You have time,' said Kent. 'The group you're pursuing has temporarily ducked under our radar.' He snorted. 'They destroyed the entrance to a hotel with a hovercraft and just walked away. Couldn't write it, could you?'

Jacob nodded. 'I was made aware of your failure to apprehend the targets.'

'My apologies. Our government tends to prioritize healthcare and schools over the military. If only you'd had a chance to apprehend them in your own country. Oh, wait...'

Jacob shook his head. 'Touché. Okay, rather than trade insults, shall we just get on with this? Tell me what I need to know and then let me go do what I do best.'

Kent grinned. 'No doubt with all guns blazing. But fine.' He fiddled with the computer in front of him. 'Now as much as I couldn't care less if you bring your own government to its knees. When it comes to my Queen and country, I am obliged to intercede. Understand this — while you are on British soil, your mission will be overseen and handled by British Special Forces, i.e. me. You are here in an advisory capacity only, and in the event of capture, as an escort. Are we clear?'

Jacob jumped to his feet. His face reddened. 'Now look here, my rank...'

'...is meaningless in this country. But if you like - are we clear, Colonel, sir?'

Jacob slapped the desk in frustration and lowered back into his seat. 'Fine, we're clear. But it will not be the last you hear of this.'

'Can I begin?' Jacob dipped his head and raised his arms in mock supplication. 'Excellent. First, I suggest you release yourself from any preconceptions you have around my line of work. I work closely with my counterparts in the US and the reality, whether or not you believe it, is that we are not alone in this universe of ours.'

Jacob rolled his eyes and exhaled. Another nut job. He'd seen plenty of them in his time at Area 51, and they all shared one thing, an unwavering belief in whatever baloney happened to be the flavor of the month. Just because this man had convinced someone powerful enough to fund his ridiculous unit, it did not make his theories any more credible.

'The reason you are rolling your eyes at me, Colonel, is because you've been conditioned to respond in such a manner.' Kent clicked his mouse and a picture of a blob of bright light appeared on the screen. 'Let me take you back to wartime England, August 5th, 1944. A RAF recon plane is returning from a mission over Germany when a strange metallic object intercepted it. The object matched the aircraft's course and speed for several minutes before accelerating and disappearing. Prime Minister Churchill was presented with a report of the incident, and on the advice of your President Eisenhower, covered it up, banning its reporting for fifty years amid fears it would cause mass hysteria.'

Kent flicked through a couple more images. Jacob sat forward; his interest pricked for the first time by one of the pictures. 'Wait, go back. Was that the Russian craft? Looks similar to the saucer they sent to Roswell to sell us this fantasy. Did Stalin try the same thing in Europe first?'

Kent snorted. 'This was the blueprint of the saucer you boys tucked away in the secret desert hangar everyone knows about. But it certainly wasn't Russian.'

'Why? Is that because the reds told you it wasn't?' asked Jacob, his voice laced with sarcasm.

'Not at all, we know because RAF aircraft helped them locate it.'

Jacob cocked his head. 'You did what?'

'We helped them find the saucer. The Germans shot the craft down, but an RAF crew retrieved it.'

'Wait, so am I to believe the Russians commandeered it as the spoils of war?'

'Eventually, yes. I understand we attempted to claim ownership, but it failed. The sheer number of Russian soldiers rendering any resistance as mere folly. They returned to the Motherland with the saucer, a selection of German scientists and any equipment not bolted down.'

'Those scientists didn't happen to include two brothers, did it?' asked Jacob.

'Indeed it did — the Horten brothers. So, you do know a little about this?' said Kent.

'I know they are alleged to have designed and built the disk-shaped craft for the Russians.'

'I take it back. You merely know the party line.' Kent smiled. 'Although perhaps more through luck, you are half right. The Horten brothers certainly helped the Russians modify and understand the internal workings of the craft, but as for the actual engineers... Whatever piloted the original saucer over Germany, we still have no idea.'

Jacob shook his head. 'Are you really asking me to accept this saucer is actually of unknown origin? The same saucer American scientists have been reverse engineering for the past half-century?' Kent nodded. 'But surely, if true, there'd be more examples, and certainly more sightings. You can't honestly expect me to believe this is, and I'm unknowingly part of, some almighty cover-up. If saucers are flying above us with any kind of regularity, how could anyone cover it up?'

Kent bent over his lectern and gazed directly into Jacob's eyes. 'Colonel Carmichael, worldwide there are over five thousand reported sightings every year. Although I am willing to concede the majority are explainable, only a fool would be unwilling to concede one or two might not be. And don't forget these are only the "reported" sightings.'

Jacob pouted and brushed both hands through his receding hairline. 'Okay, if I concede to your logic, I don't see why you are telling me all this. Why is it relevant to this manhunt?'

'Again, I will be blunt, Colonel. I am afraid you have inadvertently got yourself snagged on the coattails of a conspiracy. A conspiracy designed to undermine your government, your military, and pave the way for an eventual invasion.'

Jacob looked for a hint of humor in Kent's face. There was nothing. 'You are kidding, right? Who would be naïve enough to attempt something like that?' He scratched his cheek and considered his own question. 'I guess if the various terror groups around the world came together, they could take out a few high-profile targets, but a full-scale invasion of the USA... Not even the Russians could be that stupid.'

'Funny you should say that.' Kent called up the next slide; ironically, a map of Russia with a series of arrows thrusting west into Europe and east into the United States. 'Your CIA and our MI6 have been concerned about a reprisal of cold war feelings ever since Putin assumed power. His KGB background is of major concern to the Western world.'

'Fair enough. I'll admit I've had similar discussions with my fellow officers.'

'I'm not surprised. I understand the appointment made most of the world shift its collective arse in its collective seat.'

Jacob grinned. 'I'm assuming James Bond is on the case?'

'He was washing his hair,' Kent replied, deadpan. 'So they gave me a ring.'

Jacob shook his head. 'As ridiculous as this all sounds, fine. For the moment, let's just assume I am onboard. What happens now? I've had no orders other than to take down the fugitives. What orders can you possibly have for me that supersede a kill order?'

An incoming email pinged on Kent's screen. The Wing Commander closed his eyes and drained the remains of a bottle of water, throwing it with venom into a nearby bin. 'Colonel, we put your kill order in place to prevent your targets from making contact.' He paused. 'Guess what? They've just made contact.'

Chapter 34

H unter stood, open-mouthed and soaking wet under the lintel of an upmarket, cream colored, terraced house in Southsea, a suburb of the city of Portsmouth.

'Come on, Hunter, get him inside. I don't want the police catching up with you now. You should have called me sooner, Solomon. You know the importance of Yussel to the cause.'

Hunter looked sideways, eyeballing a man he really didn't know anymore. 'What the actual... Well, Solomon? Aren't you going to answer your friend, Oleg Anosov, the Russian who wanted to bury us in the desert?'

Solomon glanced at the bare wooden floor and addressed the man standing inside the doorway. 'My apologies. I did not have any means of contacting you. We were being tracked, so I just pushed ahead with the plan.'

'Okay, now all of you get inside before you catch your death.' Oleg clapped a hand on Hunter's back and grinned. 'By the look on Dr Hunter's face, I feel I may have a little explaining to do?' He paused and looked down at the frail blanket swaddled body held in Hunter's arms. 'Is that...'

Hunter nodded. 'Good men have already died so Yussel could escape Area 51.' He ascended the final concrete step into the house and pushed roughly past Oleg. 'You better have a good explanation why you had us arrested back at EG&G. You must have known they intended to execute us.'

'It was a calculated risk, Dr Hunter. A risk we were forced into taking in the wake of other events unfolding.' Oleg sounded genuinely remorseful as he made his way into the opulently decorated hallway.

Hunter frowned and shook the rain from his jacket, the droplets landing upon a lavish red carpet. There was a distinct Russian theme to the décor

— the marble bust of Lenin and gold-framed portrait of Putin leaving him in little doubt as to the political allegiance of the building's owner. Oleg ushered Hunter inside and shepherded him through an imposing pair of ornate oak doors. The decadent theme continued into the room beyond, and the opulence of the gold-plated fixtures was something he imagined only the British aristocracy might match. Incalculably valuable tapestries and portraits lined the walls, separated by sculptures and curiosities of equal paucity.

Hunter gawked at the mahogany furniture; their silken backs inlaid with intricate embroidery, which would put many of the world's finest art galleries to shame. He shook his head in disbelief. 'Wouldn't this place be considered a little lavish by your comrades?'

Oleg snorted. 'Solomon warned me you'd be feisty. I am glad to see your recent brush with death has done little to dampen your spirit.'

Hunter ignored the jibe and lowered Yussel onto a sofa, making sure his head was supported. 'He's still unconscious. Do you have anyone who can provide medical attention? He's been shot and lost a lot of blood.'

Concern replaced Oleg's good humor, and the Russian rushed to a nearby phone. 'This should have been the first thing you told me.' The call connected and he barked an order in his native tongue. He nodded at Hunter. 'Arrangements have been made. Our friend will receive the best available treatment.'

'The wound has clotted,' said Hunter, 'but I don't know how much longer he can hold on.' The double doors exploded open, startling everyone as a pair of burly orderlies entered with a stretcher. 'Solomon,' he whispered. 'Tell me this is okay?'

Solomon placed a hand on Hunter's shoulder. 'It's fine. We're in a safe space. Stand down for the moment. We will explain everything in due course.' The two men transferred Yussel from the sofa to the stretcher, exiting the room with nothing more than a cursory nod in Oleg's direction.

Hunter lowered himself into one of the extravagant armchairs and allowed his eyelids to close, finally succumbing to fatigue. Could this really be the end of the road? Were they finally safe? Was this decadent, Russian controlled, Portsmouth residence really the sanctuary he'd been craving? Serena perched herself beside him and squeezed his arm in reassurance.

'I'd say a stiff drink is in order,' said Oleg, slapping his hand against a short granite top built into the far corner of the room. 'How about a snifter of some proper Russian vodka? That'll take your aches and pains away.'

Hunter gratefully accepted and drained the double measure in one. He caught Solomon's eye and placed his empty shot glass on the coffee table. 'Can I ask how long this plan has been in the offing? Did you cook it up in Russia or was it more recent?'

Oleg raised an eyebrow and patted Solomon's shoulder. 'Shall I field this one, old boy?' He seated himself opposite Hunter and slouched into the chair as if readying himself to reminisce with a long-lost friend. 'Well, Dr Hunter, I would say it has been a fluid combination of the two. I assume you know of my past link to the Professor?'

Hunter nodded. 'He let me read his account of your time together in Kapustin Yar.'

'Excellent, I'll skip to the end then.' He shook his head, poured another shot, and dispatched it quicker than the first. 'My fellow countrymen were swift in discovering my part in the infiltration and marked me for interrogation — an interrogation I knew I had little chance of surviving.' He straightened an oil painting of Red Square and his head dropped, in what Hunter could only assume was shame. 'So I did what anyone would do in such a situation and fled, seeking asylum in the States. My willingness to divulge a few choice Soviet era secrets meant the powers that be welcomed me with open arms.'

'And once you'd divulged your secrets, EG&G took you in?' asked Hunter.

He nodded and sniggered. 'Although they believed I knew much more about the saucer than I actually did.'

'So, they were involved with the saucer?' said Hunter.

The Russian wrinkled his nose. 'Yes, but only at a low level. The CIA divvied up the contract to reverse engineer the technology between a few third parties, not just EG&G. They didn't want a situation where they could be held to ransom and therefore chose to dilute the potential power of any one company.' He winked at Hunter. 'The Americans are a paranoid race.'

'So what aspect were EG&G given? I saw nothing out of the ordinary whilst working for you,' said Serena, breaking her silence.

'Ah,' replied Oleg, 'the million-dollar question, and the reason we are all here. EG&G were tasked with replicating that poor bastard upstairs. Or rather, certain aspects of him.'

Serena frowned. 'What's that supposed to mean? You obviously haven't taken him apart.'

Hunter noticed the Russian wince. It was borderline imperceptible, but after years of reading the reactions to his various and sometimes off the wall theories, Hunter recognized the tell. 'Oh my God, they did take him apart, didn't they? No wonder the poor guy is so damaged, physically and mentally.'

Oleg exchanged a furtive glance with Solomon and received a confirmatory nod to continue. 'Look, Yussel has a unique set of abilities…' He paused, unsure how to phrase his explanation. 'To be blunt, EG&G won the tender to work in the field of genetics, or as it became known, the Super Soldier contract. They gave DARPA the physical side, muscles etcetera, and the agency became our unlikely bedfellow on the project.'

'DARPA?' asked Serena.

'The Defense Advanced Research Projects Agency,' said Hunter.

Oleg nodded. 'They received and I believe still receive a congress approved an annual budget of two billion dollars for the development of the super-soldier and synthetic police force program.'

'Am I correct in thinking EG&G has been the more successful of the two?' asked Hunter.

Solomon wiggled his hand back and forth, indicating it was a close call. 'Yes, but only because of a looser set of ethical practices.'

'Hasn't this been made public?' said Serena. 'I'm sure Clooney made a film along these lines? Men and Goats — something like that.'

Oleg slapped his thigh. 'Ah yes, "The Men that Stare at Goats." The government is very careful to release only what it wishes the public to know.' He smiled. 'And in this case, the failure was light-hearted enough to make a Hollywood comedy.'

'Are you saying that was EG&G?' asked Hunter.

'God no! There are similarities, but EG&G are much further down the line. Their success, at least for the moment, is still classified the darkest shade of black.' He grinned at Serena. 'Brad Pitt won't be playing me just yet.'

'Are you saying they've succeeded?'

'They did, or rather they have, but only recently.' Oleg broke eye contact, stumbling over his words. He rose from his seat and paced the room. Hunter watched him in confusion and caught his eye, his expression demanding an explanation. Solomon paused and faced Serena, his eyes damp. Was he crying? 'Before I continue...' He was choked up, the words stuttering as they attempted to escape his mouth. 'I must deal with the elephant in the room? I am so sorry for handing your twins over to these monsters. At the time I knew the complex was experimental but...' His head dropped. 'I'm sorry, I had no idea.'

Hunter set his jaw, his gaze flitting between Solomon and Serena. 'We know only one of our babies survived.'

Oleg cocked his head to one side. 'Solomon?'

Solomon sighed and fiddled with the damp cloth of his trousers. 'I'm afraid I may not have been entirely honest with you both.' He scratched his forehead. 'Only one survives, but technically both were around until fairly recently.'

Hunter's eyes narrowed, his heart missing a beat. 'But you claimed you knew nothing of a surviving infant when we were told. Now you are telling me both survived the initial experiments. Are you joking?' Solomon attempted to grasp Hunter's arm, but he shrugged him away. 'Get away from me, you arsehole.'

'They are the only children who survived,' said Oleg. 'And the reason I need you.'

'You can piss off as well? Are you seriously expecting my help?' Hunter strode to the window and slapped the ledge, gazing into the stream of rain beating against the tarmac of the road beyond the gate. 'Why the hell would I help the pair of you do anything? You should have been straight from the start. What did telling me my children were dead achieve? We've done nothing aside from stealing a memory stick from your office, the reason for which I still do not know.'

'It made the scenario believable for 51 and gave you a motivator to continue. Revenge can be a powerful ally if manipulated correctly.' He raised the bottle in his hand, but Hunter refused the offer. 'A drink might help settle your nerves, doctor. Try to see it from our point of view.'

Hunter shook his head for the second time. 'Your point of view? Go on then, this should be good. Please go ahead... Justify why you allowed my child to die and then risked my life for information already in your possession.'

'Come now, John, please calm down.' A man entered the room, his hand ominously placed inside his jacket. Oleg shook his head and motioned for him to stand down. The guard glared at Hunter but complied. 'Yes, it was a setup, but the theft needed to appear real. Sol and I agreed keeping you in the dark would make everything feel more authentic. EG&G needed to believe I'm still onside or they'd never have let me leave the country.'

'So the data we uploaded is real?' asked Serena, her face emotionless, as if unable to comprehend what she was being told.

'Certainly, and if plan A doesn't work, plan B will kick in and the names will go public,' said Solomon. 'I promise all those involved in this disastrous affair will be brought to justice, and the program ended for good.'

'And what of the Major? Where did he come into all this? Remember him, the guy who died to save your skin,' said Hunter.

Solomon dipped his head again, shuffling his feet on the carpet. 'That wasn't part of my plan. He knew nothing of Oleg's involvement and had his own agenda. I agreed to play along with him as his aims broadly coincided with my own.'

'And thank God,' whispered Serena, 'as without him we'd all be dead.'

'Yes,' said Oleg. 'Although his actions scuppered my own plans for your escape with Yussel.' He sighed. 'C'est la vie, it all worked out I guess.'

'You are cold, even for a Russian spy. You are cold,' said Hunter.

'What's plan A?' asked Serna. The Russian looked at her in confusion. 'You just said the data drop is plan B... So, what's Plan A?'

Oleg looked away from her and directly into Hunter's eyes. 'He's asking for you, John. You are Plan A.'

Hunter grasped at his hair and closed his eyes, taking a deep breath. 'What the hell does that mean? He's asking for me? Who? My son? The guy has met me. Instead of risking lives, why didn't you just fob him off with a fake?'

'The fake is dead.' Oleg screwed up his face. 'Along with four orderlies and six guards. Your boy is powerful, John. The Americans can't control him.' He waggled a finger at Hunter. 'But I do. I have a man on the inside who believes the blood running through your veins can tame him.'

Hunter released his hair and the breath he'd been holding. 'As tough as this is for me to say, if he's killing people, why hasn't he just been restrained or shot?'

Oleg snorted. 'You give Uncle Sam too much credit. They'd never abandon a twenty-billion-dollar weapon for the sake of a few deaths.'

'Twenty billion? You're not serious?' said Serena.

'Hang on a goddamn moment,' said Hunter. 'You keep mentioning the Americans as if you aren't part of this. Who exactly is it you're batting for? I understand Solomon's motives, but what exactly are you getting out of this? You don't strike me as a man with a social conscience, so what is it?' He slapped the window in frustration. 'And while I'm the one asking questions, why the hell do you need Yussel if I'm the designated plan A? Is he just a decoy or something?'

'He's definitely something. That little man literally holds the key to all of this,' said Oleg. 'And do not worry about my motives, I will be well compensated for my efforts.'

'Fine, but it's by whom that worries me. And I still don't understand how Yussel can be key, how can he possibly help...' Hunter shook his head as the answer dawned on him. 'Ahh, you don't know where this facility is, do you?'

Oleg shook his head. 'Very perceptive. No, we don't, all visits are made blind. I would guess South America based on the humidity and surrounding vegetation, but beyond that... I've no idea. I don't even know anyone with clearance. Even the pilots fly blind. The autopilot takes control and all they do is take off and land. Those in power wanted the location buried, and that's exactly what they got.'

Hunter shook his head. Some of the pieces were finally slotting into place. Yussel must have been one of the facility's original graduates. He was the map.

'Are we on the same page at last, Dr Hunter?' asked Oleg.

Hunter nodded. 'Yussel was a patient, wasn't he?'

'Spot on,' said Oleg. 'Poor guy was captured by a Russian team in Mexico whilst in transit with a few others back in 1946. The KGB knew what they were and carried out several experiments themselves. They proved futile and Stalin decided to expose the American human experimentation program by sending a few of them back to the USAF inside a fake alien ship. The saucer was destined for Vegas but never made it. You know the rest.'

Hunter held up a hand as a disturbing thought entered his head. 'Wait, before we continue can I just get this straight? Are you asking Serena and I to participate in the rescue of our son, or his murder?' said Hunter.

Oleg walked toward Hunter and gripped his shoulder. 'I am sorry. I can only imagine how hard this is to hear. EG&G has been tasked with building an army and your son is the prototype.'

'If they succeed, John, war will follow,' said Solomon. 'If we can nip it in the bud, we will save the lives of millions.'

'Millions is a little dramatic, don't you think? How could you know?' said Hunter.

'The wheels are already in motion,' said Solomon. 'I love my country, but to be frank, it's screwing itself into a corner. Soon the only option left will be to fight.' He poured himself another drink and addressed the room as if preaching to a packed lecture hall. 'US politics has been based on warmongering and military propaganda for decades. We love a bad guy and creating one is an easy win for our politicians during elections, and for selling copy for that matter. Now, whether that be scary black-skinned men during the eighteenth and nineteenth centuries, Nazis, Communists or more recently, Middle Eastern terrorists, it doesn't matter. Middle America is programmed to fear the unknown and the unfamiliar. Focusing on that fear is the key to unlocking power and our leaders know it. Hitler, Stalin, Mussolini, Hussein, Gaddafi, Bin Laden — it makes no odds as long as there's a perceived baddie fighting against the freedoms granted by Uncle Sam.' He paused for breath and cracked his knuckles. 'Unfortunately, since the assassinations of Bin Laden and Gaddafi, the current administration has struggled to find a legitimate threat. North Korea perhaps, but for whatever reason, possibly their size, they've been disregarded.' He strode into the center of the room for effect and clamped his hands on the back of Hunter's now empty armchair. 'As such, and perhaps inevitably, the most recent President's crosshairs have refocused back on its most infamous enemy.'

'Moscow,' said Hunter.

'Indeed,' said Oleg. 'The US government is poking a sleeping giant, and seemingly without the appreciation it actually is still exactly that, a giant. Time may have dimmed memories as to the extraordinary power once wielded by the hammer and the sickle, however, although camouflaged by the new flag, it does not mean the old is no longer there. The Union may have dissolved, but the iron fist of the people's party only lies dormant, Dr Hunter. It would not take much cajoling to rip through the velvet glove within which it now resides.'

Hunter looked into Oleg's eyes. 'I'm confused. Do you want this revolution... or are you trying to prevent it?'

Oleg smiled. 'Are you questioning my politics or my morality?'

'I'll let your answer dictate,' said Hunter.

'Don't think it hasn't crossed my mind just to let this situation just play out. After all, a shrewd man can make many a fortune from the spoils of war.' Oleg chuckled. 'A debate Solomon and I have shared over many a bottle of vodka.'

'And how we've ended up here,' said Solomon.

'Combined with a little dash of guilt?' said Serena.

Oleg drained his drink and opened a second bottle, evidently determined to live up to Russia's reputation as a nation of hard drinkers. 'Maybe.' He shook his head and snorted. 'Are any of you aware the Motherland still controls enough of a nuclear arsenal to wipe out the Earth ten times over? Forget the disarmament propaganda we are fed in the West; the weapons are still there... just well hidden. China has a similar stockpile, and as for the good old USA, they have enough firepower to destroy every planet in our solar system, let alone Earth.'

'But why does this suddenly matter now?' asked Serena. 'This has been true of the superpowers for decades?'

'Yes,' said Solomon, 'and a key reason our world has been a relatively safe place to live during the last few decades. The global stalemate effectively preventing a nuclear war.'

'Serena's question still stands,' said Hunter. 'What's changed?'

'The breakthrough in the super soldier program.' Oleg rose to his feet. 'You need to open your eyes, Hunter. I've seen the plans and I know the long-term ambition of US government is to disarm Russia once and for all and conquer its people.'

'Come on, that's conspiracy theory nonsense; the rest of the world wouldn't allow it for a start,' said Hunter.

Oleg cocked his head to one side. 'And I guess you still believe Iraq's leaders were sitting on a stockpile of WMDs? Please don't show your naivety, Dr Hunter. If a master manipulates the rhetoric, they can coerce their audience into believing any truth.'

Hunter clamped his hands to his head as, without warning, a bolt of searing pain coursed through him. He doubled over and fell to the floor, screaming in pain. The pain dissipated and disappeared altogether, leaving behind only five words etched into his brain.

"Brazil, Apuí, Mengele — I'm sorry." It was Yussel...

Hunter pushed himself upright and bolted for the door. He pulled it open as the crack of a solitary gunshot reverberated through the house.

Chapter 35

'You damned idiot,' hissed Kent. 'I said quiet. Why can't you Americans follow simple orders? Alive god-damn-it, ALIVE!'

'Fuck you, Kent,' said Jacob, nodding at a sharp pair of scissors lying on the carpet. 'If it weren't for me, those things would be buried in your forehead. Anyway, you killed him, not me.'

Kent pulled the slim blade of a Fairbairn-Sykes knife from the temple of the dead creature and picked up the bullet from the floor. He tossed it to Jacob. 'Let's call it even. Another second and that bullet would have been buried in your forehead. Just be glad its injuries meant its multitasking wasn't quite up to scratch.'

Jacob caught the bullet and grimaced as a floorboard creaked beyond the bedroom door. He nodded at Kent. 'Our cue to leave — not sure I fancy a shoot-out without cover.'

'I told you not to use your gun. That gunshot was loud enough to raise the dead.' Kent pressed the comms device fitted into his ear. 'Zulu warrior, come in. Window evac required.' There was a knock on the door. 'Shit, and make it quick. Contact imminent.'

Jacob joined Kent at the window. 'Where's the cord, Kent? Where's the cord?'

Someone shouted something in Russian from behind the door. '- Откройте дверь.'

'He's asking us to open up,' said Jacob.

'Do you think I'm stupid?' said Kent. He paused and shouted back in Russian, 'Одна минута.'

'What do you mean, "One minute"?' said Jacob. 'Ah piss it; I'm not waiting for them to shoot first.' He raised the barrel of the L85A2 machine gun strapped around his neck and squeezed the trigger. The oak door erupted into a cloud of splinters and lethal shards of wood. Screams of agony were quickly replaced by silence as the clip cycled through its deadly contents. He felt Kent attach something to his back as his rifle's ammunition dried. Jacob grabbed for a fresh clip, his eyes widening as the moonlight picked out the barrels of a pair of Kalashnikovs snaking about the doorframe. The deadly weapons cracked in unison, spraying bullets and raking the room in a show of lethal retaliation. Instead of pain, Jacob experienced only a rush of air as his body jerked skyward; his legs colliding painfully against the window ledge as something hauled him clear of danger.

***

'What the hell is that?' shouted Hunter, trying to make himself heard above the noise of the helicopter's rotors.

Oleg glanced backwards before pulling himself into the cabin of a Russian made experimental helicopter, codenamed "the Viper." 'It's a V-22 Osprey. An American tilt-rotor aircraft capable of vertical take-off and landing.' He turned and helped Serena aboard. He squinted and smiled. 'Scratch that; the extra radar is a giveaway. We're privileged to have a U.S. Special Operations crew on our tail.'

'Shit,' said Serena. 'Is that good or bad? Will they try shooting us down?'

'They could try,' said Oleg. 'But politically speaking, they would be taking a hell of a risk. This chopper is not only armed to the teeth, but it's also registered as a diplomatic aircraft. If they engage and fail to destroy us, they risk activating a political time bomb. In the current climate, it could be the final straw in reigniting the cold war or perhaps worse.' He placed a hand on Serena's shoulder. 'Don't worry though; the armor on this beast is thicker than the walls of my house. We'll be safe.'

Hunter hauled himself into a vacant seat and gazed about the Spartan cabin, noting the huge minigun mounted on the door of the chopper. He caught Solomon's eye and pulled a face, shaking his head in disbelief. This was getting beyond ridiculous now. His life was fast becoming a conspiracy theorist's wet dream. Solomon mouthed another apology. They seemed to come thick and fast from his mouth at the moment. Something fizzed above his head and sparked off the armor plating. He ducked down and pulled on the pair of headphones attached to his chair.

The pilot screamed instructions through his headset. 'Lockdown the cargo. They have a sniper. I am lifting off.'

Oleg pulled a rifle from the webbing above their heads. 'Keep your heads between your knees,' he roared above the sound of whipping rotors. Hunter didn't need to be told twice. He watched the burly Russian use the webbing to swing himself outside the chopper to find a stable shooting stance.

'What are you doing?' shouted the pilot. 'Sod the rifle, get on the mini-gun and give me some cover.'

Solomon obliged and strapped himself to the massive weapon, pointing it toward their aggressor. A second shot sparked about the cabin. Oleg grabbed at his left arm and his shirtsleeve turned a shade of red. Luckily the bullet only seemed to have nicked him. Their helicopter turned as the mini-gun roared an angry response, an array of sparks coating the big aircraft. Oleg pulled the rifle to his shoulder and fired. Hunter saw a figure fall from the Osprey. Solomon pulled the Russian inside and slid the doorway shut.

Hunter raised a thumb in respect. 'Good shooting.'

Oleg shrugged and caught his breath. 'Easy shot for an ex-Olympian - albeit one that did not medal.'

The pilot's voice crackled through the headphones. 'They have a lock on us. Taking evasive maneuvers. Strap in and brace for potential impact.'

'I guess a diplomatic status counts for little these days,' said Oleg.

The helicopter banked hard right. 'Missile away, flares away, brace for impact,' barked the pilot through his headphones. Hunter heard an explosion somewhere under his feet. The helicopter shook but remained in one piece. 'Missile evaded. I have a lock. Returning fire.' Hunter gripped his chair as the gigantic machine rattled about him, shuddering with each successive burst of ammunition.

'Calm yourself, Doc, and smile,' said Oleg. 'That's a pair of remotely controlled four-barrel Gatling guns you can hear. They fire at a rate of over four thousand rounds a minute.' He laughed. 'We'd be flying backwards if they didn't fire in short bursts. Just be glad they're not targeting you.'

A loud explosion rocked the cabin, and the craft lurched to one side. 'Jesus,' said Serena, rubbing her neck. 'I'd prefer it if the missiles weren't targeting us either.'

'They have another lock,' said the Pilot. 'Two more missiles away. Deploying flares. Brace for evasive maneuvers.' Two explosions erupted in rapid succession. Hunter's stomach lurched as the helicopter dropped like a stone, the cabin a symphony of sirens and flashing red light. Hunter screamed an expletive as panic threatened to overwhelm him.

'We're hit!' shouted the pilot. 'Rotors are stabilizing and systems are all still online.' The helicopter leveled and rose.

'Damage report?' demanded Oleg.

'We seem to have lost our undercarriage, sir. The missile must have clipped it. Landing will be rough, but we'll survive.'

Hunter regularized his breathing with a few deep breaths and checked on Solomon. 'You okay, old man?' Solomon nodded. He turned to Serena. She still had her head tucked into her lap. 'Serena?' She didn't move. Hunter felt his stomach lurch. Something was wrong, the angle of her neck. It was lolling to one side as if unsupported. He yelled for Oleg's help, fumbling at his waist to remove his safety belt. It clicked open, and he propelled himself to the side of his friend and the mother of his children. He lifted her head and felt a wave of nausea sweep over him. One of the ricocheting bullets had found its mark and entered her chest. He let her head drop back into her lap. He felt numb.

'It would have been quick,' said the Russian, feeling for a pulse. 'She wouldn't have felt a thing.'

Hunter batted Oleg's hand away. 'She didn't deserve this. She did nothing.'

'There are slower ways to die, John.' The helicopter shuddered once more, and the Russian gripped Hunter's shoulders to steady himself. 'Now return to your seat or we'll all soon be joining her.'

'Have some respect, Oleg,' said Solomon. 'Give us a moment to compose ourselves.'

'We are at war, Solomon. There are casualties in every war. You know this and I know this. Now your friend Hunter knows. Now attach your harness. We need to get out of here.' Oleg pushed Hunter into a chair and pulled straps about his shoulders, clicking them in place. 'Pilot, deploy the engines.'

There was a brief hiss of static over the headphones before the reply came through. 'But, sir, we aren't clear of the mainland.'

'I am not risking any more of our cargo for the sake of a state secret that any witnesses won't understand anyway.'

'What about the Americans?'

'They know we have this tech. They just can't admit to knowing. Now engage the thrusters before they blow us out of the sky.'

'Engines?' said Solomon.

'I suggest you both hold on tight. You may have stolen the prototype, Solomon, but that didn't stop my countryman from continuing its development.'

Hunter was only half listening as he stretched to stroke Serena's blood-spattered arm. Her fingers twitched. He froze. Did he imagine it? He punched his safety belt. Why had he let Oleg check her pulse?

'John,' shouted Solomon. 'Get back in your seat.'

Ignoring the call, Hunter placed two fingers against Serena's throat. The comforting rhythmic beating of her heart answered his touch. It was faint, but it was there.

'John, get back to your seat now,' screamed Oleg.

He looked around the cabin. Something was different. It was silent. Even the ever-present sound of whipping rotors had disappeared. What was happening? It couldn't be engine failure or they'd be spinning out of control. His brain processed Oleg's last words. The Russians continued to develop the technology. Surely not the saucer technology.

'Shit.' He lunged for his seat, grasping hold of an armrest as his legs whipped out from under him. He lost grip as his shoulders popped in their sockets and his body hurtled towards the helicopter's rear. Hunter bracing for the inevitable impact and it didn't disappoint. Pain coursed through him, but somehow he was cognizant, and more importantly, alive. Something softened the impact — some kind of net perhaps? It was all he could do to thank God for the slice of luck. He raised his head in time to see the crate drop towards him, catching him just above the ear. Everything around him faded to pinpricks, and all-encompassing darkness replaced his world.

Chapter 36

Hunter sucked in a lungful of air and scrambled to his knees, his heart beating nineteen to the dozen. He blinked in pain as beads of sweat found his eyes, blurring the unfamiliar vista surrounding him. Hunter swept away the perspiration with a shirt sleeve and massaged the stiffness in his neck. He turned to stand and started, as Oleg's beaming face loomed over him, a dripping syringe in his right hand. Hunter nodded at the device.

Oleg grinned. 'What, this? Just a little shot of adrenaline to help you on your way.'

'Adrenaline? What the hell, man?'

'Sorry, but you could have been out for hours. And, my good Doctor, time is not an ally of ours at present.'

'Serena?' stuttered Hunter. 'Is she...'

Oleg's head drooped. 'I'm sorry, John.'

Hunter balled his hands as an overwhelming sense of grief and anger swept over him. He turned from Oleg, setting his jaw and attempting to control his emotions by focusing on his new environment, a large, brown grassy clearing surrounded by dense forest. The air was thick with humidity and made breathing a little uncomfortable. He pulled at his sweat-drenched shirt, releasing it from his skin and letting it slap wetly back into place.

'She didn't deserve... and now she's dead.' Hunter swung a wild haymaker at the elderly Russian. 'Her blood is on your soul.'

Oleg stepped to his left and avoided the telegraphed attack, using Hunter's momentum to push him to the floor.

'I didn't say she was dead, John. Serena's on life support. It's not a great situation, but she'll live.' Hunter tried to right himself, but Oleg shoved him back with the sole of his boot. 'You're right, though. This particular incident could have been avoided. We could have left you alone; left to live an oblivious life for perhaps another five, maybe ten years... until the outbreak of war.' Oleg pulled a knife from his fatigues and stabbed it into the trunk of a nearby tree. 'And then you could have watched everyone you've ever met, die. Not just some random woman you don't even remember fucking in the nineties.'

Hunter spat dirt from his mouth and lunged again, but the result was similar, this time with the Russian's boot pinning him to the ground at the neck.

'Last chance, Hunter. Come at me again and I'll break you in two. You may have youth on your side, but I still fancy my chances.'

'Fine,' said Hunter, trying to wriggle free. 'Can you at least tell me where the hell we are?'

'Better.' The pressure on his throat eased. 'And hell is a pretty good guess. We're in the vicinity of the town of Apuí in...'

'...Brazil,' whispered Hunter.

'Correct.'

'Brazil, Apuí, Mengele,' said Hunter. He sat upright and rubbed his bruised neck. 'Yussel's final words.'

Oleg grinned. 'Yes. I've been waiting to hear those words for decades.' He nodded at the other side of the clearing where Solomon appeared to be involved in a deep discussion with two locals dressed in olive green military fatigues. 'Solomon was right all along; the little Jew could not only read minds but inhabit and control the actions of an individual. He must have known more secrets than God himself.'

'And amongst them, the location of America's dirty little secret.' Hunter pulled himself up using Oleg's knife, still lodged in the tree trunk, and dusted himself down. 'So, what now?'

'Now it's over to you to tame the beast. You'll have a tender father-son moment and get to save the world in the process.' He thrust his hand out. 'You in?'

Hunter took it and gave it a weak shake. 'Can I get some water? This sun is melting me from the inside out.' The Russian tossed him a water canister. He caught it deftly and drained the contents.

'Sol,' shouted Oleg, 'Have you got us any leads?'

The Professor turned from his conversation with a pair of locals and jogged to join them. 'How's John? Top of the world, I trust?'

'I've certainly seen better days,' muttered Hunter.

Oleg grinned and playfully slapped his back. 'You're alive. What more do you want?' He nodded at the locals. 'Good news?'

'Good and bad,' said Solomon, wrinkling his nose. 'Bad since they claim not to know of any military facilities in the area. However, the good news is that one of them knows of a road into the rainforest which carries a little more traffic than it perhaps should.'

'Sounds promising,' said Oleg.

'Yes, but they say it leads to nothing but dense forest.'

'Can you get a satellite feed of the area?' asked Hunter. 'I'm sure your comrades must have one or two buzzing above the USA.'

'I can put in a call,' said Oleg. 'What kind of traffic are we talking about?'

'Trucks mainly,' said Solomon.

'And do we have any idea of the cargo?'

Solomon turned to the nearest man and barked something in Portuguese. He looked pleased by the answer. 'He says they carry one of two things, food... and groups of young children. Groups of children that never reappear on return trips.'

Hunter shook his head in disgust. 'Whether or not this is the right place, morally we need to expose what they are doing.'

'Whatever helps you sleep at night,' said Oleg. 'This has got to be it. Sol, can you ask more about the trucks? Do they stop off in Apuí?'

Solomon nodded. 'We're on the same wavelength, old friend. The food trucks pick up supplies in Apuí — usually in convoys of two or three.'

'And the human cargo?' said Hunter.

'They just roll on through. I guess to avoid any tough questions.'

Hunter rubbed at the stubble on his cheek, mulling over the early stages of a plan in his head. 'Right, so we board a food truck and use it as a passport to get through whatever security they have in place.'

Solomon nodded. 'Sounds feasible.'

'We'll need a patsy,' said Oleg. He nodded at the Brazilians. 'Think these guys could enlist the help of a few local kids?'

Solomon shrugged. 'If you show them enough dollar bills.'

Hunter shot the Russian a puzzled look. 'Kids?'

'They are more likely to stop if they believe they've run down a child.'

'Okay, but why the drama,' said Hunter. 'Can't we just force them off the road at gunpoint?'

'We don't know how well these trucks are protected. If they're armored, they'll just plow through us and put every member of their organization on alert. We can't risk losing the element of surprise, John. Our team is too small to risk a full-frontal assault. This is a covert mission designed to dismantle their operation from within.'

Hunter nodded and returned Oleg's water canister. 'So how are we getting to Apuí?' The question needed no answer as the whine of a small, overworked engine reverberated about the clearing. It crescendoed as a three-wheeler tuk-tuk bounced through a gap in the trees, lost its balance and came to a skidding halt on its side.

Solomon helped the driver right the little machine and clambered aboard. 'I know what you're both thinking, and if you prefer to walk, you be my guest.'

Chapter 37

The truck lurched dangerously to one side as its driver slammed on the brakes, bringing the vehicle to a juddering halt. Twenty or so children swarmed the cabin, each of them banging on the doors in mock protest over their fallen peer. Hunter had to give credit where due — the boy's acting skills were impeccable. He took the glancing blow as instructed, vaulting up onto the truck's bonnet and allowing his body to crumple against the windscreen before rolling to the ground. His services hadn't been cheap, but given the risks the youngster faced, justifiable.

'Get out of the cab,' whispered Solomon. He glanced at the wind velocity meter in his hand and took a reading. 'Next to no wind, John. No adjustments needed. Easy shot.'

On the other side of the road, Hunter watched as Oleg broke cover, his long legs eating up the ground. Within seconds, the Russian pressed his back against the truck's rear, just as planned. Timing was everything from here on in. Hunter's grip tightened around his weapon. The VSS Vintorez, or thread cutter as it was unofficially known, suddenly felt twice as heavy as the window for his shot approached. As silenced sniper rifles went, the Soviet-made thread cutter was a decent option — easy to transport, accurate and packed a decent punch. Perfect, bar one concern. He'd never even laid eyes on one, let alone practiced with it on a range. He might be ex-military, but he'd served as an underwater archaeologist in the Royal Navy. A post requiring very little in the way of sniper training. He adjusted his sight and, allowing for the possibility of a strong kickback, tried to relax his upper body. Difficult with his heart rate rising. Missing was not an option. Oleg's life depended on it.

Hunter's index finger twitched, depressing the trigger a little as a silhouette appeared in the window of the passenger door. He regulated his breathing, slowing his heart rate just as he'd been taught on the range during officer training at Dartmouth. Relax, adjust sights, exhale fully, hold, aim, fire… Relax, adjust sights, exhale fully, hold, aim, fire. He kept repeating the mantra over and over. He'd hit his mark that day, but a straw target was a little less intimidating than something soft and fleshy.

The truck's cabin door burst open. It sprang backwards on its hinges and slapped back against the legs of an already infuriated male occupant. The man pushed it aside for a second time, sliding from his seat and onto the potholed tarmac. He was dressed in a basic olive military uniform of indeterminate allegiance. Dark patches under both arms gave away the lack of air conditioning inside the truck and in this heat, it was no wonder the man was already close to breaking point. He raised a handgun and screamed something in Portuguese at the children.

Hunter exhaled and focused on his target. A headshot was too much of a risk, even with no wind to disturb the path of the bullet. He moved the crosshairs toward the heart and his mouth twitched in frustration. The top buttons of the soldier's shirt were undone and the telltale gray of thick Kevlar body armor was on display. He no longer had a choice. Hunter exhaled and returned the crosshairs to the nose.

'Take the shot,' hissed Solomon. 'Oleg is making his move. Take him down.'

Hunter squeezed the trigger. A gunshot reverberated about the clearing and the children scattered. Hunter started, his arm jerking as a solitary bullet flew off target from his silenced barrel. 'Jesus, where did that come from?' His movement was slight, but enough. His target ducked as the glass in the truck's wing mirror shattered into pieces. He swung his handgun in Hunter's direction and grinned, steadying his aim.

Oleg roared a battle cry and charged from his hiding place. The distraction worked as the soldier jerked his gun to meet the new threat. Hunter snapped back into action, lining up his sights for a second time. His target slumped to the ground, a gapping and grizzly wound punched in the side of his head. In a move worthy of Rudolf Nureyev, Oleg deftly avoided the falling body and fired two shots through the open passenger door. He circled his hand above his head, requesting Hunter and Solomon round on his position.

'That was too close,' said Solomon.

'Sorry,' said Hunter, rising from his rooftop position to descend a ladder. 'It's been a while since I've fired a gun, let alone fired with pressure on the shot.'

'What happened?' shouted Oleg as they approached. 'How did you miss?'

'Give me a break; the mark was wearing body armor. Forced me to go for the head.'

'And?' said the Russian. 'He had a head like a melon, and you were only forty yards away. My six-year-old niece could make that shot in her sleep.' He grasped the dead man's arms. 'Help me throw this lump of meat in the back. We need to disappear.'

Hunter tried to avoid staring at the grisly hole in the side of the dead man's head and it took all his self-control to stop himself from vomiting. He gripped the soldier's ankles and helped drag the corpse to the rear of the truck. Solomon swung back the tarp and Hunter noticed his face whiten.

'What?' asked Hunter. 'Have they forgotten the wine you ordered?'

Solomon jabbed a finger into the darkness. In response, a small face appeared in the doorway, its eyes blinking as they adjusted to the bright sunlight.

'Shitting hell, Oleg,' said Hunter. 'We've been tracking the wrong truck?'

More faces joined the child and stared inquisitively at the three men. Then one of them noticed the dead man lying at Hunter's feet and screamed.

Jacob removed his blindfold and stepped from the Land Rover with Wing Commander Kent in tow. This forced collaboration with the British was annoying, but there was no way the RAF would have been so accommodating without the concessions he'd made — one of them being to keep Kent in the loop. He smiled to himself. Not that the Englishman would learn much. The real secrets lay hidden in filing cabinets and computer servers well beyond the bounds of this "orphanage". The RAF would learn nothing of value and, aside from the vague location, possibly nothing more than their intelligence operatives knew already. He'd appease Kent by introducing him to the less invasive end of the research program; the drugs and perhaps the mind manipulation trials — that would be enough.

The door into the domed, gray concrete building opened, and an orderly stepped in front of them, blocking their path.

'Can I see some ID please, sir?'

Jacob passed over his card for scanning. 'This man has visitor's clearance. He is with the British Royal Air Force. Name of Kent.'

'That'll be Wing Commander Kent.' Kent passed over his ID to be checked.

The orderly nodded and beckoned them to follow. 'Please take a seat while your ID is cross-checked. Apologies for the delay, but security has to be pretty tight around here.'

'And I thought this was meant to be an orphanage,' joked Kent.

'It is, sir, but the children we have here are prone to...' The poker-faced orderly pursed his lips. 'Being rather special.'

Jacob glared at Kent as the orderly walked away. 'What are you playing at? You know what goes on here; what's the point of trying to stir up the natives?'

'No point,' said Kent. 'I just wanted to gauge his reaction. I don't suppose they get many visitors here?'

'Are you surprised?' said Jacob. 'This facility contravenes a whole host of international laws. The US can ill afford to be linked to this place in any shape or form. Hell, even I'd be pissed off if I didn't already know the Russians and Chinese are doing the exact same thing.' He pointed at the children's drawings littering the walls. 'This absurd rainforest front and total deniability is the only way we can compete in this new, illegal and politically distasteful arms race.'

'I know, I know,' said Kent. 'I promise I'll behave. So, have you got a plan?'

Jacob let out a long sigh. 'I really don't know. I'm more worried about the possibility of this place being made public. How can we defend a facility that shouldn't exist, a research facility placed beyond our borders so US scientists can conduct illegal human research on our own citizens?'

Kent snorted. 'Slightly ironic, a Russian-sponsored team is on its way to liberate American citizens held captive by American soldiers.'

'True, but don't be fooled. The United States may be in the wrong here...' Kent raised an eyebrow. 'Okay, "is" in the wrong here, but the Russians aren't in Brazil out of the goodness of their hearts. This is win-win for them. They either acquire details of classified research or fail and expose the facility.'

'And in so doing cause worldwide reputational and irreparable political damage.'

Jacob nodded. 'The current government would implode — rioting, looting — who knows the extent of civil unrest. And then there are the sanctions. This could cripple my country for years.'

'A reasonable punishment,' said Kent.

'I cannot allow the mistakes of a few to destroy the lives of millions of innocents. This can be avoided if I simply let them walk away with the research,' said Jacob, a look of defeat on his face.

'Why are you making out this is a tough decision? I mean, realistically, what has this facility achieved in the last half-century? Where are the super soldiers? Where are the robot police officers? At present, this super soldier crap isn't anything more than a lazy plotline for some dubiously titled sci-fi novel? You achieved one result with a midget Jew and he's dead anyway. Personally, I'd be more worried about the technology in that Russkie helicopter.'

Jacob absent-mindedly drummed his fingers on the arm of his chair. 'You might be surprised at just how far we've come, Wing Commander Kent.'

Jacob's attention switched as the orderly reappeared and ushered them forward, his swipe card opening the security door separating them from the test facilities. 'This way please, Colonel. Our orders are to provide Mr. Kent with a quick insight into our work. If interested, I can point you the way of a couple of subjects currently undergoing testing.'

'Excellent,' said Jacob. 'Have the protective measures discussed been put in place? Assuming the facility has not yet been breached.'

'Nothing yet, sir. We are on high alert.' On cue, a pair of armed guards eyeballed the trio with suspicion. The orderly flashed his ID, and they continued with their patrol.

'Very good. How many guards are currently on-site?' asked Kent.

'We have ten, sir.'

'Ten? Doesn't sound like enough,' said Kent.

'Ten is enough,' said the orderly. 'This building is more like a fortified bunker than a research facility. If locked down, no-one can get in or, for that matter, out.'

'If true, why aren't we on lockdown now?'

Jacob grinned. 'Let's just say the powers that be are yet to be convinced of my theory that this place is the target.'

'You sly dog. I guess your plan can't work if they lock the place down?'

Kent raised an eyebrow. 'Careful. The walls have ears.'

The orderly paused outside a plain door. A small square plaque bore the lettering ESP. 'Here we are.' He knocked on the door.

'Enter,' barked a voice from within.

'ESP?' asked Kent.

'Extrasensory perception,' said Jacob.

'You are kidding? I've come all this way to see some idiot guess what card I'm thinking of?'

The orderly pushed open the door to reveal a young boy face to face with an older man, presumably the Doctor, across a desk. He nodded a silent greeting and swiped at a tablet computer in his hand. The boy turned his wire-covered head and stared at them through unblinking eyes. Jacob shuddered as his gaze fell inadvertently on the prominent scalpel scar circumnavigating his head. It was partially obscured by a little hair growth, but certainly not enough that he could rely on for it to be missed. He caught Kent's eye, and the Englishman nodded at the healed wound. He chose to gloss over it.

'What's going on here, Doctor? You'll have to excuse our presence. The high ups have insisted on bringing the Brits on board. Christ knows why. I was led to believe their military didn't have a pot to piss in, let alone enough to join us on this project.'

The Doctor grinned. 'Absolutely fine, Colonel.' He flicked a couple of switches and a projector hidden in the ceiling whirred into life. A playing card appeared on a screen behind the boy's head. Kent raised an eyebrow and shook his head.

'Three of clubs,' said the boy.

The Doctor nodded and four more appeared.

'King of Hearts; six of spades; nine of diamonds.'

'Yes... and finally.'

'Queen of diamonds.'

The Doctor nodded again. 'And that is five in a row.' He looked at Jacob. 'That's odds of just over three hundred and eighty million to one.'

Kent shrugged. 'I've seen this on Britain's got talent. He could be just good at reading you.' The boy turned to face the Englishman. His mannerisms were slow and calculated — almost ethereal. His vacant eyes looked Kent up and down, seemingly unimpressed by the Wing Commander's chiseled features.

'You have a sister. She is unhappy you forgot your nephew's birthday. The PlayStation you have bought is enough to appease him, but she will not forget your oversight.'

Kent shuffled his feet and glanced at Jacob. 'How did you guys... Is this a setup?'

The Doctor laughed. 'There are several clever entertainers around the world who can indeed "read people" and manipulate their actions.' He reset his computer. 'That is not what we are testing here.' He turned to the boy. 'Peter, next three please.'

'Five of clubs, ten of spades, Jack of hearts.'

The Doctor beckoned Jacob to join him at the console. 'Colonel, if you would be so good as to boot up the program again. Please confirm there is no way of me knowing the next three cards and my actions are not being directed or influenced in any way.'

Jacob nodded and double clicked on the program's icon. He looked at Peter, trying to gauge what he might be thinking. 'Where are you from, Peter?'

'D-wing, sir.'

'That's not what I meant...' Jacob paused as Kent nudged him in the ribs.

'He's right, he's predicted all three. How did he... That's crazy.'

'Peter is one of our more reliable pre-cogs.'

Kent frowned. 'Pre-cogs?'

'He has a highly developed propensity for predicting future events. A second sight, if you will.'

Jacob glanced at Kent. 'Are you starting to understand why this facility is so sensitive?'

'Because of his abilities, or because you have clearly opened up his skull?'

The pre-cog shifted his gaze to Jacob and broke the uncomfortable silence. 'The men you are seeking are already here.'

Jacob felt his stomach drop. 'I'm sorry, what?'

The boy turned back to his handler. 'The two academics and the Russian spy are in the building. Death is coming.'

Jacob lunged for the door and wrenched it open.

'Wait,' said Kent, holding him back. 'Is that creepy kid talking about us or them?'

Chapter 38

Hunter stepped from the truck, attempting to retain an air of nonchalance as he glanced at the palm reader in the guard's hand. A second guard raised his gun. This was sickening. His face contorted in disgust and he prayed the guard's focus remained on the tablet. He gingerly lowered his hand, lining it up with the outline flashing on the screen. The seconds ticked by, but nothing happened.

'Jiggle your hand,' said the guard. 'It sometimes does this.'

Hunter shifted back and forth, beads of sweat forming around his person and threatening to give him away. This had to work. They were so close. The scanner beeped and the outline of the hand flashed green.

'Cheers, guys,' said the guard. 'You're clear to proceed.' The second guard lowered his weapon and waved them forward.

Hunter nodded curtly at the two men and, with all the indifference he could muster, turned to board the truck. He slammed the door and slumped down into his seat, finally able to let out the breath he'd been holding. He glanced at Solomon and forced a smile as the facility's security gates swung open. At least this part of the plan was running smoothly.

Oleg revved the engine and forced the truck's gear stick into first. He waved at the guards as though he were delivering nothing more than pizza and accelerated into the compound. The Russian's cool façade was on another level. Hunter only started to relax once their truck disappeared beyond the walls and, more importantly, beyond the view of the guardhouse. He let the severed arm drop from his sleeve, kicking at it with his foot and scrapping it under his seat. He shuddered. 'This better be worth it, Oleg. There's been far too much bloodshed for your cause already.'

Oleg hit the brakes, and the truck rolled to a stop. 'Believe me, Hunter; there will be a hell of a lot more if our mission fails.'

A fist thumped the driver's door. 'Come on, pop the trunk. What are you waiting for? The subjects must be cooking in their skins. It's just about dinner time so I'll just take them straight to the mess hall.' Hunter eased the door open and jumped to the concrete floor. He rounded the truck and nodded at the female orderly dressed head to toe in white cotton.

'So?' she asked. 'Why so late? The other two came and went a good hour ago.'

'We had a flat,' said Hunter, thinking quickly. 'These roads are murder.'

Her eyes narrowed. 'But the tires are run-flat, you aren't meant to stop for any...' The women's final words were muffled as Oleg covered her mouth with a chloroform-soaked rag, and she crumpled into his arms.

'Close call, Hunter,' said the Russian. 'Any chance of a little more warning next time you fancy trying to blow our cover?'

'Oh, come on, how was I to know those tires were run-flats?' said Hunter. 'Anyway, no real harm done.'

Oleg withdrew the orderly's hand from her pocket. A small pen-like device dropped from her limp fingers. A ring of red light flashed intermittently about a depressed button.

'No harm done you say,' said Solomon. 'Oleg, shove her under the truck. We need to get out of here right now.'

Oleg glared at Hunter. 'Agreed. It's down to you now, Sol. Time for you to come into your own. You know this layout better than anyone.'

'I'm sorry what? What do you mean by that comment?' said Hunter, stepping in line behind his two companions. 'Why would you know the layout?' Solomon reached under the truck and, with a grunt of triumph, reappeared with the orderly's swipe card. Hunter frowned, determined to press the point. 'What are you holding back this time?' Solomon ignored him and started for the door. 'Solomon?'

The Professor paused and turned his head. 'Okay, okay - I may have acted in an advisory capacity when this place was rebuilt.'

'You may have acted in an advisory capacity?' Hunter stopped in his tracks. He didn't think Solomon could have surprised him anymore than he already had, but he was wrong. 'Who the hell are you? And why have you waited until now to tell me this?'

'The less you know, the less you can give up under duress — and don't judge me too harshly. I wasn't told what this place was to be used for.' He sighed. 'Short story, the powers that be kept tabs on me post-Roswell; first, simply to monitor my mouth, but as my career developed, they developed an interest in my research, particularly around the significance of acoustics in ancient Egyptian architecture. Sorry, John, I should have told you.'

'No, you obeyed your orders,' said Oleg. 'Nothing wrong with that. Moreover, why should you have been told, Hunter? There are no advantages, only downsides.'

'No advantages. Fuck you, Oleg.'

'I'm actually surprised someone of your supposed intelligence didn't put two and two together anyway. Didn't you ever question why Solomon was a member of this team?'

'It crossed my mind,' said Hunter. 'I just assumed you used him to get to me.'

Oleg cocked his head to one side. 'Well, yes, but more than that, he's my guide. Now get moving - unless you fancy making this loading bay your ultimate resting place.'

Solomon scurried to the compound entrance and swiped the stolen key card. A light above the door flashed green, and the door clicked open. 'I'm sorry, John. There's so much more I wish I could tell you.'

'Just get inside,' said Oleg. 'We haven't got time for this shit. Hunter's son needs freeing and the records must be retrieved or destroyed. Remember, this is about the prevention of a global war. Your petty squabbles mean nothing in the grand scheme of things.'

'We can do this later,' said Solomon.

'Fine, but what about the kids in the truck?'

'But nothing,' said Oleg. 'Someone will be along soon to check out the alarm. They'll sort them out. And if it's the morality of leaving them, forget it. If all goes according to plan, they won't be here long. It's the ones inside you should be worried about.'

'Whatever, just take me to my son. If he's alive and I can do something to save him, then at least some good can come of this mess.'

Hunter pushed past Solomon, through the door and into the space beyond. His stomach took an instant dive, and he pressed himself against the nearest wall as a surge of acrophobia engulfed him. He rarely feared heights, but this was far from normal. He looked down and instantly regretted it. The see-through, wrought iron walkway supporting his weight was hundreds of feet above the ground. So high that it wasn't obvious there was any ground below in the gloom. He took a breath and, making sure not to dip his head, looked forward at the white wall beyond the railing. Hunter's left eye twitched as his brain assessed the incredible scene opening up in front of him. This was no wall, this was the peak of an enormous, brilliant white, underground limestone pyramid. 'My god, Solomon. Was this you?'

Somewhere to his left, he heard the Professor chuckle. 'Now you can understand why I couldn't say no. Impressive, isn't she? Amazing what can be achieved with a limitless budget.'

Hunter dared to once more look into the abyss beneath his feet, following the angled sides of the monument to their end and forgetting his fear. 'Is this a replica...'

'Yup, the Great Pyramid of Giza... Stone for stone.'

He blew the breath from his lungs and grasped Solomon's arm. 'This is madness. Stone for stone you say?'

Oleg shoved Hunter aside, knocking him back against the wall. 'Yes, stone for stone. What are you, deaf? We've got to get moving. We aren't bloody tourists, and there's no time to gawk at the pretty building.'

Hunter scowled and ignored the Russian's plea. This was an incredible feat, and one may be equal to its Egyptian counterpart simply because it was underground. Egypt's Great Pyramid was nearly one hundred and fifty meters high and built from about five and a half million tons of limestone and eight thousand tons of granite. Even with modern technology, the logistics in constructing such a building in a rainforest environment were almost unfathomable. 'Did you recreate all the internal chambers?'

'You'll see for yourself. We're heading for the King's Chamber,' said Solomon, moving down the walkway and pulling Hunter along with him.

'My son is in the King's Chamber?'

Oleg nodded. 'Yes, my informers tell me his brain is one of only a few who can operate the chamber with any degree of success.'

'Operate it? Jesus, just exactly what theory of yours are they testing, Sol?'

Solomon rubbed at his face but refused to make eye contact. Whatever he was hiding, it can't have been good. Hunter let the silence press him into answering. 'Okay, but you can probably guess,' he said finally, buckling under the pressure. 'I was engaged to advise on the acoustical properties of the Great Pyramid and the effects they might have on the human mind. The King's Chamber obviously took center stage.'

Hunter took a sharp breath. It was well documented the King's Chamber possessed special acoustic properties, and he'd attended numerous lectures on the subject, some given by Solomon himself. If he remembered rightly, the local Arab guides used to hit the sarcophagus and make it ring as far back as the 1600s. 'The sarcophagus?' asked Hunter.

'Not just the sarcophagus,' said Solomon. 'The entire structure holds onto sound better than Carnegie Hall. Voices or even footsteps can make the chamber resonate in harmony throughout its length. I found a musical note whose resonance was so startling it scared the wits out of several of my students. Some even ran for the exit.'

'Really? You've never told me that anecdote.' said Hunter.

'It was weird, that's why. The rock literally shifted under us. One student even lost his footing, and all I did was pluck a G-string on a double bass.'

Hunter frowned, not yet convinced. 'Have you built this version using all the same materials?'

'To the last pyramid inch,' said Solomon, with a twinkle in his eye. 'The granite is the key though — as a quartz-bearing rock, it is renowned for its relationship with sound.'

'And you actually still believe these vibrations can send someone into a trance? Or open the mind, or whatever it is you believe?' With no answer forthcoming, Hunter took the opportunity to gaze about the massive cavern once more, taking in the sheer scale of the remarkable endeavor. A dark dome sat atop the pyramid's peak, dark and foreboding. Probably concrete covered by tons of earth and forest debris to disguise the extent of what lay beneath. A circular hole had been punched into its center, possibly for ventilation or perhaps to allow the tip to protrude. At the pyramid's base, he could see a series of spotlights but they barely penetrated the darkness. The only actual light came from the row of windows cut into the wall surrounding the structure. They appeared to be a mixture of labs, offices, and residential quarters. Solomon's back momentarily obscured his view and brought Hunter's train of thought back to their conversation. 'I thought you dropped this line of research years ago. It was never exactly credible was it?'

'And your Atlantis research was I suppose?' It was a low blow, but fair. Hunter wasn't exactly in a position to preach about acceptable subjects in academia. After all, not too long ago his own theories resulted in him being removed from his Cambridge post. 'I never dropped it, John. I proved it; proved it inside this pyramid with pages of irrefutable proof. Although I never understood the how and the why, I can tell you without a doubt that vibrations elicited through something as simple as repetitive chanting can induce an altered state of consciousness.'

Hunter shook his head in disbelief. 'Are you suggesting the Egyptians built this thing as some kind of grandiose crack pipe or an ancient alternative to LSD?'

Solomon turned his head and grinned at Hunter. 'God, no, merely an unexpected benefit I expect enjoyed, and therefore recorded by the high-ranking priests of the time. No, the truth is I don't believe the Egyptians even knew what they were building. Something else was at work here.'

'Aliens,' whispered Hunter, mocking his former mentor.

Solomon shrugged, the shrug not the action of someone dismissing the possibility. 'Maybe. It is bizarre, but the frequencies the chamber responds to best are far beyond the scope of a mere human voice. There is still so much more to discover about this structure; so much that I doubt it will ever yield all its secrets. The chamber's architecture suggests far grander ambitions than mere mind alteration, ambitions which for whatever reason have never been fully realized.'

'What do you mean by that?' said Hunter, stumbling as they hit a set of downward steps just as he attempted to match Solomon's pace.

'Off the top of my head, think about the four roofs stacked one on top of the other above the King's Chamber. They alone comprise twelve hundred tons of granite. Twelve hundred tons which, from an engineering point of view, are not required structurally.' He paused and glanced at Hunter. 'So why are they there?'

Hunter shrugged. 'Decoration?'

'Maybe you're right, and to be fair no worse than any other guess, but for now, it remains one of the pyramid's many mysteries lost to father time.' The walkway suddenly deviated ninety degrees and Hunter once again grabbed hold of a handrail, his legs refusing to carry him further. The empty space engulfed his senses and all he could focus on was falling. He fell to his knees and felt Solomon's rough hands pull him back upright.

'For Christ's sake, Solomon. You didn't tell me he'd be this much of a liability.' Oleg's voice broke the silence and grasped Hunter under the other arm and together the two eldest members of the group pulled him toward the small entranceway cut into the limestone. They arrived out of breath and dropped him to the floor. Oleg glanced at Solomon. 'It's down to you now, old man. Destiny awaits. Now, where do we go?'

Chapter 39

Hunter ducked and entered the badly lit entrance. He blinked as his eyes adjusted to the gloom and noticed the trails of LED lights lining the passage. He stroked the smooth reddish-pink granite walls with his fingertips, impressed by the level of workmanship. Surely this can't be the same rock quarried from Aswan. Did that mean the highly desirable White Tura-limestone coated the pyramid's surface? If so, the budget must truly have been limitless. If his calculations were correct, the three of them must have just entered the northern entrance to the Great Pyramid. Hunter crouched down and tentatively moved forward, smiling as he felt the passage slope underfoot. He adjusted his balance to compensate for the angle and eased his body through the three-foot square passage. Somewhere ahead he heard an expletive as Oleg tumbled in the tight space and Hunter turned on his torch, catching his companions untangling themselves in its beam. Gingerly, he continued his descent, joining them as the passage opened up a little and split into two.

'Which way?' said Oleg.

Solomon glanced at the first of the identical granite corridors, and then at the second. He needed to get his bearings, thought Hunter. There were no clues as to the correct choice — even the limestone mortar patterns seemed indistinguishable from the other. 'The first continues towards a reconstruction of the Subterranean Chamber,' said Solomon with confidence.

'And the other leads us back up into the pyramid's heart,' said Hunter, 'taking us past the Queen's Chamber and onto the King's Chamber beyond.'

Solomon nodded. 'There always used to be a soldier posted at the next junction. I suggest you both be on your guard.'

'Just one,' said Oleg. 'Shouldn't pose too much of a prob...'

A piercing scream interrupted the Russian, and Hunter froze in his tracks. The distinct sound of footfalls approached their position. They were approaching fast, the owner of the feet evidently running, and running hard. Oleg positioned his torch alongside the barrel of his handgun and pointed it toward the sound. Hunter caught a fleeting glance of a lab coat, brilliant white against dark granite. This was no threat. Instinctively, he shoved Oleg's arm to one side. A shot rang out, the sound reverberating through the Pyramid, its report worthy of Thor's hammer. Hunter fell to his knees, tinnitus ringing painfully in his ears. He glanced up, raising an arm as the lab coat, still looking in the other direction, rammed into him.

They crashed to the roughened granite floor together, and Hunter caught a glimpse of the man's manic, blood-spattered face in the flickering torchlight. He wore an expression of wide-eyed horror, an expression chilling Hunter to his very core. The scientist's eyes were wild in their sockets, his gaze darting furtively about the passageway, searching for an escape.

The man grabbed Hunter's shirt and leaned into his ear. 'He's dead... they're all dead.' A second shot shattered the silence and the scientist's head exploded, splattering Hunter's cheek in gore. Oleg grabbed a handful of Hunter's hair and pulled him upright, pinning him to the wall with his forearm. The Russian pulled Hunter's gun from its holster. 'Do that again, Dr Hunter, and my next bullet will be between your eyes.'

Hunter tried but failed to shove the larger man away. He nodded at the dead man lying at their feet. 'Fuck you, Oleg. You want to shoot me, then shoot me. This man was unarmed and posed no threat.'

'Not true,' said Oleg, releasing him. 'Now he poses no threat. You'll do well to remember this is not a civilian facility. Everything and everyone is a threat.' He pulled Hunter's lapels and shoved him down the corridor. 'Now move before I shoot you anyway.'

Hunter stumbled into the semi-darkness and exchanged a glance with Solomon. 'Is this what you signed up for? These are your own people this man is slaughtering.'

'I said move,' said Oleg, raising his gun.

'Please, John, let this go,' said Solomon. 'If this man had escaped the pyramid, the entire facility would now be on lockdown. We'd be dead men walking.'

Hunter scowled at Oleg and reluctantly continued, straining to discover the source of the dead man's anguish. But the pyramid was as quiet as the tomb it was meant to be. Whatever spooked the scientist had apparently disappeared or at least chosen not to pursue. Oleg urged him onward with the barrel of his gun. He grudgingly complied but took it slow. Who knew what lay at the end of the trail, and caution seemed the more sensible course of action.

Hunter paused, stopping in his tracks as a repetitive banging sound cut through the silence. He strained his eyes, focusing on the never-ending darkness lying beyond the range of his torch. 'What's that?' Solomon shrugged as the noise faded.

'It's gone now, so who cares? Move your butt,' said Oleg.

'If you don't care, maybe you should be out in front,' said Hunter, continuing the ascent with added caution. The rebuttal was ignored, and they continued in silence until the passage opened up and split for a second time. Hunter paused to stare down the route boasting a level walkway. 'Why can't they be hanging out down there in the Queen's chamber? Walking at this angle is playing havoc on my shins.'

Solomon lowered himself to the floor for a brief rest, his breathing labored after the climb. 'The King's Chamber lies on the other side of the galley. We're not far off now.'

Hunter stared into the darkness ahead of them as the banging noise started up again. 'The point of no return and that damn banging is back. What the hell is it?' He shot Oleg a suspicious look. 'Or do you already know? What are these people doing to my boy?'

'Expect the worst,' said Oleg. 'They've employed an expert in this field.'

'An expert in what field? Banging pans?' Hunter grinned to himself and rolled his eyes as the Russian raised his gun in response, aiming at his midriff. 'Come on, do you really think that thing is necessary? Where do you think I'm going to go?'

'Sorry, John, but after your little stunt, I will not give you even the sniff of a chance to compromise this mission.'

'Surely there's a better chance of succeeding if I'm armed as well, or...'

Oleg pressed the barrel of his Glock into Hunter's stomach. 'Just keep walking.'

He obeyed but paced himself to take in the majesty of the Grand Gallery. Solomon's reconstruction was exquisite. As good as the original, and given its lack of use and maltreatment, possibly better. In keeping with the original, bar the swirling patterns indicative of rose granite, the dim strip-lights lining each passage served only to highlight the bizarre lack of any decoration. Unlike the tombs littering the Valley of the Kings, the pyramids contained no type of art, even devoid of the hieroglyphic inscriptions so prevalent in tombs during this period in Egyptian history. It was certainly not what one might expect to find when entering a structure allegedly erected to house a deceased pharaoh. Then again, Solomon, along with many others, didn't believe the King's Chamber ever actually housed the body of Khufu, the pharaoh often associated with building the Great Pyramid. If true, it would certainly go some way towards explaining why the innards of the pyramid had not been decorated.

Hunter scrambled forward, pleased as the depth of the passage finally rose enough to allow him to stand without a stoop. Almost immediately, it sloped away; disappearing into an inky black void above him. He swept his torch beam around the space, revealing the high and imposing ceiling of the Grand Galley. It was an inspiring build and not for the first time, he wondered how such an ancient civilization could have created such a mighty structure. Surely not with mere ropes and pulleys? It seemed unfathomable — the sheer amount of rock quarried, shaped and shifted to create just this single pyramid was mind-blowing on its own. Almost six million tons, if he remembered correctly. And they'd built three in this location alone and over a hundred more along the course of the Nile.

He stopped in his tracks as an unfamiliar voice jolted him from his thoughts and back into the here and now. 'Stay back — just stay back.' It seemed to come from the King's Chamber. He looked over his shoulder at Oleg. The Russian put a finger to his lips and pointed at the chamber entrance. Hunter grimaced and headed for the doorway where the floor finally leveled out and crouched down as directed. Oleg mirrored him and slumped down on the opposite side. The tension was palpable, and they both jumped as something wet slapped hard against the rock floor in the chamber beyond. It sounded close. Hunter risked a quick look and immediately pulled back, holding back vomit. It was a body, the blood fresh and pooling about its recently severed head.

***

Jacob checked the number of rounds in the magazine of his M11 pistol. The brushed metal tips of the thirteen 9 X19 Parabellum cartridges glinted in the spotlights illuminating the pyramid's entrance. He shoved the magazine inside the handgun with a satisfying click and watched as Kent did the same.

'This complex is crazy,' said Kent. 'How the hell can your government justify building a full-scale replica of an Egyptian pyramid?'

Jacob smiled. 'Don't be so naïve. The White House knows nothing. They just agree the $40 billion budget and away we go. Black operations are never made public for national security reasons. There is no oversight and no culpability... and this place... this place is as black as they come.'

Kent nodded. 'And you are lucky enough to be in the loop.' He looked toward the pyramid's summit. 'So what are you expecting to find inside this monstrosity?'

Jacob wiped a few stray beads of sweat from his forehead. 'A patient.'

Kent narrowed his eyes in disbelief. 'You can't be serious? Singular? Just one patient? Then why are we waiting for backup? Surely the two of us can handle one man.'

'Even with backup, I'm not convinced we can handle this particular man,' said Jacob. 'And don't forget our three intruders. They're in there somewhere.'

'Two academics and a pensionable ex-squaddie. Forgive me if they aren't making me quiver in fear.' Kent ran a hand through his hair and flicked off the safety on his gun. 'Can you tell me what this particular patient can do? I'm assuming it's a little more than guessing my birthday.'

'A little more, yes.' Jacob blew the breath from his lungs. 'Wing Commander, you are about to come face to face with the world's first successful incarnation of a super-soldier.'

Kent raised an eyebrow. 'You succeeded? Why didn't you say earlier? What can he do, fly or something?'

'No, he can't fly — not yet anyway,' said Jacob, without a hint of humor. 'He's much stronger than the average male. This was expected, but...' He paused, as if unable to find the words. 'Look, I don't know how much your intelligence services know about the Roswell test subject. Are you aware he evolved an ability to manipulate his surroundings?'

'I heard the rumors. Is it true he can deviate the path of a bullet?'

Jacob nodded. 'More than that, he could redirect them. The USAF lost a few good men in a shoot-out at Roswell when our guest escaped. His power didn't stop him from getting shot though, but I believe that was more to do with the number of projectiles fired at him.'

'Guest is such a pleasant and unassuming way to describe someone you imprisoned for the entirety of their natural life.' Jacob broke eye contact and looked at the floor. 'Theirs is not to reason why...'

'Theirs is but to do or die. Tennyson,' said Kent with a derisive snort. 'Impressive... and I thought you were just another illiterate red neck.' He shuffled his feet. 'Although who am I to judge? I doubt my paymasters would have done anything differently.' He changed the subject. 'Are you thinking this patient of yours has the same ability?'

Pleased he'd not been forced to defend the indefensible, Jacob forced a smile. 'He's not quite at the same level, but he's evolving. He can already occupy the minds of his enemies and control their actions. It started as a means of non-verbal communication but he's already weaponized the technique. I advocated assassination, but the CIA believe him to be the future of covert soldiering. The potential of occupying the minds of a few foreign leaders is seemingly worth a few American lives.'

Kent shrugged. 'I get it, though. Imagine controlling the orders and speeches given by Putin, for example. With great power comes great responsibility, and all that. So, you Americans really are intending to play judge, jury and executioner to the world.' He shook his head. 'It's not really a surprise the Russians are trying to stop you.'

'Which I can understand,' said Jacob. 'But it works both ways. There is no way we can allow the Russians to leave this base and use our own weapon against us.'

'How did they find out?'

'The Russian guy was on our payroll,'

Kent shook his head. 'You couldn't write this. Did you really hire an ex Russian soldier and not expect him to be a spy?'

'He doesn't, or at least didn't, know everything,' said Jacob, his sharp reply coming over as a little too defensive. 'Unfortunately, our Roswell friend filled several blanks by hacking our computer systems. They still have gaps in their knowledge, but that's how they discovered the location of this place.'

'How are the two academics involved?'

Kent snorted. 'It's almost laughable, but the older one was involved in the initial build of this place. His link to the Russian came via a successful conspiracy to break into a high-security Russian base. They stole what they thought was alien technology.'

'The ship they crashed into the Solent?'

'The very same,' said Jacob. 'America offered the Russian asylum and a post overseeing the USA's attempt to recreate the technology.'

'And it turns out he was a double agent all this time.'

'I know,' said Jacob. 'Shocking abuse of our trust.'

'I'm sure you have one or two in the Kremlin yourself.'

Startled, Jacob lifted his M11 as a blood-curdling scream echoed down the passageway. 'What the hell...' He clasped his hands to his ears as a thunderclap followed the scream. 'That was a gunshot?' He looked at Kent. 'I don't think we can wait for backup. We've got to deal with this now or risk losing the asset.'

The pair dove inside the dark entrance as a second shot reverberated through the pyramid.

Chapter 40

The banging stopped and a voice, devoid of emotion, broke the silence. 'It is okay for the three of you to enter, the subject is sedated.'

Hunter glanced at Solomon and whispered, 'What's going on now? Who's speaking? Do you know him?' The Professor shrugged. Oleg took a different tack and smiled, standing to dust himself down. Without warning, he grabbed Hunter's arm and yanked him inside the chamber.

Hunter lost his footing and fell, jarring his back on the granite surface. He lifted his head, taking in his new surroundings and the majesty of the duplicate King's Chamber. The room was rectangular and entirely lined and roofed with smooth granite. He knew the measurements by heart and didn't doubt they'd been replicated to the millimeter; 10.45 meters by 5.20 meters, and 5.80 meters high. Built to resist the enormous pressure of the weight above, it was, and still stands as an impressive feat of architecture, its flat roof fending off over four hundred tons of masonry. It is to support this weight that traditional theorists attribute the existence of the five "relieving" chambers above the ceiling. However, others like Solomon believe this is too simplistic an explanation and claim the chambers are not structural.

He raised his head and saw the red granite sarcophagus and alleged resting place of Khufu. Estimated to weigh about 3.75 tons, it followed the design of the time, a flat-sided box with an indentation inside to support the lid. However, like the original, the sides were not finished to the same meticulous standards as the rest of the pyramid. The reason is unknown, but it suggested they did not lay the Pharaoh to rest in this location. Two stone-topped rectangular tables stood out as the only anomaly at the room's center. He raised a brow, wondering why they were there, interfering with what was otherwise a perfect reconstruction.

'Dr Josef Mengele,' said Oleg. 'Meet Dr John Hunter.'

Hunter grimaced, partly registering the pain from his fall but partly because he recognized the name. Diverting his focus, he could make out a pair of brown shoes perched behind what looked like a trolley one might find next to a dentist's chair. 'Josef Mengele? It can't be,' he whispered, the name finally registering. 'The Nazi angel of death.'

A stocky, dark-haired man stepped from the shadows. 'The angel you reference would be my father.' The corners of his mouth twitched, hinting at a smile. 'I am the less infamous, Josef junior.'

Less infamous was an understatement. Mengele senior was a German SS officer and the senior physician in the Auschwitz concentration camp during the Second World War. His name had been high on the Allies' most wanted list because of his penchant for human experimentation — experimentation that more often than not resulted in the death of his subjects. He enjoyed the tag, "the angel of death," so given due to his insistence in selecting test subjects immediately upon their disembarkation from the Auschwitz trains. His starched white physician's coat distinguishing him as an 'angel' when set against the drab clothing worn by the Jewish prisoners around him. From what Hunter remembered from his history books, the man was particularly partial to twins. Hunter's blood ran cold — Twins...

'I thought Mengele only had one son?' Hunter searched for the name. 'Raif, Rolk?'

'Rolf,' said Mengele, spitting out the name. 'Bastard denounced us and ratted father out to the papers. He kept my existence a secret. Now there are so few survivors left to care, for I have chosen to reclaim his name. I'm proud to be a Mengele. I shouldn't have to hide it.'

Hunter pushed onto his haunches. 'You're proud to be associated with a known child murderer and war criminal? Do you have any idea what he did during the war?'

Josef junior cocked his head and exchanged a smirk with Oleg. 'Mr... Hunter was it? My father did his duty.' He paused for effect, flapping his lab coat in a manner his father was once famed for. 'And in doing so made advances in the field of genetics and transplantation that many modern research facilities would kill for.'

'An apt turn of phrase,' said John, ignoring the jibe at his title.

'Granted, his methods were sometimes crude.' Mengele stared at Hunter, his icy blue eyes devoid of any emotion or guilt. 'But they achieved results.'

'Sometimes crude! Are you mad? He killed every patient he experimented on.'

'Don't be so naïve, human experimentation is still a daily occurrence. I could name labs in North Korea, Africa and parts of the Near East whose activities make mine look like daycare. Hell, historically it wasn't long ago the so-called "first world countries" tested the effects of biological and chemical weapons on live subjects. I'm talking Japan, the Soviet Union and if you look carefully, you may even find evidence of the involvement of the good old Uncle Sam.'

Hunter didn't know what to say. He couldn't prove or disprove the assertions. 'Is this how your father justified his crimes to you?'

'Just how do you think the world's military learnt to combat chemical weapons, Hunter?' Josef punched a clenched fist into his other hand. 'Trial and error, that's how. This facility saves lives. You may not find our methods ethical, but I'm happy to sacrifice the few to save the many. Countless soldiers survive as a direct result of the research carried out in our laboratories.'

'Are you seriously justifying the murder of all the children you ship in here?' Hunter stepped forward and into Mengele's personal space, the red mist descending. 'Including the murder of my own children?'

'Fuck you, Hunter,' Mengele shoved him in the chest, forcing him backwards. 'My conscience is clear. I play the odds for the good of the majority, not the few. As for your "children," you didn't even know they existed a week ago.'

'Well said,' interrupted Oleg. 'Come on, Hunter, don't forget who's been keeping your son alive all these years. Without Josef, the boy would have been on the streets, probably offering his body for a cheap high.'

Hunter lunged at the Russian, swinging a wild punch at the older man's jaw. Oleg batted the strike away, bashing the butt of his handgun hard against Hunter's temple. The archaeologist's legs crumpled, and the room faded to black, two pinpricks of light all that separated him from unconsciousness. He shook his head and his faculties stabilized, yet not enough to retaliate. Hunter felt his body rise as rough hands lifted him from the ground and dropped him onto a hard, cold surface. He felt an edge with his hands. Was he on one of the two tables? Oleg's face loomed into focus and he yelped as a stinging slap reinvigorated his groggy senses.

'What the hell? What was that for?' He moved to retaliate and failed. His left wrist was bound. The Russian pulled a second leather strap about Hunter's right wrist, and he saw a malicious pleasure in the man's eyes. A thicker strap was pulled taut across his chest and two more secured his ankles. Hunter felt akin to an extra in a cheap hammer horror; Mengele playing the part of the stereotypical shrink threatening electro-shock therapy amid a thunderstorm.

He pulled at his bonds and noticed Solomon in his peripheral vision, cowering in the shadows. 'Get these bastards off me! Why are you just standing there like some kind of fucking lemon?'

The Professor looked shell-shocked, his jaw locked in a perpetual state of shocked disbelief. He blinked and shuddered, jerked back into reality by Hunter's voice. 'Oleg, what the hell are you doing?' he shouted. 'He's been nothing but willing so far. You only need a little blood for this to work.'

Hunter looked up at the Russian, confused as a final strap slapped against his forehead. The rough leather bit into his skin, locking his head in place. Oleg winked and pulled his handgun free of its holster. 'I think we've all had enough of your mentor.'

'Sol, watch...' The warning arrived too late. Oleg found his target and fired. A rasping scream filled the chamber and Hunter heard a heavy body crumple to the floor.

'Sorry, Solomon, but your ride is ending here,' said Oleg.

'What are you doing?' said Mengele. 'Garnett was mine. Remember our deal?'

'I know what I'm doing,' said Oleg. 'It's not fatal... look.' There was the sound of a boot meeting flesh, and Solomon let out a second cry of labored pain.

'Traitor. What deal?' said Solomon, his voice strained. He coughed and spat blood. 'We need to destroy this facility for the good of mankind. We cannot allow... this technology... to escape this place. You can't give this to Russia.'

Oleg reached down and pulled something from Solomon's jacket. He must have removed his gun, thought Hunter. 'Who said I was?' He laughed. 'Putin is no better than Stalin. Give him the means to conquer, and he will. I love my country, but this weird communist oligarchical cross they've adopted is bull-crap.'

'What's the end-game, Oleg? What deal have you made?' said Hunter. 'Steal whatever this is, sell it to the highest bidder and retire to some sun-soaked rock in the Pacific.'

'Not a bad idea, John, but no.' said Oleg, returning to the table. 'I have no need for money.'

'So, what then? Is it power? Let me guess, you want to conquer the world?' Hunter wrenched in vain, pulling against the straps holding him down. 'Try it — you wouldn't survive the night.'

Oleg grinned. 'You'll have to take this up with Dr Mengele. I honestly don't care what he does afterwards.'

'Afterwards?' said Hunter.

'After I'm saved,' said Oleg.

'Saved?' said Solomon.

Mengele laughed and stepped into Hunter's eye line, tutting. 'Have you not guessed? Your friend is dying. Poor man is riddled with cancer. It's a minor miracle he's made it this far.' Hunter narrowed his eyes in disbelief.

'It's true,' said Oleg. 'I met Dr Mengele in Area 51 a few years back. I'd just been diagnosed and his work pricked my interest into disease prevention for soldiers in the field. He told me of his father's work and how he'd discovered a way of fighting diseased cells simply by harnessing the power of the mind.'

It was Hunter's turn to laugh. 'And so you bought into the lies of this snake-oil salesman?'

Oleg raised an eyebrow and nodded. 'You're right, I did, and he's since admitted to talking the purest form of bullshit.' Mengele shuffled uncomfortably under Oleg's fierce gaze. 'Turns out he was just making a good old-fashioned play for additional funding. He'd heard of my misfortune and took full advantage.'

'And yet you continue to trust him? You are a fool,' mumbled Solomon.

Oleg bristled at the comment and kicked out again, silencing the Professor. 'Let's just say I uncovered elements of truth to his claims and one procedure in particular.' He pointed his gun at Mengele. 'Junior agreed to help me carry out the procedure, but with a couple of caveats.'

Hunter looked at Mengele. 'And I was one of them?'

'Oh no, Dr Hunter, you misunderstand.' Oleg grinned, tapping Hunter's forehead with the barrel of his handgun. 'You're here for me.' He jabbed a thumb in the Professor's direction. 'Solomon is here to pay off my medical bills.'

'Me?' Solomon coughed again. He sounded awful and close to losing consciousness. 'Why? I don't even know this man.'

Hunter twisted his head, fighting against the strap to watch the broad-shouldered Russian crouch beside his old supervisor. 'You should never have told me, Solomon.' The Professor cried out as Oleg patted his wound and shoved him to the floor. He turned to Hunter and shook his head. 'This old fool has kept you in the dark about many things, John. Such a shameful abuse of trust.' He playfully slapped Hunter's cheek. 'Do you recall his little aside about frightening some students inside the Great Pyramid?'

'Oleg, no,' said Solomon, his legs collapsing under him as he tried to find his feet.

Oleg tutted and shook his head. 'Naughty boy, Solomon. Didn't your mother teach you to tell the truth?' Hunter fought against the strap as the Russian stroked his forehead, his clammy touch making him feel sick. 'When Solomon told you he was given unprecedented access to the Giza Pyramid, he really did mean unprecedented. The Egyptians even granted him the right to lift the sarcophagus. Three point seven five tons of red granite — no mean feat.' He paused and acknowledged the dying archaeologist. 'Tell him what you found, Sol. Tell us all what you found?'

'Don't do this, Oleg. You don't know what you are doing.'

Oleg kicked Solomon in the ribs. 'He found the key, Dr Hunter, the key to unlocking the secrets of this chamber.' He kicked him again, harder this time. 'But instead of revealing the secret like a good little archaeologist, he hid it away and kept it for himself.'

Solomon wiped bloody spittle from his mouth and, tapping into what must have been his final energy reserves, got to his feet. 'And for good reason. The information is too dangerous to be publicized.'

'Yet you recreated it within this very structure. Apparently not so dangerous when the US government is lining your pockets I guess.'

'What have you done, Solomon?' whispered Hunter.

'Forgive me, John, I did not know.' He wobbled and took a forward step. 'I've been played.'

Hunter closed his eyes, fearing the answer, but knowing he needed full disclosure. 'Solomon, tell me what you've built?'

'The Great Pyramid...' said Solomon, pausing in ultimate defeat, '...was built as a giant acoustical key.'

'A key doesn't sound so bad. What does it open?' asked Hunter.

'Revelation thirteen one.' Solomon whispered.

'I stood upon the sand of the sea,' said Oleg, his voice booming about the silent chamber. 'And saw a beast rise up out of the sea, having seven heads and ten horns, and upon his horns ten crowns, and upon his heads the name of blasphemy.'

Hunter swallowed. It was a Bible passage he knew well; a passage often cited as a reference to the apocalypse, the second coming of a lost civilization and the rebirth of a civilization or city conspiracy that theorists the world over know as Atlantis...

Chapter 41

Hunter's head was reeling; he'd been caught up in a scenario involving supposed Atlantean technology before and knew it was something not to be trifled with. The now notorious criminal, Hans Hoffmann, employed him to research and unearth an ancient weapon of mass destruction. Although the weapon turned out to be nothing more than a library, the papers which Hunter uncovered shocked the religious world to its core. The incident placed him on the radar of a clandestine group formed in the wake of the fall of Atlantis, the Order of Atum-Ra. In an act of self-preservation, they threw money at the situation, branded him a fraud and discredited all his finds, leaving him to languish in academic obscurity. Could they be involved here?

'If you set this thing off, you will destroy humanity,' said Solomon, holding the gunshot wound, blood oozing through his fingers. 'What has this idiot told you? Because whatever it is, Oleg, they have misled you. You're literally tying a bow on the world's big red button and handing it over. This place isn't what I thought; what we thought. It must be destroyed.'

'Ignore the old fool,' said Mengele, dismissing Solomon's rhetoric with a flick of his wrist. 'This structure will expand your mind beyond the realms of self. It'll make you stronger and fitter than you could ever conceive, furnishing you with a level of power limited only by your imagination. You saw what the Roswell freak was capable of - imagine that tenfold.'

'Fake news,' Solomon grunted. 'He needs you to activate and channel the pyramid's power downward. You're a sacrifice, Oleg, nothing more. I was wrong to help build this place. It does not have the security of Giza. We didn't recreate the water-filled tunnels they have in Egypt. I made a grave mistake in underestimating their significance.' Solomon was panting, the blood loss affecting his speech and making him slur his words. 'You must believe me, Oleg. Yes, the Giza complex was built to raise Atlantis, but here... here, nothing more than global catastrophe will result.'

'Then why continue to build it?' snapped Hunter, a flash of anger sparking in his eyes. Solomon had dropped the ball here and maybe paying the ultimate price was what he deserved.

'I only continued the mind expansion program. Mengele is correct; with the right subject, the chamber can activate nearly 60% of the human brain. No one has come close to results on that scale. The average human can only access 10%.'

'So, nothing to do with a sacrifice.' Oleg snorted in disgust and patted Solomon's head. 'You really need to keep your story straight. Now be a good boy and tell my friend here exactly how to activate the features you held back.'

'You must be joking,' said Solomon. 'You may be an idiot, but I won't see you killed for it. Oleg, please stop this. You haven't got the right genetics to survive.'

Oleg slapped Solomon derogatorily round the face and shoved him back to the floor. He crouched beside the Professor and smiled before twisting his thumb into the weeping bullet wound. Solomon screamed. 'Don't play games with me, old friend, or take me for a fool. We don't have the time. You and I both know you worked out a way to activate this place, and the transfusion from Hunter will allow me to do it safely.'

'Go screw yourself,' hissed Solomon.

'Come now, I thought you were a clever man,' said Oleg. He pushed deeper into the wound and let the fresh blood ooze through his fingers. 'This doesn't seem too clever to me.' He relaxed the pressure and Solomon slumped to the ground, barely conscious. 'You must understand that Mengele plans to activate this place with or without your help. You, therefore, have a choice. Either we do it safely... or you can sit here and watch the world turn to shit.' Hunter watched him rise and nod at the Doctor. 'First thing's first, we need to sort out the subjects and take their blood. Where is he anyway? I assume he was the one making all that noise earlier.'

Mengele nodded. 'For whatever reason, the patient didn't believe Hunter was here and threw a tantrum. We must be careful, Oleg. I have no control over his behavior. I sedated him, but not before he killed my guards.'

Oleg shrugged and glanced in Solomon's direction, a tinge of anxiety clear on his face. 'You are sure this transfusion will work?'

The question went unanswered as Hunter rattled his wrist restraints in frustration. 'What do you want with my blood? What the hell are you freaks doing here?'

Oleg caressed his forehead. 'Calm down, Doctor. We won't be too invasive. You will die of course, but take heart in that you will save my life... and the life of your son.' He sniggered and rubbed some dust from his shoulder. 'Well, you'll prolong it at least.'

Oleg turned at the sound of a set of squeaky wheels in need of oil. A hospital trolley covered by a large white sheet crossed Hunter's line of sight, pulled from the shadows. How had he missed that? His heart skipped a beat as he saw a large, military-style boot protruding from one end. Oleg whipped off the sheet and turned to him, grinning from ear to ear.

Hunter strained to glimpse the boot's owner and immediately wished he hadn't bothered. Conflicting feelings of anger and pity coursed through his body. What had they done to the poor boy? Multiple operation scars covered a hairless, misshapen skull and framed wide, emotionless blue eyes, a malformed nose and thin chapped lips. Mengele lifted the patient's muscular right arm and connected a catheter. Within seconds, a flow of dark blood snaked its way through the attached tube and dripped into a waiting bag.

Mengele turned and rolled up Hunter's sleeve, slapping his arm to bring up a vein. 'As you may have already guessed, Dr Hunter, this man is your son. Like you, not much to look at, is he?' He snorted at his own joke. 'We call him Adam. Felt appropriate since he was the first.'

Something sharp pricked Hunter's arm. He set his jaw, gnashing his teeth as a translucent tube redirected his blood toward his son. 'So good of you to do this by the way. He gets yours and in turn, I get his,' said Oleg, squeezing the bag as it filled. 'I am genuinely humbled by your sacrifice.' He tapped Adam's shoulder. 'And I'm sure your boy would say the same.'

'You are nothing but a simple fool. You honestly think a transfusion will cure you. Listen to Solomon, this man is going to kill you.' Adam's arm twitched violently, and he foamed at the mouth. Hunter pulled at his bonds in a frenzy. 'Let him go. What are you doing to him, you bastards?'

Mengele feigned surprise. 'What do you mean? I've done nothing but maximize his potential.' He cleaned the spittle from Adam's face, his touch almost tender. Did he see himself as the boy's father? 'Admittedly he's on the prototype end of the scale, but once I've perfected my techniques, the next batch will look closer to what might be considered normal.'

'You're crazy.' Hunter rattled his straps as Adam's body convulsed, tensing his muscles in another futile attempt to free himself.

'Calm yourself, John, if I can call you John,' said Mengele. 'It's only your blood entering his system. We're still working on the why, but there's something in the blood from your lineage which Adam requires when rebooting. His blood contains an imperfection previously countered by transfusions from the other twin.'

Hunter's eyes widened, his heart skipping a beat. 'The other twin is alive?'

Mengele shook his head and wiped blood from Adam's nose. 'I'm afraid not. Subject two was a runt. I don't think it could cope with the continued blood loss and recently passed.' He paused and bent to Hunter's ear. 'That's why I needed Daddy.'

A tear slid down Hunter's cheek. Mengele grinned, his eyes sparkling as he reveled in the pain he'd caused. He turned to Oleg. 'I suggest you take your chance while you can. The facility's guards will be gathering as we speak.'

Solomon coughed and wiped blood from his mouth. 'Don't do it, Oleg. You're being played. He's doing this for himself. He needs you to unlock the weapon.'

Mengele grinned and perched himself on Oleg's right. 'Come now, Professor, I am offering your friend an improved and extended life. Who are you to deny him such a thing?' He eased the needle of a syringe containing Adam's blood into Oleg's arm and pointed to a painted spot at the chamber's center. 'This is it, time for your rebirth.'

'It'll kill him,' said Solomon, pulling at Mengele's trouser leg.

He kicked him away. 'Don't listen to them, Oleg. I'm on your side here. You are already dying. I am trying to extend your life.'

Oleg spat in Solomon's vague direction. 'Leave it, Sol. You have lost. I will not let this cancer kill me.'

'You do this and it definitely won't.' Solomon made one last desperate attempt at changing the Russian's mind. 'Think about it. Why do you think they've only got one super-soldier?' Solomon lifted his arm and made another grab for Mengele. 'Ask this murderer what happened to the others?'

Mengele beat the arm aside. 'Hold your tongue, my patience is wearing thin.'

'I suggest you listen, Oleg,' said Hunter, guessing from the spark of concern on Oleg's face that his foolhardy confidence in Mengele was fading. 'Whatever this psychotic prick has promised you, it's all bullshit. Solomon built this place — what reason has he got to lie to you now?'

'Jealousy,' Oleg countered.

'Stay on the mark,' said Mengele. 'I am offering you power beyond your wildest dreams. If you don't take this opportunity, cancer will kill you anyway. What do you have to lose?'

'He needs your blood!' shouted Solomon. 'Look where you are standing. It's going to drain into the four corners. You aren't standing in the position for the enlightenment procedure.'

'Turn it on,' said Oleg, his voice wobbling. Mengele flipped a switch and a singular note resonated around the chamber.

'Do you not find it odd he hasn't enlightened himself if limitless power is on offer?' Hunter yelled, struggling to be heard above the sound.

Mengele cupped a hand over Hunter's mouth and whispered. 'What makes you think I haven't?' He turned and raised an open hand in Oleg's direction. The Russian's body rose from the floor, his arms and legs spreading to resemble Da Vinci's Vitruvian Man. 'The diluted blood of Atlantis runs through my veins and I need this for stage two. It worked for Adam, it'll work for me.'

'It's happening,' shouted Oleg. 'It's really happening; I can feel the power coursing through me.'

'It is so easy to manipulate a man without morals.' Mengele shook his head and slowly raised his right hand above his head. He snapped his fingers into a fist and wrenched his arm downward. Hunter closed his eyes. He heard a popping sound and a series of loud cracks reverberating about the chamber. A brief silence prompted him to risk opening his eyes. A jet of bile rushed to his mouth and he vomited. The hovering form of the Russian was no longer recognizable, the head now a pulpy mixture of blood, bone, and brain tissue.

'Fool. You have to wonder how he thought this would end any other way.' Mengele relaxed his arm and Oleg's body went limp, crumpling to the floor in a tangled heap of deformed limbs, his blood seeping along each of the four shallow channels and into the four corners of the chamber.

Hunter heard a scraping sound and strained against his strap to find the source. It was Solomon. He'd used the distraction of Oleg's death to pull himself upright. Something sharp glinted in his clenched fist.

Mengele spotted the blade and laughed. 'What are you intending to do with that?'

Solomon slashed at the air in front of him. 'You need to be stopped.'

Mengele beckoned him forward. 'Come on then, I'll give you one free shot. But if you miss...' He lifted a scalpel from an instrument tray and twisted it menacingly in his hand.

Solomon lunged, thrusting the knife at Mengele's chest. The Doctor deftly sidestepped the attack and plunged the scalpel deep into Solomon's back. The battle-worn academic fell heavily atop Hunter and knocked the breath from his body. 'I'm so sorry, John. I did not know. Forgive me.'

Mengele rolled Solomon off Hunter, unsheathing the sharp blade protruding from his back as he hit the floor. He winked at Hunter and raised the scalpel, primed to deliver the death blow. 'You can't say I didn't warn him.'

'Stop,' shouted Hunter. 'Surely you need him to activate this place?'

'No, John, all I need to activate this place... is you.' 'My experiment with Adam worked, but only partially. I am certain I can cure the mental instability side effect with the injection of purer blood.' He smiled and raised the scalpel above his head.

A barked order exploded through the gloom of the chamber. 'Freeze. Drop the blade or I'll drop you.' Mengele paused and gazed in confusion at the chamber's dark entrance.

Hunter punched the hilt of Solomon's knife into the side of Mengele's head, catching him unawares and knocking him to the floor. Working as quickly as he could, he sliced through the strap pinning his head and whispered a word of thanks to his old Professor. Solomon had sacrificed himself to sever the strap on his right wrist. He made quick work of his remaining bonds and pulled the needle from his arm.

'You as well, Hunter. Now you're free, lose the knife.' The knife clattered to the floor. He sat upright, his back to Mengele, but facing Adam. His heart skipped a beat. Did he just see one of Adam's fingers twitch?

Chapter 42

Hunter turned from Adam and watched in a state of numb shock as the same American Colonel he'd last seen in the Area 51 hangar, entered the King's Chamber. The piercing beam of a torch attached to the Colonel's handgun raked the walls, searching for more threats. Hunter could only imagine the man's mental state, particularly if he'd witnessed the decimation of Oleg's hovering corpse.

'Kent, keep covering the guy in the white coat.'

'He's not going anywhere. He's out cold,' said Kent.

'Just keep your gun on him. He may have killed Solomon, and Christ only knows what he did to the headless corpse.'

Kent shook his head in disbelief. 'At least you now have definitive proof your research program worked.'

The Colonel blew the air from his lungs. 'Not entirely sure the creation of psychopathic murderers was a key deliverable.'

Hunter turned, his lip quivering in rage. 'That's exactly what you bastards coveted. You just didn't count on the psychopaths ignoring your orders.'

'Dr Hunter? Is that you?'

'Spot on, Colonel. We really must stop bumping into one another; I might start thinking you're following me or something.'

'Why were you strapped to the table? You're part of this.'

Hunter slid from the table, his feet planting with a satisfying bang against the granite floor. He nodded at Mengele. 'Your employee wanted to drain me of my blood. Thought it would turn him into a demi-god or something.' He tapped Adam on the shoulder. 'I'm told this one is my son. The Doctor drugged him for killing a couple of guards.' Hunter knelt beside Solomon and felt for a pulse. 'You up to speed, Colonel?'

'Jesus, Jacob.' Kent whistled as his torch lit the blood-splattered chamber. 'Someone has certainly done a number in here.'

Solomon wriggled under Hunter's touch. 'I think most of it is mine,' Solomon spluttered.

'You are a tough old bugger,' said Hunter, mopping sweat from the old man's brow. 'I don't know if I should thank you or slap you.'

Colonel Jacob Carmichael laid his gun down and ripped Solomon's shirt open, exposing dark blood seeping from a deep cut just above the hip. 'Okay, it looks like you could do with a couple of band-aids.' He pressed the torn material against the wound. 'Can you hold this to stem the bleeding?'

'Thanks,' said Solomon. 'But the bastard did worse to my back.'

'I won't move you anymore,' said Jacob. 'You seem stable. Medics are on the way.'

Relieved, Hunter stood and moved to check on Adam. He lifted and cradled the enlarged skull in his arms.

'You sure he's just unconscious?' asked Kent.

'Yes,' said Hunter. 'Mengele injected him with something before our arrival.'

'What was the blood transfusion for?'

Hunter shook his head. 'No idea. I think he was testing a theory... believed something in my blood would make Adam easier to control.'

'He's a blue blood,' whispered Solomon.

'A blue blood?' asked Jacob.

'Atlantis,' Solomon coughed. 'Hunter's ancestors... they designed this place... but in Egypt.'

'As much as this sounds important, can we work through the details in somewhere other than Freddy Krueger's front room?' said Kent.

'No, you must hear this, John.' The Professor raised his head and grasped Hunter's trouser leg, forcing him to kneel. 'Activate this pyramid and only those with blue blood in their veins will survive. It was designed as a last resort to ensure the survival of their race.'

Hunter wriggled free of Solomon's grip. 'Come on, that's too much now. There's no way the Giza Pyramids can be a tool for genocide. If they are, are you seriously telling me you collaborated with a Nazi to create a replica?' He glanced about the chamber, grimacing as his brain focused on the weird noise Mengele had initiated a few minutes earlier. 'And can someone turn that sound off? It's like listening to a kid with its finger stuck on an electric keyboard.'

I'm on it.' Kent peered at a console set into the wall. 'Is this where it's coming from?'

'There must be an off switch?' asked Jacob. 'Just bash some buttons.'

Solomon convulsed as he tried to speak, but any sound was lost amidst a fit of coughing. Jacob twisted as a heavy boot crunched down on a loose rock. He stumbled backwards, fear overwhelming his features. The bloodied face of Dr Josef Mengele emerged from the gloom, his eyes wild and full of vengeance. He raised his hand and swatted the air. Jacob doubled over and flew into the far wall, an invisible force pinning him a few feet above the floor. Blood dripped from his lifeless head. Kent continued to flick switches, oblivious to the threat.

'Turn around, nice and slow,' hissed Mengele. Kent turned as Mengele drove his hand toward the British officer. Kent's head crashed against the console and his unconscious body slid to the floor.

Hunter looked on helplessly, his gaze skipping between the incensed Doctor and the now convulsing body of his son. The note resonating about the chamber deepened, and the room shook under his feet. Adam's eyes bulged and flickered open, narrowing as they focused in the semi-darkness.

'Where are the sedatives?' screamed Mengele. 'We must find them or we're all dead.'

'Ten minutes ago you wanted me dead, and now you want my help?'

'John,' hissed Solomon, struggling to be heard over the developing crescendo. 'Help him and turn off the machine. The pyramid is focusing sound waves to a point deep under our feet. The Egyptian pyramid has a structure on the opposite side of the planet to capture these waves and focus on its targets. Here there is no such luxury. With no check and balance, the frequency will literally shake the core of our planet apart.'

'We need a serious talk when this is all over,' said Hunter, shaking his head in disbelief. 'Do you have any good news?'

'Just get on with it. Oleg's death was phase one. Phase two is the endgame.'

On cue, the ground shook and jolted Hunter from inaction. He scrambled to Solomon's side. 'Tell me what I need to do?'

Solomon grimaced. 'Forget the console...' He paused, riding a wave of pain. 'Cut the electrics. There is a wire set into the doorway. Cut it. The longer the pyramid is active, the more destructive it will be.' Hunter nodded and picked the scalpel from the floor, cleaning it on his trousers. In front of him, Mengele fiddled with a syringe, seemingly having found the sedative. This was his chance. He made a dash for the entrance.

'Stop,' barked an unfamiliar voice, deep and venomous. Hunter slid to a halt, mere centimeters from his target. He turned to see Adam shove Mengele from his personal space, knocking him to the floor. He hadn't spotted Hunter. 'Get away from me, you murderous bastard.' He stood and kicked out at Mengele's midriff. 'Nowhere to run, Doctor?'

'Adam, no,' said Hunter, his voice impaired by emotion. 'They'll kill you.'

Adam glanced in his direction and cracked his knuckles. 'I see you've brought me a few new friends to play with.' He nodded at Solomon and sneered. 'Although I doubt that one will put up much of a fight.' He raised his arm and clawed his fingers.

'I wouldn't do that if I were you, Adam,' said Mengele. 'Remember I promised you a meeting with your father...' The deformed patient paused, his forehead creasing as he focused on the faces of his perceived foe. Hunter shouted a warning as Mengele sprang to his feet, but to no avail. The Doctor lunged; the glistening tip of his syringe arrowed at Adam's heart. His aim was true... until a second tremor pulled his feet from under him.

Adam eyeballed Mengele and pulled the needle from his shoulder, smiling as the lifesaving tremor continued to rumble about him. He faltered as the tranquilizer took effect, but righted himself and grabbed the Doctor by the throat. A flicker of fear flashed across Mengele's face. 'All I have to do is squeeze.' Mengele raised his hand, feebly striking out at his aggressor. Adam laughed. 'You know your powers are no match for mine.'

'Don't do it,' said Hunter.

'Are you parenting me, Daddy?' asked Adam, his voice laced with sarcasm. 'It certainly is swell to finally meet the man who abandoned me...' He waved his hand about the chamber. 'As you can see, I've had one hell of an upbringing.'

'Don't do it,' Hunter repeated.

'This man killed my brother,' roared Adam. 'If you are my father, he killed your son.'

'He deserved it.' Mengele countered, managing a smirk. 'It was almost as arousing as the day I took his innocence.'

Adam's grip tightened. 'Ignore him,' shouted Hunter. 'Death is too good for this man. Any idea what they do to rapists and child killers in prison, Doctor?'

'Nothing compared to what I did to your children... And your so-called friend just let me have them.' He coughed, grinning as much as the hand about his throat would allow. 'How... How does that make you feel, Dr Hunter?'

A knife rose from the ground, its sharp blade pointed at the back of Adam's head. 'Behind you,' shouted Hunter. The knife shot forward, but instead of sinking into its target, it shattered into a shower of metal flakes.

Adam grinned and without warning ducked his head, pulling Mengele's face hard against his forehead. The Doctor's nose exploded on impact and Hunter looked away as a gruesome mixture of blood and cartilage splattered across the floor. Adam launched Mengele at the wall of the chamber with a roar of pure, primal rage. He turned on Hunter. 'Did he inject me with your blood?'

Hunter shrank back in the wake of his gaze. 'I... I don't know. Maybe.'

'You should leave, and if anyone else still lives, take them with you. I'm going to end this once and for all.'

Hunter pulled at his hair in frustration. 'You surely can't still intend to activate this place?'

Adam nodded. 'Of course. The pyramid can cure me. My brother's blood kept me alive for years and now he's gone. I will die unless I initiate the rebirthing process.'

'But this isn't the pyramid you think it is,' interrupted Solomon. 'Adam, you must believe me. Your plan may work in Egypt, but this is a flawed replica. Activation will destroy the Planet. They have lied to you. This place can only give life to the apocalypse. No one will survive, not even you.'

Adam waved the comment away. 'I was told people would try to stop me. Just leave. The next wave of sound is extreme. Your ears will be unable to withstand the frequency.'

'Adam, you can't,' said Hunter. 'Billions will die. There will be earthquakes, floods, tsunamis... no-one will survive.'

Adam's eyes bore into him. Was he considering his words or was it simply hate? Hunter returned his gaze, his heart filled with both shame and pity as he took in the many scars covering Adam's scalp and torso. 'Why should I believe you? Even if I believe this fool of a doctor and you are my father, I still don't know you. Why should I believe you? These shallow quakes happen all the time when I'm in here.' His eyes narrowed, and he nodded at Mengele's prostrate body. 'How do I know you're not working with him?'

Hunter shrugged and patted Solomon. 'We helped free one of the forerunners of this research program. A man named Yussel. He could manipulate individuals by invading their thoughts. Have you got the same ability?' He opened his arms, appealing to his son. 'Search my memories... I have nothing to hide.'

Adam pursed his lips, his eyes locking onto Solomon. 'You might not, but your half-dead friend certainly does.' Adam's eyes glazed over. Hunter stared in horror as Solomon's body convulsed and a stream of blood dripped from his nose.

Hunter ran at Adam, barging into him and trying to shake him back into consciousness. 'Stop! Please stop it now; you're killing him?'

Without warning, Adam sucked in a breath of air and returned to the present. He gazed at Hunter, his distorted features paralyzed in a look of horror. 'It was him,' he whispered. 'He gave us to that monster. He's the reason I'm here.'

Hunter looked at the floor. 'I know, and it's haunted him for years. But you must forgive him. He is the one behind this rescue. He wants to make amends for his many... many mistakes.'

Adam stepped back and pushed Hunter away. 'How much did you know?'

'Absolutely nothing. I've only known of your existence for about a week. I was devastated.'

Adam reached out and grasped the rear of Hunter's head, pressing their foreheads together. 'Well then... Daddy.' He spat the word, his loathing obvious as it passed his lips. 'You need to see this.'

Chapter 43

6th September 1958

Dr Solomon Garnett shifted in the back seat of the black Mercedes EG&G sent to collect him. The phone call received the previous afternoon was weighing on his mind. What they were offering was certainly an intriguing proposition and, given his previous history with the Company, it was not altogether unexpected that they came to him first. Solomon's reputation as a renowned Egyptologist specializing in pyramid technology must have piqued their interest. There were a few academics around the world with similar CVs, but none with the balls to lay their career on the line to participate in a project of this scope.

Gravel crunched under the limousine's wide wheels as the car passed through a massive pair of iron gates. Solomon gazed through the tinted window, impressed by the tree-lined driveway and surrounding parkland. Wherever he was being taken, the location certainly wasn't lacking in grandeur. Perhaps there might be a chance of a little hunting.

The car drew up alongside a tall, bespectacled man in a gray pinstripe suit and dark sunglasses. He opened the rear door and nodded at Solomon as he alighted on the steps leading up to the house. Solomon blinked in the bright sunlight, rubbing his eyes as they became accustomed to their new surroundings.

'Dr Garnett, I presume?' Solomon turned to greet the owner of the plummy English accent and smiled as he saw a monk, a real live monk dressed in a brown cassock, striding in his direction. The monk held out his hand. 'So pleased to make your acquaintance.'

Solomon took the man's hand and shook it. 'The pleasure is mine. And who do I have the pleasure of addressing?'

'So sorry, where are my manners? My name is Nathanial Knight.' Solomon nodded. 'I head up an organization which has taken a lot of interest in your field of research.'

'Are we talking EG&G or do you represent someone else?' asked Solomon.

'Not important, old boy. All you need to know is that we have more money than God and direct access to the Great Pyramid of Giza.'

Solomon nodded 'Okay, and you need me to...?'

Nathaniel put an arm around his shoulders and grinned. 'Help us build another one of course.' He guided him towards the stately home's grand Doric columned entrance. 'Come, I have taken the liberty of ordering tea. I expect you have questions.'

$$***$$

Hunter stumbled backwards, pulling free of the connection with Adam. He stared in disbelief at his former mentor. 'You jumped in bed with the Order of Atum-Ra?' Solomon coughed a spray of blood, unable to respond. 'You are aware that Nathaniel Knight ordered my execution... hell, he even tried to kill me himself!'

'That... position... has... has changed,' said Solomon, barely able to get his words out.

Adam pulled Hunter back toward him and again forced their heads to meet. 'We aren't done,' he hissed.

$$***$$

October 12th 1992

Solomon eased aside the plastic awning and entered the King's Chamber. He grinned, processing the familiar sight he'd previously only seen in books. Could this be his Howard Carter moment? If his calculations proved correct, he might exit the chamber having proven the existence of a previously unknown civilization — a civilization operating at a time when academia believed mankind was only capable of flint knapping. He opened his fist and gazed at his prize, his fingers framing the fabled bead of orichalcum. Orichalcum, the key to unlocking both the power of the chamber and instigating the dawn of a brighter future for Earth. All the texts pointed to enlightenment and a rebirth for the world.

Solomon shuddered his heart rate racing. He knew he shouldn't have stolen the bead, but what other choice did he have? Nathanial's stubborn refusal to bend to his will forced his hand. How could he be expected to complete the Brazilian pyramid without a working knowledge of the capabilities of the original? This was definitely the right course of action.

He nodded at Colin, a postgraduate student under his supervision. 'Are you sure you want to do this, Colin? There is an element of danger and I don't want to be accused of forcing you to stay.'

Colin's toothy smile appeared through the whiskers of his wispy ginger beard. 'I'm fine, sir. More than ready to take my place in history. You've taken my blood, so let's do this thing.' Solomon nodded and wished the young Texan could at least have treated himself to a haircut. If the chamber behaved as expected, both he and Colin would dominate front pages all around the world. It would have been nice if he'd tidied himself up, at least in anticipation of succeeding.

'Good lad,' said Solomon. 'Now if you would please lie down in the casket and we'll see if this theory is worth the paper it's printed on.' He returned to the plastic awning, poking his way through to find Sarai, a dark-haired Egyptian, and another of his students. Aside from her impeccable academic record, he'd discovered her to be a technical wizard and so she'd become an essential member of the team. 'Sarai, can you get in here, please? Stop messing about with the camera and just start shooting. We're in once in a lifetime territory here. Pull this off and you and your descendants will be giving interviews about this moment until the end of days.'

The awning flapped open and Sarai pushed past Solomon, looking flustered. She tipped the heavy Sony video camera and inserted a blank VHS tape, slamming it shut with purpose. 'Ready to roll, Professor.' She pressed something on the back of the camera and a red light blinked above the lens. 'Live.'

'Awesome,' said Solomon, enjoying her accented English. He moistened his lips, his mouth suddenly dry as he stared into the dark camera lens. How many people might view this footage, thousands... millions? He couldn't afford a mistake or risk being the joke of every blooper reel on the planet. He cleared his throat and took a sip of water. 'For the benefit of the tape, my name is Professor Solomon Garnett of Florida University. The local time is...' He glanced at his watch. 'Two thirty-three on the morning of October twelfth, 1992. Welcome to the Great Pyramid of Khufu on Egypt's Giza plateau. This is the King's Chamber.' He extended his arm, moving aside to allow the camera to explore the space. Solomon coughed and swore, pausing to moisten his throat with more water.

'Don't worry,' said Sarai. 'I can edit later. No problem.'

Solomon smiled and continued, hoping she was right. 'I am here, with my team, to bear witness to the culmination of many years of fieldwork and countless hours of research.' He paused. This was the moment of truth. 'I intend to activate the Great Pyramid and instigate what its ancient architects called "the apocalypse." Now...' He chuckled. 'Before I cause anyone to run out into the street, arms flailing, this is not the end of the world as commonly misconstrued. It is more accurate to view an apocalypse as a rebirth — a fresh start for a planet which has lost its way.'

Solomon held the orichalcum bead up to the camera. 'This priceless artifact and a vial of blood taken from my volunteer are the vital components required to kick start the process.' He frowned, adopting a look he hoped would come across as both serious and thoughtful. 'Many years ago, I received an invitation to view a private collection of Egyptian artifacts. Although extraordinary in scope, I was stunned to discover the undoubted jewel to be none other than a full set of papyrus plans for the Giza complex here in Egypt.' He paused for effect. 'Now, leaving aside their astonishing historical and immeasurable monetary value, what struck me most were the number of previously unknown oddities which the plans referenced. One, in particular, set my heart racing...' Solomon strode to the chamber entrance and tore down the plastic awning, theatrically pointing to a carving hidden in the lintel above his head. 'Found in the gothic cathedrals of Europe and signifying the sacred feminine, this is the empty eye of Isis, also known as the giver and taker of life. The plans specifically pinpointed the empty eye of this important deity.'

'Got it, sir,' interrupted Sarai. 'Do you want me to keep the camera on you? Or shall I move to Colin and the chamber?'

Solomon shot her a withering glance. He was in the zone; why couldn't she have waited until the end of his monologue? 'For your sake, I hope your editing skills are exceptional, young lady.' She nodded. 'Just keep the camera on me and focus on the chamber when the main event kicks off.'

He hesitated, inadvertently rolling the orichalcum between his fingers. How could a structure the size of the Great Pyramid be bound to something so innocuous? And bound to such an extent that its absence was enough to render it inoperable. He held it to the camera for a second time. 'Ladies and gentleman, this is orichalcum.' Sarai shifted her position and Solomon imagined her zooming in on the bead. 'A rare rock famously introduced to modern historian by Plato and his work, Critias. Second only to gold in value, orichalcum mines were only found in one location... and if you know the story, you will know where I'm going with this... Atlantis.' He wiped away the sweat beading on his forehead. It was certainly getting hotter in the chamber with all the lights set up.

'These plans have convinced me the Giza complex was not the work of the Pharaoh Khufu. He may have realized the project, but there is no way the vision originated under his reign. There is still much to uncover, but I am certain our flint knapping ancestors co-existed during the Epipaeleolithic alongside a technologically advanced society. Although my peers will refute my claim, I am hoping this demonstration will be enough to open at least a few minds.'

'What will happen when you turn the Pyramid on, Professor?' asked Sarai.

Solomon smiled, pleased she'd remembered her cue. 'A good question, Sarai, and one I cannot answer without placing my orichalcum bead inside the empty eye. The papyrus plans state this pyramid and this chamber, in particular, were both built to facilitate the expansion of the human mind. An expansion, and I quote, "designed to shake the very core of the now and bestow rebirth on the worthy".' He waved in Colin's direction. 'In our case, Colin.'

The postgrad rose from the casket and gestured at the camera. 'Howdy.'

Solomon shook his head, once again questioning the professionalism of his younger colleague. 'I believe something, perhaps an energy of sorts will be channeled through Colin via the chamber.' He walked over and slapped the edge of Colin's casket. 'But rather than hypothesize, I suggest the time for clarity has arrived. Colin, are you ready?'

Colin stuck a thumb in the air and settled back down, proclaiming in his broad Texan accent, 'Sure am, Professor. Let's make our Mamas proud.'

Solomon crouched at the chamber's center, shaking his head. Something else for the cutting room floor. 'Okay. First, the papyrus states that blood given voluntarily must be gifted to the Pyramid.' He tipped the contents of the vial into an almost imperceptible grouping of four channels snaking towards the four corners. He rose, and smiled for the camera, satisfied he had completed part one of the instructions.

Dusting himself down, Solomon walked to the chamber's entrance. He felt for the eye of Isis and gently eased the bead inside as his fingers located the vacant slot. There was an audible click, and the bead locked in place. Forgetting the camera, he rose and scanned the bare chamber walls for signs of a reaction, a giddy mix of excitement and unease building in his stomach. A calm and eerie silence continued to pervade the space. There was no change in temperature, no strange lights, no clunking of machinery... no nothing.

'Maybe it is broken,' suggested Sarai. 'The structure is thousands of years old and yet I see no evidence of activation. It may not work.'

Solomon let out a slow and deliberate breath. 'Colin? Can you feel anything?' He paused but received no response. 'Colin? Shit, Colin.' He peered inside the casket and waved Sarai over, indicating she should move in with the camera. Colin was in some kind of trance. His eyeballs rolled into his head, akin to a stunt from a cheap horror film.

Solomon glanced at his camerawoman, wringing his hands as his body numbed. 'Bloody hell, Sarai. Bloody hell. What do we do?'

Sarai stepped backwards, her face pale. 'I do not like this. What did the papyrus say about this phase?'

Solomon scratched the back of his head and bit into his lip, thinking hard. 'My mind is blank. It referred to something I translated as, "the purest blood", but the hieroglyphs were so badly damaged towards the end the context was lost... Jesus.' He stepped backwards as blood spurted from Colin's nostrils and the ground rumbled underfoot. An otherworldly musical note resonated around the walls. It sounded like the G-string on Solomon's double bass.

'Shit,' said Sarai, struggling to keep her balance. 'Maybe it is a reference to the descendants of the builders. A racial term like the Aryan of the Nazis.'

'Oh Christ,' said Solomon, reaching for Colin's arm. The young Texan wouldn't budge, his body stuck as if glued in place. He pulled a tissue from his pocket and held it to Colin's nose, stemming the flow of blood.

'Let us hope Colin's distant family raised more than cows,' said Sarai. The ground shook again, the quake lasting a few seconds longer.

Solomon lost his balance, careering into the chamber wall and knocking his head. His surroundings dipped in and out of focus. He saw Sarai discard the camera and pull what looked like a penknife from her pocket. She ran to the chamber entrance. 'Pry out the bead,' he whispered. The ground shook again. Something hit his shoulder, and he yelled out in pain. It was a piece of granite. He gazed at the ceiling and watched in horror as a larger piece freed itself and dropped.

Chapter 44

Hunter pushed against Adam's shoulders, forcing him to break the connection. He turned to Solomon. 'What happened to Colin? They didn't make it out, did they? Solomon, what happened to Sarai and Colin?'

Solomon held his wound and raised his head. He was weeping. 'I don't know. Colin died. Extreme blood loss and then...' He nodded at Oleg's mutilated body. 'He ended up... like that.'

Hunter shook his head. 'October the twelfth, 1992? Why does that date ring a bell?'

'Tell him,' interrupted Adam. 'Tell Hunter what happened in Cairo on that day, Solomon? Or would you prefer it come from me?'

Solomon sniffed and wiped the tears from his eyes, smearing blood across his cheek. 'There was a minor earthquake.'

'Minor,' exclaimed Adam. 'Your experiment caused a five-point eight magnitude earthquake.'

'Okay,' said Hunter. 'Is that bad?'

'Not if you live in a quake proofed city. Unfortunately, Cairo is not blessed by such advanced engineering.'

'Oh god, Sol, how many?' whispered Hunter, fearing the worst.

'Five hundred and forty-five dead,' said Adam, no emotion in his voice. 'Six thousand five hundred and twelve injured and over fifty thousand homeless.' Hunter let out a breath and rubbed his face in disbelief. 'Worth it for the bump it gave to your life expectancy though, wasn't it, Sol?'

Solomon's voice cracked with emotion as he tried to get his words out. 'I didn't know it would extend my life, and certainly wouldn't have risked all those lives if I had.'

'I guess I should have put two and two together,' said Hunter. There's no way a man of your age could have been capable of half the things we've accomplished since your funeral.'

'I should have told you everything, but I couldn't risk you running.' He winced and took a breath. 'There's one more thing you should know. Most of those losing their lives on that day shared... I'm sorry, John, but they all shared a common blood type.'

Hunter closed his eyes, second-guessing what was coming. 'Colin's blood type.'

Solomon nodded. 'Only those of pure blood can fully activate the pyramid and survive. However, in doing so, I believe all other blood types will be targeted.'

'And so, ensure the rebirth and second coming of Atlantis,' said Hunter.

Hunter picked on the vial still containing his blood and held it to the light. 'So, the Order are looking for someone who can activate the Great Pyramid and then what... destroy the world and reshape it in their own design, or... what? I don't know, just use it as a threat? This is crazy.' He shook his head. 'Ironic they now need me after all the attempts made on my life.'

'I know,' said Adam.

Hunter frowned and managed a brief smile. 'You accessed my memories.'

Adam's demeanor mellowed with a nod of his head. 'I'm impressed. You found and activated the Atlantis library. Just a shame you didn't manage to expose this Order for what they are.' He smiled. 'At least now you know why they left you alone.'

'Because I'm the key to slaughtering most of humanity. Great. But how did they know?'

Adam took the vial of blood and examined it. 'Only a pure-blood could have activated the Brazilian chamber you discovered. But global genocide isn't the only reason they let you live. Ironically, your media campaign misdirected the rest of the world from their real purpose, and not only that, but it strengthened the resolve of those determined to accept the mainstream reasoning.'

'Their real purpose?' asked Hunter. 'Are you saying that killing a few billion people is what... just a sideshow?'

'Absolutely not,' said Adam. 'But their ultimate goal is to raise the Motherland.'

Hunter's gaze flitted between Solomon and his son. 'You're joking? No way. Not possible. We don't even know the island's location.'

'It's something Mengele often shared with me. I guess he didn't count on me having anyone to tell.' Adam stared at the Doctor, his expression hardening. 'They still need the Great Pyramid's capstone, but they do know the location...' Hunter looked confused. 'You found a map engraved into the wall of an underground pyramid in Brazil. True?' Hunter nodded and slumped against the wall; the significance of Adam's words suddenly taking hold. He put his head in his hands. 'They obtained the coordinates from your photos.'

Hunter rubbed his face. 'Let me get this straight. The Pyramid will raise Atlantis and kill off anyone not in the right blood group?'

'They need more than Giza. Mengele told me three such pyramids exist around the world.'

Hunter looked at Adam through his hands. 'Three?'

'And a key is required to unlock the power hidden within each structure,' continued Adam.

'Three pyramids?' Hunter's mind couldn't quite keep up with the volume of information he was receiving. 'Are you implying we're the keys?' Adam shrugged. 'But there's only two of us? So, there's a chance of stopping this?'

'My blood is not pure enough to constitute a key. That's why Menegele weaponized me. Your friend Yussel was the second, but you are correct, they still need another.'

'Yussel,' said Hunter, a little surprised. 'But they killed him.'

'The Order didn't kill Yussel.' Hunter turned, gripped by panic. 'And they still have me.' A gunshot echoed about the chamber. Solomon's body slumped, and the bloodied lips of Josef Mengele junior curled into a sinister smile, his eyes narrowing above the bloody pulp once making up his nose. He pulled the trigger again, and the weapon kicked in his hand, a flare of flame preceding the second crack of gunfire.

A searing heat engulfed the left side of Hunter's face. He touched his cheek and stared in shock at the coating of blood on his fingertips. Was he dead? Surely Mengele couldn't have missed from such close range.

Mengele stared past him. 'Obey me or the bullet will continue its course.'

Hunter saw the 9mm bullet suspended an inch from his forehead and staggered backwards. He collided with Adam, tripping over his feet and falling to the ground. The bullet rotated above him, its tip following his every movement.

'Whatever happens,' Adam whispered, 'you must not let the Order activate the three pyramids. I will deal with this one.'

'Oh, do behave,' said Mengele, his German accent piercing his American facade. 'Could you be more melodramatic? Enough of these games. You have your orders. Now throw him in the casket. You know it's the only way the pair of you will survive this place. Do it or your dearest papa bear will die. A shame now you're so well acquainted.'

'You wouldn't kill a key,' said Adam, raising his hands.

'Try me.'

'With pleasure.' Hunter's eyes widened as Adam's hands pulled at the empty air in front of him. Mengele's gun was wrenched free of his grip, and twisted in mid-air, its sight settling upon its former owner. The trigger depressed and a second bullet entered the fray, this time twitching in front of Mengele. Overwhelmed by panic, Hunter scurried backwards, desperately trying to widen the gap between himself and the deranged Doctor. Adam and Mengele each made a sweeping gesture with their hands. Mengele's bullet targeted Adam as he released his hold over the handgun. It dropped, clattering inside the replica casket of Khufu. Hunter followed suit, vaulting inside and praying he'd not been spotted.

He felt for the gun in the darkness, a wave of relief washing over him as his hand clutched a rubberized grip and his index finger slid over a trigger. He peered out of the casket and took aim.

'Move to the wall!' Hunter shouted. Mengele burst out laughing. 'I said move.'

'What are you doing? Get out of there, you idiot,' said Adam, throwing a punch. 'That's where he wants you!'

Mengele dodged the attack and pinched his thumb and index finger together. 'You're making this far too easy.'

The gun barrel crunched and flattened at its tip. Hunter lost his nerve and threw the weapon, ducking down into the relative sanctuary of the granite casket. Above his head, the distinctive G note resonated louder about the chamber. He closed his eyes in disbelief at his stupidity. Colin — Pure Blood — Casket. Adam was right, he was exactly where Mengele wanted him. He tried to push himself into a seated position, but his limbs felt like lead. He couldn't move. Adam's face appeared above him, his fingers clawing at Hunter's limbs and trying to pull him free. The world about him blurred as his son's body went limp and slid from view. It was replaced by Mengele, a bloodied fragment of rock in his right hand.

'Shame,' said the German. 'I'd intended to use your son to complete my journey. But you'll do. I can explain your death away.'

'What are you doing?' said Hunter, fighting to stay conscious. 'You're crazy. You know this won't work. This place isn't designed for enlightenment or to grant superpowers. The pyramid's purpose is apocalyptic.'

'So naïve,' laughed Mengele. 'Adam barely scratched the surface of what this place can do. Don't you think I knew he was in my head? I fed him enough to keep him interested, nothing more. Adam's power came from sacrificing his brother. You've seen what it granted him. He has no idea of what he is capable of. I need you as the catalyst to fuel my own ascent to such superhuman abilities.'

'You can't be willing to trade billions of lives to quench some misguided lust to live out your days as some Nazi superman?'

Mengele laughed. 'I admit genocide is a welcome extra. My father would be proud, don't you think? His offspring will both initiate a super race and, in so doing, will slaughter all those deemed unworthy. In theory, it's a perfect storm for the resurrection of the Reich, don't you think?' He clapped his hands. 'But who needs theory? The Russian's blood is in place, so let's prove it.'

Hunter twitched his fingers, desperately trying to move as the Doctor lifted into view, mirroring the Vitruvian position adopted by Oleg. Hunter closed his eyes, his limbs refusing to bend to his will. He couldn't move, an unseen force pinning him to the base of his granite prison. The drone of the solitary musical note bordered unbearable and he could do nothing to block its relentless tenor.

The casket base shook under Hunter's body and a piece of the ceiling hit the floor to his left. A wave of energy swept over his body, leaving him gasping and fighting for breath. He fought a surge of panic but could do nothing about the claustrophobia threatening to engulf him.

'Fight it.' Hunter blinked, searching for the source of the voice.

'Adam?' he rasped.

'Looks like I share Yussel's ability. Mengele is right. I still have much to learn. We have little time. I can see the link between the two of you, and it's strengthening. I have a plan.'

'And the other two,' whispered Hunter. 'If they are still alive…'

'I will try. Now brace yourself.'

Hunter tensed. Two bodies dropped out of the darkness, their dead weight momentarily crushing what remained of his senses. His world flipped, and the upturned casket dropped against the granite floor, sealing the three men from the horror of the chamber beyond. The ground shook, this time continuing to shake as a piercing, guttural roar replaced the monotony of the musical note. He could hear blocks of stone raining down and the thunderous sound of cracking rock filled the chamber. How the casket remained intact, Hunter would never know. He could only put it down to Adam.

A chink of light appeared through a crack appearing where the casket met the floor. The force holding Hunter above the unconscious men yielded. He fell against them, eliciting a grunt of pain. At least one of them had survived. The earthquake eased as a final block tumbled from the pyramid's peak, crashing its way towards the chamber. It dropped the final few feet and smashed into the corner of the casket, flipping it for a second time and catapulting the three incumbents across the debris-strewn floor.

Hunter rolled onto his back and stared into the cloudless sky above him. The pyramid had been decimated, all semblance of its former glory reduced to rubble.

'Adam.' He croaked out the name. 'Adam.' A block of granite shifted a couple of inches, scraping against the floor. His heart fluttered; hope stimulating a surge of adrenaline. He dragged himself toward the noise and shifted the loose rock. Adam's eyes blinked up at him, his legs and stomach trapped beneath a large slab of immovable rock. Hunter gripped the underside and heaved in vain.

'I'm so sorry.' Blood dripped from Adam's mouth, pooling under his head.

'Move it with your mind,' said Hunter. 'You can do this. I can't lose you now, not after surviving all this.'

'I'm too weak.' He coughed, and Hunter wiped his mouth. 'I took control of Mengele.' He paused again, clearly using what remained of his depleted life force. 'They are missing the power source to activate Giza. They constructed this pyramid as a workaround. The project is considered a failure and all funding has been pulled. You were Mengele's last-ditch attempt to prove the technology.'

Hunter grabbed Adam's hand. 'It's not important now, you just concentrate on staying alive.'

'It's too late for that, Daddy,' spat an all too familiar voice. Something whipped past Hunter's ear. Panic took hold as his gaze flitted between the bloodied outline of Dr Mengele and the hilt of a scalpel embedded in the center of Adam's chest.

Hunter screamed and tried to rush his nemesis. 'Tut tut, I thought you were intelligent. You are no match for me.' Mengele raised an arm, stopping Hunter mid stride behind some kind of invisible force field.

The pyramid rumbled underfoot, its stability still questionable. He caught a movement in his periphery and noticed an enormous slab teetering on a ledge above their heads. He smiled at Mengele and nodded skyward. 'I might not be, but...'

The Doctor followed his gaze, glancing up as the slab overextended and toppled forward. He raised his hands, releasing Hunter as his focus shifted to the rock, taking control of it before it crushed him. Hunter darted forward, lunging two footed at the man's midriff. Mengele took the hit and stared in disbelief as the archaeologist used his momentum to push himself clear. The German dropped to one knee and screamed as his connection with the rock was severed. Hunter landed heavily, rolling to safety as several tons of rock instantly reduced Mengele's body to nothing more than pulp.

Fearing the worst, Hunter limped to Adam's side and gazed into his son's cold blue eyes. He gently brushed the eyelids shut and held his son's head, letting the tears flow. A spot of rain hit the back of his neck, quickly joined by another and then another. Soon, the scene was awash with rainwater. It pooled around the outline of the still torso, merging with Adam's blood. Hunter bent forward, placing Adam's arms across his chest. He paused. Was that a twitch of strength in Adam's fingers? He placed two fingers against the neck, and elation took over. There was a pulse.

Adam's body convulsed, and he grasped Hunter's head, pulling their foreheads together. In an instant, Hunter found himself in a forest glade, the tip of the pyramid intact and behind him. Adam stood at his side.

'What is this?' Hunter asked. 'Is this real?'

Adam grasped him at the elbow and led him forward, walking further from the facility and into the forest. He could hear voices; angry, excitable voices screaming some sort of command. They rounded a thick cluster of greenery and Hunter paused at the sight of a dozen soldiers brandishing guns.

'TURN AROUND,' one of them ordered. The man thumped the butt of his rifle into the skull of one of the faceless creatures they seemed to be herding. 'I said, TURN AROUND.'

John stepped forward and squinted at the creature. What was it? 'Why can't they see me?' he asked, looking back at Adam. 'Is this one of your memories?'

Hunter looked back and dropped to his knees, a tsunami of emotion washing over him. The creatures were no longer out of focus and he now faced them, their young eyes pleading, tears streaming down their cheeks as they implored him to somehow stop the inevitable. The soldiers raised their weapons and a volley of shots rang out.

Hunter briefly closed his eyes, opening them to find Adam's teenage face pinned against his own.

'You must... avenge this.' The boy gritted his teeth and mustered all his remaining strength to speak once more. 'Find the sword. The sword of Khufu is key.'

Adam's eyes rolled back in his head and his body fell limp. Hunter pulled the boy into his chest. Someone shouted his name in the distance. He turned to greet this new danger, his mind awash with a dangerous cocktail of pain, fear, anger, and vengeance. Something sharp thumped into his neck, catching him just under the jaw. He pulled it free. It was a tranquilizer...

Epilogue

'Are you seeing this?' shouted a slender man sitting halfway down the mahogany boardroom table. 'We've lost the Doctor and the prototype. That's near on a billion dollars up in smoke.'

At the head of the table, a dark-haired man sucked on a cigarette. He leisurely blew the smoke from his lungs and dismissed the comment with a wave of his hand. 'It is of no consequence. We know of other possibilities and the Doctor was becoming a liability. The plan is still on track.' He smiled. 'After all my meticulous planning, I didn't expect the prototype to turn against us. We will not make the same mistake with the brother.'

The slender man returned to his seat and looked up at the high definition images streaming live from the replica chamber thousands of miles to their South. 'On the upside, our misinformation campaign appears to have worked. The prototype must have detected the honesty in Mengele's belief of the brother's death.'

'What do we do about Hunter?' said a third man. He was dressed in an Air Force uniform, but with an anonymous rank. 'My men are awaiting orders.'

The Chairman nodded. 'We let him go.'

The Air Force man shifted in his chair. 'Is that wise? He is a key man after all. We could just hold him until the rest are discovered.'

'Hunter will do as his genetics dictates. Remember, purebloods share a common link and are always drawn to one another. It is the only reason why any still exist. There is a pureblood woman out there he will find.' The man shrugged. 'And when he does, they will breed.'

'So you are saying just wait and watch?' asked the slender man.

'Why not? This organization has waited for over twelve thousand years; what's another ten to twenty?' He rose from his seat and strolled to a nearby window, draining the plastic cup of water in his hand. He stared at the logo emblazoned on the floor far below and read the motto, "And you shall know the truth and the truth shall make you free." The man smiled to himself. 'The puppets are in place and the time has come to recover the capstone. We are closer than we've ever been and all resources must now go into its discovery.'

The Air Force man nodded. 'Could Hunter help with the search?'

'I want him to head it up. He has proved himself worthy of his bloodline once before, so why not again? As for right now, have your men sedate him and pull him from the pyramid. Clean his police record and send him home.' He blew the air from his lungs in mock exasperation. 'But make sure the cover story is convincing. I need him to believe he has evaded us and has allies.'

'Consider it done.'

'Then I want the facility razed to the ground. Destroy everything.'

'What about the patients and staff?' asked the slender man. 'And then there's the prototype's mother. She's still in hospital recovering from a bullet wound.'

The Chairman turned to stare at his subordinates. He lifted the plastic cup and crushed it in his hand, dropping it to the floor.

THE END

Did you enjoy this book? You can make a huge d ifference!

Reviews are the most powerful tool in an author's arsenal when it comes to getting attention to their books. Much as we'd like to, we don't have the reach or bottomless budget of a London publisher. We cannot take out full page ads in the Times or put posters on buses.

(At least not yet!).

However we do have something those big publishers would kill to get their hands on. your honest opinions.

Reviews help bring books to the attention of other readers, and if you've enjoyed this book, we'd be very grateful if you could spend sixty seconds leaving a review on the book's Amazon page.

Thank you so much for your support.

Download a free story

Building a relationship with our readers is the greatest reward for us in this industry. We occasionally send newsletters with details on new releases, special offers and other bits of news relating to our authors and the characters they create.

We would love you to sign up to our mailing list and in return as a thank you we would like offer you a free download of Hamilton Jackson's upcoming action adventure novel, Wonder Weapon.

If you are a fan of Steve Berry or Robert Harris, you will love his latest offering.

You can obtain your copy by signing up at https://t.co/3UAOyYEVS7

About the Author

Mark is a qualified solicitor who splits his time between protecting the rights of academics, writing thriller fiction and raising five super children. He studied Archaeology and Ancient History at the University of Birmingham with a nod towards alternative theory, focusing on the relationship of Giza complex to the stars; portolan maps; and the origins of civilisation and religion. It was within this flame the plots for his future novels were born.

Mark's writing career extends back over a decade and his diverse portfolio includes three novels, a number of short stories and even a six-part sitcom. Long listed for the Amazon Breakthrough Novel Award, prior to publication he was a featured author on the popular writing website, Wattpad, and his work was used at the 2014 San Diego Comic-Con to promote the US Network TV show, DIG. Up to now Mark has considered writing as a creative outlet for the myriad of characters and ideas roaming about his head. The time has come to tease them out of hiding and breathe a little life into their lungs.

The Atlantis Deception was published by Unbound in 2018 and succeeded in achieving the number one position in its category on Amazon, sitting above Tolkien no less!

https://twitter.com/MarkJackson873

https://markjacksonauthor.com/

Printed in Great Britain
by Amazon

11346054R00172